D1565341

Dear Readers,

Since we first started advertising *Scarlet* books we've had a lot of positive feedback about our covers, so I thought you might like to hear how we decide which cover best fits each *Scarlet* title. Well, when we've chosen a manuscript which will make an exciting addition to our publications, photo shoots are arranged and a selection of the best pictures are sent back to us by our designers.

The whole *Scarlet* team then gets together to decide which photograph will catch the reader's eyes and (most importantly!) sell the book. The comments made during our meetings are often intriguing: 'Why,' asked one of our team recently, 'can't the hero have even more buttons undone!' When we settle on the ideal cover, all the elements that make up the 'look' of a *Scarlet* book are added: the lips logo, the back cover blurb, the title lettering is picked out in foil . . . and yet another stunning cover is ready to wrap around a brand new and exciting *Scarlet* novel.

Till next month,
Best wishes,

Sally Cooper

SALLY COOPER,
Editor-in-Chief – *Scarlet*

PS I'm always delighted to hear from readers. Why not complete the questionnaire at the back of the book and let me know what *you* think of *Scarlet*!

When **Tina** heard that we wanted to buy her novel, she was so excited she rang us to make sure that she wasn't dreaming! We were delighted to confirm that we thought *It Takes Two* was a great story and would make a wonderful addition to the *Scarlet* list.

Tina has a college degree, is married and has two children. She's been to Bermuda, Mexico and the West Indies, and has travelled around the United States. Like Annie, the heroine of *It Takes Two*, Tina hails from Texas and her native land is obviously a great source of inspiration to her. We hope you'll enjoy reading Annie's and Zach's story as much as Tina liked telling it.

It Takes Two

TINA LEONARD

IT TAKES TWO

Enquiries to:
Robinson Publishing Ltd
7 Kensington Church Court
London W8 4SP

First published in the UK by Scarlet, 1996

A copy of the British Library Cataloguing in
Publication data is available from the British Library

ISBN 1-85487-482-9

Printed and bound in the EC

10 9 8 7 6 5 4 3 2 1

CHAPTER 1

'The Aguillar landowner is proving to be the most difficult,' stated Carter Haskins, with a shake of his head. 'We can't get him to budge.'

Zachary Rayez eyed his employee patiently. The man was leading up to something, but he was afraid it might be awhile before they got around to the heart of the matter.

'And I don't mind saying it's become something of a Mexican stand-off between us and the Aguillars. As long as their property remains privately held, the other landowners continue to refuse our offers, too. For the most part, anyway.'

Zach glanced out the window of Carter's spacious office, letting his mind wander temporarily while his colleague ranted about the difficulties of getting folks to sell their land. Some of those farms had been family landholdings – and usually homesteads – since the early 1800s. Zach knew sentimentality didn't concern Carter Haskins. With a new state highway going in, and land deals turning over at outrageous prices,

3

upwardly mobile Carter scurried to buy as many innocent people out as possible – all for the sake of 'progress.'

It was more for the sake of Carter's reputation – and to line his pockets – than for any real gain to their corporation, Ritter International. The sweetener for politically savvy Carter was how good all this brokering flurry made him look to his friend, the governor. Carter could point to his sales as stimulating industry. The governor could claim, 'New jobs! Texas is back in the saddle again!', always dropping Carter's name to folks interested in buying up Texas land. It was a let's-rub-each-other's-back fraternity.

Nobody would bother to count the minority who had to find a new way of life. A new way to make a living. To solder new ties to old memories.

Zach sighed to himself. Privately he could sympathize with the landowners. But it was his job to ensure that everything went smoothly at Ritter International. And as far as helping indecisive folks make up their minds, Carter Haskins was good at his job. Occasionally, damn good.

Carter's thundering voice brought Zach out of his musings. 'I couldn't even get the Aguillars to consider an offer.'

Zach slid his gaze cautiously to Carter's face. Zach had given a notice of resignation to Ritter's board over a month ago. Slick salesmen – reminiscent of carpetbaggers – were a breed he intended to cut ties with as soon as his tenure here was over. He'd made

4

plenty of money, but now he wanted to make some he could feel good about. He wanted to go to sleep at night without being haunted by the faces of people he'd come to know and respect, mostly small land-owners he'd persuaded into selling out in the name of progress – concrete and steel for highways and businesses. Being president of Ritter International had felt wonderful, in the beginning, before he'd realized that people were drowning in the sea of green bills washing them out of their homes and heritages.

'Carter, if you're hinting for help on this, don't. I can't go out to Desperado. With my wedding to LouAnn coming up in a month – never mind my last day here is in two weeks – ' Zach slipped in smoothly, 'I just can't afford the time away.'

Zach shifted in his chair, arranging an appropriately regretful expression on his face. Inside, he was re-lieved. Life married to LouAnn Harrison was going to be very sweet. She was calm, with none of the hypertensity his colleagues usually exhibited. He liked that. And she had no aspirations for him poli-tically. His future included taking over the family business from her old man, which was cushy in-deed. Zach looked forward to that rosy picture, and getting delightfully plump and blonde LouAnn preg-nant every year. She might not be the most intellectual woman he'd ever met, but he could get warm just thinking about how her soft little hands eagerly reached for him at night. Thanks to LouAnn, he

5

could dodge this last manipulation of Carter's and finish his work in Austin.

Then he was going to try his damnedest to forget about all the lives he'd helped ruin.

Carter sat down behind his massive mahogany desk, sighing. He pulled out a fat Mexican-brand cigar, stuffing it into his mouth unlit. Zach's words hung in the room, and he appeared to consider them before speaking. 'You know, I've always thought of you as a good friend, Zach.'

Carter peered at him through grey eyes that shone with sincerity, and Zach shifted uncomfortably in his seat. Carter's smooth sales talk had been helpful in making Ritter International financially secure in a tough political and financial climate, and in return, Carter had benefitted greatly from Zach's ability to induce highly placed people to see his side of things. It had been a mutually advantageous relationship, businesslike and efficient. But if Carter was pulling on his emotional strings now, something had to be up. Something big.

Zach nodded, acknowledging the other man's sentiment and going along with the game for the moment. Carter apparently was satisfied, for he continued, 'If we want catch the attention of the business world on this one, Zach, we ought to move quickly. Ritter International stands to became an even bigger name player if we can close sales in that area of Texas. We'll be able to bid to bring large corporations to that region, now that the state highway is almost certain

6

to run right through it. Think of the effect on commerce in that region, and the tourists that might be drawn there.'

Zach didn't want to see where any of these points were leading. Ritter International stood to gain some additional cachet, perhaps, maybe some clout for the commercial real-estate deals they could pursue. But an uncomfortable itch at the back of his neck told him that the person who would gain most from these ambitions was Carter. Zach raised a brow, but remained silent.

'The Aguillars have been an ornery thorn in our backsides that we've tried to be gentle about removing, but it's not working. The race for the governorship is going to be dirty this coming year, and those damned Democrats are going to shoot at us with everything they've got. With Texas suffering so much financially, we could dry up like a puddle in the sun if the leadership changes hands and we lose our inside track.' Carter stared at Zach intently. 'These transactions could be the ones that push Ritter International over the top in the real-estate game.'

You mean you need to make hay before your highly placed connection gets the boot. Zach shook his head, unwilling to jump to the trumpet call Carter was sounding. 'My wedding is in four weeks, Carter,' he reminded him, his tone definitive. 'This job might take that and likely longer.'

Carter rolled his cigar pensively in his mouth. 'This deal should be so easy you could do it with

7

your eyes closed. The old man who owns the property'll probably kick off any day. And you've got the rest of your life to make up for your absence to LouAnn.'

Resentment curled through Zach. LouAnn would be more than unhappy. She'd be livid. There were enough showers and supper parties in the next four weeks to fill up an old maid's calendar – not that he cared about any of the peripheral merrymaking surrounding his impending nuptials. But it mattered to LouAnn, so it mattered to him.

'Look, Carter,' he began, his tone assertive, 'I gave the board my word I'd stay through the next two weeks. But that was to tie up loose ends, dammit, not to go running off to some godforsaken patch of yellow land nobody's ever heard of before. If wooing them by phone isn't working, then go call on the Aguillars in person.'

Carter listened to him patiently and reclined in his chair, kicking his boots up on the desk. 'They already hate me just by the sound of my voice. This sale is going to take real finesse if it's going to happen.'

And they both knew that finesse was something Zach Rayez had in abundance.

Zach shook his head. 'No.'

Carter leaned forward across the desk. 'It surprises me that you won't take the time to see that your creation is positioned where it should be, at the top of the competition.'

Zach returned Carter's stare. He could feel Carter's

speculative gaze on him, appraising him like a snake about to strike an unsuspecting victim. 'Your point is convincing, Carter. So convincing that it makes me wonder what the real story is. Is there a detail or two you'd like to fill me in on?'

'Nope.' Carter shook his head. 'Just that, as you know, the stockholders are hungry to get this first major sale in that area.'

'How does it have my name on it? Just because I started Ritter?'

'It just as easily has mine, Zach. But the Aguillars hang up on me when I call. I figure, you go apply your usual charm to this deal, and I'll have the easy part. There'll be a lot of brokering to do if you can push this first sale through.' Carter grinned.

Zach frowned. 'Let's try to remember that I'm the president of Ritter International, Carter. You don't make decisions for me.'

Carter shrugged. 'Even vice presidents have their uses, Zach. One of mine is that you hired me to do your haggling with our country clients. Your dirty work, in other words. This time, the job is eluding me. I think you could handle it in your sleep. But, do whatever you want.'

Damn. Carter's points were salient. It would be a wonderful edge if Ritter could get ahead in that region. But LouAnn would be a witch on a broom for days over this sudden business trip. A sparkly gem or two would make up for his absence, of course. Something to show off at those ridiculously shallow cocktail parties. Hell, everybody had a price. LouAnn's was jewelry and real fur.

Two weeks of Zach's time, to figure out what the Aguillars' price to sell out was, would be a minor inconvenience he'd hardly even notice.

Ignoring Carter, and not about to concede that he would be going to Desperado, Zach slid his jacket on. He also ignored the small voice accusing him of being glad of the opportunity to escape from the claustrophobia of the wedding plans his fiancée was enjoying to the fullest.

'It is not necessary for you to make a trip out here, Mr Rayez,' Annie Aguillar spoke into the phone. 'The right of eminent domain can't be applied to our land. We are willing to fight our case in court, if we must.' She hung up, her hands trembling.

'Who was that, Annie?' Travis Cade walked slowly into the room and waited for her answer. Almost eighty years old but still the handsome man he'd been in his younger days, her father kept a vigilant watch over her and her six-year-old daughter, Mary. The cane he was supposed to lean on was carried in his hands instead, as if he were prepared to fight an unseen enemy.

Annie smiled at her father's protective instincts. 'The same old thing, Papa. A Mr Rayez wants to come out and smooth-talk us out of our land. I told him he was wasting his time.'

'Good girl.' Satisfaction gleamed in Travis's worn

pewter eyes. 'Don't let those oil-slick city boys intimidate you.'

'What's a right of empty domain?' Mary asked from her perch in a windowsill overlooking the front of the house.

Annie glanced at her only child fondly. 'Well, it means that if the government wants to take your land for people to use, they can. They have to pay you for it, but it's just not the same. Money is never the same as heritage. But don't worry, Mary, nobody's going to take our land,' she said fiercely, more to herself than to her daughter.

'Oh.' Mary looked out the window again, her curiosity turning to other things. 'Look, Mama! A snake!'

Annie crossed to the little girl's side and glanced out the window. 'It's a big one, too. Stay in the window, Mary, while I go catch him.'

She quickly pulled on knee-high boots and grabbed a long-handled pole from a closet in the kitchen. Making certain Mary was still sitting in the window, Annie hurried out the front door.

'Be careful, Annie,' her father called.

A rifle cocking punctuated his words and Annie knew her father would watch at the window with the same grave excitement as Mary. If she couldn't catch that rattlesnake alive, her father would make sure its skin ended up adorning a pair of cowboy boots.

The fat old rattler had picked a spot near the house to sun himself in, and Annie crept forward. The snake flicked its tongue in warning and bunched itself into a tight, gleaming coil. The rattles began to shake. Annie halted and carefully extended the pole. The snake drew back to strike, and she slipped the loop over its head, tightening it with quick hands. The rattler flailed in the sun-baked dirt, desperate to escape the noose.

From inside the house, she could hear Mary clapping. Annie knew her father's eyes would be crinkled at the sides with proud amusement. For their benefit, Annie lifted the snake high and it thrashed angrily, exhibiting its diamond-shaped markings and impressive length. A rattler this size would bring a good price, for its venom as well as for its skin.

Zach narrowed his eyes against the sun as he drove up the long, dirt-packed lane to the Aguillar landholding, not ten minutes after he'd called them from a pay phone at a nearby bait store. Stopping the car, he held his breath, thinking the endless drive in the Texas heat had induced an unsettling mirage.

A very tall, jeans-and-boots clad woman with a fall of black hair streaming down her back appeared to be holding up a long pole with a furious snake attached to it. The woman was so engrossed in the snake-handling she hadn't heard the smooth purr of the rented Cadillac he was driving. Quietly, he got out of the car and walked a few feet closer, noticing how calm she was as she angled the pole so the man and child who were watching from a nearby window could have a better view. Obviously, he'd stumbled on to a ritual of some kind, and Zach hesitated.

What in the hell had Carter gotten him into? Were these devil worshippers? Was that snake intended for a sacrifice, or the dinner table? Was fear of these people the reason Ritter was having trouble buying the Aguillars out?

Zach cursed in two languages before walking forward. The front door of the house opened.

'Annie, we've got company,' an old man shouted, coming out on to the porch, armed with a rifle that hinted Zach's business better be brief.

Rattler and all, the woman whipped around, and for the first time in his life, Zach knew what the phrase 'devastatingly beautiful' meant. *Annie*. The woman's name resonated through his suddenly feverish brain. Rattlesnake Annie was a grown man's erotic fantasy come true, in please-dear-God-can-I-touch-her flesh. Shorter than he by four inches, maybe, but he was six foot three, so her height alone was impressive. He guessed she was of some Native American heritage, with that long, black hair. Deep, indigo eyes spoke of a dose of Anglo genes, trimming her features into a patrician loveliness. She was graceful and willowy like a runway model, and if she hadn't been holding that damned snake, he would have been as hard as the pole she was holding.

'Can I help you?' she asked coolly, apparently not struck by the same feelings of wonder that were ripping through him.

13

Zach marveled that she didn't even offer him a smile. Usually ladies at least managed a smile and, more often than not, a come-hither expression. Her tone implied he was a nuisance. 'I'm looking for Mr Aguillar,' he said, cursing the thinness in his voice.

The woman frowned and walked away for a moment, opening a wood-and-mesh box where she deposited the irate snake. Securing the lid, she set the pole against the house before approaching Zach. 'I'm sorry. You must have gotten the wrong address,' she informed him.

Zach shook his head. No. There could be only one structure like the Aguillar house in Desperado, Texas, so named for the dozens of outlaws who had bunked in barns and around the countryside, hiding out from the law in the early days of Texas history. The bait-store employee had been admiring in his description of the homestead. Built before the turn of the century, it was a building of wonderful angles, set whimsically on a small hill surrounded by fields of black-eyed Susans. A smooth sheet of tin roof added a modern touch above dormered windows. The grey, worn wood gave the house a weathered look, but it still retained its gabled charm. No, he didn't have the wrong address. This was the very dwelling.

'This is the right house,' he said. 'Maybe I've got the wrong name. I thought this was the Aguillar house.' Zach stopped, thinking for a moment about how the woman's voice lilted with a soft accent.

14

'Didn't I speak to you on the phone earlier?'

Her eyes narrowed and Zach knew that she'd recognized his voice, too. Having figured out who he was, Annie wasn't anxious to welcome him on to the property. He glanced toward the porch. The old man stood there still, his shotgun ready. Zach figured that was Mr Aguillar. Annie was obviously protecting the old buzzard, but it looked like he could take care of himself.

'You're Mr Rayez, then,' she said, drawing his attention back to her. 'But no Mr Aguillar lives here.'

'Who owns this property?' he asked brusquely, tired of playing guessing games.

'I do.'

The words were said with a quiet pride and Zach admired Annie's grace and determination. She was fully aware of the meaning behind his presence, and she wasn't going to go down without a fight. The pool of regret that had been building inside him for the past several months suddenly felt deeper, smothering. Almost as if he were drowning in his own recriminations.

Damn. Usually it was some sun-toughened, rangy old man he had to deal with, like the one waiting on the porch. Zach sighed, wishing he could discuss matters with him instead, in the man-to-man style he was used to. If this woman owned the land, his job would be that much dirtier. Rattlesnake Annie, with her exotic beauty and appealing pride, was someone he might find difficult to railroad. In another time and place,

15

he'd probably be trying to bring a smile to her lips. Instead, they were at opposite ends of a heated emotional spectrum. For the second time that day, he inwardly cursed Carter Haskins. It seemed trust was in short supply where his vice president was concerned.

But now he'd boxed himself into doing this job. 'So, what's your name, besides Annie?' he asked, hating himself for injecting friendliness into his tone. As if they could ever be friends.

'My name is Annie Aguillar,' she replied. 'Not Mr Aguillar.'

'No, definitely not mister,' Zach agreed, trying to sound light. The least Carter could have done, he thought bitterly, was give him correct information. 'I was misinformed as to who owned this property.'

'I'm not the least surprised,' Annie said, resentment steeped in her tone. 'We don't have *names*, or faces, to you people who want our land. We are merely pawns to be moved around at your whim, numbers in transactions. I said your time would be wasted by coming out here, Mr Rayez, and I meant it. Nothing you can say will induce me to sell this land. It has been handed down for three generations through the women in my family, and I intend to see that my daughter's children grow up here.'

According to Carter, her land would be central to the project Ritter wanted a piece of. The highway would wind through the entire state, and was planned to run right through the heart of Desperado, with

Annie's property smack in the middle. If they had their way, tall buildings housing commercial ventures would be popping up all over her property. Regret tore through him, that his position in Austin brought him here and put him in such a difficult situation with Annie Aguillar. Zach turned his gaze away from her to look instead over the gently rolling land alive with yellow-petaled sunflowers.

Her words were brave but inside, Annie's heart was racing. This handsome man with windswept hair and glinting sable eyes wasn't like the last land grabber who had come to call. That man's chubby fingers and oily complexion had repulsed her so badly she'd had bad dreams for two nights – dreams that she had died and little Mary was left to beg in the streets of Desperado. She'd awakened, fighting her way out of twisted sheets, her mouth dry. Heart-pounding fear had sucked the moisture from her. Only going into Mary's room and placing a warm kiss on her head had been able to slow the pounding of her heart.

The slamming of the front door startled them both. Apparently, Papa had decided to get out of the heat and watch from the window at Mary's side. Annie was glad. There was no reason for her father to suffer heat-stroke because of this stranger. The rattlesnake had been more difficult to handle than this Zachary Rayez would be, she told herself.

'According to the law – '

'The law,' she sneered. 'I recognize the laws I choose to. Do you really think I care what you, or those wealthy toads in Austin, call laws? All citified white men, who've never had to do a hard day's work in their life. You know nothing of *my* life. Don't come on my property and start spouting "laws" to me. You're only here to make a sale. Threatening me with eminent right of domain won't work, because no one from the state has been out to see me.' Her smile was mocking. 'I'm not so ignorant that I can be taken in by a mere salesman, a wolf in sheep's clothing.'

Whirling around, she pointed to telephone lines in the distance. 'See those lines?' At his nod, she said, 'When the citizens of Desperado came to me and wanted to run those lines over my land, I said "yes." I was happy to do that. When they came and asked to cut an acre of trees to build the new elementary school desks locally, I said "yes." I have never denied use of my property for the people of this town. But you,' she said, her tone dripping with venom, 'you want me to sell out so you can pour concrete over this land. You and your money-hungry friends in Austin who don't know me, or my family, or one person in Desperado. This time, I say no.'

'What if folks here disagree with you? What if they think the new highway will be beneficial in bringing commerce to this area? It could have an impact on the tax base, since big business will probably follow close behind the building of the highway.'

'They are welcome to sell their land and let the state highway be built where their homes used to stand,

18

have their children play in the shade of skyscrapers. But not me, Mr Rayez. And frankly, I don't understand why my one hundred acres is of such necessity to those plans. Surely you can find someone else who is willing to sell out in Desperado.'

She'd called his bluff and they both knew it. Most people in the town resented outsiders coming to bid unsolicited on their property. Zachary Rayez would look long and hard for enough people in this town to see his side of things.

The man looked defeated. Surely not because of her, Annie thought. He had to have known the impossibility of his expectations. After all, she'd warned him. Weariness appeared in thread-like lines around his eyes and in the rough curl of his mouth. The suit he was wearing was ridiculously out of place on her dusty farm, and she knew he had to be hot. Why she cared she didn't know, but it couldn't hurt to offer him a drink before sending him on his way. Letting him see how they lived might even make Zach Rayez realize he was dealing with people – not unfeeling numbers. It was a message he could relay to the big bulls in Austin, Annie reassured herself.

Now that she'd explained her stand, she relaxed a little, allowing herself to admire the height of the man, and the chiseled lines of his face underneath dark, wavy hair. His dark eyes studied her, and she wondered if she saw admiration in his gaze. Surprised, Annie recognized a tiny part of herself that she thought she'd buried with her dead husband coming to life, straining like a new plant to break through hard soil and seek the sun. Something about this man was making her feel . . . alive again. It was a good feeling, a spreading warmth of response she regretted she couldn't allow herself to enjoy.

But surely ten minutes more, savoring the unexpected feeling of womanliness Zach Rayez brought to her, couldn't possibly be wrong. Offering him a little hospitality would only show this man that she wasn't an ill-bred country yokel. 'Mr Rayez,' Annie said softly.

He'd turned his head away for a moment, breaking their eye contact. Now he looked at her again, his gaze sending a tingle of excitement jumping through her. Annie drew a deep breath, knowing she was treading on dangerous ground but needing to just the same.

'Why don't you come inside and cool off for a while?'

CHAPTER 2

Zach struggled to decline Annie's too-tempting invitation. If life was a chess game, he was a black piece and the landowners were white. There was no gray area on the board. Zach knew himself well enough to admit that accepting hospitality from Annie would be tantamount to venturing on to their side of the board – which meant risking an emotional checkmate.

Late afternoon sun shimmered on the sloping tin roof of their home and Zach squinted at it thoughtfully. Stepping inside that house would bring him into the intimacy of the Aguillars' lives. He suspected Annie was fully aware of the implications of her offer. It was to her advantage to draw him into her world. The Aguillars would become more than mere names on paper if he accepted the refreshment she offered.

He would learn how their house was furnished, whether the carpet was thick and soft, or if there were hardwood floors instead, gleaming with care and lemon polish. He'd be able to observe Annie as she moved about her kitchen, if she offered him a drink. The thought was strangely erotic in a male chauvinistic sort of way. He liked the idea of Annie waiting on him, bringing him something cold to drink in those capable hands of hers.

Zach stared at Annie, impressed with her beauty and courage. It was a situation that required delicate handling, because getting to know the Aguillars on a personal level meant he might start to care about them. It was better to remain distant.

And Zach acknowledged that he wouldn't be going inside this house to wrangle over details of a sale. He'd be going inside solely to spend a few more moments with Annie.

Even now, she waited for his answer. Eyes the color of bluebonnets watched him, perhaps trying to fathom the reason for his hesitation.

What the hell – he was supposed to be a cold-hearted guy, wasn't he? If she was throwing out some sort of a challenge by inviting him in, he could take it. Emotions weren't a problem for Zach Rayez.

'That sounds great,' he finally said. 'The drive out here was longer than I thought it would be.'

Annie nodded and turned toward the house. Zach followed, enjoying the sway of her curved hips encased in the worn-out jeans. Some raw, untamed part of him burned to know more about this woman. He found that surprising, because he'd been completely faithful to LouAnn since the night he'd proposed to her. There hadn't been a doubt in his mind that she was the right woman to share his life during their serene, nine-month engagement.

Now he looked at Annie's trim, jeans-covered thighs striding into the house, and he desperately tried to conjure up the pleasurable image of LouAnn's marshmallow-soft legs wrapped around his backside, urging him toward his pleasure. The memory seemed more distant and faded than the horizon in Desperado.

The snake, still in its prison by the steps, seemed to promise revenge, the forked tongue trembling as Annie walked inside the house. Zach hurried past the serpent as fast as he could.

'Would you like some iced tea?' Annie flung the question over her shoulder as she glided into the kitchen.

With great difficulty, Zach snapped his attention away from her enticing posterior and back to where it belonged. On his job. 'Tea is fine,' he answered.

She got out glasses and a pitcher. The old man came into the kitchen, along with the child, whom Zach thought looked heartbreakingly like her mother.

'Papa, this is Zach Rayez, the man I told you about earlier. Zach, this is my father, Travis Cade.'

'Hello, sir,' Zach said, extending his hand.

The old man ignored it, leaving no one in any doubt of what he thought of Zach's presence in his house. 'Come on, Mary, we'll go play outside,' he said instead, walking out of the kitchen. The little girl followed behind him.

Annie turned unblinking eyes on him. 'I suppose an apology is in order for my father's behavior. However, surely you can understand his feelings.'

'I do,' Zach replied. 'I understand them all too well. I'm sorry I had to meet him under these circumstances.'

It was true. He was no more welcome in this house than that old rattlesnake outdoors was, and he couldn't blame the old man for feeling that way. Annie handed him a glass of iced tea, which he took, grateful for the coolness of the glass and the sensation of her warm fingers barely brushing his.

She opened a closet in the kitchen and tossed her boots inside, putting a pair of worn-out leather sandals on her feet. Annie's feet were brown to begin with, but had seen lots of sun too, turning them a toasted almond color. Currant-colored polish on her toes complemented the earthiness of her skin. Zach thought about LouAnn's little white toes and her delicate white feet that rarely saw any sun except in St Tropez, and he wondered why he felt attracted to Annie. She was nothing like what he aspired to have in his life for himself.

After setting a plate of brownies down in the middle of the table, Annie sat down across from him. Her fingernail scratched at an old scar in the table, as if she were trying to think of something the two of them had in common they could talk about.

Although Zach usually was a master at the art of conversation, especially with women, he didn't know what to say, either. There wasn't much that he and Rattlesnake Annie had in common. And sitting there, simply gazing at her seemed to be enough for him. An odd feeling of contentment settled over him.

Annie's gaze rose to meet his with the slow, gentle grace he found so fascinating about her. He watched in amazement as her eyes traveled over his shoulders, across his cheeks, skimming down to where his shirt disappeared inside his belt. It felt strange to sit and observe her considering him so carefully, with those indigo eyes of hers. He endured her perusal, though, without minding it. For a quick second, when it seemed that she forced her eyes to meet his again, he saw what he thought was admiration in them.

Dawning wonder filled him. Was it possible that, against her will and in spite of the fact that he'd come on a mission that pitted them against each other from the start, Annie was attracted to him?

He found that thought intensely flattering. He sensed Annie gave neither body nor heart easily. He wished, with all his soul, that he were in a position to explore the secrets veiled behind her eyes.

Zach struggled to contain his lustful thoughts. Papa and his rifle held more than a touch of menace, and he didn't feel like becoming target practice for some redneck farmer in Desperado, Texas. Zach reminded himself that he'd done this type of job, and had the conversation he needed to have with Annie, in many a blue-and-white gingham kitchen. He was making it harder than it had to be.

Zach looked into Annie's eyes, knowing that his words would quickly chill the admiration he'd seen there. 'I understand your reluctance,' he began.

'Do you?' she asked, her eyes appraising. 'Do you really?'

He hesitated, knowing he was treading on dangerous ground. 'I understand probably as well as anyone can. However, I'm prepared to buy your land at a fair price. My job is to make certain that you feel good about this deal.'

'You can't possibly make me feel good about selling my land.'

'Then you're aware that Ritter International may take you to court on the premise that your refusal could be blocking a major state project. A court battle would be emotionally involving, not to mention costly.'

The reference to cost had to be made. It was obvious from looking around at Annie's furnishings that she wasn't a wealthy woman. She was probably scraping by, crop to crop, like so many other farmers in Texas. The threat of legal hassles was doubtful, but one Zach wanted to mention anyway. He was fairly certain Carter had an eye on his presidency at Ritter. One poor little farmer like Annie wasn't going to stand in Carter's way of impressing the board with his finesse.

'I will do whatever it takes to make certain that this land stays in my family,' she vowed with quiet assurance.

'If you sold your land, you'd be well off financially – '

'That might play a part in your consideration, but it doesn't in mine,' she assured him. 'Not where my heritage is concerned. Can't *you* understand that?'

Instantly, Zach realized she was referring to his obvious Hispanic background. Zach looked at his tea glass for a moment, unwilling to discuss that with Annie. How he felt about his heritage was a personal topic he wouldn't talk about with someone he was trying to broker a deal with. 'What if you lost your land? You'll always have that fear, that threat, hanging over your head. At least my way, you could sleep at night, knowing Mary's future was secure.'

That was probably his trump card, he thought. If Annie was this loyal to her heritage, she'd most likely be fierce where her family was concerned.

'Mr Rayez – '

'Please, call me Zach,' he inserted smoothly.

She swallowed and glanced away for a moment, seemingly reluctant to use his name. 'Zach,' she said, 'I realize that growing up in the city and being city-bred, you may not understand about land. But there's a history involved. I'm one-quarter Indian. I feel honored to have a piece of America. I own a piece of the land the Native American people were deprived of. That means more to me than you might be able to imagine.'

She measured him with a glance and took a sip of her tea. He watched, fascinated. Her natural, berry-colored lips were full, and endlessly pouty in the center. Just right for sealing themselves around a man's mouth and hanging on for a good, long kiss. LouAnn was a practiced kisser, but her little doll-baby lips didn't quite fit his much wider mouth. And when she pouted, it was downright unattractive.

'Secondly,' Annie said, bringing him out of his musings, 'there is my family to think about. My parents lived in this house, as did my grandparents. In fact, the land comes through my grandmother, who was white. My grandfather was full Comanche Indian. They fell in love, much to the dismay of my grandmother's family, who once owned a great deal of this valley. Their wealth and social position made it unbearable that their daughter would fall in love with an Indian, and they cut her out of their lives and out of their will, giving her this one hundred-acre parcel and nothing more. "Good riddance, and don't come back, as long as you have that Injun slavering after you," they told her. When I think about giving up this land, I think I would be betraying my grandmother's suffering. It would hurt her to know that all she'd had in the world to pass down had come to nothing.'

It was important for everyone to own land, or something of value. Half-Mexican himself, and struggling in an Anglo-oriented business climate, he'd had the need to call something his own. He understood the willingness to fight to get ahead.

He understood ambition.

What Zach didn't understand was the overpowering

28

attraction he felt for this lovely woman. He wanted Annie, wanted her in the worst way. With the same driving need that he'd wanted his successful climb to the top, he wanted her.

But he would never cheat on LouAnn. He would never cheat on anyone. Not that he was suddenly ingrained with a moral streak, or anything like that. But that was his one principle. Cheating on a woman didn't do any good – his own father had proved that theory. And he wouldn't dream of hurting Annie by acting on his desire for her. He wanted to kiss the ground her burnished feet walked on; he wanted to pour her bathwater into a martini glass and drink it.

These were fantasies he could hold close to him at night – because he would never hold her close during the daytime, in the harsh light of reality.

Zach knew he could never have Annie Aguillar.

Deep in her heart, Annie recognized that the emotions Zach Rayez stirred up inside of her were unhealthy. She tried to tell herself it didn't matter what he thought about her, that their worlds were so different he couldn't possibly understand a way of life that mattered greatly to her. Yet, some need inside her wanted Zach to appreciate why she felt the way she did.

'Would you like a tour of the farm?' she asked suddenly.

Zach hesitated and for one awful moment, Annie was sure he was going to refuse. She perceived her invitation was out of the ordinary. Land deals required cool participation on the part of both parties; there was no room for sentiment. She knew that, but the truth was, it was the only excuse she could think of to entice him to stay a little longer.

'Sure,' he said easily, looking at her with his intense gaze. 'I've got some time to kill.'

Shivers of something akin to pleasure tingled her spine. Intuition told Annie that Zach was glad for the excuse to linger. Of course, he might welcome a chance to view what he was supposed to be purchasing, Annie reminded herself.

She stood up and walked out of the kitchen. A wave of self-consciousness swept over her when Zach followed. Did he find her appealing at all? Was she too tall and lanky, her hair and skin too dark to suit him? Or did he feel the same tightly triggered response she did whenever they stood close enough to touch?

Walking on to the porch, she held the screened door open, allowing him to pass by her. His hard-packed physique brushed her arm, and the scent of an enticing musky aftershave made her mouth go dry. Annie slowly let the door close, with the sharp recognition that part of the reason she was lapping up this man's sex appeal like a starving kitten lapping milk was the fact that there weren't many men like him in Desperado. Most of the men from around here were good ol' boys, with no more sophistication than the cows they raised. Zach had a keen intellect, she sensed, sharpening it to manipulate people into doing what he wanted them to do.

And while nice enough, the males in Desperado who weren't already married were a picked-over lot, too – although that wouldn't have mattered if she'd had a mind toward marrying again. The major problem was she'd grown up with these folks, learned her letters in school with them and outran them during recess. She felt brotherly toward the men she knew. Zach raised a different kind of emotion in her altogether.

He stepped off the porch, cursing when the snake flicked a maraca-rattle warning at him. Annie smiled as he strode away from the wooden box and turned to wait on her.

'What are you going to do with that damn thing, anyway?' Zach asked sharply when she reached his side.

She laughed at him and received a grim smile in return. Tossing a casual wave at her father and Mary, Annie turned toward an open field, lightly touching Zach's arm to guide him. 'There's a man in town who buys rattlesnakes. I'll call him to come pick it up tomorrow.'

'It's hard to imagine why someone would collect rattlesnakes.'

The muscles in his arm had bunched at her touch, and Annie withdrew her hand reluctantly. It felt so good to have this handsome man's attention to herself – even if it was just for an hour. 'Crazy Cody has several markets for snakes, with more demand than he can usually satisfy,' she replied absently, her mind on the man beside her whose long stride, she noticed, matched perfectly with hers. 'The University can use them for research. Medical laboratories need the venom for making antidote to snake bite.'

They stopped walking at the edge of a corn field, which began maybe five hundred yards from the house. Zach gazed down at her, and Annie's heart beat a little faster. The scent of sun-warmed man reached her, filling her with body-aching desire.

'Good for Crazy Cody. But why do you have to catch them?'

Did the gruff tone of his voice imply he was worried about her safety? A thrill ran over her at the thought and she smiled into his eyes. 'The money comes in handy,' she said simply. 'And I like to keep them off the land, anyway. I worry about Mary getting bitten.'

Zach's lips tightened and Annie realized she'd given him the perfect opportunity to drive in another reason why she should sell her land. Not for a moment did she give Zach any credit for his self-control. Something told her he was merely waiting for the right, most ripe moment to make his case again.

Her smile was light as she turned her gaze away from him to look over the tall green stalks of corn plants. As much as his purpose for coming here should alarm her, Annie wasn't intimidated by Zach. In fact, she admired the intensity with which he pursued what he wanted.

Silently, she walked forward, knowing he'd follow. The corn field stretched forever, with its sea of green-flagged leaves. Annie felt pride and a stab of worry as her eyes automatically searched for blight and for bugs. With a wave of her hand toward the field, she said, 'I'm counting on this year's corn crop to be my big moneymaker.'

Zach made no reply, and Annie walked forward without further comment. Banking on the fact that the world's population was increasing, and the recent disturbances of wars around the world, Annie had felt corn was the crop to plant. Now she could only wait and see if her prediction would prove correct.

'Do you oversee the crops?' Zach asked.

'My father and I do that jointly, so we don't have to hire someone else to do it. It saves money, and I enjoy the challenge.'

For a couple more miles they walked, with Annie pointing out various items about the farm she thought Zach might find interesting, until they circled back to a small shack in a clearing, set under a growth of willow trees. Made mostly of wood, it was a typical foreman's house. A few cactus here and there served as landscaping. Annie nodded toward the bungalow.

'When we had a foreman, he lived there.'

Without any further description, Annie walked around to the back of the house, where the waters of a small pond whispered to the overhanging trees. After the blazing sun, the quiet shade was comforting. She lifted the hair off her neck, appreciating the peaceful stillness. Gazing with satisfaction at the water, she noted tiny bubbles as fish rose to the top looking for insects. 'Mary and I come here to feed the fish sometimes,' she murmured, lulled into sharing that about herself by the serenity of the glade.

'I thought fish fed humans,' Zach said.

His tone was teasing, but Annie didn't smile. Of course, he wouldn't understand that this was a place for dreaming, a place for solitude, where the worries that clasped her chest like an iron band could be forgotten. In his rush-rush life of making deals, what would Zach Rayez know about slowing down enough to enjoy the calls of birds in the trees, the low rumble of a tractor in the distance? 'Mary enjoys tossing corn kernels in for the fish to eat,' she replied, ignoring his comment.

'The country version of the city playground, I guess.'

Now she did smile. He made it sound like Mary was deprived of childhood joys, when actually she had so much more here than Zach could comprehend. 'I suppose so. Are you ready to go back?'

He started to say something, then closed his mouth and stared at her. Annie waited for him to answer. She looked at the firmness of his chin and the way his dark hair fell over his forehead, and wondered why fate had sent such an attractive man to carve up her life. The last man, the oily one with his pungent cigars and demeaning manner of speaking, had been so much easier to send away.

'I know why you brought me here, Annie.'

'I knew you would.' He was referring to her attempt to make him *feel* why she just couldn't sell her land, but she didn't feel any guilt about the ploy.

He put his hands on her shoulders. The light pressure sent tremors of warmth shooting through her. If only this man had come for a different reason –

'Annie, my job is my job. Unpleasant as it may seem, I owe it to the stockholders – and myself – to make certain I've done my best to purchase your land.'

'Landowners are winning more rights in court every day,' Annie replied softly, not really listening to the earnest appeal in his voice. She allowed her body to sway a fraction closer to his, and his hands tightened on her shoulders slightly. 'Anyway, where would we go? This is our home, Zach.'

'Okay. Just promise me you'll think about it and call me if you change your mind, all right?'

He hadn't released her shoulders and Annie perceived Zach's body was on a completely different track from his ambition-oriented brain. 'Whatever you say, Zach,' she said softly, knowing she'd never call him. Nor would he ever call her. This was the only time she'd ever see Zach Rayez.

She put her hands lightly on his wrists. Without taking her eyes from his, Annie moved her hands slowly along his wrists to the broadness of his shoulders, smoothly moving herself into Zach's arms.

Zach found himself in a delicious embrace with Annie so fast he didn't have time to explain about his fiancée – not that he wanted to. The last thing he wanted to do was talk about LouAnn. The strength of a freight train was roaring through his head, and all he

35

could do was pull Annie more tightly to him. Hesitantly, he lowered his lips to hers.

He'd been right about her lips; they fit his like she'd been born for him. Pliant and sweet, her mouth demanded and searched with the bewitching power of a woman's hunger. He could only try desperately to hang on to his willpower. The foreman's shack stood behind them, empty and waiting. Only a few steps separated him from what he knew would be exquisite ecstasy.

Annie moved against him with a small moan, taking her lips from his to look into his eyes, questioning. Her rain-washed fragrance teased him. The womanly pressure of her breasts against his chest tormented him. The warm angle of her womanhood pressed against his upper thigh was sheer agony, because he knew that he would find ready welcome there. But the look in Annie's eyes, all soft, inquiring innocence, was what stopped Zach from scooping her up into his arms and carrying her inside the shack. Panic filled him, paralyzing his desire. Though his body screamed for satisfaction, he could only end up hurting Annie. End up hurting LouAnn. And in the end, hurting his conscience too badly to salvage.

Regretfully, he pulled her arms from his neck and put a few inches distance between them. Zach tried for a smile, but only managed a grim twist to his lips. 'If you're trying to get my mind off my job, you succeeded.'

She smiled, too, but uncertainty shadowed her eyes.

He knew Annie was wondering why he'd broken their embrace. Perhaps she even regretted initiating the kiss. He didn't want that, because he certainly didn't mind that it had happened. In fact, her honest approach was damned sexy and made him horny as hell. It was just that she was the wrong woman at the wrong time, and he had previous obligations. Hell, he had a previous *life* that had no intersection with hers.

'Come on,' he said, his voice feeling very rough in his throat. 'Walk me back to my car.'

They returned slowly, each uncomfortable with what had happened. The shiny rental Cadillac sat in the sun, stars of light reflecting off the silver ornaments. Next time he came out here, Zach mused, he was going to drive a pick-up so he'd fit in.

Next time? Zach stopped himself. There wasn't going to be a next time, of course. He'd go back to Austin and forget that he'd ever met this captivating woman, this Rattlesnake Annie.

Mr Cade hobbled out on to the porch. He stared Zach down, obviously glad to see him leaving. Zach tossed a polite nod in his direction, then slid into the car's hot leather interior. 'Thanks for the tea,' he said, wanting to say much more to Annie but finding himself choked by the impossibility of their situation.

She nodded her head slightly and stepped back from the car. Zach stuck his key in the ignition, averting his eyes from her face. The car started, then died. He frowned, and tried again. Again the engine sputtered to a stop. Mr Cade was making his way off the porch, holding his cane like a weapon. *Blazing hell*! Zach thought, *of all the times for this to happen*! Trying again, he willed the engine to catch.

It was no good. Sighing, he got out and lifted the hood, almost resigned to a bad fate. What he didn't know about cars could fill a book.

Annie's father stood beside him, glaring at the engine. She herself stood patiently, obviously waiting for her father to diagnose the problem.

Which he did. After bending down to peer under the car – which looked painful to Zach, as old as the man appeared to be – he stood back up with a disdainful snort. 'Caught a rock in yer radiator,' he said sternly, as if Zach was phenomenally stupid to do such a thing.

'A rock?' he repeated. He'd heard a few thumps when he'd driven up the long, uneven dirt driveway to the Aguillar house, but he hadn't given the sounds a second thought. 'Can it be fixed?'

Mr Cade pressed what little bit of wrinkled lips he had into a thin line. 'Have to be towed into town.'

Apprehension began to try Zach's patience. He didn't want to wait for a bunch of small-town yahoos to try to fix the car. They'd likely do more harm than good. The rental-car company could send another, but it was a fair piece to Austin and he didn't want to wait that long either. He wanted to get the hell off Annie's farm before he succumbed to temptation.

'Drive you into town,' Mr Cade offered sourly. 'There's a small hotel there. You can call someone to come pick up your car tomorrow from there.'

'You have a car?' Zach said hopefully, almost amazed. They seemed so poor the possibility hadn't crossed his mind.

'Yep.' Mr Cade spit onto the grey-packed dirt. 'Been broke for two weeks. Got a tractor, though. Take a while to get into town, but you ain't got nothing better to do, do you, boy?'

'Papa,' Annie protested.

The old coot hated his guts, Zach thought angrily. He'd really enjoy watching Zach suffer in the heat in his business suit, while the man made certain the tractor moved slower than an ornery mule. Dammit! He should have told Carter to shove this deal – to hell with whatever was best for Ritter. It was more trouble than it was worth.

'Papa,' Annie said, her voice like a angelic song and somehow breaking through the white-hot rage that was enveloping Zach. 'He doesn't have to go into town. Zach can call the towing service from inside our house.'

'Actually, the car belongs to a rental company and they'll send someone to tow it. But as late as it is, I don't know if they can send someone today.'

'Then you can stay in the foreman's shack tonight,' Annie offered. Her expression was blank, but her offer sounded sincere.

Mr Cade looked mutinous. A vein pulsed in his forehead as he considered Annie's practical solution. Zach could tell he'd rather shoot him than have him spend one night on the property. 'Hmmph,' was all he said, turning back toward the house.

'Thank you,' Zach said to Annie, meaning it, although he'd rather stay in town, if the truth were told. Annie was too enticing, and he had a feeling she knew it. But she'd taken up for him with her father, and hearing it had made Zach's chest expand. 'I appreciate your offer.'

'Think nothing of it,' she replied, her eyes glinting like blue ice. 'I'd have done the same thing for anybody.'

CHAPTER 3

What the hell was that supposed to mean? Zach wondered. Annie had gone cold on him, sweeping into the house like a tornado. After a moment he followed her, jogging up the steps past the rattler. God, how he hated snakes. By the furious beating of its rattles, he could tell that creature highly desired to sink its fangs into him.

Throwing the screen door open, he let it bang shut behind him. Cool air from whirring overhead fans touched his skin and Zach stood still while his eyes adjusted to the dim hallway, just letting the soothing breeze wash over him.

Mr Cade's face suddenly loomed near his, startling Zach out of his relaxed state. 'If I catch you sniffing around my daughter, I'll gut you like a catfish, boy,' he warned. Casting Zach a malevolent glare to make his point, the old man turned and shuffled down the hall. 'Come on, Mary,' he called, as if he hadn't just threatened a man's life. 'Let's play cards.'

Perspiration actually moistened the skin above

Zach's mouth. The old man hated him as badly as that damned snake outdoors did, and he didn't doubt his threat. Annie was off limits. He stood rooted in the hallway until Annie returned.

'The phone's in the kitchen.' Annie's soft voice caught Zach's attention immediately. She was walking down the hall toward him, obviously coming from her bedroom. The worn-out jeans had been discarded and were replaced by a white gauze Mexican-style dress that looked cool and womanly on her. He couldn't imagine LouAnn wearing something so unsophisticated.

Following Annie into the kitchen, he watched as she tied a large apron over the dress, before pulling out a couple of pots. A glance at his watch told him it was six o'clock, and he should be getting hungry. The thought of food held no appeal. Annie's hair was woven into a tight braid, swinging down her back and revealing a delicious curve of neck. *That* was something he could imagine taking a bite of.

But by the ramrod stiffness in her spine and the way she was studiously ignoring him as she went about her chores, Annie was plainly of the same opinion as her father. Off limits.

That's fine, Zach thought crossly, sitting down and pulling the phone close to him. Woman trouble was the very last thing he needed. LouAnn was going to be fried when she found out he wasn't coming home. There was an important party being held in their honor tonight at the house of the governor's best

42

friend. Why did he have to get stuck in the middle of nowhere with a couple of prickly country bumpkins?

Absently, he dialed the rental car company and reported his problem. As he'd expected, the soonest they could come was in the morning. He hung up, and glanced again at Annie's back. Her competent hands flew as she mixed and stirred, lifting and closing lids on the hot stove. His mouth began to water as spicy aromas reached him.

Of course, she hadn't offered him dinner. He supposed he was lucky the Aguillars were willing to put him up. Sort of willing, anyway. And he could miss one meal.

Zach sighed, the delicious smells bringing to mind the sumptuous array of food that would be laid out at the banquet tonight. Which reminded him that he had one more phone call to make – to LouAnn. Shoddy as it seemed, he didn't want to call her with Annie in the kitchen with him. He wondered if she'd give him a moment's privacy if he asked. Possibly there was a phone in the foreman's shack he could use later when he was alone, yet he hadn't seen any lines strung to the house. But LouAnn deserved as much notice as possible so she could get another escort.

The fine hair on his hands electrified at the thought. Of course, she would go to the party with her parents, but she would be unattended and other men would ask her to dance. Mean jealousy tightened his groin, which Zach knew was chauvinistic and basically jack-assed.

43

LouAnn would never cast her long-lashed doe eyes with desire at another man. The only reason he'd envisioned it was because he was sitting in the house of a damned attractive woman with whom he was aching to have a frenzied session of carnal sex. Guilt by association, of course, except he wouldn't want LouAnn to go as far with anyone else as he'd already gone with Annie.

Annie slammed a lid onto the counter and covered something with foil. Perhaps his presence in the kitchen disturbed her concentration. She obviously wasn't in the mood to make small talk with him now. He thought about their kiss, which had been loaded with sexual promises, all the more exciting because the emotion had been mutual on both sides. But something had royally pissed Annie off, and he knew it had something to do with him.

She whacked at an onion rather forcefully and Zach winced. Whatever it was, he hoped she'd get over it soon. He didn't have the emotional reserves to call and soothe LouAnn and then deal with a moody woman he barely knew.

His hand paused over the phone. He really didn't want to call LouAnn right now. She was going to freak and he couldn't make kissy-kissy noises with Annie practically standing next to him. And with all the racket the woman was making chopping stuff up like she was taking chunks out of *him*, LouAnn was going to know he wasn't staying at a regular hotel.

Annie cried out suddenly, and Zach leapt to his feet,

crossing to her side at once. 'What happened?' he asked.

'I cut myself,' she said, quickly wrapping her finger in a paper towel. 'Don't worry. It's just a small cut.'

'Let me see.' He unwrapped the towel and pulled her over to the sink. Turning on the cold water tap, he held her finger under the running water. 'Keep your finger under here for a minute and then we'll look at it,' he instructed.

She obeyed without protest and after looking at Annie's face carefully to judge whether she was the type who fainted when they saw their own blood, Zach walked back over to the stove. Sliced vegetables sizzled in a pan, emitting a heavenly smell. He wondered if they needed to be stirred. Pale rose-colored beans bubbled away in another pot, with an occasional hole blowing in the thick sauce. Helplessly he turned to look at Annie, intending to ask her what to do about the food on the stove. She was leaning over the sink, her head resting on her forearm.

Hell, he didn't know any more about cooking than tossing in microwave dinners. Whatever he touched on this stove was destined to become inedible. Yet, what he lacked in the culinary department he could make up for with machismo. Annie would probably appreciate him doctoring her hand more than ruining dinner. Decisively, Zach turned off the stove and returned to Annie's side.

'How's the finger?'

'Fine.'

45

Her voice was weak, despite her positive reply. Gently, Zach took her hand and examined it carefully. Blood oozed from the wound immediately, but it didn't look severe. He put her hand back under the water. 'It'll be all right in a minute,' he soothed.

'I'm fine, really,' Annie said, glancing up long enough to glare at him. 'Don't make a big deal out of it.'

He grinned and dragged a chair across the saltillo tile, pushing her down into it. Annie was probably stoic and brave when it was someone else's blood, but when it came to looking at her own, it was obvious she was jittery. Despite her protests, she leaned her head back down on her arm, not moving an inch in the chair. Zach rubbed her back in slow circles, enjoying the feel of her firm body under the soft cotton as much as he did comforting her.

'Please just go away,' Annie murmured from under her hand. 'I can take care of myself.' Farm life was fraught with unpredictable injuries, and the cut she'd suffered was minor. If she was feeling faint, it had more to do with the heat of the day and the fact she hadn't eaten anything since noon. She was a strong woman, unused to having someone around to coddle her – although she had to admit the massage Zach was giving her felt heavenly to the sore muscles in her back.

All the more reason she wanted him to leave her alone now. His reluctance to reciprocate her advance at the foreman's bungalow stung painfully. Embar-

46

rassment at his rejection seeped through her. What had she expected? Had she imagined that, although she'd refused his buy-out offer, Zach might settle for a roll in the hay to assuage the burning sexual hunger she'd too long denied herself?

Humiliation heated the pit of her stomach. 'I'm fine, thanks,' she said, knocking away his hand and jumping up from the chair. 'I'm going to get a bandage.'

Without looking at Zach, Annie hurried down the hall toward her bedroom, trying not to let him see her face. Shakily, she found a bandage and wrapped it around her finger, the slow bleeding now only a minor nuisance. My goodness, she'd suffered much worse injuries in the past and borne them with her customary calm. Why was she falling apart now?

'Did you hurt yourself, Mommy?'

Annie managed a watery smile for little Mary who had followed her into the bedroom and stood watching her with somber eyes. The child was so serious, unlike her playmates. Mary's teacher reported that Mary often stood off to the side, watching while the other children played, although they always invited her to join them. Sometimes, the teacher had said, Mary moved from her lonely spot to collect withered, fallen leaves or to hunt for doodle bugs, but she steadfastly maintained her isolation.

It bothered Annie that her daughter's personality had completely reversed after her father's death two years ago. She'd been a normal, lighthearted child, with no larger worry in the world than whether her hair ribbons matched the dresses Annie sewed for her. Now the dark shadows of anxiety never left her indigo eyes, although Annie desperately waited for Mary to regain her childish happiness.

'I'm okay, honey. See, it's just a tiny cut.' Annie pulled back the bandage to show Mary how insignificant her injury was, hoping to reassure her.

The tiniest bit of blood instantly welled from her finger. Mary gasped and shot a panicked glance at her. 'Make it stop, make it stop!' she shouted and started to cry.

'Oh, honey, look – no, it's all right, Mary,' Annie said, reaching to hug her daughter.

The child cried out and pulled away. Pointing to the bandage dangling from Annie's finger, Mary shrieked, 'Stop it! Stop it!'

'Okay, honey, okay,' Annie said, trying to sound cheerful. Mary's reaction unnerved her, and Annie struggled to get the bandage to lay right on her skin, which only served to heighten Mary's anxiety. She rushed out into the hall, her wails of dismay echoing back into the bedroom.

'Hey, hey, what's going on here?'

In the hall, Zach's comforting voice cut through Mary's hysteria, stopping her shrieks immediately. He walked into Annie's bedroom with the child carried securely in his arms.

'Mommy's going to die,' Mary sniffled.

'What?' Annie was horrified. Giving up trying to

48

attach the bandage, she threw a shocked look at her daughter. 'I'm not going to die, Mary.' Hurrying over to her child, Annie tried to take her from Zach's arms, but the little girl wouldn't budge.

Annie darted a resentful look at Zach. He merely lifted his brows, without any indication that he intended to release her daughter to her. Furious at his intrusion into their lives, Annie ignored him. She stepped close to Mary, pushing back a lock of the child's raven-wing hair to caress her face. 'Mommy's fine, honey. Why don't you let me hold you now?'

Instantly, the child burrowed her face against Zach's chest and started to sob again. He patted Mary's back and whispered something in her ear. Mary nodded imperceptibly against his shoulder. Zach crossed to Annie's crochet-covered bed and sat down, carefully arranging Mary on his lap before looking at Annie sternly.

'Come here, Annie,' he commanded, his tone brooking no argument. 'Please,' he added more softly.

With the expectant, almost hopeful look blooming in Mary's eyes Annie didn't dare refuse, but she promised herself that when she got the chance, she was going to tell Zach Rayez where he could stuff his overbearing attitude. Stiffly, she walked forward until she stood in front of Zach.

'Sit down here,' he ordered, patting the spot beside him.

Annie pursed her lips, but finally did so despite the mutinous objection she wanted to hurl at him. He picked up Annie's hand, while Mary watched anxiously. With her daughter at a safe vantage point in Zach's lap, she made a nice barrier between Annie and Zach – which was fortunate, Annie told herself, because otherwise she just might sock him a good one.

Carefully, Zach uncurled the tight fist Annie had unknowingly made of her hand. With the skill of a surgeon, he lightly pressed against Annie's finger, drawing the two sides of the spliced skin together. Annie could feel Mary's little body taking in deep drafts of air beside her, but the child watched every move Zach was making. Deftly, he pulled the bandage over the cut and secured it.

'There,' he said, his voice expressing satisfaction. 'See, Mary? Your mommy's good as new, now.'

With a last uncertain glance at her mother's hand, Mary smiled and snuggled up against Zach. Annie snatched her hand away, glaring at him. He sounded so smug, so proud of himself, as if he were a great physician who'd just successfully completed an intricate operation.

Deep resentment shot through Annie. 'Are you through playing doctor?' she asked, her tone sarcastic.

Zach smiled, an arrogant light dancing in his eyes. 'We're through, aren't we, Mary? Come on, let's go into the kitchen. You're probably hungry after all that excitement.'

But before they could leave the bedroom Annie's father appeared, red-faced and furious, in the doorway. 'What in the name of Sam Hill is going on in

50

here?' Travis yelled, his voice jagged with anger. 'I warned you, boy – '

'Papa, wait,' Annie said quickly, hurrying to put a calming hand on her father's arm. The last thing she wanted was for Mary to watch her grandfather rip Zach from limb to limb. 'I cut my finger, and Zach and Mary helped me bandage it. All the excitement's over now. Come on, Papa, let's eat. I know you're starved.' She gave her father a gentle shove, and after a long pause during which he stared Zach down, he turned reluctantly toward the kitchen.

Directing a last pointed glance at Zach, Annie followed her father down the hall. Her heart ached as she watched him settle himself painfully into one of the hard wooden chairs circling the kitchen table. He took protecting her far too seriously. She was more than capable of taking care of herself – and Mary, too. She'd have had Mary's fears soothed momentarily if Zach Rayez hadn't butted in.

Snapping the stove burners on again, Annie watched as Zach settled Mary into a chair at the table, seating himself next to the child. Mary's delighted smile struck pain into Annie's heart. For one overwhelming and selfish moment, she hated Zach for giving her daughter the comfort she herself could not. Mary's reaction had startled her. All that talk of death –

Annie shook her head. Mary had been playing at a neighbor's house when her father had suffered his fatal injury in a tractor accident. Annie had done her best to staunch the never-ending flow of blood until help arrived, finally pressing herself in desperation against the wounds in a vain, half-hysterical effort to stop the very life from flooding out of her husband. She'd known it was hopeless, even before the paramedics from Desperado's volunteer fire department had taken Carlos to the hospital. Mary had come into their bedroom later, questioning Annie about the blood-stained towels lying on the floor. Her innocent question had broken open the icy dam of fright Annie had been shielding herself with, and tears of helplessness and rage had poured from her eyes. Very possibly, her inability to comfort and reassure Mary at that time was responsible for her emotional upset today, Annie thought guiltily. She hadn't handled the matter very well, not then, and not today, either. Her gaze unconsciously flew to Zach's face, who sat watching her with an expression of concern.

'Can I help you put the food out?' he asked.

'No, thanks,' she replied stiffly, not wanting any more assistance from him than he'd already given. She placed a plate in front of Mary, then her father, then Zach, then laid one for herself. Briefly, she considered telling Zach he could wash the dishes – a forty-five-minute process at best, since they didn't have a dishwasher – but quickly discarded the notion. He had soothed Mary's fears and, when the smoke of her resentment cleared, Annie knew she would be grateful for his kindness to her daughter.

Hatred lined Travis's face as he stared at Zach,

furious that he was going to have to share dinner with a man he despised. Hoping to turn her father's attention to something else, Annie quickly put a plate of soft flour tortillas in front of him. Steam rose from a skillet as she ladled sliced green and red peppers and onions on to each plate, before laying a sizzling iron plate of shredded beef in the center of the table.

'Eat it while it's hot,' she instructed, noting with purely female pleasure that Zach seemed appreciative of the fare. He'd removed his tie and suit jacket, laying them over the back of the chair. His shirt sleeves were rolled up, revealing muscled forearms. Longing rose inside Annie, but she told herself it had more to do with the fact that Zach was occupying the place where her husband had once sat than any further attraction she might feel for him. Her pride had been too badly injured by his rejection. She had put Zach in a bad spot with her advance, probably embarrassing him as he obviously wasn't attracted to her, and the thought made her stomach burn.

Vowing never to make such a fool of herself with Zach again, Annie began laying out bowls of salsa. The spicy condiment was her specialty, made from ripe red tomatoes she grew in her garden behind the house. The tangy garlic in the sauce was fresh also, blended with chunks of jalapeno and just the right layering of grassy cilantro, all planted by her with a little help from Mary. The salsa recipe was greatly coveted in Desperado since she'd won the blue ribbon at the State Fair, but Annie had declined to reveal her secrets. Instead, she sold jars of her home-made salsa down at the local market. Each month she said a prayer of gratitude for the extra dollars her salsa earned.

Zach didn't fail to notice how mouth-watering Annie's cooking smelled and looked. He loved fajitas and, although they were a common enough occurrence around the state, easily ordered anywhere, he had the feeling he was about to sample something a cut above common Tex-Mex offerings. Impatiently, he waited for Annie to be seated and begin eating before he dove into a tortilla packed with beef and garden-fresh vegetables. A sigh of delight rose in his throat, but Zach held it back, knowing Mr Cade wasn't in the mood for him to praise Annie's skills.

Taking a bite of the warmly seasoned beans, Zach allowed his gaze to touch Annie's face. Why had she kissed him, anyway? It hadn't been a momentary emotion she'd been satisfying, he knew, from the intensity of her kiss.

No. She'd kissed him like she'd been hanging on for dear life, but he didn't know why. Pulling his gaze away from Annie, he accidentally locked eyes with Mr Cade. The old man appeared ready to erupt in a murdering rage any second. Zach pondered whether he should just forgo the rest of his dinner and head on down to the shack since he was obviously upsetting his host so much.

'Will you please cut my meat for me?' Mary asked sweetly.

Zach looked down into the little girl's face and

smiled himself. 'Sure, sweetie,' he replied. 'You like fajitas, do you?' he asked conversationally as he cut the grainy meat into small squares. For a moment hazy imaginings that one day he'd be doing this for his own child drifted across his mind. What would it be like to be a father? Would he be any better at parenting, do things differently – better even – than his father had?

Remorse suddenly smote him. This small, disjointed family was functioning on its own. All they had was each other – and this dusty land, mainly fit for rattlesnake habitation.

The salsa he'd been enjoying developed an instant taste of flatness. Almost everything he was wolfing down at this table came from the hard work of Annie's hands. Mary accidentally bumped his elbow and he glanced down at the mocha-colored little face, accented with fine brows and delicate lips. He'd noticed Mary's dress hung awkwardly this afternoon when she was playing ball with her grandfather, and assumed she was outgrowing it. A closer glance told him the flowered print dress was home made, as were the fraying ribbons in her hair, straggly bows painstakingly tied there by loving hands – Annie's hands, which struggled to take care of an old man, raise her daughter, run a farm.

They had so little, and Zach's entire mission was to take away the only way of life they knew.

Slowly, he placed the fat tortilla back on to his plate. Without realizing he did it, Zach's eyes found Mr Cade's. The old man was watching him strangely, the

55

glare of hatred gone. Zach stared back, wondering what the crusty old codger was up to now. The expression in those worn gray eyes was changing to the frozen and dilated surprise of pain. Incredulously, Zach watched as Mr Cade tried to stand up, clawed once at his chest, and slumped unconscious in the chair.

'Papa?' Annie asked, alarmed. 'What's wrong?'

'Grandpa?' Mary's tiny voice echoed her mother's.

Zach sprang into action. Leaping from his chair, he shouted, 'Call for help – I think he's having a heart attack!'

Twelve hours later in the community hospital, Zach wearily remembered he hadn't called LouAnn. Somehow, it didn't seem to matter anymore. Another emerald ring to match the green in her round eyes would buy him entree back into her bed. And, after all, with their wedding in just under four weeks, it wasn't like she was going to end their relationship just because the demands of his job had interfered with his promise to call.

Bull. His job wasn't interfering with a damn thing, Zach forced himself to admit. He'd allowed himself to get drawn into a personal situation when the whole job should have been as cut and dried as frigging beef jerky. Now he sat, wasting time in a Lysol-stinking hospital in God-knows-where, Texas, because he was a jerk.

A greedy jerk, if anyone was adding adjectives.

Mr Cade had suffered a major heart attack, but the emergency-room physician had felt certain he would survive it. Fortunately, a cardiac specialist had been reached and was on his way to the hospital, so Mr Cade would receive the best possible care. The whole long evening still felt bizarre and unreal to Zach. One moment he'd been wondering how he was going to get through the night without the old man cutting out his gizzard, and the next thing Zach knew, he was sleeping in a cracked vinyl chair in a crappy little hospital.

A small voice inside Zach kept pointing out that the whole mess was his fault. He guessed it was so. Hatred and anger must have exploded a frothing cauldron of stress in the old man's chest. Even now the situation didn't seem real to him, as Zach played it over and over in his mind.

Behind the paramedics' truck had come a car, a black-painted station wagon-looking thing, so old that Zach had been intrigued by its ancient appearance. A wiry man about Zach's height had popped out of the rusted antiquity, sporting a feather-earring hanging from one ear and raven hair to the middle of his back. Annie had run to throw her arms around the new-comer, shocking Zach further.

To his greatest amazement, she'd quickly bundled Mary into the car. It was only when the car pulled away that Zach had realized the damn thing was a hearse. He had started to protest at little Mary going off with the eclectic character, but Annie had jumped

57

into the ambulance, seating herself in a cramped space next to where her father was laid out on a stretcher. Somebody had shoved Zach to the right-side door of the vehicle, and an impatient hand had pointed to the seat. For a moment Zach had balked. He had no business going to the hospital. The Aguillar family's pain wasn't his. This wasn't his concern.

A moan from inside the ambulance had caught his attention. He glanced to the back of the vehicle, and the sight of Annie's strained, frightened face illuminated by the fluorescent lighting decided him. She was a strong woman, but this wasn't simply a cut finger. Annie didn't have a soul in the world right now to lean on – and one further second didn't pass before Zach had decided he wanted to be there for her if she needed someone.

Now he waited impatiently for Annie to come out of ICU. *Hot, blazing hell*, Zach thought, glancing at his watch. It was seven o'clock on Sunday morning. LouAnn wouldn't believe the outlandish tale of what had happened to him in the last twenty hours. He was going to have to dream up something more believable to tell her. He imagined LouAnn tucked into her pristine, white-lace bed at her folks' house, tuckered out after last night's festivities. It was too early to call her because she was a beast if awakened before noon. In fact, the housekeeper wouldn't dare to disturb her if he called right now.

For the moment, that suited Zach fine. He needed a little bit of time to make up a plausible excuse for why

58

he'd neither shown up nor called her last night. However, he should call Carter. The man was a type-A personality who slept little and was probably awaiting Zach's call anxiously about how things had gone, anyway.

Taking out his calling card, Zach went to the lobby pay phone and punched in Carter's telephone number. Drawing a deep breath, he waited, his gaze darting down the hall to watch for Annie. As he expected, Carter answered on the first ring, sounding wide awake.

'It's me, Carter,' Zach informed him.

'How's it going in Desperado?'

Zach winced. 'I ran into a small snag,' he said, suddenly not wanting to explain his whole ridiculous-sounding predicament. He was bone-weary, and his business suit felt like it had become part of his skin. An injection of coffee would become a necessity soon. 'It's not anything I can't handle.'

'I knew you'd make short work of the thing. When will you be back?'

Zach rubbed the back of his neck. As badly as he'd wanted to leave, now he felt like he owed it to Annie to hang around, at least long enough to make certain her father was going to live. What else could he do – take a taxi from the hospital back to Austin and say, 'Too bad, Annie, hope your father makes it?' Especially since he had to face the fact he'd probably been the catalyst, if not the sole reason, Mr Cade was close to finding pennies on his eyes.

Shit. If he even had the pennies to spare.

He popped his knuckles, the sound like gunfire in the empty corridor. 'I don't know, exactly,' Zach hedged. 'For one thing, my rental car is out of commission. I'm going to have to wait until they can send another one down, which won't be any later than this afternoon, I hope. But I haven't exactly nailed this deal yet, so I may stay and throw a little more wood on the fire, so to speak.'

Carter laughed heartily and Zach frowned. 'You do that. If anyone can convince those people, it's you. Say, you missed a real humdinger of a party last night.'

'Yeah?' Zach didn't really care about the party at the moment, but felt obliged to listen to the details.

'Yeah,' Carter confirmed. 'It was a real nice affair. And LouAnn looked gorgeous, but I could tell she was missing you.'

'I couldn't break away to call her,' Zach said. 'I hope she had a good time.'

'Well, I'm sure it would have been better if you could have been at the party, Zach. However, LouAnn was flaunting a pair of emerald earrings she'd just received from her fiancé – that's what she was telling everyone, she was so proud. So I don't think she'll be too angry with you for not showing up. You just give her a call later and smooth things over.'

'Yeah.' Zach closed his eyes, hoping the pain lancing his head wasn't a major migraine coming on. 'I'll call you later and let you know what's happening.'

'I'll be waiting.'

Zach hung up and leaned his head against the black pay phone, dimly aware that it smelled dirty, like a thousand hands had clutched it over the years, transmitting panic and worry into the very plastic. Suddenly Zach felt nauseous, and he wondered if he'd ever be able to wash the stench of dishonesty off his own skin.

'That was loverboy checking in,' Carter said with a chuckle.

'How's the job going?'

The light, female voice pleased Carter, especially so near his ear. Only seconds before the phone had rung, his ear had been receiving the most sensual tongue-tickling it had ever experienced. 'Everything's going right as planned,' he said with satisfaction, before tugging her delicious curves closer to him.

With the possessive enjoyment of a man in total control, Carter closed his palms over the woman's ripe breasts, squeezing the nipples lightly. He smiled at her expected moan of delight. 'We've got nothing to worry about now,' he continued, more to himself than his companion. 'That nacho-eating spic is going to seal this deal for us faster than you can shed your clothes, honey.' Carter felt pure satisfaction well up inside him. Life was interesting when one knew how to play the game.

The woman was trailing teasing fingers along the rigid line of his erection, and Carter nuzzled his lips in her hair with contentment.

61

'How did you know Zach would be able to get the Aguillars to sell out, Carter?'

He laughed and rubbed his lips against her forehead. 'Because it takes a spic to know another dirty spic, honey. They know how to talk to each other.'

'They're from Mexico, too?'

Carter shrugged, dismissing Zach's heritage along with the Aguillars'. 'I reckon. Aguillar's a Mexican name.' He drew a deep breath of anticipation, as much from the knowledge that the contract would be signed as what the woman's manicured hand was doing to his penis. 'Anyway, don't you know God quit passing out brains south of Texas, honey?'

She giggled a little. 'Ritter International would flip if the newspapers ever caught one of your priceless quotes, Carter.'

Carter grinned and ran his hand over her stomach. Racial issues weren't his problem. He knew how to avoid touchy matters like that. Since Zach's and his law school days, he'd immediately seen possibilities in the brash young law student. Later, when Zach had started the corporation that was to become Ritter International, Carter had read Zach's name in the *Wall Street Journal* and decided to put the touch on an old school chum for a job. It had all worked out very well – but now, Carter planned on riding Zach all the way to the presidency of Ritter.

Oh, Zach thought he was ready to retire from the big business arena. But Carter knew ambition ate at Zach like a disease. He might run from it but there was no cure and sooner or later, Zach would return to doing what he couldn't escape from – trying to prove himself. A short spell away from the monstrous company Zach had created, then who knew what creative venture might spark itself in him, to make Ritter bigger and better than ever? He could return to Ritter with a position on the board with a higher title and salary. Zach thought his entrepreneurial spirit would be satisfied by trying to make a success out of the rinky-dink million-dollar company LouAnn's father owned. But the glamour, the allure of Ritter would be lacking. Zach would figure that out soon enough.

Carter, meanwhile, would be sitting firmly in the president's chair.

Carter turned his attention to the white, silky woman lying beside him. He had never seen skin so alabaster in his entire life. She looked like she'd been carved from untouched winter ice, with no scar of mixed heritage.

Whether Zach would ever admit it to himself or not, LouAnn's precious white skin and obvious blue-blood purity was what Zach craved so mightily. Befriended by the powerful, wealthy, and listed in the elite social register, LouAnn personified what Zach Rayez hungered for. Zach would spend the rest of his life trying to escape from the pain of half-breed illegitimacy, and marrying LouAnn was one way to rise above his birth. Gaining business clout was another. Carter hadn't had to think too hard to figure out what was driving Zach's behavior. Zach's rudimentary motives would make matters that much easier for Carter in the long run.

'Come here, gorgeous,' Carter suddenly said, taking the blonde in his arms to feel the wonders of her white-velvet body against his once more. 'Ah, LouAnn,' he murmured, 'let me make you speak in tongues again.'

CHAPTER 4

Annie watched the monitor above her father's bed, unable to decipher exactly what the screen was revealing about his condition. Her ten minutes in ICU were almost up, but desperately she clung to her father's hand, hoping he'd acknowledge her presence.

Unfortunately, the heart attack he'd suffered was severe enough to warrant a quadruple bypass, scheduled to take place as soon as the appropriate medical team could be assembled. Any minute now, they'd come to wheel her father away. Annie felt like she was caught between a rock and a hard place. Certainly she wanted her father to have the operation he needed to live – but would he live through the trauma of surgery? Although in her eyes Papa would forever be the tall, striking man who could pitch a softball with unerring accuracy and do more work in a day than Paul Bunyan, the insistent worry gnawed at Annie that her father just wasn't as strong as he'd once been.

Annie pressed his hand to her forehead, trying not to allow freedom to the hot tears stinging her eyes.

'Annie.'

Annie glanced up instantly at the gruff, hoarse voice. 'Papa,' she whispered, the held-back tears immediately spilling over.

'Don't cry, gal.'

'No, no, I'm not,' Annie sniffled, wiping at her face with the edge of her dress. Selfishly, the tears wouldn't subside and she held her breath, trying to choke them back.

Travis sighed and shifted slightly. 'Dammit,' he cursed. 'Best fajitas we've had in a long time and I missed mine.'

'I'll make you some more as soon as you're feeling better,' Annie promised, fervently hoping there would be a next time.

'Yeah, but that steak had just the right texture to it. I told Cody he should just shoot that damn cow and put it out of its misery. He let the damn thing graze on his good grass and grain like it was some kind of Hindu religious object, some kind of frigging pet.' Travis sighed. 'So the cow finally kicks off and what do I get, but Cody bringing around the best meat I've ever tasted to show me what I don't know about cows. Boy howdy.'

Annie knew her father was trying to make her laugh, but all she could conjure up was a thin crook resembling a smile. 'Rest, Papa. There's almost a full side of that cow in the deep freeze. You have to get well first.'

Travis was silent for a moment, his eyes closed and his face so still Annie thought he'd fallen asleep again.

Just as she started to reach up with her hem to wipe the tears away, his eyes opened again, piercing her with their glinting greyness.

'I'm worried about you, Annie.'

'Oh, Papa. You don't have to worry about me. You've always said I had more stuffing in me than a scarecrow.'

The bright, grey gaze intensified, holding her gaze. 'Don't let that city slicker get to you, Annie,' he warned. 'I know you're lonely, honey. I know there hasn't been much for you since Carlos died.'

Her father stopped and heaved a sigh that sounded painful. Annie started to speak, wanting to deny the truth in her father's words, but he shook his head. 'You've been isolated, Annie, and Lord knows you've worked yourself to a frazzle with the farm. You should have an easier life. You and Mary should have pretty dresses and shiny shoes, and a life not worrying where the next dollar's coming from. But Zach Rayez isn't the man for you, honey. There's something cold, something almost bitter about him. I'm afraid he wants to take more than your land.'

'Papa, you shouldn't be upsetting yourself,' Annie interrupted, more frightened by her father's waxy color than his words. 'You know I wouldn't sell out for anything.'

'I've seen you watching him, Annie. I know what you're seeing. He's not Carlos, baby, despite those dark good looks. That face has probably lifted a thousand skirts for Zach Rayez, Annie. Yours

67

wouldn't be the first – nor the last.'

The nurse came in and darted a measuring glance at the screen. 'Mr Cade should rest now,' she announced in a no-nonsense voice. 'We're going to prep him in about an hour.'

'Oh,' Annie murmured, relieved and frightened all at the same time: relieved her father's surgery was imminent; frightened that he might not make it; relieved that she could leave the room and not hear words she feared to be true coming from her father's lips.

'Don't worry, Papa,' she whispered, pressing a last kiss against his harshly weathered cheek. He seemed so weak, so helpless, lying there that the tears pressed against her eyes again. 'Everything's going to be fine,' she assured him. 'I'll see you in a little while.'

Hurrying from the room, Annie held on to the barrage of sobs located in the middle of her throat, clamoring for release. She had to find a ladies' room, a broom closet, any place, so she could sit down and release the choking storm of fear threatening to lay waste to her self-control.

Strong arms suddenly circled her. Annie knew whose arms those were. Without hesitation, she turned and buried her face against Zach's chest so hard she could feel one of his shirt buttons pressing against her forehead. Somehow, the discomfort kept her from completely falling apart.

Zach started walking and she did, too, willingly propelled by his strength. Seconds later, he gently pushed her down on to a hard bench in an almost-deserted hallway. The only other people in the hall were an older couple locked in their own grief, completely unaware of their surroundings. Assured that her worries could be vented in the most privacy she was likely to find, Annie accepted Zach's shoulder and let the tears quietly slip down her cheeks.

He said nothing until her grief was spent, for which Annie was grateful. His silent companionship was more bracing than any words of sympathy he might have offered. Now she felt up to dealing with whatever lay ahead.

'Buy you a doughnut and some coffee,' Zach offered.

Annie nodded. 'Let me wash my face first.'

'I think there was a ladies' room around the corner,' he said, helping her to her feet with a guiding arm around her shoulders. 'I'll wait here.'

'Thank you.' Annie was grateful for Zach's solid presence. She needed to feel that something around her was strong right now, capable of bearing her up should she fall prey to anxiety. Funny that Zach would be the person comforting her right now, when his initial purpose had been to take her property, her strength. Why, why, did she have the insane feeling that Zach's heart had never been in his mission? Annie wondered as she walked away.

Five minutes later she left the restroom and returned to the dimly lit corridor. The woman who'd looked back at her from the mirror had seemed distant and somewhat frail, with eyes haunted by worry. Annie had commanded that woman to be gone, and within moments of a briskly cold face-washing and replaiting of her long ebony braid, the confident and serene woman she was normally gazed out again from the mirror's glass.

Relief showed plainly in Zach's eyes at her approach. 'You look like you feel better.'

'I do,' Annie assured him. 'In fact, I'm looking forward to that doughnut and coffee you promised me.'

'Come on, then.' Zach jerked his head to indicate the hallway. 'Cafeteria's this way.'

They walked to the cafeteria in silence. The clatter of plates punctuated scattered conversations around the room, and the normalcy relaxed Annie. Following Zach's lead, she selected a doughnut and a large plastic cup of coffee from the serving line. He was quick to pay for her food and she let him without any protest. Ordinarily, she would resist accepting a meal from a man she'd known barely twenty-four hours, but at this moment, accepting his chivalry felt right. In fact, being with Zach made her feel better than she'd felt in a long time.

Zach nearly spilled his coffee as he sat down in one of the hard, orange chairs. Annie's pallor had concerned him and for a moment, he'd wondered if she herself was strong enough to survive her father's heart attack. Guilt ground in upon him. Any minute now, her initial shock was going to subside and Annie was going to realize she wouldn't be sitting in this hospital if it weren't for him.

'Your supper was cut short, so you're probably hungry. Let me know if you want anything else,' Zach said. He took a sip of the bitter coffee, watching Annie nibble at her doughnut. Obviously she wasn't going to say much, but there was something he just had to make sure she knew. 'Annie,' he began carefully, 'I want you to know how sorry I am. I wouldn't have wished anything bad – '

'I know,' she interrupted with a sad smile.

He was acutely uncomfortable. 'Is there anything I can do?'

'You've done enough, Zach.'

There was a trace of cynicism in her gaze for a split second – or perhaps remorse was making him look for things that weren't there. Zach wasn't sure. She had resumed picking at her doughnut, but he doubted she'd ever get past the glazed frosting. His appetite was non-existent as well. The best course of action would be to stand up, shake off the blame, and take a taxi to the Aguillar homestead to wait on the replacement rental car. Another glance into Annie's deepwater eyes decided him. 'Will you be all right?' he asked, suddenly anxious to be on his way.

'We'll be fine,' she said. 'We've hit hard times before and survived them.'

Zach went very still, his curiosity overriding his desire to escape. 'Is there a problem?'

'Well,' she began, looping her fingers casually

through her coffee mug, 'we don't have much health insurance, of course.'

Zach couldn't pull his eyes away from her lips. Why was she telling him this?

'I wish I could say Papa's heart attack was unexpected, but truthfully, it could have happened at any time. He's had a history of high blood pressure, high cholesterol. I should have increased our coverage . . . but foolishly, I didn't.' Her voice faltered. 'It's hard for me to accept that my father is elderly, or in ill health.'

The fact that Annie felt her father's heart attack could have occurred at any time washed a wave of relief over Zach. His portion of blame in the situation could be downgraded from major cause to unfortunate catalyst. The old man could have gotten angry tomorrow over birds pecking at the corn fields and the results might have been the same. Zach knew he was deliberately justifying his innocence in the matter. But he still wished Mr Cade had waited just a little longer to have his coronary, even as he recognized the selfishness behind the thought. He'd have been back in Austin then, and Annie might have called him to say she'd experienced a serious financial setback and needed to sell. That was a situation he could have taken advantage of. But here he was, with a prime opportunity to make his case again – and yet, he couldn't do it. Something inside him wanted Annie to come out all right.

'Ah, well,' Annie said, appearing embarrassed. 'I'm

talking too much. My mind is running around in circles, and I guess my mouth just popped out with what I was thinking.'

'Annie – '

She shook her head. 'I'd better get back to the waiting room.'

Annie stood up, and he followed her lead, not knowing what to say. They cleared away their trays, before walking down the hospital corridor silently. The whole mess was so damned awkward, Zach thought, and there was no easy way out.

The waiting room was empty. Zach sat down but Annie paced around the room, shuffling through a magazine before tossing it back down. Plainly she was so distraught her concentration was shot. He wasn't close to his own father – not that over the years he hadn't tried to change the fact. Reaching out to his father was like reaching into a black hole in space – there was nothing there. But if he *had* ever been able to establish a bond, an emotional connection with his father, Zach knew it would have meant the world to him. Despite their lack of closeness, it would still hurt if anything happened to his father now.

He could imagine the depth of Annie's pain and he wished there was something he could do to ease it. Unfortunately, there wasn't, and waiting around here wasn't the answer, either. He rose to his feet, intending to tell Annie he was going back to Austin.

The waiting room door opened and Zach and Annie both immediately turned to see who was coming in.

Surprised, Zach realized the newcomer was the same man who'd driven away last night with little Mary. Annie's response even duplicated last night's: She went rushing into the man's arms.

'Cody! I'm so glad you came,' Zach heard her murmur against the man's broad chest.

'Ma said she'd keep Mary for awhile so I could come down. How are you doing, Annie?'

Cody tipped Annie's chin to look into her eyes, and a small sting of unreasonable jealousy pierced Zach. Who was this character, anyway? If Ye Olde Store wooden Indian had suddenly come to life, he would look just like this man.

'Zach.' Annie's soft voice cleared a path through the haze in his mind. 'This is Cody Aguillar.'

The two men sized each other up warily. 'So you're Slick,' Cody commented.

'Slick?' Zach repeated.

Cody jerked his head in the direction of the hallway. 'The old man calls you Slick.'

'Ah,' Zach said, the syllable not conveying much rancor for the insult. 'And you must be Crazy Cody, infamous collector of rattlesnakes.' He couldn't help wondering what the relationship between Cody and Annie was. They seemed very fond of one another, but something told Zach this man wasn't Mary's father.

'You've been talking to Papa, Cody?' Annie asked eagerly.

Cody didn't take his eyes from Zach. 'Yeah. He seems to be doing all right, all things considered.'

'Then I better hurry,' Annie said, not appearing to notice the uneasy sparks flying between the two men. 'If he can still have visitors before his surgery – '

'He's not supposed to,' Cody informed her. 'I slipped in for a second. Your pa told me about ol' Slick here.' He crossed his arms and leveled a hard stare at Zach. 'What are you hanging around for anyway, city boy? You a vulture waiting to pick the old man's bones clean?'

'Cody!' Annie protested. 'Zach's not . . . like that.'

The sudden uncertainty in Annie's tone was a dose of reality for Zach. In his mind he'd known once her dazed and shocked state passed, she'd remember that they were on opposite sides; she'd easily believe the comfort he offered was to insinuate himself into her good graces, like the snake in the Garden of Eden which wended its way into Eve's trust. Zach wouldn't trust himself, either, if the truth were known.

'Come on, Slick. I heard you're waiting on a rental car. I'll give you a ride back to the farm. Sooner you're out of here, the better for everyone involved,' Cody stated.

Annie was silent. As much as he might wish otherwise, Zach knew Cody was right. The Aguillar family couldn't get back to normal while he was around, stirring up ill feelings.

'I appreciate the offer,' Zach replied. He stared at Annie for a moment. She met his gaze unflinchingly, pride obvious in her stiff height and crossed arms. They were two pieces on the chessboard again, the momentary closeness between them evaporated. 'Goodbye, Annie. I hope everything turns out all right,' he said, ignoring Cody's sarcastic snort.

'It will,' she replied calmly.

Zach realized she wasn't going to say anything else. It was as if she'd never leaned on him for emotional support – certainly never pressed her lips to his seeking affection. Yet that moment by the pond was burned into his memory – Annie's hungry acknowledgement that somewhere in the middle of their different worlds, desire had pulled them together just for a moment.

As he turned to follow Cody out of the waiting room, Zach Rayez, master manipulator, wondered who'd been checkmated.

CHAPTER 5

'I missed you, darling.' LouAnn snaked her arms around Zach's neck the moment she walked into his house. He breathed in her ever-present perfume while automatically lowering his lips to hers. This was sanity, this was safe, he told himself. Although he'd only left the Aguillar farm yesterday, Zach felt like a million years had passed since he'd held a bewitching woman named Annie.

He must have been out of his mind to let her get to him. She'd wrung sympathy out of him, sympathy he hadn't even known he was capable of feeling. How it had happened, Zach wasn't sure, but he'd allowed a long-buried sense of justice to get in his way just long enough for him to get suckered.

His fingers roved over LouAnn's body, hungry for the familiar feel of her. She stepped back slightly and shook a finger at him. 'Not so fast, Zach.'

He blinked, trying to clear the mind-numbing sexual attraction he was feeling. LouAnn's pose was slightly antagonistic. For a moment, fear tingled

Zach's skin, fear that LouAnn knew his common sense had almost been overruled by another woman's touch. Just as instantly, he knew that wasn't true, and remembered why LouAnn had cause to be upset with him.

'LouAnn, I tried to make the party.' He guided her to a sofa, prepared to talk about the situation until she forgave him. The unhappy look in her eyes bothered him. 'I got into a mess at a farm I was calling on. If I'd had any idea – '

'You've never not called before.'

He nodded, admitting that he hadn't tried to call. 'Let me tell you about it, because this was the weirdest thing that's ever happened to me. Carter was anxious for me to visit this farm, so I went. It was supposed to be an easy deal, almost cut and dried with a little persuasion.'

LouAnn patted his leg and smiled at him. 'Carter is in awe of your ability to close difficult deals. He knows you'll get the job done.'

Zach nearly smiled at the wifely pride in LouAnn's voice. But she was far from the mark, unfortunately. 'That's just it. I didn't get the job done this time, not anywhere close. The old man had a heart attack at the dinner table, and – '

'Oh, Zach. How horrible!'

'Yeah. The farm itself is in bad shape, too . . . and I guess I've been so happy lately . . .' he paused to brush a light kiss along LouAnn's cheek '. . . I didn't have the desire to . . . to . . .'

Oh, he'd had plenty of desire – for another woman.

'To upset the old guy,' LouAnn offered. 'Of course you didn't. It was just bad timing, Zach, and when that man is feeling better, I'm sure you can talk to him again.'

Zach shook his head definitively. He wasn't ever setting foot on the Aguillar land again. 'My work is over in less than two weeks, and in six weeks I'll be a part-owner in the Harrison family business.' He leaned his head back against the sofa cushion and sighed deeply. 'I can't wait.'

LouAnn was silent for a moment. Then she snuggled up against his side, leaning her head on his shoulder. 'Don't you think you should go back out there?'

'I don't give a damn.' His voice was harsher than he intended, and Zach nearly apologized. LouAnn didn't deserve to bear the brunt of his frustration.

'You're just tired right now, sweetie. In a few days, you'll be dying to get back out there and try again.'

Somehow Zach doubted it. But how could he explain why he felt that way without mentioning Annie? Changing the subject suddenly seemed very appealing. 'How are the wedding plans coming along?' he asked. 'Is there anything I need to do?'

LouAnn's fingernails traced lightly along the hairs at the nape of his neck. The sensation was stimulating yet somehow relaxing, and Zach felt the tension go out of his shoulders as she caressed him.

'Plan on getting your tux fitted this weekend,' she

instructed. 'Oh, Zach, responses to the wedding invitations are beginning to pour in. Today we received a stunning crystal water pitcher from Tiffany's, and yesterday four place settings of our sterling pattern were delivered.' He felt a flutter of excitement in her hands as her fingers brushed his skin more rapidly. Receiving gifts was one of his fiancée's most fervent delights, and she was enjoying her position as affianced socialite to the hilt. Her bliss made Zach happy, made him want to drown himself in her pleasure. He turned to her, taking her hand from his neck and placing it where he more preferred it at the moment.

LouAnn giggled, reading his desire. 'I didn't know you'd get so excited about receiving wedding gifts,' she teased.

Zach pushed aside her blond, fluffy hair, baring her neck to his mouth. Tiny nips along the slender column of her throat brought a sigh from LouAnn. 'I don't give a damn about gifts, and you know it,' he growled into her ear. One of the earrings he'd given her brushed against his chin, reminding him that he hadn't seen her wearing them yet, just for him. Maybe, just maybe, some sexual fantasizing would help stir the passion he needed to feel to forget Annie. He pulled LouAnn up off the sofa and drew her into the bedroom. 'Right now what excites me is seeing you wearing nothing but emeralds, LouAnn.'

She pulled him down upon her when he laid her on the bed. Their hands tangled in the urgency to shed each other's clothes. Zach struggled mentally, then tried to ignore that same struggle, as he tried to fan his desire into running so hot he would feel like he was on fire, feel like a runner who has run so long his muscles burn and ache with the effort.

The way he'd felt when Annie had given a piece of herself to him.

Desperately, Zach urged himself to forget what had happened, and bury himself in LouAnn's pale flesh the way an ostrich buries its head in the sand. He poised above her, and almost tigress-like she bared her teeth. Winding her arms around his neck, LouAnn pulled him closer, licking her tongue over her lips.

Whatever desire he'd been trying to capture emptied out of Zach like water. Unbidden, the fervor of Annie's kiss again came to mind. She had been so hungry, so willing to share her desire. He'd felt a part of her emotion, perhaps even understood it though he wasn't free to share in it. LouAnn's passion seemed single-mindedly lustful; although that had never bothered him before, it did now.

Slowly, carefully, Zach rolled off and lay staring at the ceiling. LouAnn laid her head on his shoulder and began stroking his chest, making noises about how she understood his tiredness, that it would pass and they'd try again. The air conditioner turned on, blowing across the perspiration on his chest in a sudden, chilling caress. The satin sheets beneath his back felt cold, and the woman beside him too close. Irritated,

Zach wondered why the emotional relief he'd sought wasn't as simple as a mere climax.

Several hours later in the darkness of his bedroom, Zach tossed for the hundredth time. LouAnn had gone home and was probably asleep in her own bed even now, wrapped in wedding dreams, no doubt. In the past couple of years, the ability to sleep had all but deserted Zach. The problem plaguing him, he suspected, was stress, related to his job, stress he was bringing on himself, but no less disturbing because it was self-inflicted. Getting into a new line of work was imperative, or he might never sleep again. In the last year, he'd noticed an occasional stray pain shooting across his chest. Zach didn't doubt he was working himself up to pop a coronary like Mr Cade had.

Zach's mind drifted to Annie. He wondered how she was coping. A fleeting desire struck him to call her and check on how she was doing, but Zach decided against it. It would be unethical, he decided. And most likely an unwanted intrusion. Annie Aguillar would probably resent a phone call from him, since he was associated with the misfortune that had befallen her.

For a moment, he imagined helping Annie out financially. The shining knight in armor scenario played itself out in his imagination, complete with Annie gratefully kissing him for his largesse. Shoot, the money he'd spent on LouAnn's earrings alone would represent a great deal of money to the Aguillars' predicament. Zach could very easily imagine himself in the role of her savior, not just because he *could* help her, but because he really would like to.

However, Annie would never allow it. Zach knew that, and he let go of the shining-knight fantasy. LouAnn would always take his gifts with a delighted smile. But he'd get no thanks from Annie. Her pride would be distressed by any attempt from him to help her. The only assistance he could give Annie would be simply to leave her alone.

With a sigh, Zach rolled over. The stress and guilt from what he did for a living already kept him up all night long, every night. Feeling confined by his relationship to LouAnn was a new sensation. But he'd never suffered a wilt in his desire for her before. Zach lay still, unsatisfied, watching the illuminated numbers on the digital clock by his bedside flip over, one by one by one.

'Maybe you didn't try hard enough,' Carter remonstrated.

Zach ground his teeth. So far, Carter refused to accept that he was simply not the man for the Aguillar contract. 'I did try, dammit.'

'Just because a small health issue popped up is no reason to give up on the deal,' Carter stated. 'After enough hospital bills pour in, they'll be glad to see you.'

'Well, I won't be in this job long enough for the bills to hit their mailbox, Carter. Remember, I'm getting married soon.'

'I know, I know. Maybe you should just give it a few more days before you decide, Zach. For all you know, that girl might call you up, begging to buy her land. This discussion would be moot then.'

Zach leveled a stare at his vice president. 'I get the strangest feeling you aren't taking my intent to resign seriously, Carter. But I am no longer going to be a part of Ritter in just a few short days.'

Carter sighed, shaking his head. 'You've been a good friend to me, Zach, you know that. And you're the best deal-maker around. I hate to break up our team. Naturally, I'm hoping you'll change your mind in due time, maybe after a few honeymoon trips with your new wife.' Carter leaned back in the leather chair, lighting up a cigar. 'Life is full of surprises.'

'Don't count on me being one of those surprises,' Zach warned. Carter's complacency worried him. It was almost as if the man knew something Zach didn't, and he couldn't shake the niggling feeling it had something to do with this latest deal.

'Is your father coming to the wedding?' Carter asked.

The question surprised Zach. He slipped a wary glance at Carter. He knew his entire history with his father; had, in fact, met him on the few occasions when his father visited him at the office. Ah, those monthly visits, always under the guise of gruff, fatherly love. Once Zach's check was in his father's hand, it never failed to surprise him how quickly his father disappeared. Until the money ran out again, of course.

Whether or not his father would extend himself to attending his only son's wedding, Zach couldn't say. He simply wished Carter hadn't asked the question. A disinterested shrug of his shoulders communicated the only answer Zach was prepared to give.

'Ah.' Carter took a deep drag on the cigar, exhaling slowly. 'I'm sure he'll make your big day, if he can.'

Zach pushed back his chair, standing up without commenting. 'I'll see you, Carter. I'm going to go make some calls.'

'All right. Tomorrow's another day.'

Zach was almost to the door when Carter's voice stopped him. 'By the way, have you seen LouAnn yet?'

He turned around. 'I did yesterday.'

Last night was more the truth. However, Zach didn't see any need to mention that.

'She forgive you for not showing up for the big party?'

LouAnn hadn't seemed to be holding any grudges when they'd attempted to make love. Zach shrugged again. 'Didn't seem to be too much of a problem.'

Carter's eyes twinkled. 'I'm not surprised. She's a generous woman, Zach. LouAnn'll make you a fine wife.'

Zach nodded in brief agreement, then turned around and walked out the door. He didn't want to think about LouAnn and her premium qualities to be a first-rate wife, a suitable life-partner for him.

In the parking lot, he pulled off his jacket as he loped to his car. If he hurried, he might catch his father before the bingo parlor opened for Monday night games. There were many things he wanted to discuss with his father, but today, one thing in particular weighed on his mind. Carter's question had stirred up a buzzard's nest of anxiety. For once in his life, would his father be capable of acting like a father? Or was the knotty, selfish old man who shared Zach's name going to remain an eternal pain in the butt?

Surely he'd show up for the damn wedding, Zach thought. Even his father wouldn't stoop to embarrassing Zach in such a manner. The car ate up the white lines faster as he drove out of the Austin city limits.

The old man had better act right for once in his life, or Zach wasn't going to be responsible for his actions the next time his father showed up with his hand out. Very possibly, Pop would be the recipient of a one-way trip out Zach's office window.

By the time he pulled up in front of the dingy shack, tension had threaded itself into Zach's shoulders and neck. Paint that had once been white now flaked off the weatherbeaten wood of his father's house in uncertain curls of disrepair. Anger deepened the taut feeling in his chest. Where in the hell did all the money he gave his father go every month? As far as he knew, alcohol soaked up some of it, but it wasn't like his father was fond of Chivas Regal. Bingo was his only source of entertainment, but Monday nights couldn't amount to much. No cable, few groceries, not even a daily newspaper – yet every month or so, his father asked him for a large sum of money, which Zach always willingly wrote a check to cover. Each time hoping, somewhere in his soul, that his father might acknowledge it with a nod of thanks, even a terse smile.

He stepped onto the porch and knocked. The door creaked open at his touch. Stale liquor smells reached him as he poked his head inside. 'Pop? You home?' he called, stepping inside.

The shambles of the darkened living room dismayed him, though he'd seen it one hundred times before. After all, this was the room he'd grown up in – and finally escaped from.

'What are you doing here, dammit?'

A slightly bent figure staggered into the hallway. Zach flicked on a lamp, searching the glare on his father's face for any sign of reluctant welcome. It wasn't there.

'I said, what are you doing here?'

'Just came by to check on you, Pop.'

'What for?' the old man demanded suspiciously. 'Who appointed you my guardian?'

Zach ignored the jibe and sat down on the sofa instead. The seat sagged with his weight and he realized the springs were shot. 'Your sofa's busted.'

'And Santy Claus has balls. In my day you didn't have to go to a fancy college to figure out when something was broken,' his father stated.

'Come on, Pop. I was surprised, that's all. Don't take it personally.'

'I don't need you coming around here with your nose in the air. I didn't ask you to come.'

'You never do,' Zach pointed out. 'I need to talk to you.'

'Well, whoop-de-do. Mr Important wants to talk to his old man. What's the matter? That flashy suit scratching your tender skin? Maybe your shoes didn't get shined the way you wanted.' His father spat, barely missing Zach's black shoe. 'There. There's some shine for you.'

'Damn, Pop!' Zach shot up from the sofa. 'What in the hell is your problem? What did I ever do to you?'

'It's your holier-than-thou attitude, Zach. Whether you like it or not, this is my house. I don't need you coming in here acting like you're some kind of king. If what I got ain't good enough for you, then get the hell out.'

Zach sighed, massaging the back of his neck. 'Look. I'm sorry, okay? How you live is none of my business. But for chrissakes, I give you enough money – '

'I wondered when you'd bring that up. You want to know what I do with that money? I got me a fancy whore, same as you. I buy her expensive earrings so she'll keep her legs open, and – '

'Shut up!' Zach's command sliced the air. 'Your filthy mouth is going to lose some of its teeth if you ever talk about LouAnn like that again.' Furious, he crossed the room to his father's side, noticing that he shrunk down as if fearing Zach would touch him. 'How did you know about the earrings?'

His father shook his head.

'You *are* going to tell me, or the freeloader's payroll closes its doors. How do you know about the earrings?'

'Carter came by yesterday.' His father twisted away and went to a cabinet, grabbing out a paper bag. He tipped it to his mouth for a long gulp.

Zach watched him, trying to assimilate that information. Why would Carter come here? Instantly, he realized his father was probably lying. 'Give me a break, Pop. Are you saying Carter came over for a glass of tea and some friendly chit-chat, and the two of you discussed earrings?'

'We discussed what a screw-up you are, if you want to know the truth.' He laughed, the sound mocking. 'Oh, I heard all about the land deal. If you ask me, that blonde bimbo of yours has sucked out your guts.'

Zach strode to the front door, afraid he was about to lose his temper and flay his father. He started to leave, but then slowly turned around. With clear enunciation, he said, 'I don't recognize you as my father any longer.'

His father threw back his head and laughed. 'I never recognized you as my son, so that just about makes us even.'

A web of suspicion trapped Zach at the front door. 'What are you saying?'

'Why do you think I never gave you my name?' His father's chip-toothed grin told Zach how much he was enjoying this moment. 'I never married your mother

89

because she was a slut. God only knows who your father is.'

'That's a lie.' White-hot fury whipped through Zach. He took two steps forward before he realized what he was doing and stopped. 'Why are you lying?'

The grin on his father's face turned to a snarl. 'Because I hate you, boy. I always have, I always will. Your sleazy mama thought I'd marry her if she was pregnant. She was wrong. No way was I falling into that trap. That's all it was, a trap. You were the bait, but I was too smart to bite.'

'You must have felt something for her. She lived here until I was eight years old.' Zach's mind denied that his father had hated him from conception. Vague memories of his mother holding him, crooning lullabies to him in Spanish, surfaced. He'd grown to love the spicy food she cooked, and how the house always smelled of warm flour. His mother represented the only softness he'd ever known in his childhood.

'I didn't make her leave. She ran back to Mexico, fast as her little brown legs could carry her once she figured out I wasn't her ticket to a green card,' his father snarled. 'Left me with a bastard to raise who didn't look a thing like me.'

'Where is she now?' Hope wavered inside Zach that after all these years he might be able to find his mother.

'How the hell do I know? Don't you think I would have found her if I could have?'

For a fleeting instant, Zach thought he saw regret,

or something like it, in his father's weathered eyes. Shock rose inside him. Did his father regret the way he'd treated Zach's mother?

His father saw the expression on his face and laughed cruelly. 'Oh, no. Don't you go thinking that I wanted her back. I tried to find her so I could give her back the little *frijole* she so kindly left behind.'

'My mother wouldn't have left me. She would have taken me to Mexico with her.'

His father turned away and took a long draught from the brown-wrapped bottle. 'Yeah, well, believe that if you want to. The fact is, your mother left me – and she left you, too.'

Something wasn't making sense. His father seemed to be deliberately twisting the story, or maybe his mind had simply changed it over the years. He was certain his father had thrown his mother out. Vaguely, he remembered his parents having a terrible argument one night while he was in bed. The shouting had been frightening to an eight-year-old, although he was used to witnessing their disagreements. But not like this one. It had started out with another woman's name being tossed around, which was how all of them started. But it had quickly escalated into something more violent. There had been shouting and a loud crash – Zach's mind blocked the memory. All he remembered was that the next morning his mother was gone. He'd never seen her again.

But she wouldn't have left Zach if there'd been any other way around it. His heart knew that with an abiding certainty. Gradually, the knowledge calmed him, and Zach realized what was really bothering his father. 'She didn't leave me, Pop. She left you. You ran her off with your drinking and whoring. Every weekend it was a different bar, a different perfume Mama had to smell when you finally dragged yourself home in the morning.' He stepped close to his father and jabbed a finger on his chest. 'You've never forgiven her for leaving you. And you've spent all these years feeling sorry for yourself and blaming it all on me.'

Zach turned and strode to the front door, jerking it open. He stepped out into the soft summer twilight. 'By the way, don't bother coming to the wedding. We both agree I'd be lying if I introduced you as my father.' He let the door slam and walked to his car. As usual, the simplest conversation between him and Pop had escalated into a battle. Zach started the car, throwing it into reverse hard enough to feel gravel grinding under the tires. He could never get away from his past fast enough.

CHAPTER 6

Annie's emotions were strung tight from sitting in the hospital for hours on end. Although her father had made it through surgery in good condition, waiting to see if complications would crop up was wearing her down.

There was little to do in the hospital except wait and stare at the drab yellowed walls, and she found her mind drifting to Zach despite herself. Even when he'd worn a solemn expression, she caught herself staring at his lips, remembering their stolen moment by the pond. Oh, no doubt those lips had seduced many women; she herself had wanted to believe every word that had come out of Zach's mouth.

Kissing him had been a dizzying experience. Carlos had loved her deeply, and she had known delicious passion with him. But the taste of Zach had sent her spinning into deep waters of forbidden hunger. He was so confident, so self-assured, so strong and handsome.

Annie understood why her father feared Zach's

presence. Zach Rayez was a man who would rarely suffer a setback once he set his mind on a goal. If his looks didn't get him what he wanted, his personality could. Carlos had been extraordinarily handsome, too, but Annie had enjoyed being the one true love of his life. He was as solid and unchanging as the earth he'd tilled.

So why had the fangs of attraction bitten her so deeply from the moment she'd laid eyes on Zach? Conventional wisdom warned her that a man like Zach would never settle down; his heart would never be one woman's. He'd always be searching, striving.

Yet, her woman's wisdom denied that interpretation of Zach Rayez. She'd sensed his desire for her – and also his fierce determination not to touch her. He had been concerned for her, and she'd seen real pangs of distress in his dark eyes when her father had become ill at the table.

Yes, Zach had come to Desperado to buy her farm. But he'd left without doing his job, and it stood to reason that he would reject the idea of one woman standing in the way of what he wanted. Technically, she'd handed him an embarrassment he had to take back to Austin. The question was, why hadn't he tried harder to change her mind?

Annie crumpled up the plastic cup she held in her hand and tossed it into a trash can. The waiting-room clock indicated it was time to visit her father, so she hurried down the hall.

'Hi, Papa,' Annie said, after the nurse had nodded

her inside. 'How are you feeling?' The touch of grizzled, spiky hairs along his face brought tears to her eyes. He seemed to be aging overnight.

'Hi, baby,' he replied. Travis shifted the hand with the IV slightly on the white sheet and squinted open his eyes. 'I'm fine. Doing just fine.'

'Are you comfortable?'

'Hell, no. Is anyone in a hospital?'

His querulous words brought a smile to Annie's face. Her father sounded almost normal again. 'Is there anything you want? Anything I can do for you?'

'Stop fretting, for one thing.' A worn smile slipped across his face before disappearing. 'And tell me that city-slick has gone back to where he belongs. Under whatever rock that is,' he mumbled under his breath.

Annie reached up to fuss with her father's hair, smoothing it into place as best she could. 'He's gone, Papa,' she confirmed softly.

'And he ain't coming back?'

'Can't imagine why. What is there to come back for?'

Travis grimaced and sighed heavily. 'Seemed like he had his sights set on you, gal. 'Course, a man with his brains between his legs probably has his sights set on a girl in every town.'

Annie kissed her father's worn cheek. She could only fantasize that Zach's sights might have been set on her. The truth was, Zach had felt obligated to stay with her at the hospital, or he'd have already been cutting a trail back to Austin. 'Don't worry so, Papa.

You're just giving your ticker something to act up about.'

He sighed. 'I'm getting sleepy again, dammit. I'm like a baby, taking naps so often.'

'Rest, then. I'll be back to see you soon.'

Annie kissed her father one more time, then stood up. Her eyes traveled from his closed, wrinkled eyelids to his sheet-covered legs. He seemed so frail, and she'd leaned on his strength all her life. Suddenly, she felt very alone.

Turning, she walked quickly out of the room. A tide of hunger and exhaustion swept over her; it was as if she was depleted. The best thing to do would be to go home, take a shower, and rest for awhile. Then she could head over to Mrs Aguillar's house to visit Mary. Holding her daughter would make her feel strong again. She had no choice but to be strong for Mary's sake – and her father's. They were all she had. And she needed them as much as they needed her.

Annie had nearly reached the hospital exit when a hand grabbed her arm. For a split second, her heart leaped with hope that Zach might have returned.

'Whoa, slow down, Annie,' Cody said.

'Oh, Cody,' she said, tracing a smile onto her face to cover her disappointment. 'Guess I wasn't looking where I was going.'

'That's okay.' His expression was concerned. 'Are you all right?'

'I'm fine. I was just on my way home.'

Cody tipped her chin up. 'You should have called

me. I would have been glad to come and get you.'

'I know, and I appreciate that. I was going to call a taxi. I didn't want anyone to have to come down here just to take me back to the farm.'

His eyes sparkled knowingly in the sidewalk lights. 'You didn't want to bother anyone. Come on, I'll take you home.'

Her brother-in-law's hearse was easy to spot in the parking lot. They walked toward it and Annie waited while Cody opened the car door for her. She climbed in and sat down, twisting her hands in her lap. Cody got in beside her and started the car, driving away in silence.

After about two minutes had passed, Annie felt like she had to make an attempt at conversation. 'I'm not good company tonight, I'm afraid.'

Cody didn't take his eyes off the road. 'No one's asking you to be.'

She sighed. 'But I really do appreciate you taking me home. I was dreading a cab ride.' Not to mention it would cost about twenty bucks to get her to the farm, and Annie wasn't sure if she had that much in her purse. All she'd been thinking about was getting home and changing into something clean before hurrying over to kiss Mary goodnight. 'How's Mary doing?' she asked.

A smile tugged at Cody's lips. 'Driving Ma crazy.'

'Oh, no! She's not misbehaving, is she?'

'No way.' He shook his head. 'But you know how it is when little kids visit their grandmother. There's something fascinating in every closet, every drawer. Ma's having the time of her life trying to keep up with her. Today they made popsicles and Mary put hers outside for the birds to eat. Ma finally convinced her that the birds would rather have something else for dinner.'

Mary's antics brought a real smile to Annie's face and she relaxed, finally able to let some of the tension ebb out of her. 'Your mother's awfully good to Mary.'

'She'd do anything for her. You know that, Annie.'

Unspoken words hung in the air. *Nothing changed because Carlos died.* Yet, Annie never felt comfortable asking Mrs Aguillar for assistance of any kind. A lingering resonance of guilt that Carlos had died too young, too soon, trying to help her hang on to the farm kept Annie from wanting too close of a relationship with her mother-in-law.

'I know,' she replied. 'Mary's lucky to have a place where she can go and just be a little girl.' Far away from the worries that plagued her mother.

Cody nodded, seeming to understand the meaning behind her words. 'How's Travis?'

'He's taking this whole thing like a trooper. If no complications appear, the doctor says he'll be able to go home in a few days.'

'I'm glad to hear it.'

'Yes. I was, too. Papa's chomping at the bit to get out of the hospital as it is.'

'He's going to be chomping when he gets home, too. Have you figured out what you're going to do about his recovery?' Cody slanted a questioning glance at her.

Annie sighed. 'Frankly, no. Everything's happened so fast that I've been surviving moment to moment.' She pushed a hand tiredly through her hair, noticing that the braid was mostly undone. A few fingernails were chipped, and her denim skirt and white blouse looked like she'd worn them for a week. No, she hadn't thought about her father's rehabilitation, nor much of anything else beyond surviving the panic of the first few days.

Cody patted her leg briefly. 'Ma and I'll be glad to help you any way we can. Just tell us how, when you figure it out.'

'You're doing enough by taking care of Mary. I'll be all right, really.'

Cody didn't reply as he pulled into the long driveway. There were no lights on to herald a safe haven. Annie wondered if she'd ever feel right again, if the sense of overwhelming confusion would ever go away. It was like she was walking a crooked path blindfolded without any sense of what lay in store for her at the end.

'I'll wait for you.' He turned the car off and folded his arms. 'Take your time, nothing's pressing me.'

'Cody . . .' Annie stared at him. 'I'm going to take a shower and change my clothes. You can't wait on me all that time.'

He leaned his head back against the headrest. 'Sure I can. Get something to eat while you're in there.'

She couldn't let him do it. 'Please, I'll be fine. You go on – '

'You walking to my house?'

Annie put a hand to her forehead, rubbing lightly. 'How silly of me, the car's broken. I'm not thinking.'

'You're thinking fine. You've got a million other things to think about right now. Go on.'

She managed a tired smile. 'I think there's some leftovers in the fridge, and maybe a soft drink or two. Come on in, so I won't feel bad about you sitting out here.'

He grinned at her before opening the car door. 'At least if I'm foraging in the kitchen I might convince you to eat a bite.'

Annie shrugged and got out of the car. 'I can't think about food until I've had a shower. I feel like the smell of the hospital is clinging to my skin.'

He waited while she unlocked the front door. She reached to turn on a light. Nothing happened. 'That's strange,' she murmured. 'Maybe it's burned out.' Gingerly, she moved into the hall, stepping into the kitchen to feel along the wall. She flicked the switch, but the ceiling light didn't come on. 'I wonder what's wrong?'

A hot flash of panic enveloped her. She didn't need this right now, didn't know if she could handle one more problem, trivial as this probably was.

'Hang on. I'll check the box.'

She heard the sound of a lighter flaring, and a tiny flame illuminated Cody's features. Annie drew in her

100

breath. She'd forgotten how very much Cody resembled his brother. Without being able to see the shoulder-length raven hair and the feather earring Cody sported, he looked disturbingly like Carlos. Although Cody was like a brother to her, it hurt to see the resemblance. She turned away, unable to look at the face of the past. 'The box is in the kitchen closet, and there's a flashlight on the wall.'

He edged past her into the kitchen. A moment passed before he came back out of the closet. 'I don't see any problems.'

Annie frowned. 'I don't get it.'

'Me, either.' In the flashlight beam, she could see concern in Cody's eyes. 'I feel dumb for asking, but did you pay your electric bill?'

She closed her eyes, suddenly feeling inadequate. 'It's still sitting on my dresser where I put it to be mailed.'

He chuckled. 'Stress'll do that to you. Still, it seems like they shut you down awfully fast.'

Annie turned away, not wanting her embarrassment witnessed. 'We're not what you would call a good credit risk, I guess.'

Cody pulled her gently around. 'What are you saying?'

It was almost more than she could bear. Confessing her treacherous financial position would make it real, would make it impossible to ignore. She'd been holding on for so long, fighting, praying, desperate for anything to keep the monetary wolves at bay. But

101

the pitiful wall she had erected against the odds was crumbling. 'Things were bad when Carlos was alive, despite everything he did to save the farm. He almost had us solvent when he . . . had the accident. But since then – ' Annie choked to a stop, fearing tears would spill from her eyes any second. A sense of nervous anxiety rose inside her, and she felt weak, defeated. 'I've done everything I can, but it's not enough. It's never enough,' she whispered.

Cody gathered her into his arms. 'You're doing a great job, Annie. It's tough for a lot of people right now. You haven't done anything wrong.'

Sobs racked her body. 'You don't know.'

He patted her back soothingly. 'The banks are full of people desperate for assistance. You've done the best you can with almost nothing.' Cody leaned back, touching the flashlight beam to her face.

Annie was ashamed of the tears streaking down her cheeks, ashamed that she was falling apart. She looked a mess and felt worse, like an incompetent fool. Ducking her head, she tried to escape the searching glare of the light. 'I've made so many mistakes.'

'Everybody makes mistakes.' He put the flashlight on the kitchen table, so the beam pointed to the ceiling. 'I make mistakes, too,' he said, sliding into a chair. 'So what? This one's easy, anyway. I'll go down to the electric company tomorrow and pay the bill.'

'I can't let you do that, Cody.'

He pointed her into a chair. She complied, feeling

102

too defenseless to stand up. Despite her reluctance to bare her disastrous economic situation, it felt wonderful to be able to unburden herself to someone she could trust.

Not like Zach. He would never understand how someone could get into such a bind. What did he know about sacrifice, about hard times? He'd pity her for being such a fool. And maybe his pity would be deserved.

'You *can* let me do it, Annie. I insist. You can pay me back later.'

Cody's voice broke into her ruminations, spurring her memory. *If you sold your land, you'd be well off financially.* Ah, Zach's honey-smooth voice, working to get what he wanted. Her land, her pride – her very soul.

Yet, how much would all that be worth if she had to go begging to family relations for hand-outs? Annie's back stiffened at the thought. A small loan now to cover the electric bill, next week a little more to cover groceries. Then there would be the discreet charity: new school clothes for Mary, a pair of shoes now and again. All under the well-meaning guise of familial love, but she'd know. And it would cut her soul.

'I can't let you do that, Cody. But you're kind to offer. The check's on my dresser, and I'll run it down tomorrow.'

He shook his head. 'Let me do it. You need to be at the hospital. It'll take some time to argue with them about reinstating your service.'

Cody got up and crossed to the refrigerator, pulling out some soft-drink cans. Annie picked at one of her ragged nails. He was right, she did want to be at the hospital for the few short blocks of visiting time she was allowed. Allowing Cody to run the errand wouldn't be such a great drain on her pride if she didn't allow it to be. 'Thanks. I'd really appreciate it.'

He popped the top, setting the drink in front of her. 'Now that we've hashed that to death, why don't you go take that shower? It'll be shorter than you might have wanted, since the water'll be cold, but maybe you'll feel better. Or you can get a change of clothes and shower at our house.'

Annie jumped up from the chair. 'No, that's all right. The water won't be too cold if I'm fast. I'll be right back.'

Cody moved around the kitchen, guiding himself with the lighter. 'Take the flashlight. I can find food in the dark.'

With uncertain fingers, she picked up the flashlight and walked slowly down the hall. Annie knew she'd feel more comfortable bathing in her own home, despite chilly water. She felt suffocated, as if it were almost a fact that she was going to become a philanthropy of the Aguillars'. A charity case. Annie knew Cody didn't intend to make her feel that way, but she also had a funny feeling that her check was never going to be the one cashed by the electric company. Yet she'd acquiesced, realizing the fight was slowly ebbing out of her.

Ten minutes later, Annie made her way back into the kitchen with her mind and body stingingly refreshed. Cody had dug out an old kerosene lamp from somewhere and was opening a jar of salsa. Tortilla chips were in a bowl on the table, next to some cut vegetables.

'It's not much,' he said, jerking his head toward the table, 'but I'm afraid to make sandwiches. I don't know how long the electricity's been off.'

'It's okay, I'm not that hungry. What you've put out looks great,' Annie said. She said down at the table and shot a pointed look at Cody. 'When you run that errand for me tomorrow, be sure you use my check,' she instructed.

'What are you saying?' Even in the dim light, she could see he appeared confused.

'I don't want you paying my bills, Cody. Please understand that I have to be responsible for my own family.'

'I was planning on it.' He sat down across from her. 'But I hope you realize what a long haul you're in for.'

Annie picked up a carrot and munched it absently. 'I think I do.'

Cody stared at her. 'I talked to the doctor myself at one point. Even though your father came through his operation fine, he's still got a long way to go. The doc says the recovery side is the hard part.'

Awareness crept into Annie's brain. Cody was talking rehabilitation, which she'd figured meant working with her father some to keep his muscles fit. But the way he was talking, it sounded like money might be involved. 'What else did he say?'

'You're going to need some physical therapists to come and help you, Annie. You can't do it all.'

'I always have,' she replied tartly.

'Okay.' Cody picked up a chip and dipped it into the salsa before eating it. 'Let me get this straight. You're going to raise Mary, take care of your invalid father, and bring in those crops all by yourself. Just trying to get Travis to do his exercises is going to be a major chore,' Cody said with a grin. 'He's not going to let you tell him what he's supposed to do, Annie, and you know it. And did you get the part about your father having to wear shorts so his legs can heal where they stripped the veins for the bypass?' Cody broke into a snort of laughter. 'I'll be older than your father before I ever see him wearing anything but jeans for work and trousers for church.'

He shot her a wry glance. Annie sat still, feeling glued to the chair. Somewhere in her mind, she knew Cody was making sense, but didn't want to acknowledge it. *I can do it* had always been her motto. It hurt not to be able to say it now and know it to be true.

'As I said earlier, I haven't thought much past the urgency of the moment,' she said, feeling very weak even as she fell back on the truth.

Cody ran a hand through his hair before giving her a searching glance. 'I know, Annie. God knows you haven't had time to do much of anything. But your pride may cost you if you're not careful. You're going

106

to have to let Ma and me help you out.'

Her shoulders sagged. 'Maybe you're right. But how are you going to run two farms?'

'I have some help I can spare. Plus my farm's in good shape.' He stopped a moment, dragging his hand through his hair once more.

'You'll run yourself ragged going back and forth,' Annie pointed out. 'And you're talking about a lot more than just helping me over a rough spot.'

Cody leaned back in his chair, studying her by the soft yellow light of the kerosene lamp. 'It won't be too much of a problem. But I've thought about this a lot, and getting married might make matters easier on both of us.'

CHAPTER 7

Zach ripped a check out of his checkbook, stuffed it into an envelope with his father's name on it, and tossed it on the edge of his desk for the secretary to mail. It was insanity, plain and simple, but after all this time he still felt responsible for Pop. A vision of the man he'd grown up with, hungry and without basic necessities, haunted him into writing that check.

Zach glanced around the office, noticing with relief that the calendar on the desk showed there were only a few days left until he was a free man. Two weeks after that, he'd be married and on to a new, better phase of his life.

The door opened and Carter poked his head in. 'Got a minute?'

Zach nodded. Something his father had said was bothering him and he wanted to ask Carter about it, so the visit was timely. 'Sure. What's up?'

'I just got a phone call that the bank is going to foreclose on the Aguillar land if the taxes aren't paid up by the end of the year,' he said, strolling confidently into the room.

Carter paused, obviously expecting some reaction from Zach. When he didn't respond, Carter sat down in a leather chair facing the desk and leaned forward. 'This is a hell of an opportunity for us. It could be the sale we need in that area to put Ritter in a direct position to compete for commercial real-estate deals along the new state highway placement.'

Zach shook his head. 'No. Fortunately for the Aguillars, they're sitting on a bumper crop of corn. They'll make their taxes. And anyway, I'm out of it.'

'You're giving up on an opportunity Ritter should have.'

Zach shrugged.

Carter held up a hand. 'Let's talk about this.'

'I have nothing to say. Wrapping up my client load will keep me busy enough for the next three days. Someone else will have to go out there.'

Carter pursed his lips, studying him silently. 'You're awfully opposed to this. Did something happen out there you're not telling me about?'

'Hell, no.' Zach wasn't about to sit and have a tête-à-tête about the effect the Aguillar family had on him. 'I've got a lot to do, and I wasn't hot to take on another deal in the first place.' Zach met Carter's eyes firmly. 'LouAnn and I have a lot to do to get ready for the wedding, and it's nearly impossible for me to be away now.'

That was all very true, but it wasn't the real reason he wanted to wash his hands of the Aguillar deal. The whole thing had been a mess from start to finish – he'd never had a deal go south on him as fast as that one had. And he'd never expected to find a ravishing, courageous woman on a run-down, dusty little farm in the middle of nowhere. The desire to bed her had risen up out of some primal place inside him he couldn't name, nearly blinding him to common sense and decent behavior.

Hell, no. He wasn't going back there.

He shook his head decisively. 'LouAnn and I've got some details to iron out, so I'm taking her to dinner tonight. I may be in a little late in the morning,' he added.

Carter ignored that comment. 'Let's not be hasty. You might change your mind.'

Don't hold your breath, was Zach's immediate thought. Aloud, he merely said, 'I don't think so. And while we're talking, what were you doing at my father's house the other day?'

For a moment, Carter eyed him thoughtfully. Then he picked up the envelope Zach had finished addressing to his father, studying it for a moment. He looked at Zach, then purposefully held the envelope up to the hot, bright light streaming through the office window. Even Zach could clearly see the outline of a check through the paper.

Carter put the envelope back on the desk. 'I wasn't far from his neighborhood, so I stopped to let him know you'd been held over in Desperado. I didn't want him worrying about you.'

Zach snorted. 'Cut the crap, Carter. He hasn't worried about me since day one. Pop told me you'd mentioned the land deal to him, and that it had fallen through. And you also told him about the earrings I gave LouAnn. Since when did you two become such bosom buddies?'

Carter gazed at him with soulful grey eyes. 'Your father's lonely, Zach.'

'Oh, jeez. Give me a break.'

'Well, he is. What does it hurt me to stop by and spend a few minutes with him?'

'What does it *gain* you, you mean. You told my father more about my life than I ever have. What I can't figure out is why.'

Carter stood up. 'I like your old man. And as I said, I was in the neighborhood.'

They started at each other silently for a few minutes. Then Zach said, 'Getting my father to goad me into finishing that deal isn't going to work, Carter. I'm way past caring what Pop thinks about me.'

His vice president appeared to think about that for a moment, before shrugging and ambling to the office door. 'It wasn't my intention to try to sway you by using your father. I've known you long enough to know that wouldn't work. Though I do hope, selfishly maybe, that you'll change your mind about the deal.'

Zach took a deep breath. 'And I hope that this conversation doesn't surface between us again, or you may find that my last act as president in this company is to make sure you no longer work here.'

The threat was clear. *Don't try to screw me, Carter.*

After several shocked moments, Carter moved past the doorframe and closed the door. Zach had a feeling Carter wasn't telling the truth about the visit to Pop. Something else was going on, but he sure as heck didn't know what. The only thing he was certain of was that Carter didn't make friends unless he needed them. What possible motive could Carter have for getting buddy-buddy with Pop?

The phone rang, startling him. He picked it up. 'Hello?'

'Darling, I'm downstairs at the curb, if you're ready to go to dinner.'

Despite the static of the car phone, Zach could hear the anticipation in LouAnn's voice. Well, dammit, he was going to be excited about their dinner plans, too, and he wasn't going to let Carter ruin it for him. 'I'll be right down,' he said.

'Hurry, darling.'

The phone went dead and Zach hung up, shrugging into his suit jacket. He started to pick up the envelope containing his father's check, then stopped. Why was Carter so interested in his correspondence with his father? Since the beginning, when Zach had met the struggling law student, his associate had known of the difficult relationship he had with his father. At some point, Carter had taken it upon himself to fill a void in Pop's life. Now Carter had gone too far in his friendship with Zach's father and something felt sinister about it.

112

Zach made it to the door when the phone rang again.

'Dammit,' he murmured. The last thing he needed was to get held up on a business call. If LouAnn was at the curb, she'd have to keep circling the building or risk a ticket. Too many times having to circle would take the curl right out of LouAnn's blonde hair, and they'd start the evening off at odds.

'Hello?' he said briskly.

'Zach? Zach Rayez?'

He frowned, not recognizing the voice although it sounded familiar. 'Yes?'

There was silence for a moment, before the quiet voice spoke again. He had to press the phone hard to his ear to hear. Then he knew that voice, knew it like he'd heard it all his life. 'Annie? Has something happened?'

'No.' She sounded like she was at the point of tears. 'But I wondered if you had a moment to talk.'

Zach was speechless. The one thing he'd never imagined happening was this. Annie sounded so distressed that he was worried. 'Are you all right?'

He heard a sniffle, before she said, 'I'm fine.'

'Nothing's happened to your father, has it?'

'No, he's doing much better.'

So it wasn't urgent, although he certainly wanted to talk to her and make sure she really was fine. 'Listen, I really do want to talk to you, but I need to leave the office now. How about if I call you back tonight? Will you be home?'

She was silent. Zach wondered if she'd heard him,

113

but then Annie softly replied, 'I'll be home after nine.'

He wouldn't be home quite that early, but maybe he could call her from the restaurant. Suddenly, he remembered LouAnn was waiting on him – impatiently, no doubt. 'All right. I'll call you back this evening.'

It sounded like Annie said 'thank you' and then the phone went dead. Zach tossed it down and strode to the door. He caught the elevator as it was closing. Quickly, he got on, hoping to catch LouAnn before she had to move out of the way of traffic. Her little white sports car was just pulling up to the curb. He squeezed himself into the car, giving her a quick peck on the cheek.

'I got caught on the phone. Sorry about that.'

LouAnn smiled, obviously in a good mood over something. 'It's okay. I've got something special planned for you tonight.'

'Oh?' Zach glanced at LouAnn's perfectly styled hair and fingernails. A sudden thought occurred to him that he couldn't remember ever seeing LouAnn without the full complement of cosmetics she always wore. She was beautiful, of course, stunning enough to make heads turn whenever they walked into a function – but he wasn't sure what lay beneath the veneer of makeup. He wasn't sure what her skin smelled like without the scent of perfume and hairspray clinging to her; even her cheeks smelled like expensive lotions and powders.

Suddenly it seemed urgent that he get to know this

woman – the real LouAnn – before he married her. Hesitantly, he asked, 'What did you plan?'

'Something at your place, where we can get comfy, and be alone,' she said suggestively. She slid her hand up his leg. 'I'm having dinner delivered, too, so we don't have to be bothered while we're trying to talk about our wedding plans. How does that sound?'

Zach caught her roving fingers deftly in his, on the pretext of wanting to hold her hand. How was he going to call Annie with LouAnn hovering around? 'Sounds great,' he murmured.

'I knew you'd be excited,' LouAnn said, her cherry-colored lips stretched into a smile. 'I can't wait until we're married. I'm going to surprise you like this all the time.' She reached into the back of the car, handing him a small bag. 'I got you something to get you in the mood for discussing wedding plans, Zach. Open it and see.'

Reluctantly, Zach released LouAnn's hand, hoping it wouldn't wander back into his lap. He opened the bag. Underneath the white tissue lay a pristine, lacy white pair of crotchless panties.

LouAnn giggled. 'So, shall we go talk wedding?'

'The faster the better,' he replied, knowing that was the expected response. LouAnn laughed, and the little car sped through a yellow light. Zach closed the bag and returned it to the back seat, wondering why he suddenly felt a little nauseous.

* * *

115

Carter waited until Zach left, then strolled into his office. The phone call Zach had just received had been very interesting. He'd listened shamelessly through the door, realizing almost immediately from Zach's reaction who was on the other end of the line.

Zach had sounded so concerned that Carter pondered the conversation again. Something *had* happened while Zach was at the Aguillar farm. Surely he hadn't allowed himself to go soft over that Indian woman. Zach had never once looked at another woman since LouAnn, and the Aguillar woman was a direct contrast to the trophy female he'd caught himself. Zach would never cheat on LouAnn – but something just wasn't making sense.

The check on the corner of the desk drew his eye. Oh, he knew all about the row between Zach and his father. They'd finally had it out, the sore in their relationship festering over the years until it had finally reached painful proportions. That Zach still felt responsible for the worthless old man who shared his bloodline amazed Carter. It was possible being in love was making his boss go soft in the head.

Carter's eyes widened. In love, yes, but possibly not with LouAnn. Zach's behavior hadn't altered in the nine months he and LouAnn had been engaged; he'd been as ruthless and deal-hungry as ever. Suddenly, he'd had it out with his pop and was still willing to front the old toad, and he had a lack of hunger where a deal was concerned. All since he'd gone to Desperado.

All since he'd met the owner of the Aguillar farm.

Was it possible, was it even conceivable, that Zach had fallen a little bit for that black-haired, countrified witch of a woman?

It was too strange to bear thinking about, and would certainly throw a kink into Carter's plans. Decisively, he strode to Zach's desk. The envelope bearing Zach's father's name he opened, staring at the amount written there.

'Stupid fool,' he muttered, before tearing it up.

She shouldn't have called him. Embarrassment flooded over Annie like water from a burst dam. Zach's voice had sounded so distant over the phone lines that she knew the small bond she'd imagined between them had never been real.

She glanced at her father, who lay peacefully sleeping in his hospital bed. It was eight-thirty in the evening. Cody would be waiting for her out in front of the hospital. Annie picked up her purse and leaned over to touch her lips to her father's forehead. He didn't move, so she silently drifted out the door and down the hall.

As she'd expected, the hearse was parked at the curb in the fire lane. Cody obeyed no authority in life except that imposed upon him by the sun and the moon. A slight breeze brushed her legs as the hospital doors slid open and Annie walked faster, anxious to leave the hospital behind.

'Hiya, Annie,' Cody said as she got into the car.

'Hi, Cody.' She gave him a smile before leaning her head tiredly against the headrest. 'I appreciate you giving me a ride home.'

'No problem. It's on my way.'

She turned to look at him, her eyebrow arched. 'This is most certainly not on your way.'

He shrugged and pulled out of the parking lot. 'But it's not far enough to make a difference, either, Annie. I'm glad to do it.'

The distance between his farm and the hospital was about twenty miles, Annie calculated. Add to that the driving distance to her farm and it was a round trip of about sixty miles. She pursed her lips, feeling guilty. Cody shouldn't have to do for her. His mother was already keeping Mary, and that was enough of an imposition. The weight of her responsibilities bore down upon her, and a little resentment, too. Never before had she felt so dependent, so helpless.

Unaware of the emotions he was stirring up, Cody said, 'By the way, I took your check by the electric company. Everything's straightened out now, and when you get home, you should find lights and hot water waiting for you.'

Annie smiled weakly. 'Your efficiency is impressive, to say the least. Thank you.'

He turned his head to look at her. Illumination from occasional city lights chased the shadows from his face. Cody was handsome, in a rough-hewn sort of way, all the more attractive because his countenance spoke of hard work. But Annie felt no spark inside her soul for Carlos's brother, despite the softness his smile held just for her.

'I don't need any thanks, Annie. You're family, and family pulls together.'

Yes, but she was a drag on the line. 'I can't help feeling bad for everything you and your mother are having to do for me. I'm disrupting your lives.'

He ran a light finger down her cheek before pulling onto a main road. 'And what would you do if my mother was in an accident of some kind?'

'Oh, my goodness,' Annie murmured. 'Well, I'd cook for her, and try to get her to let me clean the house. Mary would want to color her a hundred get-well cards, and – '

'Now, then,' Cody interrupted smoothly, 'you'd feel the same way we do about helping you out while you're having difficulties. Everybody goes through hard times, eventually. You're just suffering a little more than your share right now.'

His smile was kind and wise. Annie took a deep breath, trying to calm the raging sea of worries inside her. Cody was right. In the end, everything was going to work out fine.

Suddenly, she felt more awkward than ever that she'd placed that call to Zach Rayez. Since when did a little misfortune knock her off her horse? Since when had she forgotten to get right back up and ride like hell?

Never again was she going to bow to the pressure of self-pity and anxiety, Annie vowed.

119

'Well, here you are,' Cody said. He pulled the hearse in front of her house. 'I'll go inside with you and make sure the electricity has been restored.'

Annie started to say it wasn't necessary, but Cody had already opened his door and gone off into the darkness, muttering something about hell to pay if it wasn't. She sighed and climbed out of the car, relieved to be home. Tired as she was, Annie appreciated the sense of comfort and welcome that seemed to resonate from every corner of her home. Home. That's what this small, hard-baked piece of land was, and just setting foot on it sent strength welling up inside. Whatever insidious doubt had caused her to weaken, to pick up the phone and call Zach she didn't know, but when he returned her call tonight, Annie knew she would stick to mundane matters and never mention what she'd really been calling about.

She would never admit, with her dying breath, that she'd actually considered selling a tiny portion of the land that was hers by right of birth.

'You comin', Annie?' Cody called. A warm flood of light radiated from the porch with his words.

Annie hurried toward the house. 'I'm right here.'

He met her at the door. 'Everything's in order. You can spend the whole evening relaxing.'

She put her purse down on a table, meeting his smile. 'I don't know if I'll actually relax, but it's definitely nice to have the lights back on. Thanks again, Cody.'

'Well, I guess I'll be going, unless there's something else you need.'

Shaking her head at his wistful expression, Annie said, 'You've done enough.'

'I'll do a lot more, if you ever say the word,' he replied huskily.

Annie cast her gaze down, unwilling to witness the hope she saw in his expression. 'You're a good friend, Cody,' she murmured.

After a moment, he sighed before walking to the front door. 'I've got a small surprise for you, so I'll pick you up around nine in the morning. How does that sound?'

She allowed her eyes to finally meet his. 'Wonderful.'

'Great. See you then.'

The sound of his boots thumping down the porch steps brought a feeling of relief, because now she could truly be alone with her thoughts. Sooner or later, he was going to require an answer to the startling proposal he'd offered her. Annie sighed, trying to force herself to relax in her little home.

Yet, strangely enough, a feeling of loneliness pervaded her. The house was too empty. Too quiet. Mary's laughter was missing, and so was Papa's gruff encouragement.

Still, Annie warned herself to be strong. Giving in to alien feelings of weakness was what had preyed on her before. Like vultures, there were people circling, waiting to take advantage of the slightest crack in her defenses.

It was so good to be home. She could get strong again here.

And then nothing could get to her.

Not even Zachary Rayez and the memory of his lips against hers, the feel of his man's need pressed against her. He'd wanted her, Annie knew with certainty, but that kiss would have to sustain her through many lonely nights. It would only make her miserable to dream about something that was never going to happen again.

Pressing her lips together, Annie realized she hadn't remembered to get the mail when they'd driven up to the house. Cody hadn't thought about stopping at the little mailbox at the end of the drive, and neither had she. Walking down there in the darkness could be dangerous, despite the fact the night breeze blew sultry in the inky sky and a walk would be refreshing and nice.

She thought about the overdue electric bill which had caused such problems, then hesitated. Cody had removed the rattlesnake at some point, leaving the box empty for its next inhabitant. There wasn't much chance of her coming across one if she stayed on the rock-and dirt-packed lane. Annie shook her head. There were other bills she hadn't paid in an exact and timely manner. Likely there was nothing in the mailbox that couldn't wait until morning.

And besides, she might miss Zach's call. Annie instantly frowned. Why did she feel like it would matter?

Suddenly, silence pressed in upon her. It was too damn quiet; it felt like she was in a tomb. And maybe that was why she wanted to be sure she caught Zach's call.

To reassure herself that she was still alive.

CHAPTER 8

Sleep came uneasily to Annie that night. It was as if she were holding her breath; she tossed and turned, never fully awake.

In the morning she rose feeling sluggish. The rejuvenation that she so desperately needed eluded her. Annie realized she'd never fully relaxed when she'd finally gone to bed – because her subconscious had been listening for the phone to ring.

And it never had. Zach never returned her phone call.

Bitter disappointment washed over her, all the sharper because it shouldn't have mattered, and it did.

'What a fool I am,' Annie whispered to herself, raking her long, black hair into a careless braid. The mirror reflected a woman too tired and too tense to have any contentment inside her soul. She sighed, deeply. 'I can't say Papa didn't warn me about Zach.'

Her pride stung all the more when she remembered their kiss, how he'd refused to take what she'd so plainly been offering – sexually. What he wanted was her land and that he couldn't have, so he'd gone away without making the conquest he'd wanted.

And she was no more than a name on paper to him now.

Loud honking outside drew Annie's attention to the window. Cody's hearse was pulling up, and he had a passenger. With a glad cry, Annie ran to the door, flinging it open in her delight. 'Mary!' she cried, running to the car to open it and pulling the small child inside into her arms.

Annie breathed in the strawberry-sweet scent of Mary's hair, noting that her daughter's shoulders felt small and frail as she clutched her. 'Mommy's missed you so much,' she murmured.

'I've missed you too, Mommy,' Mary replied. 'When can I come home?'

Annie winced at the question. 'I don't know, sugar. Aren't you happy at Grandma's?'

'Yes.' Mary's nod was definitive. 'But I miss you. I miss my grandpa. I want to come home.'

Annie pulled Mary back into her arms for another tight hug. 'I know you do. Mommy wants that, too. I love you so much.'

After a moment, Mary pulled back slightly and stared into Annie's eyes. 'The snake got away.'

'What?' Annie was shocked. She glanced toward the mesh-and-wood box, remembering that she'd assumed Cody had taken the snake away. She glanced at Cody for confirmation. 'What happened to it?'

He shrugged and shook his head. Annie looked back

to Mary. Solemn indigo eyes gazed at her. 'Will it ever come back, Mommy?'

Annie was perplexed. She was certain she'd securely closed the box. That had been one of the fattest rattlers she'd ever seen, and she wasn't sure she could comfortably allow Mary to play outside, knowing the granddaddy of all snakes was on the loose.

'I don't know, sugar,' Annie said with a frown. 'But if it ever does come back, Mommy'll kill it. I won't let it get away again, I promise.'

'You'll kill it dead?'

'Dead.' Annie nodded decisively.

'And we can bury it in a *really* deep hole?'

Annie smiled. 'After we make your grandpa the fanciest hatband and boots he's ever seen.'

Mary clapped her hands. 'For when he comes home from the hospital!'

'Exactly. Now don't you worry about that old snake again. Likely, he's so glad to be free he's gone back to wherever he belongs and he's never coming back.'

'Good.' Mary tucked her hand inside Annie's, and together they walked inside the house. 'He was really scary.'

'I have to agree with you about that.' Annie went into the kitchen and opened the refrigerator. New jars that had never been opened sat in neat rows inside the rail. Several bottles of juice stood beside a new jug of milk.

Slowly, she turned to look at Cody, who'd followed them inside. 'You didn't have to do this.'

He shook his head, appearing vaguely uncomfort-

126

able. 'Just about everything spoiled in the refrigerator when the electricity went out. Fortunately, the deep freeze stayed fairly cold, so you just needed some little odds and ends.'

Annie started to protest, but Cody waved her silent. 'When do you have time to go to the store? Every one of your waking minutes is spent at the hospital, as it should be.'

She bowed her head. Cody was right – and yet, she felt so impotent. Never had she needed to rely on other people for so much.

'Thank you,' she murmured.

'Don't mention it,' he replied, his voice very gruff and not welcoming further comment.

'Can I have a grape soda?' Mary asked, pointing to the purple cans on the bottom shelf.

'Sure, sugar.' Annie popped the top and handed the can to her daughter. Mary took it happily and climbed into a seat at the table. 'The least I can do is offer you a drink, Cody. What'll be?'

'I'll have one of Mary's grape sodas.'

'Yuck.' Annie grimaced and Cody laughed. Annie's awkwardness fled. Deftly, she pulled out a can and tossed it to him. 'I can see you and your mother have been spoiling my daughter.'

Cody caught the can, grinning. 'You betcha. And having a heck of a time doing it.'

A sudden snapshot in time flared in Annie's mind. Cody, Mary, herself – the three of them a family. The image was grainy, distorted. As much as she liked

Cody and yes, even loved him, she loved him like a brother. Carlos's brother. In her heart, there was no way she could ever love him the way she'd loved Carlos. Maybe Cody didn't expect her to, but she couldn't accept his marriage proposal without loving him. Hers and Mary's life would be a lot easier, but Annie would always know that she'd cheated Cody of experiencing the joy of a woman who loved him with all her soul.

Cody was a good man who would shoulder family obligations without complaint. But being an obligation was more than she could bear.

She'd have to tell him, soon. 'Cody,' she said, forcing her mind to another pressing matter, 'there's a chance the hospital may release Papa tomorrow.'

Cody crushed the soda can between his palms and tossed it into the trash with a smile. 'That's great news! Good for the hospital, because they're probably ready to see the last of that ornery cuss.'

'What's a cuss?' Mary asked, her eyes rounded.

Annie laughed. 'Cody is saying that your grandfather is stubborn, kind of like that mule we had once that kept getting into the corn.'

'That's not very nice, Uncle Cody,' Mary admonished.

Annie and Cody shared a laugh. Cody crossed the room and hunkered down in front of Mary. 'I'm teasing, ladybug. It's not meant to hurt anyone's feelings. Like when I call you ladybug. You're not really a ladybug, are you?'

Cody tickled under Mary's chin when she tried to answer, and Annie was relieved to see the solemn expression on Mary's face lift for a moment. 'No,' Mary said, between a gale of giggles.

'And you're not really a bag of sugar, either, are you? You're sweet, but you're not really sugar, or what's going to happen?'

'I don't know!' Mary managed between delighted shrieks, as Cody continued tickling her.

'Well, I know. The horses will think you're their treat, and they'll want to nibble on you!'

Mary squealed with laughter. Cody gathered the little girl into his arms and slid on to the plank bench, brushing the ebony hair out of her eyes while she caught her breath. Happiness shone in her deep blue eyes, and Annie felt gratitude to Cody well up in her heart.

Gratitude, but not love.

Mary looked up at Cody's face, adoring. 'I guess Grandpa was only teasing then when he called Mr Rayez snake-eyed vomit.'

A tiny smile hovered at Cody's mouth. 'Surely he didn't say that about Mr Rayez,' he said with a grin Annie's way.

'Uh-huh, Uncle Cody.' Mary's voice was certain. 'Grandpa said, "If that damn fool snake-eyed vomit – "'

'Hang on a second, Mary,' Cody interrupted. 'I believe you, honey. There's two things we gotta get square here. I'm teasing you when I call you a ladybug, because I love you. You know that, don't you?'

Mary nodded and waited.

'I don't reckon your grandaddy loves Mr Rayez, though, do you?'

'No,' Mary answered, the solemn shadows back on her face.

'So, I guess I have to say he wasn't teasing when he called him a snake-eyed varmint. However – and I believe Travis would agree with me here – your grandaddy was very upset that day, and I think he said some things he probably didn't mean. Probably he was so angry, he wasn't thinking before he said them, okay?'

'Okay.'

'Good. Now, why don't you run into your room and get a few more of your stuffed animals to bring to Gran's house tonight?'

She slid down off his lap. 'Sure, Uncle Cody.' Before she could leave the room, Cody said, 'And, Mary . . .'

'Yes, Uncle Cody?'

He bent close to Mary's ear, but whispered loudly enough for Annie to hear. 'I don't think Travis meant to say damn, either. You don't want to be saying that around your mother, okay?'

'Okay.'

She skipped out of the room and Annie smiled gratefully at Cody. 'You handled that like a real parent.'

'Well, I love Mary like she was my own.'

The statement was true, had always been a fact. Yet it hung heavy upon the air, and Annie knew she had to clear away the question that was certain to come up again. 'Cody, I think the world of you. You're everything good a woman wants in a man. I wish I could make myself feel differently, but as much as I care about you, I could never feel the way about you that I did about Carlos.'

'I'm not asking you to,' Cody said softly.

It was the answer she'd expected and prepared herself for. 'He'd always be between us, Cody. I'd always feel like I was betraying him somehow. I can't live that way – and it's not fair to you.'

An eternity of silence met her words. Cody ran a hand over the long, black braid of his hair, automatically checking for the feather at the end. He stared at her with bright, knowing eyes, seeing much more than Annie wanted revealed.

He sighed deeply, getting to his feet. Shaking his head, he appeared at a loss for words. Finally, he said, 'I'll do whatever I can to help you, Annie. There's got to be a way to get you out of this mess that I haven't thought of yet.'

Annie was relieved. Cody didn't really love her. Oh, he loved her like family, but she wasn't breaking his heart with her refusal. She'd been right: he'd been offering out of a feeling of family loyalty. And that wasn't a sound enough reason for him to hitch himself to her for ever.

'I don't know the answer, Cody. But with good

friends like you, I know we'll make it through this.'
The phone rang, and Annie turned to pick it up. 'Let me get this real quick, and then we'll get on our way,' she said. 'Hello?'

'Annie, it's Zach Rayez.'

'Oh.' Annie's startled gaze skittered to Cody. She'd put the fact that she'd called Zach out of her mind. 'How are you doing?'

'*I'm* fine. The question is, how are you?'

'Oh, I'm about the same.' She shot a rather guilty look at Cody. How she wished she could talk to Zach without Cody hearing every word of their conversation!

'You had me worried last night. I wish I could have called back, but . . . I had a dinner obligation.'

'Oh, it was no problem. I went to sleep as soon as I got home, anyway,' she fibbed.

Cody shrugged and left the kitchen. She heard his boots on the floor as he headed down the hall toward Mary's room.

'Still, you sounded upset, or something. I was afraid your father's condition was on the decline.'

'No,' Annie said softly. What the devil was she going to say her reason for calling him had been? 'I shouldn't have called. I don't know what I was thinking about.' There. That was close to the truth.

'Well, I'm glad you did.'

'You are?' Annie asked.

'Sure. I've been wondering how you were getting along. How's Mary?'

She smiled. 'Today is the first day I've spent any time with her. She wants to come home, and I think she's ready for everything to get back to normal.'

'Well, that sounds like a little lady who knows what she wants.'

'I think so, too.' Annie thought about Mary's quiet, almost sad, demeanor and decided to change the subject. 'Well, I – '

'How's your father, by the way?'

Was there the slightest echo of concern in his voice? Annie was surprised, since her father had done everything he could to bait Zach while he'd been at their house. 'He's getting stronger. The doctors may release him tomorrow.'

Zach let out a sigh. 'I'm glad to hear it. When he started clutching at his chest, I thought – well, hell, it doesn't matter now. Suffice to say I'd rather Travis be fit enough to curse me again than turning bluebonnets up with his toes.'

Annie smiled. 'Shall I convey your sentiments to Papa?'

Zach chuckled. 'No, thanks. Let's just let sleeping dogs lie, all right? Or should I say, sleeping snakes?'

'Our snake got away, so we're back to regular farm animals around here.'

'You're kidding! How'd that happen?'

Annie shrugged, though Zach couldn't see it. 'That snake was old, old and wise enough to have learned a few things about survival. I should have set something heavy on top of the cage.'

'You're giving me the creeps. Not that it's any of my business, but I guess you'll keep an eye out for Mary when she's outside for a few days, in case that thing's still slithering around?'

His concern for her daughter warmed her. 'Mary's staying at her grandmother's, but yes, I'll be keeping a sharp eye out.'

'Good.' He sounded gruff. 'Keep your boots on, Annie.'

Was he worried about her? Zach would be shocked if he knew that her call to him hadn't been merely social, if he knew the real reason she'd called him in the first place.

The fleeting thought that, if Zach knew she'd considered selling a portion of the land, he most likely would pay another visit to Desperado flew across her mind. She closed her eyes, remembering Zach's determined eyes. The memory of his mouth, pressed hard against her lips, flared her nostrils. She thought about him in his stiff business suit, and knew their lives were too different to intersect.

'I'll keep my boots on, Zach,' Annie murmured. 'Thank you for returning my call.'

'You call me if you need anything, all right?'

She opened her eyes a bit sadly. 'Sure thing. Well, goodbye.'

'Goodbye.'

Hanging the phone up, Annie allowed herself to feel regret. What was it about Zach that made her turn all quivery inside? What was it about him that made her

134

feel like she'd met her match, the other half of her soul?

It was so impossible it was ridiculous. With a curious sense of longing, Annie turned to start tidying the kitchen so they could leave for the hospital.

'Mary's about got her toys packed,' Cody said, coming back into the kitchen. 'Are you all right?'

'I'm fine,' Annie replied, keeping her expression bland.

'I take it that was the snake-eyed varmint.'

Annie smiled at Cody's blatant use of Travis's words. 'How did you guess?'

'Well, you looked startled when you answered the phone. Then you looked like you wished I'd get the hell out of the kitchen.'

He smiled, but Annie could tell Cody was probing out of a sense of protectiveness. 'It's okay, really. That was Zach Rayez, and he was calling to see how Papa was doing.'

'Clearing his conscience, I guess.'

'Cody! You know as well as I do that Papa hasn't obeyed any doctor's orders in the last ten years. He's too stubborn to change, despite numerous warnings about his health. Zach may have ignited the situation, but then again, it could have happened the next time a snake appeared on our porch.'

'One and the same, to my mind,' Cody grumbled.

Annie laughed and finished wiping the counters. 'Nobody around here is going to claim Zach as their best friend. He was doing his job, and that's the end

135

of it, okay?' Cody nodded reluctantly, and Annie couldn't help teasing him a little. 'Zach wasn't real impressed that you dismember reptiles for a hobby, either, so you two are about on equal ground.'

She could tell Cody was trying to hide a smile by the wry twist of his mouth. 'Okay, enough said about Zach Rayez,' he agreed. 'Shall we go pay a visit to Travis?'

'Absolutely. Mary, honey, it's time to go.'

'All right, Mommy,' Mary's voice filtered down the hall.

'Do you mind stopping at the mailbox at the end of the drive so I can get the mail?' Annie asked. 'I forgot it yesterday, and was too chicken to walk down there in the dark.'

'That's showing good horse sense. No telling what might be out there,' Cody said, his tone stern. 'It's no trouble to stop.'

'Thanks.' The three of them walked to the car, and after Annie strapped Mary safely in, Cody started down the road.

Dust plumes flew up as the hearse crunched over the small rocks. 'We could use a good rain,' Annie murmured.

'I know. I'm getting worried about the crops,' Cody confessed. 'It's been years since we've had this hot and dry a summer.'

She glanced out at the miles of untouched earth that ran east and west of her home. 'Surely we'll get some rain soon. I've spent so much time in the hospital, I guess I hadn't noticed the weather.'

'Well, it's been hot enough to bake beans, I can tell you.'

Annie looked at him. 'I know you've been coming over to water the animals and check my crops. You're a good man, Cody.'

'Yep.' He shot her a grin. 'Grab your mail.'

She rolled down the window and opened the mailbox, snatching out the single long, white envelope sitting on top of a pile of junk mail. 'Hmm, this looks official.'

'Maybe you won the lottery,' Cody joked.

'I don't think so, but I sure could use it,' Annie replied. A small thread of uneasiness tightened her abdomen. This couldn't be more bad news. It didn't look like an overdue notice – and yet, something told her it wasn't anything she wanted to read.

'Well, open it, so you won't sit and worry all the way to the hospital.'

'You're right. I'm sure it's nothing.' Annie slitted the envelope with a fingernail and pulled out the paper inside. Her heart suddenly felt shriveled and cold.

Cody put a hand on her shoulder. 'What is it, Annie?'

Her lips felt numb. She could hardly press the words out. Tears filled her eyes so that she could hardly read.

'I'm overdue on my taxes, as usual,' she whispered. The fear became full-blown. 'But this time the bank wants to take my land.'

* * *

137

Zach hung up the phone, dissatisfied. Something told him that Annie hadn't called for social reasons. There had been an underlying strain in her voice, very different from the confident demeanor he knew Annie to have. He'd waited, paving the way with idle chitchat should she decide to unburden herself to him.

Yet, she hadn't, and he'd known she probably wouldn't. Annie might have a heavy load to bear, but he was not the person she would choose to confide in. She was strong, she was determined, and she would overcome her problems with courage despite the sinkhole beneath her feet. And he would cheer her on, admiring her from a distance.

Zach glanced out the window, absently noticing the cars on the ribbon-shaped highway many stories down. From his high perch, they looked like ants scurrying to get wherever they needed to go, determined in their blind, yet driving need. He ground his jaw, his teeth tight together. Should he have hinted to Annie about the newly precarious position Carter had mentioned she was in? Would a warning have helped a woman who was already struggling to do the very utmost she could to save herself and her family?

Most likely he would be stretching an ethical boundary by telling Annie that the bank was seriously considering her land as a foreclosure. On the other hand, Zach sensed Carter wasn't dealing with an honest pack of cards on this deal. The man was far too interested, far too keen on the Aguillar land. He'd always been just a cut above dishonest, but never before had Carter displayed the slavering intensity he was showing for this particular deal. Zach's mouth curled. Could it hurt to stack the deck a little in Annie's favor, or would he be doing more harm than good?

He catapulted to his feet, pacing the glassed-in office. It was possible she could make her taxes in time. Farming wasn't something he knew a lot about, but Annie had been enormously proud of the acres of corn she'd shown him. She was banking on the corn to be a major staple in the world food market. Zach felt her theory was as good as any, maybe even sounder than most. Annie was forthright and shrewd about her decisions. If blight didn't get her, or birds, or whatever other dilemmas farmers faced, she had as good a chance as any to hang on to the world she loved.

Perhaps he was in a position to tip the scales just a bit in her favor, though. Zach left a message on LouAnn's answering machine, before grabbing up his car keys. He'd wound down most of the business he'd come in to take care of, especially since he wasn't fielding new calls. Retiring from the big business arena was something Zach looked forward to greatly, hungrily even. His responsibility to Ritter would be a thing of the past, even was nearly so now. He didn't owe them part of his future, though Ritter had been his brain child in the beginning. Too many things had changed in the growth process, with boards and stockholders and slimy sales deals. It wasn't the baby he'd birthed and Zach didn't think a thing about turning himself to a new project.

Of course, he didn't owe Annie anything either, but after all the people whose land he'd bought, it would make him feel good to help one woman hang on to what she loved.

And Desperado was but a road trip away. Maybe a drive would clear the web of incessant wedding preparations from his head.

'I tell you, he's acting different.'

Carter narrowed his eyes at the stunning woman. LouAnn was in a royal snit over her silly preoccupation with Zach Rayez. He nearly sighed with boredom. 'I'm sure you're just imagining things, LouAnn.'

'I'm not, Carter. Damn it, will you listen to me? Something's going on, and I'm worried.'

'What's going on? What's different? I can't help you if you don't give me more concrete examples than that.'

'Damn you, Carter Haskins, don't talk down to me. If I knew what the frigging problem was, I could fix it myself.'

She flicked a pointed fingernail in his direction. Carter held up a hand, shaking his head. 'Calm down, LouAnn. Let's be rational about this. Zach's probably suffering from wedding overload. Didn't you just say you couldn't wait for this silly circus to be over? What makes you think he feels any differently? Most likely, he's anxious to get on the honeymoon with his beautiful bride.'

'Yes, I said that, but only because I'm getting scared, Carter. I want this thing to be over so I've got Zach's ring on my finger.'

He smiled lazily. 'Ah, yes, the noose around his neck, so to speak. What happened, LouAnn? Did you let yourself fall in love with our ride to the top? Does that Tex-Mex give you a thrill when he lifts your skirt?'

She frowned and crossed her arms. 'I wouldn't know, lately.'

Carter leaned forward in the chair, examining her closely. The woman was stupid, but in her own idiotic way, he realized she was doing her best to tell him something. 'What do you mean, you wouldn't know – lately?'

She bowed her head, appearing supremely ashamed and uncomfortable to be having this discussion with him. Carter frowned, sensing real trouble.

'Zach and I haven't made love since he went to Desperado.'

Carter leaned back, clenching his teeth. Damn that Indian woman! Was it even conceivable that Zach would be remotely attracted to her, when he had the wondrously pink and blonde LouAnn waiting back home? Carter held back a curse, wondering if he'd miscalculated the situation. Surely LouAnn was wrong about Zach. The man probably wasn't losing interest in her – and yet, Zach had been plenty interested in her sexually since the day he'd met her. If he was passing up golden chances to slide into a woman made like a soft, welcoming loaf of warm white bread, then indeed, there was a huge problem.

He cleared his throat. 'I assume you've done what you can to get him into your bed.'

She nodded, spreading her hands in confusion. 'At first I thought Zach was simply tired. But when sexy lingerie didn't do the trick, either, then . . .'

Her voice drifted into silence. Damn the silly bitch. She was the perfect vehicle for Carter's ride to prominence and power. Paired with the lethally handsome and likeable Zach Rayez, they'd be a socially elite and powerful duo to be reckoned with, and, as Zach's good colleague and friend, Carter would be positioned for a plum appointment in the next round of corporate musical chairs. If Zach was shedding Ritter International, it just meant that something else was lurking in the ambitious Hispanic man's brain. Carter would continue to ride Zach's coattails whenever it was beneficial to do so.

But at the moment Zach was suffering from some kind of sexual inertia, and tight, cold apprehension swept Carter.

He picked up his phone, jabbing in some numbers. 'What are you doing?'

'I'm calling Zach,' he replied tersely. 'Maybe I can figure out if anything's up by having a brotherly one-on-one with him. Could be you're just imagining things. Bridal nerves, or something like that.'

'I don't think so,' she murmured softly.

The phone rang until it kicked over into the phone-mail system. Carter listened intently, then hung up, swearing viciously. LouAnn jumped, but he barely gave her a glance.

'What is it, Carter?' she asked.

He stared at her, seeing eyelashes glued together and lipstick smeared from crying. LouAnn's hair was mussed from her picking at it. The woman was a mess. Could it be she'd actually fallen for their brown-skinned pretty boy? The man she was marrying for financial security – a necessity when one spent more than their trust fund held – and continued entrée to important social circles?

Even more inconceivable, could Zach have fallen out of love with a trophy woman men far wealthier than he had pursued?

At the moment, Carter found he didn't harbor much desire for LouAnn, either. He bit the inside of his mouth, resisting the urge to smack some sense into her. 'Better get used to sleeping in your own bed, honey. The chicken's flown the coop.'

CHAPTER 9

'Try to put it out of your mind, Annie,' Cody said, indicating the tax notice she held between trembling fingers. 'The bank's sent you those before, and you've always paid up on time.'

That was true. But there were so many things in her life sliding out of whack that Annie felt like she was struggling just to hang on to normalcy. In the back seat, Mary murmured to her stuffed animals, her conversation pitched in the soothing sounds of a mommy voice. Annie closed her eyes, feeling sick. Something had to get better. Somewhere, somehow, there had to be a piece of good news with her name on it.

Cody patted her hand. 'The corn crop's going to be a big one, Annie. It looks like rows and rows of profit to me. There should be plenty to pay off the bank, with some to spare. And you know you can count on me to help bring it in.'

Annie nodded, dutifully fixing a smile to her face. 'You're right. I shouldn't let myself get so thrown off balance.'

'That's my girl. We wouldn't be farmers if we weren't tough.'

'I'm tough, too,' Mary called from the back seat.

Annie glanced around to give her daughter a reassuring smile. She looked so pretty, all done up in a new red-stripe dress and matching hair bow her granny had made. Annie's mouth went dry. For the slightest second, the old nightmare froze her brain: Mary begging in the streets of Desperado, a bedraggled orphan with no one to care about her.

Annie pressed her lips together. That menacing nightmare was impossible. Mary had family who would take her in, should something ever happen to Annie and Travis. Mary had family, true – yet why couldn't Annie provide a more reassuring future for her only child?

'I *am* tough, too, right, Mama?'

Annie managed a nod and a smile for her daughter, seeing only the delicate bones in the child's face and the innocence in the wide, questioning blue eyes. 'Yes, sugar. You're as tough as a corn cob.'

'Ooh, gross,' Mary giggled.

'Well, you could be as tough as Grandpa Travis's toenails, and that'd be grosser,' Cody commented with a grin.

Mary squealed and Annie managed a slight smile. Cody pulled up in front of the hospital. 'You two go ahead and get out. I'll park the car.'

Annie slid out, helping Mary on to the sidewalk. They clasped hands together and walked into the hospital, Annie barely aware of Mary's questions about how the sliding doors worked and why couldn't she bring her toys inside with her. The child became quiet as they walked into Travis's room.

Mary ran straight into the outstretched arms that were waiting for her. 'Gosh, Grandpa, this place doesn't look like much fun.'

'It ain't Disneyland, that's for sure. When am I getting out of this jail, Annie?' he demanded.

'I need to reconfirm with the doctor, but I think tomorrow, Papa.' She walked toward the bed, fluffing the pillow behind his head and trying to straighten the thin blanket covering his body.

He waved her away impatiently. 'Don't start fussing after me like I'm a corpse, girl. I can do for myself. I'm right as rain and ready to get home. If I stay here any longer, all these ignorant nurses and doctors are going to kill me.'

It was plain to see Travis was chafing to resume his independent lifestyle. Annie sighed, knowing he had every right to complain. She patted his arm before sitting on the foot of the bed. 'I know it hasn't been pleasant for you. Maybe we should take you home today, if we have to sneak you out in the night.'

'Who's sneaking out of here?' Cody asked, coming into the room.

'We may need to borrow your car, Cody,' Annie said. 'Papa can't take another minute of all this peace and relaxation or he's going to explode. I guess we

146

could pretend you've come from the mortuary and need to pick him up – '

'Hell, no,' Travis cursed, interrupting her attempt at black humor. 'I ain't sneaking out of here like some dog that got caught in the chicken coop. I'm walking out of here like a man, and anybody doesn't like it, can kiss my – '

'Good afternoon, everyone,' a plump, wiry-haired nurse said, stoically entering the room and pinning Travis with a no-nonsense stare. Her demeanor was stern, but her eyes lit with playful affection as she looked at her patient.

'Hi, Gert,' Travis grumbled.

'I hear you're ready to go home.'

'How'd you guess?' he asked, his expression surly.

'I could hear you bellowing about it down the hall. So could every other patient in the hospital. Did you know that getting upset like that isn't recommended for a man who's just had bypass surgery?'

'Mind your own business. You ain't giving me any more lip after today, Gert.'

'Since you've been reading your chart, you know it doesn't say the doctor's releasing you.'

'I'm releasing myself,' Travis growled. 'The doctor can bill some other fool for his services. The hospital's going to be the death of me.'

The nurse shrugged, throwing Annie an I've-done-my-best look. 'Well, it happens to be your lucky day, anyway, you mule-headed patient of mine. I just saw the doctor in the hall and he says it ain't doing you any good to stay around here when you're so all fired up to leave.' She shot him a playful grin. 'So, do you think you can get dressed in civilian clothes by yourself, Mr Cade?' she asked.

'Keep your claws away from me, Gert. I'm more than capable.'

Ignoring his outburst, Gert stepped away from the bed. 'Fine. I'll go get a wheelchair for you.'

Indignation furrowed his forehead. 'I ain't going out of here in a wheelchair.' He jabbed a finger at the nurse. 'Don't you even think about it.'

'I'm sorry, Mr Cade. All patients leave the hospital in a wheelchair.' She turned her back on him, directing her attention to Annie. 'Could I see you in the hall for a moment, please?'

'Cody, will you keep an eye on Mary?' Annie asked, knowing he would have, anyway. It wasn't a question that needed to be voiced. Yet, she felt like nothing could be taken for granted; the day would come when she no longer had to ask favors of anyone, she swore.

She followed the nurse into the hall, who now gestured toward the waiting room. Annie followed her inside, relieved to see that the smoky room was empty for once.

'Ms Aguillar, there are a few things I want to go over with you about the care your father will need.' At Annie's nod, she pulled a list from her pocket. 'It's important that these precautions are followed to allow for proper healing, since the veins that were used for

148

the bypass were taken from Travis's – I mean, Mr Cade's legs.'

Annie took the paper, scanning it carefully. 'This all seems pretty simple,' she said.

'You'll also note that he'll need some therapy. It's important for him to try to walk a little every day. Not too much at first, of course, but building gradually as he gets stronger.'

At Annie's silent nod, the nurse leaned forward, her gaze penetrating. 'I want you to be aware of one other thing. Don't be surprised if Travis's recovery is difficult. He thinks he's stronger than he actually is, and unfortunately, the surgery isn't the hardest part of solving the problem. The patient's recovery is almost always the most difficult link in this process.'

'I see,' Annie murmured. 'Thank you for your advice.'

The nurse stood, her no-nonsense expression back in place. 'The healing process can be emotionally traumatic for the patient, and in this case, you're dealing with a very stubborn, independent man.'

The nurse's candor made Annie smile. 'Yes, I am. Papa isn't going to be an easy case, I know. I don't expect any less of him.'

After a moment, the nurse nodded, her smile understanding. 'I'll go get that wheelchair now.'

Annie walked back into Travis's room, not a bit surprised to see her father sitting on the edge of the bed, dressed in street clothes. Mary was sitting beside him, contentedly swinging her legs, while Cody lounged against the door frame.

'We'll have you home within the hour, Papa,' Annie said.

'It's about time. I'm beginning to molder around here. I want a hot meal that has some substance to it, no more of this disgusting baby food crap. I hope you've got some of your salsa made up, Annie. My taste buds are like to die of disuse.'

She nodded, walking around the room opening drawers to make certain nothing was left behind. 'There's some salsa I made a few weeks ago on the pantry shelf.' She turned around, pinning him with a worried stare. 'Is salsa okay for you to eat? Aren't you supposed to be on a special diet, or something?' Worriedly, she dug the list out of her pocket, scanning it. 'This is about therapy, but I don't see anything about food you're supposed to avoid. I should ask the nurse.'

'Don't do that!' Travis bellowed. 'I had a heart attack, dammit, not an ulcer or something. Besides, if you ask that ornery woman, she'll say, "No spicy food, no fatty food" – ' he mimicked the nurse's voice ' – just to irritate me. I've been complaining for days about the food around here. I swear they send it over from the nursing home when the old folks turn it down.'

He crossed his arms and glared. Annie sighed. Although she suspected her father's diet was important, he was a grown man. If she fixed him the kind of meal he enjoyed tonight, it was one less thing to argue about, thereby keeping his blood pressure down.

150

'Okay,' she said. 'For dinner, I'll fix something you'll be able to taste.'

'Good. I want some more of that cow Cody butchered. I feel like having fajitas for my coming-home dinner.'

Cody grinned. 'I can get you some of that real easy, if you've run out.'

'Just make sure there's enough for Cody to eat dinner with us, Annie,' Travis commanded.

Cody looked to Annie with a raised eyebrow. Hurriedly, she seconded her father's gruff invitation. 'By all means, have dinner with us, Cody. It'll seem like a celebration for Papa.'

'I'd like that a lot.'

Mary slid off the bed, clapping her little hands. 'Hurray! A party!'

Annie laughed and Cody joined her. Travis nodded his pleasure. In her mind, Annie began ticking off the ingredients she had at the house that hadn't been ruined when the electricity had been turned off. The doubt that her father should have so much excitement on his first night home from the hospital began to wear off. He could sit in his easy chair and watch television, after all, and being pent up in the hospital had been far more stressful to him than having a hot meal for dinner would be. *I'm getting to be like one of those women who worry about everything*, Annie thought. *When did I turn into such a grey cloud, anyway?*

'Okay, a homecoming party it is,' Annie said, 'but

151

just dinner, and no excitement. Understood?'

She threw her father a daunting glance, but he shrugged it off. 'A real meal is excitement enough for me,' he answered. 'A quiet, cozy family event, and an early bedtime sounds like heaven.'

'You're sure you don't mind me horning in?' Cody asked. 'We could do this another time.'

'Hell, no,' Travis replied. 'You're not horning in, Cody, you're family. If I didn't feel like a mile of torn-up track, I'd be up to more company and your mom could come over, too. We certainly owe her a month of paybacks. But I believe even if Archangel Gabriel showed up at my door for dinner tonight, I'd have to ask him to come back another time.' He sighed, and rubbed his wrists in a tired motion that concerned Annie. 'Heck,' he said quietly, 'I'm actually starting to feel like Father Time's ticking down on me.'

Loud knocking at the front door that evening startled Annie. She got up from the dinner table with a frown. 'I wonder who that could be?' she murmured. 'We weren't expecting company, and no one knows you're home from the hospital, yet, Papa.'

Walking down the hall, she opened the door. For a moment, she couldn't speak for the astonishment flooding through her. Butterflies jumped into her stomach at the uncertain look in Zach Rayez's eyes. 'Well, you're certainly the last person I expected to see,' she told him, trying to keep the tingle of excitement she felt from her voice.

152

Her tone made him grimace. 'I should have called – '

'Yes. You should have.' Because then she would have had time to gather up her tattered emotional reserves to see him again.

Zach shifted on one foot, then jammed his hands into his jeans' pockets. 'I think I needed the element of surprise on my side to make myself come do this. I've been wanting to see you, to see how you're doing, but I was afraid if you knew I wanted to come, you'd say no.' His grin was reluctant, somewhat unsure. 'And we didn't get too far over the phone.'

Annie placed a hand against her midsection, trying to calm the quivers twisting in her stomach. Happiness? Nervous excitement? Fear of what Cody and her father would do to Zach once they discovered him here? A firestorm of emotions was assaulting her, but for the first time, Annie admitted to herself that she was genuinely glad to see this troublemaker of a man.

'Come on in,' she said.

He obeyed, following her down the hall to the kitchen. Cody laid his fork down silently, but it was her father she was worried about. With a hand out as if to ask for tolerance, Annie forestalled Travis's explosion. 'I'm sure everyone remembers Zach Rayez.' Nobody moved. She then turned to Zach. 'I'd offer you something to eat – '

Zach shook his head, immediately refusing. The last time he'd broken bread at Annie's table, all hell had busted loose. With the old man staring daggers at him, and Cody looking like he might leap over the table and try to strangle him, Zach figured he was better off making himself scarce. Even little Mary, whom he'd thought liked him, was giving him a startlingly cold shoulder for one so young.

'I'll wait in the car until you finish,' he said.

'Oh, no, don't do that,' Annie said. 'At least sit on the porch, or take a walk down to the fish pond. We'll be finished soon.'

Zach nodded and showed himself out.

'Have you lost your mind, Annie?' Travis roared. 'Inviting that son of a bitch to eat our food when you know what he wants? Haven't you ever heard of somebody bitin' the hand that fed him?'

Annie seated herself and began eating her beans. 'Upsetting yourself is only going to make you sick again, Papa,' she said calmly. 'Zach says he wants to talk to me. I handled what he had to say the first time he came. Don't you think I can handle him this time?'

Travis pursed his lips, obviously not liking it one bit. Cody shrugged and went back to eating. Mary inched closer to her on the plank bench.

'I don't feel like eating anymore, Mama. May I be excused?' she asked.

Annie ran a loving hand over her daughter's hair. 'Sure, sugar. Are you feeling all right?'

Mary nodded. 'I'd like to go play.'

Annie hesitated. There could be snakes out there, specifically the granddaddy of all snakes, which was still an escapee. 'I don't know. Can you wait until I'm through eating?'

'Okay, Mama. I'll go play with my dolls in my room.'

It sounded like she was accepting a penance. Annie's heart felt squeezed. 'I think Mr Rayez is sitting on the porch. Why don't you go talk to him for a minute, keep him company?'

Mary glanced uncertainly toward the door, then slowly shuffled out of the kitchen.

Annie frowned. Her daughter had cozied up to Zach quickly on his first visit, to the point where Annie had been bitten by tiny pangs of jealousy. Now her child appeared reluctant – or was she simply retreating into that shell she'd pulled around herself when her father had died, and never really let go of?

Outside, Zach seated himself on the wooden porch, which despite a coat of grey paint, was worn and weathered. He glanced up at the evening sky which was quickly assuming the protective shades of night and wondered for the hundredth time if he was doing the right thing. Did he have the right to warn Annie? Would she welcome his involvement in her problems?

The screen door creaked open. 'Hi, Mr Zach,' Mary said.

Zach swiveled his head to see the little girl peering at him. Her big eyes took his measure with a grave expression. Obviously, this was not a moment to be treated with latitude.

'Hey, little lady. Are you through eating?'

She nodded.

He cleared his throat, trying to gauge Mary's attitude toward him. 'Did you come out to see me, or to play?'

'There's nobody to play with.'

Zach nodded, appearing to mull over her statement. 'I could play with you. If you'd like.'

Mary looked up at him thoughtfully, releasing her hold on the screen door, which slammed shut with a loud crack. 'What can you do?'

'Well . . .' Zach tried to think quickly and resourcefully. The very brains he had used to outwit men much smarter and richer than he felt like they were atrophying in his head. 'Have you checked on the fish yet today?'

Mary shook her head. 'Mama's been busy trying to get Grandpa some dinner. He's been kinda sick.'

Zach grimaced. *Yeah, honey, and I'm the spark that lit that dynamite*. Wryly, he said, 'I hope he's feeling better.'

'He is. Grandpa says as soon as he gets some of Mama's cooking in him, he'll be a new man.'

'But you're still out a trip to the fish pond.'

A tiny smile hovered at Mary's mouth, and her eyes turned excited and beseeching to his. 'Do you know anything about fish, Mr Zach?'

'Not enough to put on the end of a hook, honey.'

'Oh.' Mary sighed, as if she couldn't understand why adults were so unconcerned about the things that

156

really mattered in life. 'If you'll walk me down there, I'll *try* to teach you about them.'

Her tone implied that Zach would be a near-impossible case in her eyes. He grinned and stood up. 'Let's go, then. There's only about an hour of sun left if you're going to knock any fish sense into my head.'

Sedately, Mary stood, allowing Zach to hold her hand. Together, they started off at a meandering pace toward the foreman's shack. Zach glanced at the small girl beside him. Rarely had he seen the child smile, although one had nearly peeped out at him tonight. Was she always so earnest, so world weary?

His childhood had been extremely grim, with very little to smile about. He hated to think that Mary was suffering in any kind of way. She was a sweet and truly beautiful little girl. Yet, she was in no way abused, that was certain. Zach knew Annie thought the sun rose and shone in that child. Cody was obviously a beloved uncle, and Mary's tough-as-petrified-cow-bricks grandfather would clearly go to his grave with Mary's name on his lips. In many ways, Mary was lucky, but growing up with adults had made her old and wise beyond her years. And something had made her sad.

They were within a hundred feet of the pond now. Suddenly, Zach had an idea. 'I think I remember how to skip,' he said. 'We could give that a shot.'

'Skip what?'

She didn't let go of his hand as they walked, just continued staring up at him. Zach felt the importance of her serious gaze as he realized the child didn't even expect him to know how to do such a simple thing.

Or maybe that frivolous occupation hadn't been a part of her childhood, yet.

'We could skip the rest of the way. If I can remember how.' Zach relinquished Mary's hand gently and saying, 'Watch this,' over his shoulder, started an awkward gait of knees up, boots down, in the direction of the pond. After skipping about twenty-five feet, he stopped and turned around.

Mary hadn't moved. Her eyes squinted with concentration. Zach didn't say anything as he waited for the little girl to react. *Come on, Mary!* he thought. *I know you've got a smile in there!* She looked at his feet, then looked back up at his face as if she were gauging her trust in him. He nodded encouragement. Mary lifted one knee hesitantly, as if she were trying to get the feel of the next movement, gave an admirable hop-and-stumble – and came to a halt.

'That was great! Try again,' he urged.

She looked uncertain. He walked to her side. 'Look, we can kind of do this together,' he said, linking his hand to hers again. 'Go!'

Together, they started off on an awkwardly jolting hop-skip motion, heading in the right direction. Careful not to go too fast and drag her down, nor to let his boots get near her little sandaled feet, Zach was too busy concentrating to notice the smile spreading across Mary's face. She laughed outright, a child's hearty giggle of excitement, and Zach looked down in amazement. Already a beautiful child, she was downright gorgeous with proud happiness on her face and the weight of whatever was bothering her lifted from her shoulders.

And suddenly, Zach realized Annie rarely smiled either. Not that she'd had any reason to since he'd met her, but he'd be willing to bet the facial muscles used for a smile were terribly out of shape in her lovely face. Annie was a survivor, not a pampered female like LouAnn, and survivors were too busy trying to keep their heads above water to open their lips into a smile. Otherwise, they'd take on water and drown in their troubles.

But damn, oh, damn, how he'd love to be the one to put a smile on her face.

Cody's eyes narrowed as he watched Zach and Mary from the kitchen window. 'The snake-eyed varmint's heading toward the pond,' he announced. 'With Mary.' He turned around and shot Annie a questioning look. 'Does that bother you?'

'No.' Annie shook her head and got up from the table. 'But help Papa into the living room, will you? I'll clean up later.'

She washed her hands and fluffed her hair before strolling toward the door, aware that Cody and her father were watching her with he-man, protective scowls. Slipping out, she let the screen door close quietly behind her. The evening was balmy with humidity that teased of much-needed rain, but Annie looked at the empty Texas sky with knowledgeable

159

eyes. At this point, Desperado required a miracle from God to bring the soothing, regular showers her crops had to have before they were ruined.

The letter from the bank popped into her mind heedlessly, flaring like a warning flag and making her frown. On the briefest puff of wind, childish laughter and a hearty man's chuckle carried to her ears. The letter was immediately forgotten. Annie walked faster, drawn to the happy sounds.

She rounded the foreman's shack, realizing that Zach and Mary sat close together with their heads almost touching. His bare feet dangled in the water, boots discarded beside him and jeans rolled to the calf. The two intently watched something in the water, most likely curious, tame fish coming to see what food was being tossed in and finding Zach's heels instead. And her daughter looked so content, sitting there beside the big man, that Annie's eyes burned with tears of gratitude.

'I thought you weren't ever coming back,' Mary suddenly said, looking up at Zach with intent accusation on her face.

Annie froze, automatically putting a hand against one of the old willows in her path.

'I didn't think I was, either,' Zach replied. He sounded uncertain and careful with his reply.

'So, why didya?'

Only willow leaves rustling against tree trunks interrupted the silence. Annie could tell Zach was weighing his answer. It was a question she'd wondered about herself.

'I need to talk to your mother,' he finally said. 'That's why I've come back.'

'Oh.' Mary nodded in understanding. 'But I liked you.'

Zach paused. 'I like you, too.'

'You didn't even say goodbye,' Mary pointed out.

'Ah, no, I guess I didn't.'

There hadn't been time, of course. Annie closed her eyes briefly, remembering that hasty flight to the hospital, with Cody taking Mary away in the hearse. Nobody'd had time to say anything.

'But I wanted to,' Zach suddenly said.

'You did?'

'Yeah.' Annie saw Zach's decisive nod. 'I wanted to say goodbye to you. I wanted to make sure your mother's finger was all right. I wanted to see if your grandfather was going to be okay. But I had to go, little one.'

'Oh.' Mary looked down at her feet, floating next to Zach's in the water. For a moment she was silent. Slowly, she lifted her gaze to the man watching her. 'My father left without saying goodbye to me, too,' she said softly.

But Annie heard. Hot tears of denial sprang to her eyes, and she covered her mouth with her hands. *Carlos didn't leave you, baby*! she wanted to cry out. *Your daddy would never have done that*! But there had been too much blood, too much agony, and she'd been unable to explain what had happened to Mary's father.

161

In slow, uncertain motion, Zach's hand lifted to pat Mary on the back. 'I'll tell you a secret, Mary.'

Annie crushed her lips together, leaning forward to hear, anxious to hear how he would soothe her daughter.

'My mother left me without saying goodbye.'

Annie's eyes widened with shock.

'She did?' Mary asked. Her small voice was filled with awe that someone older than she might possibly understand her sorrow. 'Your mother left you without saying goodbye?'

Zach's shoulders slumped. 'Yes, she did.' Annie watched as he pulled her little girl tightly to his side. 'And you know what?'

'What?'

'I was just about your age.'

'You were?'

Annie heard his deep, heavy sigh, and it resonated somewhere in the recess of her own agony-tormented soul.

'Yeah,' Zach Rayez told her baby. 'And you know what else?'

'What?' Mary's question was just a soft breath in the night.

'I have a feeling neither one of them wanted to leave us that way.'

162

CHAPTER 10

'I'll handle this.'

Cody's husky voice near her ear made Annie jump. She started to speak, but he was already walking toward the pair at the pond's edge.

'Catch anything?' he asked easily, hunkering down beside Zach and Mary.

Hesitantly, Annie followed Cody's lead and nonchalantly walked forward. She sat down cross-legged beside him, staring out at the water as if nothing was out of the ordinary. As if she hadn't just overheard searing pieces of a man's inner misery.

'Nope,' Zach replied. 'Although these fish don't look like they'd put up much of a fight if we threw a hook in.'

Cody nodded. 'They're so tame they'd jump up in your lap if you asked them to.' He dangled one hand in the water and a small, daring fish came to nibble at his finger. Scooping it up, he let Mary examine it closely for an instant before tossing it back in.

They all watched silently as the little fish zoomed

off to deeper water, enlightened about humans and their seemingly innocent appearance.

'How about some dessert, Mary?' Cody asked. 'I think your ma's got some fresh pineapple in the refrigerator.'

'Okay, Uncle Cody,' she said, getting to her feet. 'See you later, Mr Zach.'

'I'll be up at the house in a minute,' Annie said, meeting the warning in Cody's eyes with stubborn assurance. 'Save some pineapple for us.'

When Cody had taken her child away, Annie trained her gaze on Zach without sympathy for the conversation she'd overhead. There was a motive for this man to return to Desperado, and it was best not to forget that. 'So, you wanted to talk to me, Zach.'

Annie's hard indigo stare reminded Zach that there was no truce between them. How could there be? He hadn't been completely honest with Annie about anything, and she was too smart to be sucked in by a smooth line. And suddenly, he knew that if he was ever going to set things right with Annie Aguillar, he was looking at the hangman's last chance to speak.

Because she'd sure as hell never trust him again – or another word out of his mouth. And it was imperative that she believe him now.

'Yes, I wanted to talk to you,' he said slowly, admiring the way her ebony brows slanted over her eyes, silently daring him to sweet talk her. He sighed. *The first thing I want to say is how badly I wanted to see you again*. No. Scratch that. It might be true, but she'd point him to the end of the Aguillars' lane if he said that now. And he couldn't say, 'Had any bad news lately, because I have a gut feeling my employee is after your lovely toast-and-cream skin with a vengeance?'

Hell, no. Annie cocked her head at him quizzically. Zach felt like the world's biggest fool, sitting there with his tongue tied in a hundred knots.

'So . . . talk,' she prodded, the tiniest edge of dry encouragement slipping into her voice. 'You want to restate your previous offer about purchasing my land – ?'

'No.' The word was decisive and quick. And she'd given him the perfect place to start. 'I do not want to buy your land. In the next couple of days, I'll no longer be working at Ritter International.'

At Annie's surprised look, Zach nodded. He made a solemn vow at that moment to return and cut his notice short. There were only a few small deals left on his plate, nothing some junior exec couldn't handle. The Aguillar deal was the only one Carter was interested in anyway, but Zach knew that, after what he was about to confess to Annie, he'd never have the stomach to look at Carter's face again.

'In fact, my interest in your land is just the opposite,' he stated. 'I'm more interested in helping you keep it.'

'Mr Rayez, I don't pretend to understand what you're getting at. But I think it's best that, if you're not here on official business, then you leave my business interests out of the conversation.'

He set his jaw. 'Annie, I know you're a proud woman. I know it's awkward for me to be here, and that you really have little or no reason to trust me.'

She appeared a little less mulish, so he continued. 'I have nothing to base my theory on, but being that your land is sitting on a prime strip of acreage that some folks have their eyes on to acquire, at any cost, I believe you're going to need all the help you can get to keep it for another generation.'

'And you're proposing that you're the help I need.'

The suspicion was back in her voice, richly sarcastic. Zach looked at the woman who sat less than a foot away from him, proud bearing in her posture, and wondered where the words were going to come from to convince her to allow him to help her.

'I've got some ideas. Not suggestions, just some thoughts to start with.'

'None of this is necessary, Zach. My life is not your concern.'

She stood, and he did, too, hastily rolling his jeans down. 'Annie, wait. Just hear me out.'

When she paused, he said, 'There isn't any easy way for me to say this to you. But I think a vice president at Ritter – the man who works for me – is plotting to take this land. If I'm right, there won't be much you can do about it.'

'You sorry excuse for a buzzard. I should have known that you'd try some underhanded – '

'No, no.' He held up a hand. 'Annie, listen to me. I

166

was on my last two weeks in this position, when Carter mentioned he was having trouble with this deal, and maybe if I came out here and talked to you – '

'Carter?' Fury snapped in Annie's eyes. 'Carter who?'

'Carter Haskins is my employee. We went to law school together and I hired him to work for me at Ritter.'

'You're a friend of Carter Haskins?' Annie's tone was deadly. 'His boss?' In her mind, she remembered the stocky man with his nasty cigar and demeaning attitude toward her, toward her home. She hadn't let him inside, but he'd stood in the drive, coldly allowing his gaze to roam up and down her body. Mary had been in the house with Travis, thank God, and spared from contact with him. But Annie had never forgotten the look on his face when she told him to get the hell off her property before she shot him full of holes. And she would have, too, damn the consequences.

Now here was Carter Haskins's boss, the man who paid Carter to lick his boots. Carter had suggested Zach might have better success seducing her out of her land. Annie wanted to sneer. Well, the bootlicker had hit pretty close to home, because she'd nearly fallen for this pretty boy Zach Rayez. All hot, hungry man and sexual prowess that a lonely woman like her could smell, could taste, could want – and could eventually succumb to.

And find herself taken, fast and hard. Physically, at first.

Then financially.

A sibilant hiss escaped Annie's lips. Zach started. 'Were you the best your company had to send?' she demanded.

Zach appeared surprised for only a second. 'Actually, yeah,' he replied, a slow grin turning up those full, mocking lips.

'Well,' Annie said very quietly, 'you failed.'

'Annie – '

She held up a warning hand. 'I suppose it's to my credit you didn't get me in the sack.'

Zach remained politically silent.

'You know, you're a very hot man, Zach Rayez. A lesser woman might have been taken in by all these hard muscles,' she whispered, stepping close to massage his arm. Running her hand along his back and up over wonderfully broad shoulders, Annie put her lips close to his chin. 'I suppose even I was blinded for a time by all this manliness.' He relaxed under her caress, just the way she wanted him to. 'Such a hot, hot man,' she cooed, and shoved him back with every ounce of anger and strength she possessed. With a hoarse shout, Zach sprawled into the water. 'Deserves a dip in the pond,' she finished, watching him come sputtering back to the surface.

'There isn't a man alive who can make a fool out of me, Rayez, don't forget it. I *might* have wanted to bed you, but it would have been simply for my own pleasure. You still would have gone back empty-handed, Zach Rayez, without a contract.' She smiled at him coldly. 'Worn-out and drained, but empty-handed even so.'

Zach pulled himself out of the pond and sat on the edge, cursing under his breath. Stubborn, proud woman! She wasn't worth it. Let Carter take his best shots – Zach didn't need to waste any more time here in this land that God forgot.

'Fine, damn it,' he bit out. Shoving his hair out of his face and pressing the soaked strands back onto his neck, Zach shot Annie a furious stare. 'I didn't come all the way out here for my gratification.'

'Well, obviously you did,' Annie shot back. 'You say it wasn't for business. What other reason could there possibly be? A widow should be ripe pickings, after all, and too long without the wild thing makes a woman crazy. A good, hard bout of sex should put her right. Isn't that how men think, Zach?'

Zach snaked his arm out, grabbing Annie at the ankles. With a cry, she tumbled to the ground within arm's reach. He jerked her into his lap, cradling her with an iron grip. 'For God's sake, Annie. I didn't even know you were a widow. I didn't know who you were. As a final deal, I was supposed to come do a job on the owner of the Aguillar property, and I was expecting a man. A man I could deal with on a man-to-man basis. But the interesting thing about you, Annie, is that you seem to know more about how men think than I do,' he rasped against her hair. 'Let me tell you the truth. If I'd been after sex, I would have had you the first time I came to Desperado.'

169

'You couldn't. My father got too ill. But he warned me about you.'

'You should have listened to the old man, then,' he growled in her ear. Ignoring her furious struggles, Zach held Annie even tighter to his chest. 'Let me tell you one more thing. I don't know what widows are good for. You seem more green than ripe to me. As for the wild thing, Annie Aguillar, if I decided to have you, it wouldn't be the wild thing. It would be long, slow lovemaking that would make you burn from your toes to your – ' he gently licked inside the curve of her ear ' – to here. I would say your name as reverently as a baby loves its mother's breast, and you would moan my name in a whisper that begged for more loving.'

He sat her straight up in his lap, releasing her arms but fixing her with a relentless stare. 'I do not have meaningless sex, Annie. As desirable as you are, it's not in me to acquire your body without loving you first.'

Even as he said it, Zach realized his statement was fact: he was falling in love with Annie. It was only a flashing second thought that he could never touch LouAnn again, knowing this; that their engagement would have to be broken. All he could feel was waves of astonishment rolling over him that he'd done the unthinkable, the unexplainable, by allowing his heart to be caught by this woman.

Annie was as surprised as Zach seemed. Was it possible he had a conscience? 'Why?' she asked.

He shook his head, almost sadly. 'I've seen what using women like disposable cans of beer does to a man. You use 'em up, throw 'em away – but you're not the man you think you are. And after a while, well, you're trying to fill an emptiness that can't be filled.'

Annie raised a brow. Zach grinned at her ruefully. 'My father,' he said with a shrug.

'Oh.' A father with no ability to love and a mother who'd left him at some point. Zach had pushed her away when she'd first kissed him at the foreman's shack, although she had known he wanted her. Had he been distancing himself from her – or was there so much pain in his past that he found it difficult to get close to anyone?

'Maybe I said too much earlier,' Annie said, placing her hand lightly on Zach's arm. 'The name of Carter Haskins has the ability to inflame me past reason.'

'You and a passel of other folks in Texas. Forget about it.'

'Zach, I heard you comforting Mary earlier.' She stopped, wondering how to be delicate without hurting his pride. 'Um . . . you said more to her than most adults manage with a grieving child. They're usually uncomfortable and murmur trite things. But you went deeper and shared something of yourself with her, something she could relate to. You treated her like an adult, which in so many ways she's had to be. I thank you for that.'

Zach shrugged his shoulders, intently disliking the serious personal turn the conversation had taken. He wished his jeans weren't wet and sticking to him like glue, because with Annie sitting in his lap radiating warmth near his crotch, his body was starting a subtle war with his conscience. 'I like your daughter,' he said, more roughly than he intended. 'She's a good kid. It's pretty standard stuff, though. A parent leaves for whatever reason, and the kid believes he or she's done something wrong. I just wanted Mary to know differently.'

Now if Annie would only get out of his lap, he could slink back to his truck and grab some dry things to put on. A few moments away from her would be very healthy for his –

'Mary's father – my husband – was killed in a tractor accident.'

Zach stiffened in the act of scooting away from Annie's warmth.

'Um, she didn't see the accident, but she came home before I could clean up . . . the towels . . . and the . . . blood.'

'Oh, Annie,' he whispered, pulling her close into the circle of his arms. 'Oh, Annie, I'm so sorry.' He held her tightly, allowing the slight shakes he felt from her body flood into the strength of his. 'Baby, baby,' he murmured, 'don't cry. Please don't cry.'

The woman wasn't really crying tears that he could feel or see. It was more a rocking to and fro as she suffered soul-deep agony. He felt her shudders as she tried to hold back her pain. 'Oh, baby,' he whispered against her hair, nestling his head against her shoulder, 'I'll be here as long as you need me.'

* * *

172

Annie had no idea how long she sat in the protection of Zach's hard body, wrestling with her demons. The whisper of night wind soughed through the willow branches, soothing in its near-silence. The moon shone a sliver of light on to the now quiet pond. Zach was nearly dry from his very thorough drenching, so he'd held her for a long time. Patiently.

Maybe she'd even dozed a little, when the tempest had passed through her. But he was awake, she could tell, by the alertness in his posture. Almost as if he were on guard against something.

'Zach?' she whispered, turning her head toward his. Dark eyes gleamed black in the night as he stared back at her.

She was going to murmur words of thanks for his comforting her and escape to the haven of the house when she saw something new in the instant fire in his eyes. Instinctively, Annie knew Zach had been waiting for her to awaken, waiting, wanting to kiss her. She tilted her head slightly, offering him her mouth. His lips closed reflexively around hers, almost in the instant response one would give a child. A split second later, Annie felt the hunger surge into his kiss. She sighed, welcoming Zach's strength and hardness as he searched her mouth with his. Her lips molded submissively each time he took them. Suddenly, he was kissing her cheeks, her forehead, even her eyelids, and the moan Annie heard rising from inside her was one of sheer yearning.

For sex, for love – for Zach.

But, of course, he'd already told her they couldn't be together without love. And that was something she respected about him, more this time than the last. A man with scruples was rarer than rain.

Still, she was sad when their kiss ended. He looked at her, searching her eyes, only an inch away from his lips. She smiled bravely. 'Thank you,' she murmured.

He shook his head. 'There's nothing to thank me for, Annie.'

'There's a lot to thank you for.'

'No.' His voice was brisk, and she felt him withdraw from her. 'Don't set me up as something I'm not. The truth is, I came out to sucker you. After I met you, I could not. Last year, maybe I would have. I don't know.'

Zach stopped, giving her an assessing look. Annie realized he was being as honest with her as he possibly could be – painfully honest.

'And the reason you didn't apply the full-court press?'

She won only a sharp look for her slight attempt to ease his discomfort.

'Laziness. I lost my *cajones*. The fat and easy way was calling me, and I didn't have the heart to rouse myself to make another human being miserable.' He gave a sarcastic snort, shaking his head. 'I'm getting married.'

Annie felt like someone had just jerked her backward by the hair, leaving her stunned on the ground. Zach married? Had she heard him right?

'I don't think I follow you,' was all she could manage.

'I'm supposed to be married in about two weeks. Two weeks after that, I formally take over my fiancée's family business.'

Slowly, she edged away from Zach. Why was he telling her this now, when they'd just shared the most earth-shattering kiss she'd ever experienced? *I do not have meaningless sex, Annie. It's not in me to acquire your body without loving you first.*

Of course. Zach loved another. Once again, she'd thrown herself at him, and this time, he'd comforted her because she'd been crying like a baby. But the same wonderful emotions that spun through her at his touch left him unfazed. Because there was a woman in his life who already had his heart.

Annie sighed deeply, wondering if it was possible for a heart to actually break in half. Hers felt like it was splintering in two. A different kind of pain in the heart than Travis had suffered; one that wouldn't benefit from a late-night trip to the emergency room.

All Texas's horses and all Texas's men, couldn't put Annie together again. The nursery rhyme ran through her head, bastardized by the tormenting, hateful thoughts toward that other faceless woman. Annie shook her head, angry with herself. Hearts mended. She was a survivor. Best to salvage her pride, to walk away a woman of courage.

'Congratulations,' she said, her voice soft and pleasant. 'And that you drove all the way to Desper-

175

ado to try to help me during this special time is more than you should have done. A phone call would have sufficed.'

'You're too ornery to be talked into anything over the phone.'

Annie nodded agreeably. 'You're right. Still, I should pay you for the gas money you wasted on the trip out here.'

Zach reclined on his elbows, tossing an amused look her way. 'You haven't even listened to my business idea, yet.'

She stood, brushing off her jeans briskly. 'No. But I need to get up to the house to check on Mary. And Papa. Please make yourself comfortable in the fore-man's shack, if you wish. We could discuss anything else that's on your mind in the morning at breakfast, before you leave. I feel bad keeping you from your wedding preparations.'

Annie turned away. Instantly, her arm was caught in Zach's relentless hand.

'Annie, don't be this way.'

'I'm not being any way. It's late, and I'm tired. Please excuse me.'

Reluctantly, he let her hand fall between them. 'All right. But we talk in the morning.'

She shrugged and turned toward the house. There were plenty of things she could find herself doing to keep herself out of Zach's way tomorrow. She was almost to the house when she heard Zach calling.

He came thundering through the darkness, crashing

through crackly shrubbery lining the drive. 'Wait a minute,' he commanded, catching up to her. 'Why do you sound like you know Carter Haskins so well, anyway?'

Annie turned, but Zach grabbed her arm. She jerked away. 'Let me go.'

'Annie, wait – '

Something thudded in the dirt between them. Annie and Zach jumped. A good-sized hunting knife stuck up out of the cracked earth, handle shivering.

'What the hell!' Zach swore.

'The lady wants to be left alone,' Cody said. 'So leave her alone.'

Zach could make out the big man on the porch, idly smoking a cigarette, its tip glowing brightly in the darkness. The son of a bitch hadn't moved from his spot more than an inch, yet he'd managed to send the hair on the back of Zach's neck straight up. He was going to end up with a limb missing yet.

'Damn it! You could've cut off my toes. Or hers, Cody,' he complained. 'All that drama's wasted on this city boy.'

Cody chuckled. 'Wasn't aiming for your toes or I'da hit 'em.'

Zach sighed and glanced at Annie. She stared back at him, her hands on her hips. Boy, was that woman ever mad. He reckoned she had a right to be, but he was hoping for a more receptive attitude before he broached his idea. Deftly, he leaned down and snatched the knife from its resting place, noticing

177

that it was heavy enough to have done real damage if Cody'd been of a mind to hurt him rather than scare the bejesus out of him. He handed it, handle first, back to the man on the porch, who accepted it without comment.

'Now,' Zach said, 'Annie, I would really like to know how well you know Carter Haskins.'

She pierced him with a glare. 'Carter came out here to discuss buying my land. He is a disgusting human being, and I sent him packing.'

Zach digested this news, feeling a sour ache spread through his gut. Carter had come to Desperado privately, though he'd lied, saying they'd only had phone contact. Something was rotten about the situation, but he didn't know what it was. Why would Carter disturb himself to research a deal so thoroughly – other than a possible commission on it? Congratulations from the governor? Hell, no. Carter had gone way overboard with his sneakiness this time. And running to Pop, sniveling about how Zach couldn't make the deal, like Pop's disappointment in Zach would matter two cents to him, anyway. Maybe Zach had been on top of the heap too long. There were too many ambitious men – like Carter – waiting to cut him down. Only he'd never thought this treachery would come from the man Zach had hired.

'*You know I've always thought of you as my friend, Zach.*'

Zach grimaced. Still, more than Carter's underhandedness wasn't right. He looked toward the east, scanning darkness untouched by a single wisp of cloud. It had been a while since he'd seen the original drawing of the proposed highway. Since he hadn't known Annie at the time, he hadn't checked to see where her land lay on the chart. And Desperado had meant little to him other than the name of a thoroughfare.

But as soon as he got back to Austin, Zach promised himself a good look at that proposed state highway. Because something about the whole situation was stinking to high heaven.

Yet he said mildly, 'You're right. Carter is not a nice man. My association with him is not one of the things I'm most proud of in my life, anymore. That's one of the reasons he's no longer going to be working at Ritter International.'

Zach stopped, giving Annie a chance to think about what he was saying. 'But if you've met Carter, you'll realize how important it is to listen to my idea for getting your farm fiscally secure.'

'In the morning.'

He shook his head stubbornly. 'You're already mad. I might as well go ahead and say everything that might rile you up at one time.'

She crossed her arms mutinously. 'I'm listening.'

Zach glanced at Cody. 'Is the porch the place you want to discuss business?' he asked Annie.

'Yes,' she insisted.

'Go ahead, Slick,' Cody said, tossing his cigarette to

the ground. 'There ain't crap on the evening news, so I'll just sit here and be entertained.'

'Me, too,' Travis said from inside the house.

Zach trained his eyes on the window beside the porch and realized Travis was reclining on the sofa inside. The window was up and the old man had been sitting there listening to every single word that had been said up to this point. Cagey old buzzard, Zach thought. A man couldn't let his guard down for an instant around these people.

'All right. A family caucus is as good as any way to throw my thoughts out, anyway.' He squatted down on the porch. 'The way I see this thing, some folks have gotten the notion to buy this land. They're willing to threaten you with right of eminent-domain laws, thinking that with the state highway coming through here, they have the right to pull that particular string. They may even be the reason the bank is putting the squeeze on you right now.'

'You're talking about Haskins,' Cody stated.

'That's what I suspect. Unfortunately, I believe he's got his teeth to your ass on this one, Annie. Carter isn't going to stop until he gets what he wants.'

She pointed a shaking finger at him. 'You go back and tell him to find someone else to bother. He may have his teeth to my ass, but he'll find himself wearing dentures if he tries to bite.'

God, how he loved this woman's grit. Zach shook his head. 'I've got a funny hunch on this, Annie. I'm asking you to trust me.'

Travis cursed blue, and Cody followed suit. Zach spread his hands. 'All right. Just hear me out.'

The three looked at him warily.

'If Annie can make her taxes, the land can't be foreclosed on. In fact, the more financially solvent Annie is, the less of a threat Carter can ever be.'

'How much were you going to make to come out here and do a job on me?' Annie asked.

Zach scented red-alert danger. 'Now, wait a minute, Annie. My salary isn't pertinent to your finances. First things first.'

'Don't patronize me, damn it. I know about commissions. *How much*?'

He shook his head, before looking her square in the face. 'A hundred thousand dollars.'

'Son of a bitch!' Travis shouted from the window. Annie broke her gaze from Zach's and turned her head. 'My rifle's on the porch, Annie. Shoot the dirty rustler.'

Annie folded her arms across her chest, refusing to look at Zach. 'I can't shoot him. I've kissed him.'

'That's it, you low-down, skirt-chasing, snake-eyed – ' Travis cursed as he tried to move from the sofa. 'I'll come out there and shoot you myself.'

'Sit down, Papa,' Annie commanded. 'Let's hear Zach's idea before we kill him. To give up one hundred thousand dollars, it must be a blue-ribbon winner.'

Cody hadn't moved, but then the rifle was just behind him, Zach noticed. And he'd given Cody back the hunting knife, so the big man had two promising choices of weapons if he decided Zach was merely an ink blot in Desperado's history.

'Okay,' Zach said, turning his focus to Annie. 'To get you solvent, you need a business. Something profitable, that isn't at the whim of sun or rain, or other uncontrollable acts of nature.'

'Clock's ticking, Slick,' Cody said. 'Cut the sales bull and give us the bottom line.'

Zach stared at Annie, who merely gazed back.

'I'm thinking salsa's the name of the game.'

CHAPTER 11

'Salsa!'

Cody, Travis, and Annie repeated the word in unison. From his position inside the window, Travis shook his head. 'If you mean Annie's salsa, she's been selling that locally for some time now. And making about forty bucks a month at it. Chicken feed, compared to what we owe.'

Cody shrugged. 'Nice try, I guess, anyway. I still haven't figured out why you're so determined to get on Annie's good side.'

Annie hadn't said a word. She kept her gaze trained on him, as if she knew there was more to his theory than he'd gotten to tell so far. Zach welcomed the connection he felt between them.

'I'm thinking commercial, Annie,' he stated, his voice soft, yet determined. 'Commercial with a twist, maybe a gimmick thrown in.'

'I'm listening,' she said. 'Keep talking.'

'I aim to.' He hunkered down on the porch steps and she sat close by, her eyebrows raised with interest.

'Now recently, a Texas picante sauce company was sold for a nice chunk of change. So, I know there has to be money in a good, hot recipe. Your salsa is one of the best I've ever tasted, and I've traveled most of Texas.'

'Been around a bit, have you?' Travis interrupted meanly.

'Texas is an interesting state,' Zach tossed over his shoulder. 'Be a shame to miss any of it.'

He grinned at Travis's sarcastic snort and continued on. 'The restaurant angle is what comes to my mind. What if you marketed your sauce to better restaurants, specifically those looking for a different, attention-getting product for their customers?'

'What's so interesting about salsa?' Cody asked. 'It's either good, or it's not so good, but it isn't something people are going to interrupt their supper talk over.'

'Ah, but this is Snakebite Sauce, cooked up by Rattlesnake Annie herself,' Zach said with a grin. 'I envision a big brown and gold label, with Snakebite Sauce prominently figured in the middle and with Rattlesnake Annie in curving letters over the top.'

'The Aunt Jemima of salsa,' Cody said.

'We can only pray,' Zach replied.

'Cody, you ain't buying Slick's line, are you? There's so much bull crap piling up out there, I'm gonna have to shut the window.'

Cody folded his arms over his chest, his gaze measuring as it rested on Zach. 'I've always got one ear open when a man's talking opportunity, Travis. He's obviously put some hard thought into this for no apparent reason that I can figure – unless you own stock in some kind of company that's set to make a profit off this scam, Slick.'

The growl in Cody's voice made Zach chuckle. 'Wish I had. All my investments are sunk in oil stocks and commercial real-estate ventures, and they haven't been worth dirt since the bottom fell out of the market.'

'I still don't see why Annie needs to do this,' Travis complained. 'She's sitting on a bumper crop of corn out there, more than enough to pay off the taxes this year.'

'This year,' Zach repeated. 'Could be next year won't be so great. Or the next. If you hit the market right, Snakebite Sauce might keep you from worrying your teeth to nubs every year.'

'Humph.' Travis scanned Cody's face, then Annie's. 'Ah, hell. I can see it ain't worth telling either one of you that we've always gotten by, we always will.'

Annie leaned her head back and peered up at the black sky. 'Maybe getting by isn't enough anymore, Papa. You're older and not quite as strong as you used to be.' She smiled at his curse of denial. '*I'm older*, myself. I'd like to provide better for my only child. Shoot, Papa, we don't even carry enough health insurance to get us by the bad times. If we lost that corn crop, I don't know what we'd do.' Slowly, she turned around to look at her father. 'You don't say it, but I know you think it sometimes, too, Papa. It's been

185

harder since Carlos died. I haven't been able to provide as well for us. Maybe it wouldn't matter if it was just you and me – ' her expression turned pleading ' – but for Mary's sake, it hurts to be so strapped all the time.'

Travis's face stayed set in mulish lines. 'This carpetbagger's gone and scared the horse sense out of you.' He shot an angry look Zach's way.

Annie shook her head slowly. 'No, Papa. It has nothing to do with Zach. I will admit that I've been more insecure about the future, but it started when Carlos died. There were two of us to take on the world before, but then everything changed. Haskins came out here. I began having nightmares about not being able to – '

She stopped, obviously incapable of putting into words what she wanted to say. Zach reached over and patted her knee, but inside, he was promising Carter an ear-ringing firing from Ritter International. It would be one of his last acts of kindness if he didn't throw Carter out the glass window.

'Well, we don't have to run out and find a factory tonight,' he said, his voice reassuring. 'I was just throwing out an idea. It may be stupid as hell, for all I know.' He glanced up to see a thoughtful expression on Cody's face. The realization swept him that Cody was actually giving his proposal some merit, without dismissing it the way the old man had. Strangely enough, Cody's opinion mattered to Zach.

'Aw, hell. Let's go to bed,' Travis said. 'I've been

186

home less than a day from the hospital and y'all are talking capital enterprises. Come on, Cody. Help me to my room.'

'All right.' Cody threw one last glance at the pair on the porch and went inside.

'Good night, Papa,' Annie called. 'I'll be in later to check on you.'

She grinned at her father's muttered cussing. Zach rested his head on his forearms, silently listening to Cody help Travis from the sofa. It was time to take himself down to the foreman's shack, yet he didn't feel like leaving Annie yet. He wondered what she'd really thought of his suggestion. Annie was an intelligent woman. She knew what the risks of starting a new business were – especially with a small child and an old man to care for. She also knew what the risks of relying on crops for her income were. Maybe she even had an idea of her own rolling around behind those warm indigo-blue eyes of hers.

He took a deep breath of night air just barely cooling from the heat of the day, and realized that whether or not Annie was buying the idea of Snakebite Sauce, all he really cared about was that she knew he cared about her. Really, really cared about her. This was the only way he knew how to help her, to show her he was on her side, regardless of which side he'd started out on.

He suspected Cody had figured that out, although he still sensed animosity from the big man. Annie was smart enough to realize it, too. He wasn't in a position to offer Annie any type of relationship, but she had changed his life. Much, much for the better. And he would never forget that.

Annie sighed beside him. 'So, can you find your way back down to the foreman's shack?'

'I think so.'

'There's a shower and you'll find towels in the closet.' Annie's gaze roved over him. 'Although I guess you've just finished drying out from your swim.'

Zach smiled at the mischievous light in her eyes. 'A warm shower sounds inviting, actually, despite the swim.'

She stood slowly, and Zach rose with her.

'Thank you for coming, Zach. You've given us all something to think about.' For a moment, her eyes held uncertainty. 'It's something we've been needing to face for some time. Maybe over the next few months, we can talk about your idea again.' She paused for a second, her gaze asking him to understand. 'When Papa feels better.'

He nodded. 'It's not my idea anymore. It's yours. Do with it what you will. If it helps you in any way, then I'm glad.' Slowly, gently, he ran one finger across Annie's cheekbone. 'Before I leave tomorrow, I want another tour of the corn fields. I've never seen what corn near harvest time looks like.' He removed his hand slowly. 'Actually, I think the only corn I've ever seen besides yours was in the grocery store.'

Annie smiled. 'City boy,' she murmured softly.

He chuckled. 'Yeah. Well, I'm sure you've heard the old saying that you can take the country boy to the city, but you can't take the city boy to the country.'

'I think you completely ruined that saying, Zach,' Annie teased.

'Something did get lost in the translation, I agree.'

They stood staring at each other for a moment, their eyes locked. Finally, he had to break the silence. 'So. Corn field tour in the morning?'

'Right after breakfast.'

'We could take Mary,' Zach offered. *Shame on you, using a little girl as a buffer*! he thought. 'If you think she'd like that,' he finished guiltily.

'Mary always loves to romp in the fields,' Annie told him. 'She'll tell you more about those corn crops than you ever wanted to know.' She looked toward the fields where the corn was planted, then looked back at Zach a little sheepishly. 'I had acres and acres of it planted. Corn's one of my favorite things to grow. Cotton's a good money-maker, but you can't eat it,' she said with a smile. 'If I had to, I could make meals out of that corn for a very long time. I can see it from the south and west windows of the house, and sometimes I imagine that corn is a security blanket around us.'

She sighed, before turning her wistful gaze back to him. 'Silly, huh, city boy?'

Zach clenched his hands at his sides to keep from pulling Annie into his arms. 'I'm barely resisting the urge to run through those corn fields naked in a ritual appreciation dance,' he said, forcing himself to sound light.

189

Annie laughed, the sound full of relief. 'You always say the right things.' She turned to go into the house. 'You'll be okay?'

Zach waved her on. 'I'm going to bed down in that shack like it's the Ritz, and I'm not waking up till I hear reveille. Or smell breakfast cooking.'

It was untrue, but it kept the smile on Annie's face until she closed the front door behind her. And that alone made his trip to Desperado worth it.

Annie went down the hall to her room after checking on Travis, then on Mary. The little girl slept peacefully in her bed, clutching a small bear in her arms. Annie turned the nightlight on, in case Mary woke up in the night with a bad dream. It didn't happen as frequently now, but Annie was in the habit of turning the tiny light on just in case.

She thought about Zach comforting Mary as she walked into her own room. He'd said more to Mary than anyone else had ever managed, including Annie. Although she'd tried to help Mary deal with her grief, there really wasn't a good way to explain to a child why her daddy died, or how, or why God had let it happen. And was Daddy up in heaven, watching over her?

Annie sighed and sat down on the bed to brush her hair. Of all people, Zach Rayez wasn't the person she would have guessed could connect with Mary's pain. And what he'd told the child about his own mother had brought swift tears to Annie's eyes. At least Mary still had one parent left who loved her, and then a circle of doting family.

Zach had lost both parents. No wonder he'd grown up to be such a tough character.

But not too tough to drive out to Desperado to try to help Annie solve some of her difficulties. Despite Travis's and Cody's suspicions, Annie knew Zach was on the level. He might be tough in business dealings, but she herself had seen soft underbelly. Vulnerable heart. All in all, a good man in many ways.

A man who was due to be married very soon.

Annie pursed her lips and put the brush down. White-hot pain stabbed into her heart as she thought about his fiancée. She would be beautiful, of course. She would be able to help Zach in his career. No doubt the future Mrs Rayez was loving and kind and just the woman he could entrust his heart to. The heart that had known little love as a child, and likely less as an adult. He would choose a woman who would be careful of those bitter scars and yet know how to encircle him and make him whole with her love.

She slipped into a nightgown and turned out the bedside lamp. Later, after Zach had gone, she would think again about the salsa. Later, when she knew his wedding was past and that their connection was finally severed for ever, she would think about her future.

Zach tossed and turned in his sleep. He awakened about every hour, it seemed, to glance at the watch on his arm and then try to fall asleep again. About two in the morning, he got up and walked around the cabin, uncertain as to why he couldn't relax. The fish pond was still. He walked back to the front, glancing toward Annie's house. All the lights were out, except for a small glow, like a star, in a west window. Zach smiled, remembering that Mary's room was across the hall from Annie's. He'd seen the rows and rows of stuffed animals lovingly arranged on a day bed the afternoon Annie cut her finger. Mary had been afraid of him, then. But she wasn't afraid of him now. He was glad she trusted him. A child's trust was a very important gift, and very few adults trafficked in the business of trust, Zach knew. He would treasure Mary's trust forever.

Yawning, he went back inside and crawled in the sheets. The bed was comfortable enough, with crisp, white sheets that smelled of detergent. The cabin itself was cool. Zach lay on his back, his arms crossed under his head, staring into the semi-blackness. Oh, there was a reason he couldn't sleep. He just didn't want to face it.

Annie Aguillar had started a fire in him he couldn't douse. Something about her had attached itself to his heart and wouldn't let go. Trying to think about LouAnn did nothing to improve the situation. A vision of LouAnn naked but for high heels, modeling her wedding garter, flitted through his mind. Zach winced. And made a major resolution. He was going back to Austin tomorrow and meet with LouAnn, to tell her he couldn't go through with their wedding. It was going to be a most unpleasant scene, but it had to be done. Whether or not Annie ever became a part of his life remained to be seen. But she had taught him the real meaning of love.

And he didn't love LouAnn.

He loved Annie with heart-pounding, bone-melting emotion he'd never felt for a woman. He could go mad thinking about Annie when he was lying beside another woman, a woman he didn't love any more.

Zach closed his eyes, willing himself to sleep. There was no point in thinking about it tonight. Time enough for action tomorrow.

The smell of something cooking teased Zach out of a restless dream. He smiled to himself, and rubbed his face in the pillow. What little he'd tasted of Annie's cooking was delicious, and he looked forward to eating whatever she made for breakfast. He hadn't eaten since noon yesterday, having declined dropping in on their homecoming dinner last night.

However, he would make up for that with gusto this morning. The fact that he'd be sharing the meal with Annie and Mary was the best part, of course. Travis and Cody he could deal with – easily – if it meant being with those two ladies.

He sat up groggily and rubbed a hand over his face. *There's a hell of a breeze this morning, if I can smell what Annie's cooking*, he thought. It was still dark in the cabin, yet he could see a glow on the horizon out the south window.

South. Not east as the sun rises.

Zach shot his feet and raced to the window. 'Oh, my God,' he whispered. 'The fields are on fire.'

CHAPTER 12

'Cody! Annie!' Zach stumbled toward the house, awkwardly jerking his jeans on one leg at a time. Glancing toward the corn field, he saw only bright flames and jet wisps of smoke spiraling upward in the darkness. Forcing himself to run faster, Zach gained the porch steps and started pounding on the front door hard enough to fracture the aged wood. 'Somebody open the door! The corn fields are on fire!' he shouted.

The door jerked open. 'Slick!' Cody said. 'What the hell?'

'There's a fire in the corn fields.' Zach pointed toward the south. 'It's big, too.'

'Damn it.' Cody cursed under his breath and reached over to the sofa, snatching jeans up. 'Annie!' he yelled over his shoulder.

'My God,' she said, appearing in the doorway, soft and rumpled in a gown that just swept her knees. 'What are you two doing?'

'Call the fire department. The corn's on fire,' Cody commanded.

Annie gasped and raced into the kitchen. Now dressed, Cody shouldered past Zach and hurried down the porch steps. Travis hobbled into the hall, tossing a malevolent stare Zach's way. 'What the hell are you doing, sneaking around the house at this hour?'

Annie returned at that moment. 'Papa, there's a fire in the fields. Listen out for Mary, in case she wakes up frightened. I'm going down there.'

She ran into her room, coming back out two seconds later wearing jeans under her nightshirt. She hurried past Zach, but he was at her side before the screen door slammed shut. 'I won't even ask how you knew there was a fire,' she said, not breaking her frenzied pace.

Zach halted in his tracks, staring after Annie. Her long, ebony hair waved as she ran, stretched out on the wind of her footsteps. Those feet were bare, flying over sharp rocks and uneven, prickly growth. He pounded a fist against his leg and took off running again. The woman was probably going to lose everything she had. He wanted to try to help her. Later, they could talk.

Zach heard sirens in the distance. The crackle and roar of the fire as it ate its way through the corn crop was louder, and Zach realized the fire department wasn't going to be able save enough of it to matter. The land was already parched from endless days of baking sunshine, and what might have been a small, manageable fire under different conditions was exploding into a pyro's dream.

The whine of a tractor as it started caught Zach's attention. Cody headed the tractor into the eastern portion of the field, rolling over the tall stalks in his path. Zach realized he was trying to divert the fire, but it was too desperate an attempt. 'Cody!' he cried, running behind the tractor. 'Stop!'

Most likely Cody couldn't hear him, but Zach knew he wouldn't have stopped anyway. Zach halted in the path of run-over corn and watched the tractor shove on relentlessly. Annie ran to Zach's side, her fingernails digging into his arm. 'He's going to get hurt.'

'I know.' Grimly, Zach watched the tractor slow, then come to a stop a couple hundred yards away. Heat from the fire scorched Zach's face. Cody had to be suffering worse. He counted under his breath, waiting for the big man to give up and jump from the tractor. Nothing moved. Zach got to ten and started running with everything he had.

'Cody!' he shouted. 'Cody!'

A wall of fire was steadily sweeping its way toward the tractor. Pungent, lung-burning smoke seared Zach's eyes, making it difficult to see. Heedlessly, he sprinted over the crushed stalks. 'Cody, damn it! Get out!'

The tractor engine was silent, Zach realized. He started coughing, wishing he had a shirt or anything to put over his nose and mouth. Eyes tearing, lungs bursting, he finally reached the tractor. Cody was slumped; the only thing keeping him on the tractor was his knee jammed against the steering column.

'Son of a bitch!' Zach cursed. He reached up and knocked Cody's leg away from the column until it angled toward the side, then dragged the big man off the tractor, knocking himself down in the process.

'Son of a bitch!' Zach swore again. Cody's dead weight crushed him, bringing stars of pain to Zach's eyes. With a mighty shove, he pushed Cody off of him, then pulled himself to his knees and finally to his feet. Choking, gasping, and knowing they were both in immediate danger of being overcome by smoke, Zach grabbed Cody by the feet and began pulling him, rickshaw-style, away from the fire.

Suddenly, Annie was at his side. 'Give me a leg,' she gasped.

Together, they made stubborn progress tugging the man out of danger, making their way toward the fire truck at the far edge of the field. Men were running with water hoses and shovels, but Zach knew it was too late.

When they were far enough from danger, Zach gently let Cody's leg down. Annie did the same, before running to get help. 'You stupid cigar-store Indian,' Zach said roughly, lifting Cody's eyelids. He laid his head to Cody's chest, listening for a heartbeat. There was a faint one. 'I know you hear me,' he said. 'You nearly got yourself killed. You nearly got Annie killed. Wake up so I can kill you,' he said, not meaning the last but desperate enough to say anything.

Vainly, he watched for any movement in Cody's face. Zach shook him, knowing even as he did that it wouldn't help. '*Come on, Cody,*' he ordered. 'You're too damn bullheaded to die.'

A volunteer paramedic hunkered down on the opposite side of Cody, placing an oxygen mask from a portable tank over his nose. Another man monitored Cody's vital signs. Annie crouched nearby, silver trails of tears running down her face. She met Zach's gaze over Cody's still form, but he looked away, unable to bear the despairing plea for help in her eyes.

He'd done the best he could. And come up lacking.

Suddenly, Cody coughed, a frightening, hacking sound. Zach's gaze riveted to the man on the ground. Cody spluttered beneath the oxygen mask, his eyes popping open to stare up at the heat-clouded sky. The paramedic pulled the mask away as Cody tried to sit up.

'Hey, take it easy, there, Cody,' Zach said. 'Put the mask back on.'

Cody shook his head, thumping his chest weakly as he coughed. Slowly, he laid back down. 'Sorry,' he murmured.

'Sorry?' Zach tried to sound jovial as he glanced up at Annie. She shook her head at him, so he shrugged to make light of the situation. 'What's there to be sorry about?'

'Couldn't . . . stop it,' Cody whispered.

Annie moved closer, tracing her fingers across Cody's furrowed brow. 'There's a fire truck out here that can't stop it, Cody. You risked too much,' she said.

Zach winced at the pain and held-back tears in her voice. 'Take some more oxygen, Cody. It might help you.'

'Don't . . . want it.' He waved away both the mask and the paramedic who was trying to edge him onto a stretcher on the ground.

Zach's patience was threadbare from fear that the big man was hurt more than he would admit. 'Listen, damn it,' he said, leaning over so that Cody could clearly see and hear him. 'You need medical attention. You tried to put that fire out by yourself, and damn near swallowed more smoke than a hundred packs of those crappy cigarettes you adore would have put into your lungs. Not to mention,' he said, reaching over to Cody's ear and flicking the hanging wire there, 'you singed off your earring. The feather's completely gone, Cody, and some of your eyebrows. You could have been, too. So, quit being so damn ornery and put the mask on and get your ass on the stretcher.'

Cody's gaze slid over to Zach, questioning in the darkness. 'Tell . . . me you . . . didn't do this, Slick.'

'Do what?' Zach asked, genuinely confused.

'The . . . fire,' he rasped.

'Oh, for – ' Zach swallowed the curse words, glancing up at Annie. Her doubtful expression froze him. 'You don't . . . I mean, why would I?'

Cody lay silent and still, yet his eyes wouldn't let go of Zach. 'Why would I?' Zach asked numbly. 'I want to help Annie, not hurt her.'

'Your . . . father,' Cody whispered hoarsely.

'My father!' Zach frowned. 'What's he got to do with anything?'

He looked up at Annie, but she was staring at Cody. 'Your father . . . wants . . . her land.'

Zach couldn't believe what he was hearing. 'Cody, you're out of your head. My pop is a dirt-poor alcoholic who lives in a falling-down shack across from a bingo parlor. He couldn't buy a pot to piss in, much less Annie's land.'

Cody closed his eyes for a moment. 'Owns . . . land to south.'

Zach shook his head. 'No. That's not possible. Annie, I swear to you, my pop doesn't even own the house he lives in.'

The paramedic gave one last stab at trying to move Cody on to the stretcher, but at the strength of Cody's hoarse curse word, moved away. 'Lying.'

'No. I swear it.'

'Somebody did buy the farm to the south of my property,' Annie confirmed. 'But I don't know who it was.'

'Zach's father,' Cody said. 'Sales are matter of . . . public record.'

'So I did this for my father, whom I completely despise.' Zach snorted. 'Not damn likely.'

'Blood . . . thicker than water.' Cody closed his eyes again.

'Bullcrap. The blood runs too damn thin in my family to be of any use to a corpse. If you're not going to the hospital, then let me help you up off the ground,

201

you son of a bitch. I'm not dragging your ass all the way back to the house.'

The fire was out in places, still smoldering in others. Black-edged fields and heavy smoke lent a surreal air to a place where so much hope had once thrived. Annie met his gaze silently. Zach turned his face, angry at her suspicions. Angry at Cody's. Angry at the whole sorry situation. A hacking cough tore out of Cody's throat, and Zach looked down wearily. He pushed an arm under Cody's shoulder. 'On the count of three, sit up,' he commanded. 'One, two, three!'

Giving him a hearty shove, Zach managed Cody into a sitting position. Annie crouched under one shoulder and Zach took the other. Together, they tugged Cody to his feet, and when he was steady, they slowly helped him stagger back to the house.

The firemen were rolling up their hoses and putting away their equipment. Zach could hear them muttering amongst themselves as they passed. More than anything, he felt hopeless for Annie's sake. She was a survivor, true, but now she was wiped out.

Travis was sitting on the porch, with Mary tucked up against him. Her anxious eyes flew to Cody. 'Uncle Cody!' she cried. 'What happened?'

'He's all right, sugar,' Annie said, her voice calm. Zach knew she couldn't be nearly as calm as she was trying to sound. 'Open the door, baby, so I can help Uncle Cody on to the sofa.'

Straining every muscle in his shoulders, Zach maneuvered Cody inside and to a sitting position, where the man collapsed with his head back on a sofa arm.

'Dang, but I feel . . . lousy,' Cody admitted.

'Try to get some sleep, Cody,' Annie told him. 'We can't do anything more tonight, and worrying isn't going to change anything. That goes for you, too, Papa. And you, sugar.' She tossed a light blanket over Cody, which he immediately threw on to the floor. Sighing, she helped her father to his room. Zach heard her relating the damage as they made their painful way down the hall.

Mary stood still, staring up at him with those trusting eyes. Zach put out his hand. 'Come on, Mary. I guess I'll tuck you in.'

She stood rooted to the spot. 'I don't want to.'

'Well, heckfire,' Zach muttered, trying to keep the harshness out of his voice and not succeeding. 'Nobody in this family wants to do anything they should be and . . . and – '

He halted at the stricken look in Mary's eyes. 'Oh, come here,' he said, gathering her up into his arms. 'I'm not angry with you, Mary. I'm grumpy because I'm worn out, kind of like a baby when it misses a nap. See?'

Mary gazed at him with big indigo eyes inches from his face. 'Mr Zach, I'm afraid. I heard sirens, and something smells funny. I don't want to be in my room.'

Zach groaned, knowing the child was frightened out of her wits. She'd been through so much in her short life. He tamped down the urge he was feeling to go tearing back to Austin and leave these obstinate, unfortunate people to their own devices. How could Annie even *think* for a second that he would do something as cruel as wiping out her livelihood?

But the child was still looking at him, her gaze confused and upset. Zach firmly planted his bare heels on the hard wood floor, miserably aware that he was not going to desert the little girl while she was suffering. 'Here, Mary,' he said, pulling over a ragged plaid easy chair, 'sit right here next to your Uncle Cody for just a bit. Don't be scared, even though he looks like a burnt-out scarecrow.'

Zach allowed himself a wry grin and momentary satisfaction at Cody's indignant grunt. 'Sit here quietly so Uncle Cody won't feel like the last, charred hot dog on the grill. I'm going down to talk to the firemen, but I'll be right back. I promise.'

The men were about finished cleaning up when Zach got there. Even dulled by the rosy glow of rising sun, the fields looked sickeningly empty, destroyed. He fought down a wave of revulsion as a fireman walked over to him.

'Ugly sight, ain't it?' the man asked. 'Name's Jim Crier. Known the Aguillars forever.'

Zach took the hand Jim offered. 'I'm Zach Rayez. I stayed with the Aguillars overnight.'

Jim's steady eyes didn't so much as blink. 'They don't have many house guests.' When Zach shrugged at his comment, he asked, 'Do you know who saw the fire first, Zach?'

He heaved a sigh, knowing the words were going to damn him. 'I did.'

'That so? How'd you come to see the fire?'

Zach shrugged. 'I didn't sleep well last night. Then I thought I smelled something, so I got up.' He frowned, remembering how fast the fire had spread. It was the most horrible, consuming thing he'd ever seen. 'I got up . . . and saw the fire. Then I ran to Annie's house to get help.'

'To get help?' Jim's voice was sharp. 'From an old man and a helpless woman? Or were you wanting to be the big hero?'

'I don't know.' Zach despised the helpless tone in his voice, but he had just reacted blindly. He'd have carried water in his mouth to put out the fire if it would've helped, but he'd known the fields were past saving. 'I don't know,' he repeated. 'All I could think of was that we were going to need a miracle to put that damn thing out.'

'I see,' was Jim's laconic reply.

Zach felt Annie standing beside him even before she spoke. The feeling was an instant awareness, like a coming together of pieces, and Zach wondered at the realization.

'Thank you for coming out so quickly, Jim,' Annie said.

The man hugged her briefly. 'I'm sorry we couldn't do more.'

She shrugged with a stoic smile. 'You did what you could. It might have been the house and worse, had the wind changed.'

'Thanks, Annie. You know how to make a man feel better when he's got bad news to share.'

'Bad news?' Zach and Annie repeated the words in unison.

'I'm afraid so,' Jim said, nodding. He pointed toward the fields. 'You were luckier than you think. That fire was set on purpose.'

'Oh, no! Are you sure, Jim? I – '

Annie stopped speaking. Zach felt her horrified stare clean through to his soul. He waited for her to accuse him, to damn him out loud. The weight of Jim's stare was on him too, but Zach never released Annie's gaze.

'We smelled gasoline, Annie,' Jim stated, 'so we know that was what was used to ignite the fire. You got any idea who?'

Annie was silent for a long minute. Zach waited, counting the thundering heartbeats he heard in his own chest.

'I couldn't even begin to guess, Jim,' she said quietly. 'High-school prank? Some mean-spirited person with an appetite for starting fires? I've never heard of anything like this happening in Desperado, so I'm pretty much at a loss myself.'

'Well. That's that, then.' Jim stepped back a pace before patting Annie on the back. 'You let me know if you think of anything. We'll have the sheriff out here today. In the meantime, I'd put in a call to your insurance company.' He turned, then turned around again. 'By the way, where did you say you were from, Zach?'

He hadn't. But the fireman wasn't about to forget Zach's name on his possible suspect list. 'Austin,' Zach replied shortly. 'You can find me in the phone book if you have any further questions.'

The fireman nodded, his steely gaze hard on Zach's face. 'I'll keep that in mind.'

When Jim had walked away, Zach turned to look at Annie. She was staring out at her beloved fields, her eyes glittering with unshed tears. He would have tried to offer some piece of condolence, superficial as it would have sounded considering the situation. But she turned almost at once and hurried back toward the house.

Fortunately. Because he didn't know what the hell to say to her.

Zach ground his teeth. Somehow the web was growing tighter and tighter around him. Somehow he was coming up aces in an accursed hand that bore his name. He walked into the burnt-out devastation, kicking at the blackened stalks bitterly. The fire truck pulled away, rumbling down the lane. Zach imagined every one of those men's eyes were focused on him, assessing him.

He wanted to shout that he didn't do this deed, but his gut told him no one would believe him. Cody certainly had his doubts. And Annie, although she wasn't admitting it out loud right now, wondered, too. Once she got past the moment of crisis, she too was going to look at him with accusing eyes.

'Damn it!' Zach kicked over another ruined clump of corn stalks. 'Damn it to hell and back!' He let out another more furious swear word, then stopped dead in his tracks. Crouching down, he stared for a moment at the ground. Carefully, he picked up a piece of ruined corn and pushed at something in the charred earth. When it rolled over, soggy and half-smoked and nearly indistinguishable in the muddy blackness, Zach could only stare in disbelief and amazement.

It was a cigar. A big, fat Mexican cigar. Exactly the brand Carter kept on hand.

CHAPTER 13

'What do you know about Zach Rayez, Cody?' Jim Crier asked.

Annie watched Cody close his eyes wearily. She wished he didn't have to answer any questions and could recuperate instead. The man had nearly sold his life to save her corn fields, and the debt of gratitude she owed him was too great to ever repay.

'Does he have to talk right now, Jim?' she asked. 'I think Cody ought to be resting.'

'It's just one small question, Annie. I'll be okay.'

Annie shook her head at the gritty, painful sound of Cody's voice and sat down in one of the plaid chairs. Mary promptly crawled into her lap and Annie began the comforting motion of drawing her fingers through her daughter's long dark hair while she listened.

'We don't know much about Zach, to tell you the truth, Jim. He came out here a few weeks back to buy Annie's land. Couldn't finish working the deal because Travis had a heart attack just looking at "the snake-eyed varmint", as he calls him.'

'No love lost there, eh?'

'Naw. But Travis is a mean son of a gun himself. Cares about two things in this world, and that's Annie and Mary.'

'Not true,' Annie murmured. 'He'd give his right arm to help you, Cody.'

A small smile flitted over Cody's smoke-grimed face. 'Yeah. But his two girls are the only thing your ragged old man is living for. And when Slick appeared, well . . .'

His raspy voice fell silent. Annie leaned over to examine his face worriedly.

'Jim, he's so exhausted. Can't this wait until later?'

'The sheriff'll do plenty of talking this afternoon,' Jim said, nodding. 'What I want to know from Cody here is if he thinks Zach was involved in the fire in any way?'

The room fell completely, ominously silent. Annie looked down to see Mary's eyes, huge and questioning. She shook her head so her child wouldn't be concerned, but Mary pushed herself up in her mother's lap.

'No! Mr Zach wouldn't do that!'

Jim stared at Mary, then at Annie. 'I'm sorry, Annie,' he said. 'I didn't realize the man had such a staunch supporter in the room. I'll be more careful.'

Annie nodded. Cody took a deep breath, which sounded winded and drawn. 'You know, Jim, I had my doubts about Zach in the beginning. But, like with Mary, he started to grow on me. Truth is, I'm having

210

real trouble fitting Zach into the scene of the crime.'

'Really? Based on what?'

'Nothing but a country boy's gut feeling.'

'Oh, hell, Cody, tell me what you're thinking.'

A small, amused chuckle escaped Cody. 'You remember those guys in high school who thought they were the big kings of testosterone, strutting and shooting off their mouth all the time?'

Jim scratched his head with his pencil. 'Ah, yeah, I do, Cody. You were sitting on the testosterone throne.'

Annie smiled at the sudden frown on Cody's face. 'Come on, Cody,' she said gently, 'don't waste what little breath you've got denying it. I remember our high school years the same way Jim does.'

The frown lifted a little. 'My brother never was that way, you know,' he said. 'Carlos wasn't any more a farmer than I am a rock musician. But once he married Annie, he worked like an ox to make this place the next King Ranch.'

He met Annie's dismayed gaze and she couldn't tear her eyes away, although what Cody was saying was tearing her heart into painful ribbons.

'He loved you, Annie. Whatever it was that made you happy, that was what he was going to give you, no matter what.'

Cody rubbed at his wrist absently, as if the skin there had been seared by the fire's heat. 'Some men are born salt of the earth, I guess, or somehow their character ends up that way. Others are big wheels,

211

testosterone kings. That's what Slick reminded me of when he first came here. Kinda cocky, real sure of himself.'

'Very masculine and aware of it,' Annie murmured, earning a dark look from Cody.

'I'll tell the story, if you don't mind,' Cody stated.

'I get the picture, Cody. So what's the point?' Jim interrupted.

Cody leaned back, closing his eyes. 'Well, here was this guy who acted like he had the world by the tail and I'm thinking "what a jackass". I was ready to ship him back to Austin via Seattle in a car-trunk. It was clear that he had the hots for Annie and I wasn't going to stand for some sidewinder moseying in here and – '

'Sh!' Annie commanded, her eyebrows raised to indicate Mary's listening ears.

'Sorry.' Cody looked sheepish. 'Well, safe to say I didn't like Slick much at first.'

'I see that,' Jim agreed.

'He called Annie one night. I knew he'd be back, like a fox to the henhouse. So, I did some checking up on him.'

'You did what?' Annie was astonished.

'I feel like it's my job to look out for you occasionally, Annie.'

'Was this before or after you proposed to me, that you thought Zach needed some "checking up on"?' she asked, feeling wrathful and strangely flattered all at once.

'You proposed to Annie?' Jim asked, happy interest

lighting his eyes. 'I've been wondering if you'd ever get around to that.'

'Why?' Cody and Annie asked at the same time.

Jim hastily pulled his pencil down from his ear. 'Seems like the sensible thing to do, is all,' he muttered.

Cody shook his head with a wry grin. 'Well, Annie turned me down and I'm glad she did. I want to help Annie any way I can, but I love her like a sister. I hope she loves me like a brother. I want Mary to always count on her Uncle Cody.'

Annie smiled and nodded. 'We all love you, Cody. But I'll keep the tractor keys from now on. You took your protective instincts a little too far for my comfort.'

'Okay, okay, so no wedding,' Jim prodded. 'Let's get back to Zach. You're starting to look white as that pillow case, Cody.'

Cody placed a hand on his chest, as if he was feeling some pain there. 'Well, I discovered he's engaged to be married. Soon,' he qualified, giving Annie a this-hurts-me-more-than-it-hurts-you look.

When she didn't look surprised, he continued. 'And his daddy owns the property south of here. Even though the name on the deed wasn't Rayez, I had a hunch. Called Zach's office and asked the secretary for the correct spelling of Zach's father's name for my company's mailing list.' Cody smirked. 'Sure enough, my hunch was right.'

Jim looked up, startled. 'Let me get this straight.

213

Zach wanted to buy Annie out, but she wouldn't let him. Then her corn fields get set on fire, which I imagine is going to set you back a piece.' He looked at Annie for confirmation.

'That would be putting it mildly,' she said.

'So, are we talking motive here, Cody?' Jim asked.

Cody sighed. 'You know, Jim, Slick could talk the worm out of a tequila bottle. He came in here yesterday, all fired up about getting Annie set up in a salsa-making business, and the next thing I know, I'm hearing him loud and clear. I'm actually ready to offer some rattlesnake fangs to toss in some of the jars as a gimmick, maybe in a sales promotion of some kind.' He snorted.

'And now?'

Annie waited for Cody's answer, her heart thumping nervously in her chest. She knew exactly what Cody was talking about. Yesterday, Zach Rayez had actually made her start spinning fantasy dreams about her own fancy business – and being solvent. Making it on her own, after all.

Today, reality had come crashing in upon her. But until yesterday, she'd forgotten how to dream.

She'd never forget again.

'And now,' Annie looked up as Cody spoke again, 'I still think he's slicker than a cow's teat. But being slick and being out to hurt Annie don't jive in my book. Something's not making sense here, but I haven't figured it out, yet.' Cody looked at Jim tiredly, before closing his eyes again. 'However, since you're looking for my advice, I'd say to look elsewhere for a suspect.'

'That's pretty strong support, Cody, considering Zach's probably the only likely suspect,' Jim said.

'That's part of what's bothering me,' Cody stated without opening his eyes. He turned his face away toward the window, obviously too exhausted to continue. Annie leaned forward over Mary to catch his next words.

'It's all too convenient,' he whispered. 'Too damned convenient.'

The sight of the cigar held Zach transfixed. It was the expensive brand Carter smoked almost constantly. Of course, anybody could be smoking a cigar.

No. Not on Annie's fields.

It might have been there for a long time, Zach theorized. Still, Cody smoked only cigarettes, Travis smoked nothing, and who the hell would venture this far on to someone's property to sneak a smoke?

The brand bothered Zach the most. Why did it seem odd that the local fellows would choose such an expensive brand, if everyone in Desperado struggled as hard as Annie did to make ends meet? Seemed like chewing tobacco would be the more popular choice.

Zach frowned, digging into his thoughts for logical answers. Carter was a sneaky, selfish man at the very least. But for him to go to these lengths to get Annie's land was too preposterous to think about seriously. Burning out a family would take a criminal mind.

He crossed his arms, staring up at the now-serene

blue sky. In the distance, mockingbirds scolded each other for thievery and other imagined slights.

'Carter came out here to talk to Annie, before I let him talk me into doing this job,' Zach said softly to himself. 'He never mentioned the property owner was female, or anything else about the deal. He acted like it was easy pickings, when he knew that wasn't true.'

Still, buying out the Aguillars was for the sake of Ritter International and perhaps some future commercial sales deals. It wasn't a personal vendetta.

It wasn't supposed to be personal. But at some point Carter had begun subtly pressuring him about the deal. Zach had just as subtly ignored the pressure, using his upcoming wedding as a shield against Carter's machinations.

The bank is going to foreclose on the Aguillar land if the taxes aren't paid up by the end of the year. Carter had told him that just a few days ago. Zach had shrugged it off, not even a little surprised that Carter had buddies in less-than-honest places who would give him that information.

Instantly, he realized Annie had never mentioned a possible foreclosure to him. The woman would bend like the willow trees around the fish pond in the face of disaster, but she was never going to break. Carter Haskins was not going to break Annie Aguillar.

Like a lightning flash, Zach remembered his reply to Carter. *The Aguillars are sitting on a bumper crop of corn. They'll make their taxes.*

Had he accidentally condemned Annie to this

devastating fate with his own big mouth? Zach felt like he'd been kicked in the head just thinking about his possible role in Annie's downfall.

Not possible. Probable.

The suspicion that he was more involved in this than he wanted to be broke small beads of sweat out along his forehead. If Carter truly was behind this, then the stamp of guilt lay on Zach's forehead, too.

And yet, why in hell would Carter go to such lengths?

Cody claimed that Pop owned the property south of Annie's farm. Now, that was a major piece of misinformation if he'd ever heard it. Zach shook his head, his memory automatically recalling the retching smell of sour booze and dank filth he associated with Pop.

No. Pop didn't even own himself. He'd sold himself to the devil a long time back.

And Carter had paid a visit to the old shack just a few days ago.

Zach looked down at the cigar once more. Cody was not a stupid man. Something had gotten very dirty somewhere, and if Cody said Pop's name was on a deed, then it was past time to pay a visit to Pop.

Turning, Zach headed toward Annie's house. Difficult as it was going to be, he had to face her. Had to look her in the eyes – and Mary, too – and tell them he was leaving.

Zach walked in the front door, his heart heavy. Annie, Mary, Cody and Jim Crier all looked up at him.

He felt condemned.

'Well, isn't anyone going to say "Hello, Zach. We were just talking about you"?' he asked. Too angry to stop the words, Zach knew they were misdirected. His anger was too divided to be aimed at just the people in this room. And yet, he couldn't help wishing Annie had a little more faith in him.

'Hello, Mr Zach. We were just talking about you,' Mary repeated obediently.

Her comment took the tenseness right out of Zach. 'Thanks, sweetheart. Anything else I should know about?'

He took in the four pairs of eyes watching him and sat down, not really expecting Mary to answer.

'Well, Uncle Cody says he's going to put snake teeth in your hot sauce,' Mary continued, blithely unaware that she'd made Cody's words sound like a threat.

The electricity in the room intensified to the point that Zach felt the hairs on his arms tickling. He stared at Cody, who had rolled his head to scowl at Mary's lack of discretion. Then Cody turned his eyes unflinchingly to Zach's.

'Snake teeth in my . . .' Zach stopped, realizing the precious information in what he'd just heard. 'That's a hell of an idea, Cody,' he said. 'What a great marketing tool.' He grinned, feeling a lot less condemned. Because if Cody was buying Zach's Snakebite Sauce, then maybe that meant Cody was buying Zach.

Didn't believe he'd set the fire.

218

Zach felt like leaping into the air. 'Thanks, Cody,' he said, meaning it with all his heart.

Cody merely shrugged. Zach didn't care. He slid to his knees at Annie's side to get down to Mary's level.

'Mary, I have to go home,' he said. 'Next time I come, I'd like another fish lesson.' He touched the little girl's raven-black hair, where it waved along her cheek. She stared at him with wise, earnest eyes. 'But, Mary,' he added softly, 'I *am* coming back.'

Her rosebud lips curved into the sweetest smile. 'I know, Mr Zach. Because this time you remembered to say goodbye.'

He nodded. 'Yes. I won't ever forget again.'

Slowly, Zach rose to his feet. 'Goodbye, Annie,' he said, holding her eyes for just a second. There were questions there, but he was in no position to say anything more. Not until he had answers of his own.

Zach turned his gaze to Cody. 'Bye, Cody. Give up smoking for awhile, okay?'

Cody chuckled. 'Get the hell out of here, Slick,' he said. 'And I'd be watching my back, if I were you.'

'Count on it,' Zach said. He nodded at Jim Crier. 'By the way, there's a half-smoked, expensive-brand cigar lying out in the fields you may want to take a look at. Or lead the sheriff to,' he added, before leaving the living room and walking out the front door.

'What the hell was that all about?' Jim asked curiously. 'I'm not sure he should leave Desperado if he's our only suspect. I feel certain he ought not leave before the sheriff arrives.'

219

Cody coughed and closed his eyes.

'Well, hell, Cody,' Jim complained. 'So there's a cigar out there now. How come I, or one of the other firemen, didn't see it? How do we know Rayez didn't plant it, knowing he's the prime suspect?'

'Zach doesn't smoke cigars, or anything else. He gets on my neck about it. Don't reckon he was carrying one around just in case.'

Cody rolled over on the sofa toward the window. Annie pulled Mary closer to her, knowing in her heart that Zach leaving was the right thing for him to do. He'd said he would come back, for whatever reason – and like Cody, she believed in Zach.

Despite the mean, frightened words she'd flung at him earlier.

'The man's just figured out he's being framed,' Cody murmured tiredly, sounding old and battle-weary to the point that Annie ached for him. 'Now he needs to find out who's got him by the short hairs. And why.'

CHAPTER 14

The old shack across from the bingo parlor smelled the same as always. Zach grimaced at the sour stench as he walked inside. That was something that was never going to change about Pop. The man simply had no use for clean living.

'Pop, it's me,' Zach called. 'You here?'

There was a muffled curse, then the sound of slowly moving feet. Pop shuffled into the living room, wearing a dirty, nappy bathrobe and looking much the worse for wear. 'Are you all right, Pop?' Zach asked.

His father grunted as he sat down heavily on the busted sofa. 'Well, ain't I the special one today? The Prince himself has come to pay this worthless servant a call. My, my.'

'Ah. You're doing pretty much the same, I see.' Zach pursed his lips and stared up at the cracked, grey-lined ceiling before leaning against the wall. He wasn't about to sit next to his father, and other than sitting on the heavy box that served as a coffee table, there was no place else for him to go.

221

Still, the conversation he needed to have with Pop might be long and protracted, and Zach wanted to be looking him straight in the eyes as they talked. Zach walked into the kitchen, knocked a month's worth of newspaper off a kitchen stool and dragged it into the living room.

Pop never even glanced his way. Sullenly, he picked at a torn piece in the sofa cushion with old gnarly fingers, his veined legs sticking out in front of him like flimsy kindling. Zach wondered just how long Pop could go on living like he was before he killed himself.

'How've you been, Pop? Really,' he asked gently, the unnatural shades of grey he saw in his father's florid face alarming him. Blue capillaries spread around Pop's nose and toward his cheeks, a slow testament to his years of drinking. Those alcohol scars had been present for years; yet Zach realized he was looking at the deterioration of a man he'd never really known.

Something told him his life would be a lot easier without Pop in it. There would be no sharp criticism, no accusations, no boiling hatred for whatever sin Zach represented to his father.

Still, he couldn't feel anything except bitter sadness for their relationship. He wouldn't miss Pop when he was gone, not with a sense of deep grief. But he'd always regret not having the bond a father and son should share.

Regret was a royal pain in the ass when a man shouldn't give a damn.

222

Unfortunately, Zach did.

'Look, Pop,' Zach said suddenly. 'I heard something I want to ask you about. It may or may not be true, but I want you to be honest with me.'

Pop shrugged. 'What you see is pretty much what you get with me. Ain't you figured that out by now, Mr College Education?'

'Okay, Pop.' Zach deliberately made his tone soothing, although he was gritting his teeth with the effort. 'Somebody mentioned that you'd bought some property a couple hours north of here. I wasn't aware you were interested in buying up any land, so I thought the story was far-fetched, but I wanted to ask you about it, anyway.'

Pop swiveled his head to stare intently at him, bushy white brows furrowing with anger. 'Why? Cain't I own land, same as you? Same as anyone in this damn state?'

'Hold on, Pop, that's not what I'm – '

'It's just what you're saying! You don't think I'm smart enough, or good enough, to have anything other than what I've got!' He sat up straight on the broken sofa, throwing his arms out in front of him to encompass the tiny, dirty room. 'Didya think I didn't want more out of life, Zach? I cain't do no better than this?'

Zach narrowed his eyes. 'I may have overlooked some ambition on your part, perhaps, Pop. You haven't answered my question. Is it true?'

Pop settled back down in the sofa, glaring at Zach.

'Hell, yeah, I got me some land. But Carter said he'd keep his mouth shut about the deal. Said he'd keep it between the two of us, gentleman-like. Shoulda known he couldn't keep quiet.'

'Why keep it a secret?' Zach asked.

'Everybody on planet earth don't need to know my business, specially *you*,' Pop replied meanly.

'Why would I care what you do with your money?'

'Same reason you're asking,' Pop shot back. 'You're jealous of me being in on a deal with Carter.'

'It does occur to me that it's a strange partnership, Pop.'

'Well, come on over to America, Prince Charles. A man can make a success of himself here if he's got a mind to.'

Zach shifted on the cracked yellow vinyl of the kitchen stool. 'Big deal, is it?'

Pop's grin was smug. 'Well, it ain't the biggest, but Carter said he picked the land up for a song.'

Too many things weren't fitting into place. If the land was for the purpose of selling to high-stakes business companies, Carter wouldn't have 'picked the land up for a song'. Ritter would have bought the property at close to fair market value. They weren't in the business of shaking people down. At least they never had been before.

And Pop wouldn't have been involved in the deal at all. The skin on Zach's scalp tightened as he realized there had been more behind Carter wanting him to go to Annie's farm in the first place than Carter had ever

224

let on. But, God bless Annie's stubborn soul and ornery father, Carter had been denied in his original bid for Annie's land. Apparently, he'd then moved to purchase the land to the south of Annie's farm.

Zach kicked out his legs in front of him, pretending casualness. 'Why isn't the land in both your names, Pop?' he asked, guessing that Cody would have mentioned another name being on the deed if there'd been one.

Pop pushed his bony chest out. 'We got us a limited parn–partnership,' he said proudly. 'Carter didn't want anything to have his name on it, so it wouldn't get confused with his Ritter International business. It's all legal-like. Says "George Smith and Partners" right on the document.'

Zach crossed his arms over his chest, eyeing his father. 'Well, I always wondered what you were doing with the money I gave you. Now I know.'

'Hell, no, sonny boy,' Pop denied heatedly, shaking a finger toward Zach. 'I didn't pay for nothing with any of your money. You ain't give me any lately. Carter wanted a partner, but I didn't have a dime to put in it, so he generously loaned me the money if I'd keep the partnership silent.'

'I see.' Zach *was* beginning to see. Not only was Carter hamstringing the Aguillars, but he'd now indebted Pop to himself as well.

Suddenly, the whole dirty business was beginning to feel extremely personal to Zach – like somebody had it in for him.

'Pop, I sent you a check not a week ago. What happened to that money?'

Pop shook his head belligerently. 'You ain't going to get away with making me feel guilty, Zachary Rayez. You stomped outta here last time, madder than a hornet landin' in cold water. Said I wasn't your father.'

Zach noticed Pop was leaving out his own damning words in their argument, but he let it slide. 'Yeah, and when I cooled off, I mailed you a check.'

'Sure.' His father shook his head stubbornly. 'You're saying that to make me feel bad.'

'If you feel bad about anything, it's because you cooked this thing up with Carter to cross me.' Zach stopped, his memory sharply recalling Carter holding the envelope with Pop's check up to the sunlight. Carter had been awfully interested, although at the time, Zach had put it off to one of Carter's typical maneuvers. Still, the check had never arrived, and Carter had talked Pop into putting his name on a shady limited partnership.

Zach snorted. Limited, indeed. Limited to whatever Carter could suck out of Pop. But if Carter had Pop in his sneaky grasp, then he was ultimately trying to get at Zach. If the partnership went south, Pop owed Carter money, and Pop didn't have anything but the leaky roof over his head. That meant Zach would have to come rushing in to bail Pop out. Carter knew that.

Chilling awareness flooded Zach. 'By the way, Pop,'

he said slowly, 'just how much did Carter loan you, anyway?'

Finally, a trace of conscience seemed to invade Pop, because he lowered his head, refusing to meet Zach's eyes. 'Not that it's any of your *business*,' he said, 'but Carter paid off what I owed on this house.'

Shock lanced Zach's mind. 'You mortgaged your own home, in return for your silence on a shady deal?'

Pop jumped to his feet and began stomping around the room. 'You're jealous, Zach! You don't want me to have anything but what you dole out, like I'm too pitiful to do anything for myself! Well, this time, somebody thought enough of me to make me their partner, and I don't care what you say, this deal isn't shady!' He stopped to poke a gnarled finger Zach's way. 'You think you're the only one that can live the high life, screwing beautiful women and driving that damn flashy car. Well, let me tell you something, Mr Too-good-for-your-old-man, I can do just as well without you! I don't know why I agreed with Carter to cut you in on the deal!'

Zach frowned, a red alert sign flashing in his mind. 'What the hell are you talking about?'

'George Smith and Partners – that's you *and* Carter, 'cept I tole Carter we didn't need you. I said just to give you a little bit but Carter wanted to share. Said he owed this to you – '

Zach leaped to his feet, the flimsy chair crashing over behind him, as hot, painful comprehension flooded him. Carter had made damn sure he'd closed every loop, and greedy, hate-filled Pop had made it easy for him to make certain Zach was completely under his control. Maybe it wasn't all Pop's fault, because he could never hope to match wits with Carter, had never seen past his own blind greed.

Zach could hardly rein in the bitter rage filling him. 'Fine, Pop. You'll have to eat from the hand you've chosen to feed you. Don't blame me when you find yourself hungry.'

'What's the matter? Can't face the music? Don't like your old Pop making a success outta hisself?' Pop demanded.

Zach ignored him, striding outside. He flipped his keys out of his pocket and opened the car door.

Pop made it to the porch, calling, 'You'll see! Carter says me and him are going to do more deals together! I'll be bigger than you one day, and all you'll have is that silly bimbo and her fat-cat daddy. They just want you for the political ride they're hoping you're gonna give 'em!'

At that Zach halted. 'What in the hell are you babbling about?'

Pop smirked from his position on the porch, clearly enjoying this last bit of power he had over Zach. 'Never knew, didya?'

'Never knew what?'

'That big-breasted blonde lover of yours is hoping your brown skin and good looks is going to get you a brass plaque and a desk in the state congress one day, good Republican that she and her old man are gonna make of ya!'

Pop bent over roaring with laughter at his own words. Zach slid into the hot sports car, watching the old man clutch his sides with mirth. Obviously, those words had come straight from Carter's mouth, because Pop had never had a single original thought of his own in his life.

Zach started the car, gunning it. It was past time for a heavy-duty talk with his vice president.

Annie opened the front door, expecting to see the sheriff. It took her a second to recognize the elderly lady standing on the porch dressed in street clothes rather than hospital white.

'Gert!' Annie exclaimed. 'What are you doing here?'

'Heard about your troubles from one of my nurse friends at the hospital. It's my day off, you can see,' Gert said, gesturing at her polyester pants and print blouse. 'I figured you had enough worries without trying to see to your rascal of a father's therapy, so I came out to help.'

Annie felt gratitude – and instant recognition that Gert was harboring some kind of feelings for Travis. It was something Annie might have realized at the hospital, perhaps, but she'd been too buried in her own troubles.

Gert's blush highlighted the wrinkles in her cheeks as she waited for Annie to invite her inside. Annie smiled and stepped back. 'Please come in, Gert. I'm not sure how Papa will greet you, but you are certainly welcome where I'm concerned.'

'Thank you.' Gert nodded, no-nonsense, and walked into the hall. 'What have we here?' she asked, heading into the living room where Cody eyed her cautiously from the sofa. 'You're the crazy man who tried to stop the fire with a tractor.'

Cody threw a look Annie's way that appeared pleading. 'If I didn't know better, I'd think Slick had arranged this,' he complained.

Annie hid a smile, knowing that Gert would enjoy martialing two patients in her care. 'This is Cody, my brother-in-law.'

Gert nodded sagely. 'I've heard of you. They call you Crazy Cody in town, don't they?'

Cody didn't answer, but Gert sat down in a chair across from him. 'Is the tractor story true?'

He sighed, realizing the determined woman wasn't going to allow him to escape her questioning. 'I'm sure it's been greatly embellished, but yes, slowing the fire down with empty dirt rows seemed reasonable at the time.'

Gert thinned her lips. 'Name fits, then.'

Annie placed a small end-table near Gert's chair and laid a frayed straw coaster on top of it. 'How did you hear all this?'

'Some of the firemen came down to the hospital,' she said mildly, positioning herself in the chair to have a better view of Cody.

Annie gasped. 'No one was hurt, were they?' In her

shocked state, she hadn't even thought to ask after the men who'd put out the fire.

'No one was hurt at all. Occasionally they make a run through to get supplies, whatever, maybe check on a patient they've drug in there. This time, I 'spect they was looking for *you* to give in and make a run to the hospital, Cody. But I guess being crazy doesn't necessarily mean you got sense.' Gert grinned to take the sting out of her words. Cody eyeballed her warily, probably aware that this woman was here to stay – and likely he was going to get more caring for than he'd had in his entire life.

'Now, Ms Gert – ' he began, but Annie interrupted him with a meaningful stare.

'Cody, Gert coming by is a wonderful thing. I'll be so busy talking to the sheriff and insurance company, that taking care of Papa is going to be a handful. Not to mention that I've got Mary, and, of course, your mother has her share of work cut out for her trying to hold the farm down without you around – '

Cody held up a hand. 'All right. I surrender. But please, ma'am, I've managed on my own for a good long time. I appreciate your intentions, but if you can – '

'Keep the mothering to a minimum?' Gert asked with a grin.

'If you could,' Cody replied, his smile relieved.

Gert leaned forward to whisper, 'Well, you're awfully handsome, but the truth is, I'm here to see the old man, though I wouldn't mention it if I were you. He doesn't think he cottons to me.'

'What the hell is she doing here?' Travis roared from the hallway.

Annie glanced up. Her father stood completely transfixed by the sight of the white-haired woman in his living room.

'Who let *her* in the house?'

'I did, Papa. You remember Gert, don't you?' Annie asked unnecessarily. With a smile, she turned to the nurse. 'Would you care for a glass of tea, Gert?'

'That sounds wonderful.' Gert turned a delighted grin on Travis, who hovered in the dark hall. 'Come here, you old coot, and tell me you ain't been smoking in bed and starting this fire.'

Travis's expression was incensed. Annie couldn't help a small giggle. Cody caught her eye, his eyebrows raised significantly, and Annie nodded. He leaned his head back on the sofa arm, grimacing as he focused his gaze out the window.

Annie went into the kitchen to get tea for everyone. Gert's visit would mean a couple of apple carts would be upset, but Annie needed her help. God bless the old woman for caring enough about Travis to come by. Annie put a sugar bowl and some napkins on a tray, sighing. If her father would calm down long enough to be civil, he might actually find that Gert could be a companion for him.

Unfortunately, he was a lot like Cody in that he'd gone unbranded far too long.

Quite the opposite of Zach, who was going to be

branded as a married man in less than two weeks. Why that had popped into her head, Annie didn't know, but she wished it hadn't. Slowly, she placed the tea pitcher on the tray, willing the pain in her chest away. Tiny stings at the back of her eyes told her she was feeling sorry for herself. She wasn't the right woman for Zach – but oh, how she wished she could be.

Zach turned the sports car into the parking garage. He pulled out the cardboard box he'd stopped to get. There were only a few things in his desk he wanted to retrieve and a few personal mementoes scattered about the office. After he tossed them into the box, he was going to say goodbye to his old life and start over.

Completely over.

The elevator carried him swiftly up to the top floor. He was greeted efficiently by the receptionist, whom he barely noticed as he made a beeline to his office. Tossing the box carelessly on the floor, he strode to Carter's office. The outer office was empty, although the door to Carter's private chamber was closed. Zach shrugged. His vice president obviously was out for a late lunch, because he was usually pacing in the office, shouting into a portable phone at some unfortunate person.

Zach walked to the closed door, thinking to knock on it just in case Carter was inside. After a second, he thought better of that. The receptionist would know whether Carter had gone out; it'd be better to ask her. Bearding the lion properly required an appropriate time and place other than the small, personal sanctuary where Carter kept only a long sofa and a cocktail table. It would be a poor choice for a major confrontation.

Zach turned to head back out to the waiting area and the receptionist when a map on Carter's desk caught his eye. Slowly, he approached the desk, recognizing that there was a circled town on the map.

Mesmerized, he stared down. Small dots lay along the line near Desperado, but off the area where the new highway had been drawn in. In fact, the dots formed a semi-circle, as if land in the middle was being enclosed. Pin-pointed.

Zach put his hand on the desk to peer more closely at the dots, knocking off something as he did. He stooped down and grasped the rolled-up map, automatically opening it as he stood. It was a chart with seismic data from a certain region. He glanced to the top of the map, somewhat surprised to see Desperado written there.

A chill hit the middle of his stomach, making it clench painfully. Disbelieving, he looked from one map to the other, his mind denying what he was seeing.

And yet, Zach knew, without a doubt, that at last he was holding the key to Carter's game.

If this data was correct – and this chart appeared to be recent – dirt-poor Annie Aguillar was sitting on top of something she never dreamed she owned.

Oil.

CHAPTER 15

Rage churned inside of Zach as he stared at the map showing seismic data. Carter was buying up the land around Annie, on the pretext that it was for Ritter International. But Carter's fingerprints weren't on the deal, just Zach's. He'd even gotten Pop involved so there'd be no ties to himself, and it was an excellent cover. Carter hadn't bothered to inform Pop about the oil, obviously. Zach knew that his father would have spouted that charming factoid instantly, just to be able to brag about how he was finally going to be a rich man.

It niggled at Zach why Carter had used Pop as an accessory, besides the fact that his father wasn't the brightest man in Austin, and his greedy nature made him an easy mark for Carter's scheme. There was more, much, much more that Zach wasn't seeing. He frowned at the data, wondering how he'd allowed himself to get snared in this scurrilous web. It was as if a dark cloud obscured his brain's capacity to see what he was afraid should be clear to him.

A low giggle punctuated the austere silence of Carter's office. Zach jerked his head up, surprise pulling his brows together. Where had that sound come from? Eerie silence settled once more in the room; it was so quiet Zach could feel his heartbeat thundering in his ribcage. After a moment, he shook his head, thinking that the receptionist, Judy, must have been laughing in the greeting area.

Except that he hadn't noticed her speaking to anyone. Zach shrugged and went back to perusing the data, memorizing it, hoping to see more than what the squiggles and lines could reveal. If there really was oil under the Aguillar farm, how in the hell did Carter think he could get away with buying Annie out at a fire-sale price?

Fire. Zach's intuition became razor-sharp. It would be simple for Carter to have a mineral rights clause slipped into the contract. As unsophisticated as the Aguillars appeared to be – and since they apparently had no idea of their possible wealth – they would likely sign the contract without blinking an eye at the innocent-looking clause. After all, what was their land good for, besides growing corn and harboring rattlesnakes?

Zach let out a deep, ragged sigh, remembering the blackened, destroyed fields where Annie's hopes for the future lay devastated. He could almost envision cruel, black vultures encircling her, waiting mercilessly. And when the Aguillars wouldn't sell, Carter had decided to kick their legs out from underneath them by setting the fire.

A low, sensual moan snagged Zach's attention. *That* was a female sound, one he'd heard plenty of times before. It sounded suspiciously familiar. Where the devil had it come from?

He stared at the closed door to Carter's sanctuary. As long as he'd known his soon-to-be ex-colleague, the man had never been one for entertaining females at the office. Some men mixed business and sex freely, but Carter had never allowed a woman past the leather chair in front of his desk.

Zach quietly put the maps back where he'd found them. If Carter *was* in there – entertaining or otherwise – Zach didn't want to be caught with smoking guns in his hands. He turned to leave when something glittering and green beside the desk phone caught his eye.

He froze. In the harsh fluorescent light, the object winked brightly, beckoning him. Transfixed, Zach put a hand out to touch it, to pick it up. The contact sent ice-cold shivers through him.

LouAnn's earring. One of the pair he'd given her as an early wedding present. Disbelieving, he reached around the phone, snagging its mate. The two unbelievably beautiful gems lay pristine in his palm, daring him to face the truth.

And another low, eager moan from behind the closed door forced him to face it.

Without really thinking, Zach deposited the earrings into his pocket and left the office, completely disregarding that he had come to clean out his desk.

But the sounds of lovemaking had shocked him to his core, rendering him unable to think. Already overwhelmed by the research on Desperado piled up on Carter's desk, Zach's brain had gone into overload at seeing LouAnn's earrings casually dropped by the phone.

In less than five minutes Zach was in his sports car, pushing the machine to illegal speed, as if he could outrun the trap he now realized had been woven around him. Another man might have thrown open the door to Carter's office and enjoyed the hellacious scare he could give LouAnn and her lover by ambushing them in the act. Zach preferred to wait for the cool rationale that would overtake his anger soon.

It was so much more dangerous.

At his house, Zach strode into the living room, fully aware that he needed a serious game plan. Reaching into his jeans, Zach tossed the earrings on to a nearby coffee table, where they sparkled at him insidiously.

He could no longer overlook the fact that Carter had it in for him. From being one of the fast track guys in the business, Zach had let himself be outwitted in every way. It was strange that he'd not seen through Carter's manipulations, but having known him since law school, a reminiscent zone in Zach must have assumed Carter wouldn't dare set up an old acquaintance. Major tactical error.

Zach knew Carter assumed he would take over Zach's chair as president of Ritter International. Carter wanted it badly, despite his claims that he hoped Zach would return to the corporation one day, once he got over the burn-out he presumed Zach was suffering from. He *was* burned out, but it was from dealing with chumps like Carter.

Obviously, Carter wanted the presidency of Ritter. He couldn't possibly know what Zach did, that the stockholders had already chosen a replacement, considering Carter much too green, too much of a twisted pistol to entrust with their business investments. With land prices being so volatile, they needed a cool head at Ritter's stern.

But maybe Carter did know he wasn't the chosen one. Could that be why Carter had gone after him with such a vengeance? Had he uncovered that piece of information and decided it was Zach who must appear unfit, that it was Carter who'd been running the show all along? He'd once mentioned a board member whose ear he had, but Zach had no idea who that could be. No one had raised a finger to nominate Carter for even a bonus.

Of course. He was such an idiot not to have seen the crystal-clear answer to a situation that was no Rubik's Cube. LouAnn must have been dropping information along with her hisses of delight during their trysts.

Zach sat down in a leather recliner, waiting for the black rage he knew he should feel. Stunningly, he was more angered about Carter's double-dealing than LouAnn's defection. For some reason, if he felt anything at all, it was cold anger that she possessed so little moral fiber that she would stoop to humiliating

239

Zach. But the blazing fire of fury he would expect to feel at finding his fiancée enjoying the services of another man wasn't there. Didn't get past an occasional bubble of disbelief. Something had changed for him, even before today.

Annie was the change. Meeting Annie had taught him the value of the not-so-fine things in his life – all worthless. But she'd given him a chance to witness real love, real grief, honest caring. Annie. Mary. Cody, and hell, yes, even old Mr Cade had burrowed deeper into his heart than shallow LouAnn had ever managed.

Cosmetics, perfume, silky crotchless panties – all these were manufactured to make Zach feel something for LouAnn.

He felt nothing.

Where there should be rage, though, there was relief, despite the many issues facing him. In order to fight his way out from behind the cross-hairs he knew were trained on him. Zach knew he had to be practical now. And the cold, logical response that Zach knew would come settled over him.

First, he owed a phone call to the corporation which had been his brain child. Zach picked up the portable phone beside him, dialing from memory.

It was answered immediately by an efficient secretary. 'Sam Lindale, please,' Zach said briskly.

'One moment, Mr Rayez,' the secretary said.

'Zach, buddy, how are you?'

He smiled at the booming voice. 'Fine. Need to talk to you, though. Got a second?'

240

'I have if you've decided not to resign from Ritter.'

Zach laughed. 'I'm afraid not.'

Lindale sighed. 'Guess I'll have to give you a second anyway, then.'

'I need to ask you a question. Almost three weeks ago, Carter told me about a property he wasn't having any luck purchasing down in Desperado. Relying on my instinct to do the best thing for Ritter, Carter mentioned that there were high-level commercial real-estate deals hinging on how many properties were available for sale in that area. Because of my wedding and the fact I was leaving the company, I pretty much relied on Carter's word about this. Now, I'm wondering. Do you know anything about this, Lindale?'

'No, Zach.' The man sounded honestly confused. 'I haven't heard anything about a difficult deal, although it wouldn't necessarily have been mentioned to me. For one thing, it's not out of the ordinary. We've received a great deal of resistance over the years from folks in that area about selling, as you know. They're stubborn farm stock.'

Zach grinned. Instantly, he thought of Annie, and he liked that description. It fit, and he was proud of her.

Lindale chuckled before saying, 'And another reason I might not be in the know is because we're pretty much staying out of Carter's way these days. I hate to say this, Zach, 'cause I know he's a college friend of yours, but he's simply not Ritter material. We're not going to give him any future international accounts.'

241

'That's probably a good idea. Between you and me, those college ties have frayed very quickly.'

'Oh?'

Zach crossed his legs on the recliner, glancing at those precious green and gold baubles sparkling on the inlaid teak coffee table. 'You could say that Carter has ingratiated himself with my soon-to-be ex-fiancée.'

There was a sharp intake of breath at the other end. 'Oh, hell, Zach, are you sure?'

'Very.'

'Well, that's the proverbial old hit below the belt, isn't it? Are you going to kill them?'

Zach laughed heartily. 'I have other things to do besides go to jail because of this, Sam.'

'That's the spirit. So, do you want me to fire Carter?'

'Actually, that was the second reason I called. I was planning on telling Carter today that he was no longer employed by Ritter. But not because of LouAnn. I believe he's involved in a land scam, which is where this extra money would be coming from.'

'That son of a bitch.'

'Yeah. I feel bad about not checking out his story better, Sam. I hope this doesn't hurt Ritter.'

'It won't. I won't let that happen. And don't feel too bad about it, Zach. You hired Carter to be your back leg, didn't you?'

'Yeah,' Zach said laconically.

'Well, occasionally a dog has to piss on its hind foot. It ain't gonna kill Carter, though.'

Zach rubbed his forehead, trying not to laugh. 'You're probably right. But another thought that's occurred to me is that we'd better do some additional checking into his expense accounts et cetera, since he could be embezzling. I don't know that for certain, so don't breathe a word of it to anyone you don't have to. But Carter got all that money from somewhere.'

'Damn right,' Lindale replied. 'I'll begin a very quiet investigation into this myself. Hey, I just thought of something,' he said, sounding rejuvenated. 'If you're not marrying LouAnn and taking over the family business, you still need a job, don't you?'

Zach grinned. 'Actually, my friend, no. I'm picking up a new enterprise.'

'I have never known a man with a bent for finding money like you can, so I'm not a bit surprised. What's the business this time?'

'Salsa.'

'Salsa! That's . . . why, I love that stuff.'

The laughter that spilled out of Zach was joyous and alive. 'Well, Sam, with any luck, you'll get to taste Rattlesnake Annie's Snakebite Sauce one day. It'll blow your socks off.'

'Hmm. Sounds like it. And Annie herself?'

'Pretty much the same,' Zach said with a grin.

After saying goodbye, Zach hung up, staring at the phone in his hand pensively. He had two final calls to make before he could talk to the one person he really wanted to speak with. Punching the numbers in, he

243

waited for the familiar voice of his receptionist to answer the phone. 'Ring Carter's office for me, please.'

'But Mr Haskins is in a meeting right now. He left word he doesn't want to be disturbed.'

He held back a snort. 'Judy, listen. I know Carter's in a meeting, with my fiancée.'

The receptionist let out a little gasp.

Zach continued, 'Now, you buzz that office and then take yourself down to the break room for a smoke, all right? And don't you worry about Mr Haskins either. He's not going to fire you over this.'

'Y-yes, Mr Rayez.'

A second later the phone rang. Carter picked up on the first ring. 'Damn it, Judy, this better be important.'

Zach leaned back against the headrest. 'It *is* important.'

'Zach!' Carter sounded thunderstruck. 'I'm sorry, I thought – damn it, I'm going to – '

'No, you're not. I told Judy to put me through. But I'll only disturb your important meeting for a minute.'

'What's on your mind?'

He could hear the sweat in Carter's voice. Zach relished that. He was glad to do this last thing for the company he'd started.

'Carter, you're fired. Be out of there in one hour, or security will be in to assist you. Leave all items that are Ritter's in a visible place to make the inventory easier.'

'Zach – '

244

'Oh, and while I've got you on the phone, let me speak to LouAnn, please.'

'LouAnn? Ah, she's not – '

'Dressed? That's fine. Her mouth works very well when she's naked. Hand her the phone.'

There was strident whispering in the background before LouAnn got on the phone. 'Yes, Zach, darling?'

Zach grimaced. 'I'll make this brief. I've got the emerald earrings, which I intend to take back. You can have the engagement ring, which is very generous under the circumstances, I believe. Needless to say, you can erase our wedding day from your social calendar. Goodbye.'

That felt good. Zach called security with his instructions concerning Carter, feeling better still. Hanging up, Zach relaxed against the leather headrest and closed his eyes, willing himself to relax. He told himself that he wasn't acting out of revenge. Yet, that same voice happily reminded him that this was a very small payback to Carter for burning Annie out.

Freedom. Ah, sweet, sweet freedom from the coils that had bound him. Zach breathed deeply. It was almost as if he could smell reprieve in the air. Settling more comfortably into the easy chair, he dialed one last number.

Annie answered, her voice like a balm to his soul. 'Hello?'

'Annie. It's Zach.'

There was silence for a moment. 'I wasn't expecting you to call so soon.'

'But you're glad I did?'

There was hesitation again. 'Yes.'

'How's everybody doing?' He wanted to know everything.

'We're all doing better than might be expected. The nurse who took care of Papa in the hospital – Gert – came by today. She's going to let me pay her to help with Papa's exercises, and even keep an eye on Cody, though we don't dare mention that to him.'

'Very wise of you.'

Annie laughed softly and Zach's heart pumped faster. 'Gert's been wonderful. I've been able to do a lot of stuff today, errands and what-have-you, and even play with Mary some.'

Zach felt complete relief at her words. 'I'm so glad you have help. Maybe you can hire her away from the hospital for a while.'

'I'm trying. My ace in the hole is that Gert has a thing for Papa.'

Zach chuckled. 'Travis needs someone to keep him in line.'

'I know. *He* doesn't think so, of course.'

They were silent for a moment. Zach wondered if he could express to Annie the thoughts swirling around in his mind. Did he have the right to burden her right now?

'Zach?'

'Yes?'

'I know you didn't start the fire.'

He listened to her voice, trying to intuit what she

wanted to tell him but couldn't seem to make herself say.

'I wish . . . I wish I hadn't said what I did this morning. About you seeing the fire first. I acted terribly, Zach. You've been so kind – my God, you even saved Cody's life – and I've been cool toward you. I hope you can forgive me.'

'I wasn't being kind, Annie. I couldn't bear to watch that crazy man on a tractor kill himself.'

He sucked in his breath, realizing his words might bring back visions of the way her husband had died. He couldn't bear to cause her any more pain than she'd already suffered.

'Excuse me? What crazy man? Who was the man running *behind* the tractor in his bare feet, with no shirt on, like he was invincible?' She giggled a little, the sound sweet. 'You're as bad as Cody.'

That was a compliment. 'Maybe,' he said with a smile she couldn't see.

'Can you forgive me, Zach?'

Zach closed his eyes for a moment against the distress he heard in her voice. 'I can't forgive you when you've done nothing to me, Annie. You've given me so much more than I've been able to give you. I . . . I need to see you, Annie.'

There. He'd finally put words to the feelings that had been circling around his heart since he'd met her. They were free now, free from the secure prison he'd kept them in. It was so very true. He did need to see her, to press her against him, hold her tight.

247

He just plain needed Annie.

'I don't think it's a good idea, Zach.'

'Oh. Of course not, you've been so busy today. I have business I need to take care of in Desperado. I could drive down tomorrow just as well – '

'Zach, listen to me. I really appreciate you calling. It means a lot to me that you care. And I know you had nothing to do with the fire. But, I just can't see you. I'm sorry.'

And very softly, he heard a click. Zach stared, devastated, as he realized Annie had just severed their connection.

'What the hell was that all about?' Carter was pulling on his clothes as fast as he could. LouAnn was dressing, too, putting on the black bra with pointed cups and the black garter belt and stockings he'd leisurely removed from her body with his teeth and exploring tongue. Right now, he wanted the woman to get dressed quickly. Any desire he'd been feeling had hit the road during Zach's inopportune phone call.

It was time to use his wits to save his ass.

'I don't know how Zach figured us out,' LouAnn said, sounding breathless and worried. 'You don't suppose Judy snitched?'

'No way. She's too afraid for her job. Her mother's in the hospital with some cancer thing and Judy's footing the bills, so she wouldn't dare open her mouth,' he said carelessly, his mind mulling over his plans.

LouAnn straightened in the act of connecting sheer stocking to lace garter. 'You threatened her job knowing her mother was ill?'

Carter grinned. 'Love me for it, honey?'

She pulled the low-cut dress over her head, ensuring that she didn't muss her tresses, and smoothed it down over her body. 'Not at all. You're lower than a snake's belly to do that.'

Carter grabbed LouAnn's arm, squeezing it a bit. 'You didn't mind knowing your wedding and precious socialite reputation was secure because I was discreet, LouAnn. Don't start playing the insulted virgin just because we got caught. All I'm saying is, Judy didn't blow the whistle on us.'

'Fine.' She jerked her arm away. 'Since *you're* the one who lost *your* job instead of Judy, I'll leave you to pack your things.' Slipping on her high-heel shoes, LouAnn started to sail out the door. Carter's mocking words halted her.

'Running to swear to your ex-fiancé your undying love and devotion with my cologne all over your skin? Might not be very convincing.' With a subtle pause, Carter hinted, 'I've got a better idea.'

That turned her around. She shot him a wary look. 'Your ideas have only gotten us in hot water so far, Carter. What are you thinking now?'

'Sit down for a minute, LouAnn, and let me teach you how winners cover all the aces.'

CHAPTER 16

Annie avoided looking at the phone the next morning, trying not to think about how much she wished it would ring and be Zach on the other end. Still, she knew she'd done the right thing. There could be nothing between her and Zach but certain heartbreak. If there was a man on this earth who might be absolutely the right man for her, it was Zach, but unfortunately, too many obstacles separated them – permanent obstacles.

Like the dank, now rotting fields outside her window. The rain that had teased them all month with its absence, parching the land to inferno-ripe conditions, had finally fallen in the night like tears from the sky. Annie had stood outside watching the silvery, moonlit sheets of water hitting the ground, where the moisture soaked right into the soil. She'd even cried herself, a little, for what might have been. Hours into the morning, Cody had come outside and pulled her into his arms, cradling her against his flannel-covered chest. Willingly, she'd allowed him to walk her into the house, where he wrapped a towel around her and dried her tears before fixing her a cup of hot chocolate in silence.

There had been nothing to say.

Zach hadn't started the fire, but he was under scrutiny. Until Jim Crier – or another representative she trusted – came to tell her differently, it wouldn't look good for Zach to be hanging around her or hanging around the farm. Anyone who came out to gather information would stir up hostile feelings, between Zach, between the investigators. No need for him to return to the scene of the crime until the smoke had cleared completely. She could only pray that Jim Crier and the sheriff's team had been thorough in their search before the rain washed away any evidence there might have been.

But even if the fire hadn't swept her corn fields, Annie couldn't forget that Zach was due to be married any day. The fear that she might succumb to Zach's lethal charm the next time she saw him was crippling. All she needed right now was a broken heart to nurse. Once Zach possessed her body, it would be the last barrier she had against him. Like a barrel going over Niagara, she would fall headlong in love with him.

And eventually, she would be left alone.

Even though once she might have been able to enjoy casual physical satisfaction with Zach, they had come to know each other too well for that now. It had gone much too far for her to want less than all of him. It wouldn't be fair to hinder Zach's life with her love, when he'd been honest in telling her that he wasn't available. Had, in fact, taken her arms from around his neck, setting her away from him, when she had kissed him at the fish pond in the very beginning.

'Papa?' Annie asked, walking into his bedroom. With a smile, she saw that Gert had fallen asleep in the chair beside Travis's bed. It seemed that no one in the house had gotten much sleep during the midnight showers. A constant rain like last night's was usually music to sleep restfully by, but the day's events had stolen everyone's peace of mind.

Deciding Gert and Travis would rather snooze than eat right now, Annie crossed into Mary's room. Her daughter's eyes were wide open, staring at her over the top edge of the blanket.

Annie sat down on the bed, gently pulling the blanket down to Mary's chin. 'Good morning, lady-bug,' she said, pushing the ebony locks away from Mary's rose-petal soft cheeks.

That coaxed out a smile. 'Uncle Cody calls me that.'

'I know,' Annie replied, reveling in the satin of Mary's hair underneath her fingertips. 'You are a sweet one.'

'Ladybug, ladybug, fly away home, your house is on fire and your children are gone,' Mary recited softly.

'Why, Mary! Wherever did you learn that?'

The child shrugged. 'In kindergarten last year.'

Annie caressed her daughter's forehead. 'Our house didn't burn, baby.'

'I know. And I'm not gone. So, I'm not that afraid,'

252

she said, turning her troubled gaze on Annie. 'I love you, Mama,' she whispered.

Swiftly, Annie gathered her daughter up to her, clasping her nightgown-clad body to her tightly. 'I love you, too, sugar. So much. I don't want you to be scared anymore, okay? Everything's going to be all right.'

Mary snuggled in deeper, seeking Annie's warmth. 'I wasn't too scared. Uncle Cody says you're the bravest woman he knows, so I was trying to be brave like you.' She looked up anxiously. 'But it was hard, Mama. Real hard.'

'Oh, Mary.' Annie rocked her baby back and forth in her lap. 'Let me tell you a secret. I'm not brave at all. Uncle Cody just told you that because he's blind in one eye.'

'Is he really?' Mary asked, fascinated.

Annie was glad to see the tension in Mary's face relax a little. 'No, baby,' she said with a smile. 'But Cody sees only what he wants to see. Now, here's another secret. You don't have to be brave until you have children of your own, okay? Until then, I'm taking care of you. Deal?'

'Deal.' Mary sat pensively for a moment. 'Mama? When is Mr Zach coming back?'

Annie froze and put down the silky-soft plait of Mary's hair she'd been braiding. 'I don't know, baby.'

'He said he would.'

'I know he did,' Annie said slowly, 'but sometimes people can't do the things that they really want to.'

'Oh.' Mary's shoulders slumped. 'He promised.'

'Well, I know Zach would like to come back, but . . .'

But what? How could she explain that Zach would have kept that promise – would have been here last night, in fact – but that Annie had told him not to come?

'I've been praying, Mama. I've been praying for a new daddy. I kinda thought Mr Zach might have been him.'

Now Annie's shoulders slumped. Her daughter wanted a father and Annie wanted Zach. But she said, 'I don't know, sugar. Come into the kitchen. I'll fix you some breakfast. Maybe later I can take you down to feed the fish.'

'Okay, Mama,' Mary said obediently, padding into the hall in front of her mother.

Cody sat at the kitchen table, hunched over a newspaper. 'Are you feeling better?' Annie asked. 'Less like a smoked turkey?'

'I'm fine,' he replied grumpily. 'Are you feeling better? Less like a kitten who nearly drowned herself in the rain last night? I won't be surprised if you catch a cold, and I'm not dragging chicken soup all the way over here when you do.'

Annie laughed, as he'd known she would. 'Cody Aguillar, I'd forgotten what an ornery person you are when you don't get much sleep. If I didn't know better, I'd think it was harvest time. Coffee?'

'Please.' He looked down at Mary, who'd seated herself next to him on the plank bench. 'I know

254

another little lady who didn't get much sleep last night, either.'

'Was Mary up last night?' Annie asked, surprised.

'Up? The child sat in her bed, peering out her window most of the night. Like she was trying to spy Santa Claus and his reindeer.'

'He didn't come,' Mary said glumly.

'Of course not. It's not Christmas,' Cody said.

'Never mind,' said Mary.

Annie glanced at her daughter as she set Cody's mug in front of him. 'Were you watching for Mr Zach?'

'I don't want to talk about it, anymore. Can I go outside, Mama, please?'

The child still wore her nightgown, but what could it hurt to let her sit on the porch for a little while? It was sunny now that the rains had passed and it would be good for Mary to soak up some of those rejuvenating rays. Might even lift her spirits.

'Stay on the porch, sugar. Leave the front door open, too, so I can call you when I need you.'

'Yes, Mama.' Mary slid down from the bench and left the kitchen.

'Well, that's a fine howdy-you-do,' Cody said. 'I thought she was looking to make sure the fire wasn't going to start up again. Never occurred to me she was looking for Slick.'

'It was partly the fire,' Annie said, ladling some *huevos rancheros* into a plate for Cody. 'She said she'd been trying to be brave last night. But, she was also hoping he'd come back.'

Cody was silent as he took a bite. 'Thank you, Annie, this is delicious,' he said. 'I'm starting to get my feelings hurt. I always thought I was first in Mary's heart.'

'You're an excellent uncle, friend, and the father figure Mary hasn't had,' Annie said warmly, sitting down across from him with a plate of her own. 'Unfortunately, that's what Mary's looking for. A father.'

'Whoa. Don't think that's gonna happen, is it?'

Annie shook her head.

'Well, hellfire, Annie. I'll marry you, you know that.'

'Shut up, Cody,' Annie said with a smile. 'You need a good woman and children of your own to keep you sane.'

'Insane, sounds to me.' They were silent for a moment while they ate. Cody slathered a heaping spoonful of Annie's salsa over his eggs before looking back up. 'So, is the salsa king ever coming back?'

Annie paused before meeting Cody's eyes. 'I think it's best if Zach doesn't. I told him not to come here again.'

'Fallen that hard, have you?'

'Maybe.' Annie's voice was non-committal, but she dropped her gaze. 'Yes,' she whispered after a moment. 'I'm afraid so. Crazy of me, isn't it?'

Cody sighed. 'I don't know, Annie. What I know about finding the right person could be cupped in one of Mary's little hands.'

'Oh, Cody, your lady will come along one day.'

'Ain't particularly worried about it,' he said, finishing the last bites of his breakfast. 'Now, Slick, he isn't all that bad, is he? What do you want to go and run him off for?'

Annie narrowed her eyes as she fathomed Cody's meaning. 'Since when did you decide Zach wasn't so bad? You used to think he was one tough character, too tough for me to tango with.'

'I like tough characters, myself. Anyway, can't a guy change his mind?'

'Maybe. But Papa will never change his.'

Cody laughed. 'Listen, Annie, before this rehab of Travis's is over, Gert is going to tie him up in his own bedsheets and make him her love slave.'

Annie started to laugh, but sudden shrieks from outside shot Cody off the bench, with Annie close behind.

'My God, Mary, what is it?' Annie flew to her daughter, throwing an arm around her protectively, while following the direction of Mary's trembling finger. 'Oh, my Lord. That's the snake that got out of the cage. Is it dead, Cody?'

They stared at the rattlesnake, which lay large and unmoving in a patch of sunshine. Cody kicked loose mud its way, but the reptile didn't swish a rattle. 'Reckon it is,' he said. 'But look at this.' With a boot tip, he pushed the fat rattler away to reveal a much smaller one.

Mary shivered against her. Annie pulled her child

257

tightly to her hip. 'Was it a mother, with its baby?' The thought was sad, in a way.

'Wouldn't count on it, not with it being as big as it is. Cody kneeled down to get a closer look. 'I don't know that these two snakes are related. It might have just been survival of the fittest. Or biggest, in this case.'

'What did they die from?'

He squinted against the sun, considering. 'I'm willing to bet it was the fire.'

'They got smoked out?'

'Well, the heat was pretty intense. Might have gone under the house for protection.' With one hand, he stroked along the conspicuous diamond-shaped markings. 'Some animal likely dragged them out this morning, and Mary might have scared it off when she came outside.'

Annie felt sick thinking about how that giant rattler might have been waiting, in a cozy dirt nest under the house, until it saw its chance to strike. And what struggle was being waged under the very foundation of her home last night? 'Oh, Lord, Cody. I think I'm more upset than Mary is,' she said. Feebly, she thanked the heavens her daughter hadn't fallen victim to snake bite.

Cody got a shovel out of the back of his truck, scooping the two snakes up. He tossed them into the bed, along with the shovel. 'You need some rest, is all. Come on, Mary,' he said.

Though she'd been clinging to Annie, Mary went

258

readily into his arms. 'Tell you what. You go get dressed, and I'll snag a couple of those grape sodas out of the fridge for the road. We'll go check on Grandma. What do you say?'

'Yes!'

'Are you sure you feel well enough, Cody?' Annie asked.

'I feel fine and besides, it's getting depressing around this snake pit.'

Annie laughed. 'Thanks.'

'Naw, I'm teasing,' he said, putting an arm around Annie's shoulders and giving her a light squeeze. 'But I do need to go give Ma a hand. I called her last night and she cussed me for being so stupid to try to stop the fire. I could tell she missed me.'

'I know she does. Tell your mom I appreciate her loaning you out for awhile.'

Annie took Mary inside to her room, helping her put on a little pair of denim shorts and a pink eyelet blouse. 'Grape soda for breakfast. Ugh. Will you please ask Grandma Aguillar to give you something healthy to eat?'

'Yes, Mama.' Mary grinned. 'You shouldn't be so picky, Mama. If you tried one, you'd probably like it.'

'I'm not picky, Mary, I'm particular. There's a big difference.'

Mary giggled. 'Sodas are better than that old coffee you drink.'

Annie ruffled the bangs on Mary's forehead. 'You may have a point there. Now, slip these shoes on and

259

hurry out to Uncle Cody's truck before he has to come looking for you.'

'I will, Mama.' Mary hurried outside and Annie watched the big man help her daughter into the truck. It was relatively new and expensive-looking, big all over and meant to haul whatever needed it on the farm. Cody'd bought it from a friend and was awfully pleased to have gotten it. Annie smiled and let the blinds fall back in place. He'd needed a new truck, but she thought the worked-over hearse suited his style far better.

But he wouldn't have been able to toss those snakes into the back of his hearse quite as readily, Annie thought with a shiver. The fright that had run up her spine when she'd seen the enormous length of serpent again – so close to Mary – had made her slightly nauseous. Her only child had been through so much lately. Would life ever get easier for them, be gentler to Mary?

Annie shook her head and strolled back down to check on Gert and Travis. They were both still asleep, so she made Mary's bed, enjoying placing the plentiful stuffed animals in a row along the back and over the pillow. Outside, she could hear mockingbirds rustling and chattering in the trees outside the house. The sun was shining brightly and it was a beautiful day, if she didn't have to walk past the trees and see the stark blackness of the fields.

No point in thinking about that if she could avoid it for the moment. She'd clean the kitchen after Travis and Gert ate, Annie decided. Putting on boots, she wandered outside to stare at what damage the rains had done. Slowly, she walked to where the corn had grown in neat furrows. The ground lay fallow, unnatural in its idle appearance. To Annie's eyes, it almost looked as if the very dirt was waiting, wanting the rejuvenation of roots down deep inside it. If she could get the insurance money fast enough, Annie supposed she could get another crop in of something before it was too late for the fall growing-season.

Feeling sorry for herself now wasn't going to put food on the table, though. Annie remembered how she'd once told Zach that she imagined the corn fields were a security blanket wrapped around three-quarters of the house. She'd felt invincible, knowing it was a good crop and that, even if their financial situation became more precarious, they could eat many meals off that corn.

Fervently she wished Carter Haskins had never come to Desperado. What a low-down, two-headed snake he'd been, far more dangerous than that old fat rattler which had met its end in the shadows under her house last night. Annie wished Carter could reap the rewards of the devastation he'd managed to force on her and her family – and then instantly tried to push the bitterness from her mind. It would do no good to let the hatred burn inside her for what he'd done – but it stung her pride to know he was sitting somewhere laughing at her. Waiting for the bank to foreclose now, any day.

Annie reached down to touch the earth, making a solemn vow that a new crop would be planted to be nourished by its life-giving soil. Then she stood and walked toward the house, resolute in her determination to survive this terrible setback. Somehow, some way, she was going to find a way to keep her home.

The sight of Zach's shiny sports car parked in the drive by her house stopped Annie in her tracks. Leaning against it was Zach, looking big and strong and more irresistible than ever. His arms were crossed over his chest, and in his face she read stubbornness and determination. While she'd been staring at her ravaged land, Zach had been watching her, giving her time to grieve.

But by the hard look in his eyes, Annie knew Zach wanted an explanation for why she'd said she didn't want to see him.

Chapter 17

'Hello, Zach,' Annie said.

Zach could read the wariness in her eyes. But he'd had to see Annie. Some hopeful, desperate feeling inside him said that if he could just have thirty minutes to talk to her, she wouldn't tell him to go away.

He could only hope that he was right. 'I'm chancing you won't tell me to hit the road,' he said, striving for a light tone in spite of the truth of his words. She didn't smile, her ebony brows drawn in a tight line in the mocha of her skin. Her hair, hanging darkly radiant to her waist, was held back with combs so that he could see every nuance of her expression. Annie was going to tread very cautiously with him. 'Okay. Will a bribe buy me thirty minutes of conversation with you?'

The lightest trace of a smile passed across her lips. 'You haven't been able to bribe me before.'

'You've got a point. So this time, I decided to be smart.' He reached through the open window of the sports car, pulling out a large, rectangular white box. Without a word, he handed it to Annie.

'What's this for?'

He grinned at the suspicion in her eyes. 'It's not a snake. Go ahead and open it.'

'Oh, don't even say that,' she murmured. 'My fingers shake just thinking about it.' But slowly she pulled the lid off, gasping. 'Oh, it's beautiful!' Carefully, she took out the musical carousel, three white horses on gold poles poised to spin around a glass bottom.

'It's for Mary,' Zach said quietly. 'Do you think she'll like it?'

'Like it? Zach, she doesn't have anything like this! It's . . . so stunning.' Sunshine shone off the golden bridles and hooves of the white horses, making the carousel look like a starry vision out of a child's fairy book. 'You already were Mary's hero. Once she sees this – well, it's a wonderful bribe, Zach. Thank you.'

The delighted and grateful expression on Annie's face warmed his heart. Once he'd seen the porcelain confection, Zach had known it had to belong to Mary. For a room decorated with raggedy stuffed animals and handmade dotted-swiss curtains, it was the perfect jewel in a little girl's crown. And for Mary, who had taken the time to teach a city man how to fish and who'd believed him without reservation when he'd said he would return, it was the perfect way to say thank you.

Mesmerized, Annie twisted the carousel. Pink,

peach, and lilac roses adorned the turning base, while strains of a happy, light-hearted tune melted into the hot Texas air. 'You shouldn't have bought her something so expensive.'

Zach shrugged. 'Some things are so special no price can be set for them.' Gently, he reached to stroke one dark tendril that was laying against Annie's cheek. 'Didn't you tell me that once?'

'About my land,' Annie said with a smile. 'You did understand, all the time.'

'I understand much better now. You taught me that. You've taught me a lot of things. Annie, don't turn me away,' he said, his voice husky. 'I have to talk to you.'

Annie stared into Zach's sable eyes, knowing that much more than a need to talk echoed between them. They would share, they would touch, they would laugh – Annie smoothed a finger along the painted roses of the carousel top. Part of her cried out, *This man is not the solution to your problems!* But the biggest part of her – the part where her heart resided – couldn't resist time alone with him. 'Come with me,' she said softly.

He followed her down to the foreman's shack. Underneath a potted cactus lay a key, and she opened the door. Inside, Annie turned on a light and the ceiling fan, before setting the carousel on a rough, wooden table. Slowly, she turned to meet Zach's eyes. 'I need to tell you something first.' At his nod, she said, 'When I told you I didn't want to see you, I was afraid.'

Approaching Annie slowly, the way he would a frightened kitten, Zach moved to within a few inches of her. Close enough that he could see the darkness of her eyes, see the trembling in her lips. 'And now?'

'I'm still afraid. Aren't you?'

'Yes.' Slowly, he slipped his arms around her, at once struck by how right holding her felt. 'But not of this.'

Annie bowed her head, touching her brow to his chest. 'I threw myself at you once before, Zach. I can't forget what you said – '

Stroking her lip with his finger, Zach whispered, 'I broke off my engagement.'

'Why?' Annie's voice was scarcely more than a whisper as she looked up to search his eyes.

'I discovered that my fiancée was unfaithful to me, which was the catalyst for breaking up with her,' Zach replied thoughtfully. 'But the truth is, I wouldn't have been able to marry her, anyway. Once I'd met you, my heart wasn't in it.'

She shook her head, but Zach placed his finger over her lips. 'I'm not saying that you purposefully had anything to do with my decision. What I am saying is that in you I saw faithfulness, whether it was to your family or your land. In you, I saw a woman who knew what mattered in life. I was blinded by ambition and greed and I'd forgotten what really counts, but I remember now. I don't think I will ever forget again,' he said, brushing his lips along her forehead.

Annie looked so serious that he wanted to kiss away

266

the frown shading her eyes. 'It's an awful lot to turn your back on. You must have had much in common, or you wouldn't have wanted to marry her in the first place.'

'If we'd had so much in common, both of us would have been faithful. Fidelity aside, there's a natural beauty inside you that shines clear to the outside. I realized LouAnn's beauty was very much artificial.' Zach shook his head. 'I wanted you from the moment I first laid eyes on you, Annie Aguillar. If I'd been a smarter man, I would have made love to you on the spot, right out there with the fish for an audience.'

Annie smiled. 'I think it's better that you didn't. I can trust you, Zach Rayez, because I saw that you were a man of principle. You may be used to getting whatever you want, but you have treated me with honor and respect. There was a better man inside you than you were showing the world,' she said softly, raising her lips to his.

'I'm still used to getting whatever I want,' he replied huskily.

'So am I. So kiss me, Zach.'

With infinite care, Zach joined his lips to Annie's, feeling a jolt clear through his body that was emotional as much as physical. A sense that he'd waited all his life for this woman flooded through him, and hungrily, Zach strove to get closer, to know every cell that was Annie. She matched the urgency in his kisses, winding her arms around his neck while he tangled his fingers in the satin fall of her hair, pressing her tightly to him. As if he'd been given a precious gift, Zach kissed Annie's eyelids, her nose, and returned to the welcoming shelter of her lips. He sensed no reservation in her passion, only encouragement. Knowing that Annie was offering herself body and soul sent masculine need surging through Zach. Now he was free to know the wonder of Annie. Zach knew the moment had come.

Barely aware that he was holding his breath, Zach unbuttoned Annie's blouse, letting it fall to the floor. She wore no bra and dusky nipples atop cinnamon-colored breasts beckoned him with their perfection. Annie slid his denim shirt off, lightly tracing through the hair on his chest. With desire clenching his groin, Zach cupped his hands around Annie's breasts, enjoying her gasp, as he lowered his head to kiss them.

'You're beautiful,' he murmured, pulling his head up to smooth his lips along hers. 'Annie, I want you so much I feel like a kid in a candy store. I want it all.'

'There's no sign that says "look, don't touch",' she told him.

Zach's heart pounded harder at the thought that all this wild, untamed woman could be his. 'Are you sure, Annie?' he asked, tucking one hand into the waistband of her jeans, into her panties so he could cup her closer to him. Annie's other hand he took in his, lovingly kissing each finger one by one. 'I won't do anything you don't want me to.'

'I want to make love with you,' she said hesitantly, 'but I don't have any protection.'

'I do,' he murmured, taking the hand he'd been kissing and putting it around his neck. He bent his head to press warm, searching kisses into the curve of her neck.

'You presumed a lot,' she said, tipping her head back so the area he wanted was freer to his lips.

'I *prayed* a lot,' Zach returned. 'I want you so much the bottom of my feet feel like they're on fire.'

Annie laughed. 'Let's take your boots off, city boy. That might be the problem.'

'I don't think so. Feel this?' He moved her hand down to cover his groin. 'This feel like it's on fire, too.'

Her hand turned to unzip his jeans. 'We'll have to take these off, too,' she murmured.

'I like that idea,' Zach said, picking Annie up and cradling in his arms as he carried her to the small bed. Together, they leisurely removed each other's clothes until finally they lay in the foreman's cabin, skin to skin, whispering words to each other that only lovers share.

In his dream, Zach was running, running so fast he couldn't pull enough air into his lungs. His eyes felt like they were ready to burst from his head with the exertion of trying to escape. Muscles burning, he sprinted toward the edge of the light, where he knew there was enough darkness that he could hide from his pursuer. The light grew, like a beam from a movie projector widening to fit the screen. The darkness that he craved seemed further away, more impossible to

269

reach. Just as he made it to the edge – and safety – something grabbed him by the back of his neck with sharp talons, jerking him away from the safe zone. Zach awoke, realizing with a start that he held Annie crushed to him, in a grip too hard to be comfortable. Trying to relax his grip without being too obvious, Zach tried to shake off the dream.

'Sorry about that,' he murmured. 'Did I hurt you?'

Her blue eyes widened. 'No. Are you all right?'

Reflexively, he tightened his arms around her, needing the secure feeling of solid Annie against his chest. 'I don't know what was after me,' he tried to joke. 'I'm glad you saved me, though.'

She lay against him, nuzzling her head against his neck. One hand crept down to caress the flat plane of his stomach. 'I kind of like saving you.' Their legs were twined together, so that she could feel the hard strength of his thigh underneath her bottom. Rough hairs tickled the back of her leg intimately, in a way that emphasized the fusing of their bodies. Annie looked up, meeting Zach's interested gaze with a serious look. 'Did you come all the way to Desperado just to make love with me?'

'Mostly,' he whispered against her hair. 'I have an errand I need to run in town. It was a convenient excuse for coming to see you. Actually, I wasn't sure you'd want to make love, but I was determined to tell you in person that I wasn't getting married.'

'Mary was asking for you,' Annie said. 'Are you staying until dinner?'

'I can't,' Zach said with a regretful shake of his head. 'Unfortunately, I still have to clean out my office. Plus, I need to do some financial reorganizing of my accounts.' He let his lips trail down to her neck. 'But there's something else I came to tell you, Annie. In fact, I should have told you immediately, but . . .'

She smiled a lover's smile. 'But we got sidetracked.' Her hand moved from his stomach to a lower region.

Zach captured her playful hand, giving it a kiss. 'This is serious. I must have your utmost attention.'

'I think you've got it,' she murmured, arching against him. Zach could feel his desire growing, hardening into wanting her again. Immediately. But he had to tell her this. 'Annie, listen to me,' he said, raising himself up on one elbow to look down into her eyes.

'All right,' she said obediently, her other hand lazily stroking his back.

'I went into Carter's office the other day to ask him some questions. I found a map and some graphs pinpointing Desperado. Particularly, there was information in his office indicating that your land may be a prime spot for oil. That's why he bought the land south of yours. That's why he's done everything possible to buy you out. Annie, he was never interested in the commercial real-estate ventures Ritter might have gained. I believe he intended all along to swindle you out of your mineral rights.'

Annie's eyes had widened during his words. Her

mouth had parted somewhat, as she listened intently. The hand that had been caressing his back had stilled. But Zach wasn't prepared for the relieved laughter that suddenly filled the cabin.

'Oh, Zach,' she said. 'Don't tell me that's what this has all been about. Surely, no one believed that story. My crops are gone because some idiot bought into that pirate's tale of buried treasure?' Annie sat up. 'I think I'm going to cry.'

Zach was alarmed. 'Why?'

'Because if you're right, it was all such a waste. There's no oil under my land. Years ago, they told my mother the same yarn. The townspeople had been passing that rumor since my grandmother's time. My mother let them dig up a part of the farm, drill it, virtually tear up every inch of the area where they thought the oil would be. There wasn't a drop of anything to be found, not even dirty water.' Sadly, she leaned her head down onto her upright knees. 'What a shame. And I know they'll never connect Carter to the fire. I lost the best crop I ever had because of someone's greed.'

Zach privately agreed that Carter wouldn't be tied to starting the fire. He'd covered his tracks too well, and the rains had only helped disguise his involvement. Zach sat thinking, remembering the lines and waves he'd seen on the chart. The data had seemed real, not like a pirate's story at all. Still, if they'd looked for oil once on the land, then there wasn't a reason to look again.

'I'm sorry, Annie,' he murmured, pulling her close to him. 'I was hoping I was delivering good news. I thought maybe I had the key to your dilemma.'

'Were you going to save me, Zach Rayez?' Annie asked, accepting his warm comfort.

'I damn sure thought I was.'

She raised up on an elbow and looked into his eyes. 'It's the thought that counts, Zach. Anyway, it's not up to you to save us.' Tenderly, she pressed a kiss to the hard line of his mouth. 'But thank you, for wanting to.' With a curious look, she said, 'If you needed help, would you accept it from me?'

Zach thought about that for a moment. 'I would want to solve the situation myself, if I could.'

Annie nodded. 'Pride isn't solely a man's emotion.'

Lightly, he stroked his hand along her leg, up over her delicately rounded bottom. 'But I would be glad you cared.'

'I am glad you care.' Annie pressed herself against him.

'Sometimes another person is the only one who can solve the problem, though. Like two keys that fit together.'

'That's true, too. My grandmother, Nancy Day, who owned this land originally, felt that way when she met my grandfather, Two Days Laughing. Though they in no way were accepted by Grandmother's family, she would not have lived without him.'

'Two Days Laughing?' Zach couldn't help a grin himself.

Annie shrugged. 'I don't know much about the circumstances, but my grandmother wrote in a journal that, after she married him, something happened to my grandfather that caused him to laugh for two days. So, that's what she called him. Two, for short.'

'Do you know his real name?'

'It's in a journal somewhere, I know. The name fit Grandfather so well that I never heard anyone refer to him as anything else.'

After meeting dour old Mr Cade, it was difficult for Travis to imagine the males in the family doing much laughing. 'What about your mother?'

'Oh.' Annie's eyes softened for a moment, the purply blueness turning hazy with happy memories. 'Well, she was smart and wonderful and totally in love with my father.' Catching Zach's eyebrows raised teasingly, she said, 'Believe it or not, Papa can be very lovable.'

'I know. It's clear that he adores you and Mary.'

'Yes.' She caught Zach's hand in hers and placed it on her shoulder, where he reverently dusted his fingers along the satiny skin. 'My mother lived to see me married to Carlos, but not long after that, she died of a rare blood disease. I wish she could have seen Mary when she was born,' Annie said softly. 'In all your life, you never saw a more beautiful baby.'

'I still haven't.' Zach felt as proud of Mary as if she were his own.

The afternoon sun slanted through the window of the foreman's shack, warming the smile Annie gave him. 'Are you sure you can't stay until Mary comes home for dinner? She'll be so upset that she didn't get to see you.'

Annie thought about Cody saying that Mary had sat up during the night, peering out the window to see if Mr Zach's car was in the drive. She didn't want to tell Zach that, and couldn't tell him that Mary was hoping that Mr Zach was going to be her new daddy. All this might be scary to a man who'd only recently been contemplating marriage to another woman.

She caught the direction of his glance. Zach was staring at the lovely carousel, sitting on the fragile old table in the corner. Light from the sun caught the gold of the ponies' harnesses, making magic of their beauty. She sensed his struggle. In her heart, Annie knew that Mary and Zach had connected in their souls, like those two very same keys he'd been talking about.

That thought festered the worrisome guilt Annie was feeling for allowing herself to become close to Zach. What made her happy might not be good for her daughter. Puff the Magic Dragon hadn't understood why his friend, Jackie Paper, never came back. Mary would certainly suffer when her Mr Zach stopped coming.

'I can't stay,' he said regretfully. 'What if I go by Cody's farm and say hello to her on my way out of town?'

'You would do that?' Annie said. Though she knew Mary would be delighted, deep inside she wondered if it was for the best.

275

Zach nodded. 'I'd like to take Mary her present.'

Annie thought about Cody's remark about Santa and his flying reindeer. Mary would definitely think that about Zach now. And after the fire and the rattlesnake scare this morning, her daughter deserved an extra special surprise. Annie couldn't begrudge her that. 'She would love that. It would mean the world to her.'

'And Mary's mother?'

Annie smiled, willing her uncertainty to dissipate. 'Her mother, too.'

'Cody'll be glad to see me, too.'

She laughed at his purposefully raised brows. 'He'll be delighted to see you. While you're there, ask him to show you the two little friends who were by the porch this morning.'

'I don't think I want to.'

'No, you probably don't, city boy.' Annie grew serious. 'I'm glad you came to see me.'

'I'm glad, too.'

'Are you feeling better?'

'I wasn't feeling bad.'

'What about the dream that woke you up? Is it all gone?'

He thought about the sensation of something chasing him that he couldn't escape from. He thought about the miracle of waking up safe in Annie's arms. Zach moved against her, his intentions clear. 'I think it's *almost* all past. Maybe I should make love to you one last time, just to be certain.'

276

Annie lowered her lips to Zach's, flattered by his arousal. 'Maybe you should,' she whispered, before melding her mouth to his.

'It's lunch time,' Travis Cade said from his spying nook by the window.

'So it is,' Gert replied placidly. 'What of it?'

'They're still in there.' He knew Gert was aware of what he was talking about, and she also knew it was worrying him. Her calmness about the whole matter infuriated him even more.

'If you're that hungry, Travis, make yourself something to eat. Annie doesn't need to fix everything you put in your mouth.'

'That's not what's bothering me and you know it, Gert!'

She spared him a frustrated glance while continuing to fold clothes on the kitchen table. 'Travis, come over here and sit down, for heaven's sake. All that stewing ain't going to get you what you want, so you may as well cool it.'

'Easy for you to say. Annie oughtn't to be alone with that man.'

Gert let the T-shirt she was folding droop in her hands. 'She's thirty years old, been married, has a child. Old enough, I think, to make her own decisions about whom she wants to be alone with.'

She saw the hurricane coming and blew it out with one sentence. 'Is some time alone with him too much for Annie to ask for?'

277

Travis shook his head, not liking it one bit. He knew Gert was right, but his every instinct was still to protect his only child from harm.

'I know you love her, Travis, but you can't decide what makes her happy, even if it doesn't suit you. And I know the fatherly feelings are running fast inside you right now, but Annie's got enough on her hands trying to take care of this farm without you prying into her business. I'm sure she'd die of mortification if she knew her daddy was eagle-eyeing her from a window.'

Gert went back to folding clothes. Travis scowled at her, coming to ease himself down carefully on the plank bench. In disgust, he picked up a piece of laundry and began helping to fold. 'Oh, hell. To me, Annie's my little girl. And I can't think that city slick means to do right by her. He's just too damn cocky.'

She raised her eyebrow at him. 'Ain't up to you, though. Besides, who's cocky? Are you wearing shorts, like the doctor told you, so those veins would heal, or long trousers?'

'Ain't worn short pants since I was a boy. I'm not aiming to start now.'

'See, now, if I was taking your parental tack, I'd come after you with a pair of scissors and say, "Yes, by God, you are going to wear the shorts because that's what's best for you." Instead, I'm saying to you, "Travis, you're a grown man. If you want to have to go back to the hospital because you haven't followed the doctor's orders, then that's a choice you'll have to live with." Make sense?'

The sound of a car door slamming rendered them silent in their bickering for a moment. Travis stood slightly to peer out the window. 'He's leaving.'

'Well, fine, then. And Annie's still in one piece?'

He shot her a baleful look. 'Hush up, Gert.'

She grinned and started stacking the clothes. 'Where are you going?'

Starchily refusing to let Gert see how much consideration he'd given her words, Travis didn't pause. Nor did he want to witness the serene smile he knew would be on her face as he called over his shoulder, 'I'm going to put on some of those short pants you keep babbling about, woman.'

CHAPTER 18

Right away, Zach could tell Cody's farm was in a hell of a lot better shape than Annie's, and it wasn't just the stark blackness the fire had left compared to the gently waving green leaves in Cody's fields that told the story. Cody's red-brick farmhouse, though it lacked the gabled charm of Annie's, appeared newer and sturdier. A late-model truck was parked in the front next to Cody's hearse, and a modern harvester was under the shade of a nearby pecan tree.

Three running vehicles to Annie's zero. Zach had figured Cody for a man of achievement, in spite of his lackluster attention to dressing for success. He tried to picture Cody in a board room, brawny arms akimbo, jet braid hanging, feather earring accenting blazing eyes – and failed. Just as with Annie, Zach recognized this was a setting that suited Cody perfectly. Knocking loudly, Zach waited on the wide porch, hoping Annie's brother-in-law was at home.

'Come on in,' Zach heard a voice holler, 'but if you're selling something, I ain't buying!'

It was safe to say he wasn't in the door-to-door sales category. Zach pushed the screen door open, poking his head around to peer into the hall. 'Cody?'

The big man stuck his head out from another doorway. 'Slick! What the hell are you doing here?' His surprise quickly turned to concern. 'You're not going to make me an offer, too, are you?'

Zach laughed. 'No. I'm out of the business now. I stopped by to say hello to Mary. Is she around?'

'Annie know you're here?' Cody asked suspiciously.

'How do you think I got your address?'

'Oh. All right, then. Yeah, Mary's here. Come on.'

He motioned Zach into the kitchen and gestured out a window. 'There she is, happier'n a flea in a dog's ear.'

Mary sat in a sandbox under a shady tree, intently scooping brown sand into several plastic toys and containers. An older woman, whom Zach assumed was Mrs Aguillar, sat with a sun hat on her head and her feet buried in the sand at the other end of the box.

'That looks inviting.' Zach was glad to see the peaceful happiness on Mary's face. Now she looked like any normal six-year-old girl might who was enjoying a day at her grandmother's.

'Well, it's fun if you don't mind sand all over the place. Ma wanted Mary to have something special for the times she's here, so she talked me into putting that thing in. Mary'll even have sand in her hair by the time she's finished, and Ma'll spend half an hour getting her clean, but as you can see, they'd both raise hell if I tried to dismantle it.' Cody shrugged. 'Ah, hell. You're only young once, I guess. Besides, I think Ma gets as big a bang out of sitting in the sand as Mary.'

'It does look like she's enjoying herself.' Zach thought Cody sounded like a proud papa over the sandbox himself, despite his grumbling. Briefly, he wondered why Cody and Annie had never developed their obviously close relationship into anything more serious. A cold sensation instantly shot into his stomach at the thought. Zach decided it wasn't a scenario he wanted to linger on.

'So, been to see Annie, have you?'

Zach turned his head to meet Cody's gaze. 'Yeah.'

'She didn't seem positive you were coming back.' Cody's expression was laconic.

'I told her I would,' Zach said in some surprise. 'Why wouldn't I?'

Cody shrugged. 'Why would you?'

'Because I . . .' Zach stopped, somewhat uncomfortable with Cody's questioning. *Why would he come back*? That was a stupid question. Anyone with two eyes could see how he felt about Annie. Zach registered the concern in Cody's expression and told himself to relax. He should be able to recognize purely brotherly concern when confronted with it, though momentary sparks of jealousy were blinding him. 'I always keep my promises,' he said simply.

Cody seemed content to let the matter drop. 'So,

you heading back over there after you see Mary?'

'No. I had an errand I needed to attend to in town. After I see Mary, I'm going back to Austin.'

'I see.' Cody nodded his head toward Mary, who was now industriously burying her grandma's toes in deeper piles of sand. 'Ladybug's getting attached to you. Could be you doing the do-drop-in occasionally might put dreams in her head.'

Zach jerked his head around. Though he sensed Cody wasn't criticizing but trying to alert him to something, it still stung. 'What the hell are you talking about?'

'You just gonna keep waltzing in and out of her life? And Annie's? Annie, she's a grown woman, better able to handle the situation. But a little girl like Mary, now, she needs regular people in her life.'

Zach snorted. 'Like you.'

'Keep your dander down, Slick. Didn't you mention once that your daddy hadn't been any ribbon-winner for putting security in your life? All I'm saying is that Mary's been through a lot in her childhood, more than I've liked to see her go through. It isn't any of my business, because Annie's the one to tell you, but you need to be doing some serious thinking here, friend.'

'Cody, I don't like the direction this is heading.'

The man pulled at his earring, pursing his lips. 'Look, Slick. I'm beholden to you for pulling my ass out of that fire. And I think you've got your heart in the right place about a bunch of things. But that white box you dragged into the house and set on the table wasn't a hostess gift for me, was it?'

Zach shook his head. 'Hell, no.'

'Well, then I suspect it's for little Mary. And she's going to love it, 'cause it's from Mr Zach. And she's already got stars in her eyes about getting a new daddy, if you get my drift. What do you think your unexpected call out here and that present's going to do to those stars?'

'I think she'll be very happy,' Zach said tightly, his voice defensive.

'Sure she will. This time. But if you keep dropping in, and bringing doo-dads for her, there ain't no way she can help from getting dreams in those beautiful blue eyes of hers. And Slick, I just can't bear to see her be disappointed.' He shot Zach a keen look. 'Reason I'm telling you this, is because I don't think you want that, either. I believe that you'll think about what I've said, and you'll know I'm right.'

'You're telling me I either step up to the daddy plate or hit my ball on out of the park.'

Cody frowned. 'It ain't as pretty as I'd say it, but you got the gist of it.'

Zach felt two emotions roaring through him hard enough to make him feel queasy. One, he knew Cody was probably right. Two, he wanted to knock the farmer clean to the ground for having so much common sense, and having the guts to tell Zach how he felt.

And fast on the heels of those thoughts was that

Cody was suggesting Zach should marry Annie Aguillar. The realization made him turn his head back to the window, mouth open, as he stared at the tiny, wonderful girl in her sand playland. Son of a gun. He'd be a husband and a father all at once – pretty amazing stuff. Except that his father credentials were sorely lacking. Pop hadn't been a shining example of what a father was supposed to provide emotionally or otherwise to his offspring. Would Zach fare any better?

'Need a beer, Zach?' Cody asked kindly. 'You're looking a bit peaked. It's hotter out here than in Austin,' he continued in a conversational tone, which Zach knew was to save his feelings, ''cause you city folks are used to air conditioning. We don't seem to notice the heat so bad. Our skin has learned to perspire more.'

Hell, yeah. Only Zach felt like he was sweating bullets. 'Have you got some tea or water?' he managed to croak.

Outside, Mary looked up, catching Cody and Zach staring at her. Her bare feet burst into action as she flew around the side of the house and into the kitchen. Flinging herself at him, she gleefully yelled, 'Mr Zach! You did come back! I knew you would!'

Zach gathered Mary into his arms, accepting her delighted hug. 'I saw you playing in the sandbox. It looked like fun.'

Mary nodded enthusiastically. 'It is. How'd you know I was at Grandma's?'

'Your mother told me.'

'Oh. That's good.'

'Your Uncle Cody's got a nice place.'

'Mmm-hmm. No snakes.' Mary got down from Zach's lap with a pensive look. 'I was supposed to wash the sand off before I said hello to you. I'll be right back.'

Zach smiled, even as he realized there were sprinkles on his jeans and his shirt collar felt a little gritty where some sand had shaken in during their hug. 'It's okay. I'm not going anywhere.'

Mary turned around, amazed. 'You mean, you're staying for good this time?'

His smile suddenly became an effort. 'No. I meant that I'm not leaving yet.'

'Oh. Okay.'

The disappointment on Mary's face was deep and heartfelt as she left the room. Zach didn't dare glance at Cody. He concentrated instead on drinking the iced tea Cody had placed on the table in front of him.

Cody sat down silently at the table, allowing Zach to absorb his thoughts. Suddenly, Zach wondered if he was in way over his head here. Part of him thought the whole idea of getting hooked up permanently with Annie was pretty wonderful.

The other part of him was whispering, 'You bastard. Why didn't you think this through before you seduced Annie?'

Because that's what he'd done, plain and simple. Wanton seduction. He'd admitted as much to her.

'Mr Zach,' Mary said, walking back into the kitchen, 'why do you look so sad?'

Swallowing a lump the size of Rhode Island in his throat, Zach replied, 'I'm not really sad, Mary. Sometimes grown-ups only smile when their favorite little girl comes in the room.'

'Oh. I see.'

Zach could tell Mary liked the notion that she was extra special by the big grin on her face. 'There's a box on the table in the hall that's for you. Can you carry it by yourself?'

'Sure!' Eyes alight, Mary scampered down the hall. Cody remained silent.

Carrying the package back into the kitchen, Mary sat down at the table next to Zach. 'What is it?' she said, her voice a reverent whisper.

'Can't tell you,' he whispered back. 'You have to open it and see.'

'Now?'

'Now.'

The delight on Mary's face as she lifted the lid off tore at Zach's heart. Her little hands reached in and gently took the carousel from its bed of paper tissue. The sun streaming in the kitchen window twinkled on the gold paint. A few dainty musical notes magically pealed into the air. Completely astonished, Mary murmured, 'Oh, my. Look, Uncle Cody! Look what Mr Zach gave me. Isn't it wonderful?'

Cody smiled at Mary. 'It's as pretty as you are.' Then he shot Zach an inquiring gaze that he couldn't fail to understand. Special presents and an occasional visit weren't going to be enough for Mary. Eventually, he would hurt her by his absence. Nor would it be fair to Annie, who deserved far more than she'd ever gotten.

Mary took great care in setting the carousel on the kitchen table. Then she hopped up into Zach's lap, taking his face between her tiny hands. 'Thank you so much,' she said, planting a kiss on his cheek and then wrapping his neck in a tight hug.

Zach's eyes burned. He tried to push down the tidal wave of emotion rising in his chest, nearly choking him. Mary's joy was wonderful – alive and infectious – and he was glad he'd made her happy. But had he done the right thing? Uneasily, he patted her on the back. 'You're welcome, Mary.'

She pulled back far enough to fasten her indigo eyes on to his. Dark lashes framed eyes so penetrating that he could tell exactly what Mary was going to say even before she said it. 'I love you, Mr Zach.'

'I love you, too, honey.' The response was natural and true and Zach meant every word of it. Mary nodded, their communion complete. Sliding down out of Zach's lap, she said, 'I'm going to go show Grandma. Is that all right, Uncle Cody?'

'It's fine, honey. Be very careful carrying it.'

'Oh, I will,' Mary said breathlessly.

Zach stared at the empty white box pensively. His gift had been meant to be special, but it might imply promises to a hopeful little girl. The truth was, he didn't know what would happen between him and Annie. Didn't even know if he was ready to pursue another relationship with the frosting still sitting on the wedding cake for this weekend. There were so many loose ends to tie up right now that he really couldn't make any promises about the future. He simply didn't know.

Zach pursed his lips, setting his chin. 'Guess I'll be heading out, Cody. Thanks for the tea,' he said, avoiding the other man's eyes.

'Gonna say goodbye to Mary?'

Lilting notes floated down the hall into the kitchen. Zach paused, considering. 'I think I should just let Mary enjoy her present for a while.'

Cody shrugged. 'Suit yourself.' Silently, they walked outside to Zach's car. He got inside, not knowing what to say to this enigmatic man whose life he'd saved, who saw so clearly inside him.

'Here, Slick. Got a souvenir for you to take home,' Cody said, handing something through the open window of the car.

Zach took the snake teeth in some amazement. 'They don't look so frightening once they're not connected to reptile, do they?'

'Nope. Good luck, Slick.'

Laying the fangs on the dash, Zach said, 'Thanks, Cody.' With a brief nod, he pulled out and headed down the dirt road, trying to ignore the chilling sensation that he'd just run off on Mary.

* * *

289

Annie dialed the tax assessor's office, her fingers trembling. It hurt her pride to have to make this phone call. Knowing it had to be done, she could only pray that the officials would listen to her with kind ears.

The secretary was someone she'd gone to school with. 'Schula? It's Annie Aguillar. I'm fine, thank you. How's the family? Oh, we're all fine, here. Well, the fire was a bit unplanned, but we'll get along. Thanks for asking, though. Is Mr Barland in? I need to talk to him about my tax situation.'

'He's not in right now, Annie. Can I leave him a message for you?'

Annie hesitated. 'I guess so. Will you tell him that I'll be down to the office tomorrow to pay on the taxes I owe?'

Thankfully, some of her salsa money had come in. It meant she'd have to impose on Cody for a ride, but he wouldn't mind. He was becoming used to having two families to care for, she thought unhappily.

'Um, Annie, I thought your account was paid up to date.'

She frowned. 'No, Schula, I haven't paid anything, yet.'

'Well, let me check. I thought for certain that gentleman who was in here this morning was paying off your taxes. Here's your folder. Let me see . . . Aguillar, Annie, balance zero.'

Shock tightened Annie's chest. She felt cold, leaden. 'There's been a mistake somewhere, Schula.

Believe me, I wish it were true. But there's no way – '

Suddenly, a bizarre thought hit Annie. Oh, there might be a way all right. She just couldn't envision it. Surely Zach hadn't taken it upon himself to pay her debt? Not after the conversation they'd just had in the foreman's cabin. *If you needed help, would you accept it from me?* she'd asked him.

Zach had thought about that for a moment. *I would want to solve the situation myself, if I could.*

And she'd replied, *Pride isn't solely a man's emotion.* A vision of the carousel, wonderfully elaborate and more expensive than Annie could ever afford, flashed into her mind. A carousel for Mary, a clean account for her mommy.

Did a few hours of delicious lovemaking mean Zach thought he had to dip into his wallet for Annie, too? Her face burned with shame. Apprehensively, she asked, 'Are you certain it's my account that's paid in full? The papers haven't gotten confused with Cody's farm?'

'No way,' Schula said cheerfully. 'I was here and got the paperwork for Mr. Barland myself.'

Dismay threaded itself into Annie's chilled heart. *Were you going to save me, Zach Rayez?* her own teasing words mocked her. 'Can you tell me who paid off the taxes?'

'Well,' Schula sounded uncertain, 'since it's your account, I don't see why not. It was a man, a real handsome man. Tall, dark, and fascinating, you might say.' She gave a purely feminine giggle.

'It wasn't Cody.' Annie's voice was flat.

'No. Hair was shorter and he looked, I dunno, kinda citified. You know what I mean? No dirt under the nails, I guess. Ah, here it is. Zachary Rayez. Cash payment. Anything else you want to know?'

Annie closed her eyes, astonished by the pain she felt inside. 'No, thank you, Schula. I appreciate your help. Say hello to your folks for me, please. Goodbye.' She hung up and slumped her head over into her hands, thinking that having her taxes paid and a big cloud lifted from over her head should make her deliriously happy. Unfortunately, it only made her sad. And furious with Zach.

And ultimately, she just felt taken.

CHAPTER 19

Zach got out of the car and walked up the cobbled sidewalk to his house, his mind pondering everything that had happened in Desperado. He wished Cody wasn't right about how Mary played into the equation, but he was. Mary and Annie were a package deal, and what Zach did with Annie ultimately affected Mary. It could be a positive effect, of course, if he thought out the consequences of his actions. But a periodic roll in the hay with Annie would affect Mary adversely at some point. Cody was damn smart to realize Zach and the little girl had forged an important emotional bond.

Hell. They all had.

Zach was worrying so hard about this new concept of a permanent relationship with Annie that he at first didn't realize the lamps inside the house were on, dimmed to a romantic glow. He'd left them off, since he hadn't known how long his business in Desperado would take. There was only one person who had a key to his home, yet he didn't want to take for granted that he knew who was – or had been – in his home. Leaving the door unlocked behind him just in case he wanted to make a quick exit, he glanced around, cataloguing changes in the room since he'd left.

The emerald earrings had vanished from where he'd tossed them on to the teak table. A sudden, subtle tease of a perfume he recognized well lingered on the air. Slowly, like a man who knows he's being ambushed, Zach walked toward the bedroom.

LouAnn lay stretched out in the bed, wearing a black negligee that could only be described as nothing. The earrings dangled at her ears, beckoning. Zach took a deep breath, commanding himself not to pick her up and throw her from his house.

'What the hell are you doing, LouAnn?'

Seemingly unfazed by his harsh tone, LouAnn simply smiled. Running one palm down a length of white thigh, which moved her breasts enticingly under the lace, she said, 'Waiting on you, Zach. I know we had harsh words earlier, but you didn't give me a chance to tell my side of the story. Come here, lover, and tell me you were just jealous. There isn't anything between Carter and me, you know,' she whispered huskily.

Zach stared at the red of LouAnn's lips as she smiled at him. All he could think of was the taste of Annie's mouth, bare and clean of cosmetics, delicious to his taste. He wasn't sure if he'd ever tried to get past the satin-slickness of Chanel Red to discover the true LouAnn. He'd known the glamor had gone along with the girl, and he hadn't looked past the mirage.

It had been a grievous mistake.

'I think I got your side of the story, LouAnn,' Zach stated. 'You wanted more than I could give you. You wanted the whole pie. For a while, you got it. But now, the party's over. Get the hell out of my bed.'

'Is that any way to treat your fiancée? Zach, we're getting married this weekend. You're suffering from cold feet. Let me warm you, all over.'

She sat up, reaching her arms out toward Zach. Rosy nipples called to him, and he could see the dark triangle at her thighs, waxed into its usual heart shape. Once that had been an appealing notion. Now, the realization that LouAnn had given to someone else what he'd thought was his alone turned Zach off. Shaking his head, he backed up a step. 'I'm giving you five minutes to get dressed and be out of my house. Leave the earrings and my key on the table in the den. Five minutes and then I'm calling the police.'

'Zach, wait!' she called, leaping from the bed to rush to his side. Throwing her arms around his neck, she pressed herself against him, pleading, 'We were meant to be together.'

She swayed and, automatically, his hands went to her waist to steady her. His voice rough, Zach replied, 'I thought so once, too. That was before I knew there were three of us.'

Click. Click. Whirr.

The second Zach heard the sounds, he swiveled his head, realizing he'd been set up. Before he could react, the photographer squeezed off another set of shots, then hurriedly made his escape.

He stared down at LouAnn, frozen by what had just happened.

'Actually, there were four of us. But you weren't going to be honest about that, were you, lover?' With a sinuous motion, LouAnn detached herself from Zach. She gave her hair an idle fluff, smiling cat-like at him. Enraged, Zach snatched the earrings from her ears, but LouAnn just shrugged and turned away. 'I got what I came for, Zach. If you thought you were going to embarrass me by calling off a wedding that everyone who is anyone has already bought an evening gown for, you were wrong. You thought you'd just leave me holding the bag, having to send back all those wonderful wedding gifts with pathetic little explanatory notes attached. Wrong plan.'

Blinding rage tore through Zach. 'Excuse me, LouAnn, but I did think fidelity was part of an engagement. I'm not marrying a woman who's cheap.'

'Oh, honey, I'm not cheap at all. This little escapade is going to cost you plenty.' She waved a red-tipped fingernail at him. 'I was plenty good for you when you had your eye on rebuilding Daddy's business. You switched mid-stream when you found a better venture. I know you, Zach. You're like a magnet, only the attraction is to money. And I didn't stand a chance against a woman who had oil under her land, just waiting for some lucky man to discover.'

LouAnn had dressed quickly during her speech of

296

fury. Hips swaying, she walked to the front door. 'The pictures are insurance, Zach. I want you to be a good boy from now on. If you dare to even *think* about not showing up for the rehearsal dinner and our wedding, I'll see that your brown-skinned slut gets these photos. In fact, I'm so pissed by the way you tried to dump me, I may do it, anyway. See you Friday night, lover.' With a thin smile, she sashayed out.

Zach listened to the sound of LouAnn's high heels clicking down the sidewalk, his heart sinking. True to form, she was determined to have her way. Unfortunately, LouAnn having her way meant a whole lot of other people could – and probably were going to – get their feelings hurt. He thought about Annie and closed his eyes, feeling sick. She'd be terribly distressed to think he'd lied about ending his engagement. Never would she trust him again, and he couldn't blame her. And Mary. What could she possibly think if she were to see a picture of a lace-draped, almost nude, woman clinging to her Mr Zach?

He sat down on the edge of the bed, trying to think of an escape hatch before this time bomb exploded. No easy answer came to mind. Hot, boiling wrath filled him, made worse by the fact that he could still smell LouAnn's perfume clinging to his sheets. Zach leapt to his feet, tearing the linens from the bed as if he could exorcize LouAnn and her deviousness that simply.

Problem was, he was only obliterating one half of

what was angering him. Carter's mark was all over LouAnn's actions.

All Zach could do now was wait for Carter to make his move.

Two hours later, Zach sat thinking in the dimly lit den, his body unable to relax in the comfortable easy chair. He was caught in a metal-teeth snare, into which he'd stepped blindly. The only person who'd ever been able to make him feel more miserable than LouAnn was Pop. With a start, Zach realized he needed to talk to Pop about the wedding. They'd had harsh words about Pop attending, but Zach had never stopped hoping in his heart that some of the shell around his father would crack and he would want to be present. Now, Zach could tell him there wasn't going to be a wedding.

Because that was the painful decision he'd made. Annie or no, he couldn't be strangled by LouAnn for the rest of his life, now that she'd shown her true colors. Either way he turned, Annie was lost to him. LouAnn had greatly miscalculated her plan, though. Knowing that he was going to lose the woman he cared deeply about had left him no motivation at all to try to appease LouAnn. He'd called and left a message on her answering machine, once he'd gotten his thoughts straight. *No wedding*. All he could hope for now was that she'd been bluffing about sending the pictures. Surely there was a core of decency in LouAnn somewhere.

Even he knew that wasn't a likely scenario. Briefly he considered calling Annie to warn her, then realized what an idiot he'd sound like. Once more the red sign flashed neon in his mind: *End of road, Zach.*

Turning off the lights, Zach stepped out into the darkening twilight. Humid air hung around him, suffocating. He got into the car listlessly and headed it toward Pop's. There was a chance Pop might be home this early, unless the heat was keeping people at the bingo parlor later than usual. Even so, he could go over there and drag Pop out so they could talk, though the old man would be none too pleased about the interruption.

The house was dark and lonely against the shouting and laughter coming from the bingo parlor. Zach glanced that way, deciding he'd check inside before going across the street. 'Pop!' he called, pulling open the door.

'No need to shout. I'm sitting right here,' Pop replied laconically.

Zach let the door close quietly as he peered into the darkened living area. Pop sat on the broken chair, his head resting on his hand, as if extremely important matters were weighing on his mind.

With a jolt of realization, Zach realized his old man was stone sober. There was no haze of wrath hanging in the air, ready to explode; no twisted grimace of hate on his face. For once, the fetid smell of liquor was absent from the air. He could remember no other time in his life that Pop had been in a decent condition.

'Are you all right?' Zach asked. 'I . . . do you want me to turn on a light?'

Pop sighed and pointed to a box. 'Leave the light off and pull up a seat. I'm fine, I just want to sit and think for a while.'

'All right,' Zach said cautiously. 'I'm kind of in a thinking mood myself.' He sat, mostly resting his weight on his outstretched legs in case the flimsy wood should break. Astonishingly enough, it appeared that the most fragile object in the room at the moment was Pop. Never had he seen worry lining his father's face. Only the distortion of moodiness that came from drinking too much.

They sat in the dark for maybe five minutes before Pop finally spoke. 'Well, Zach, as much as I hate to admit this, you were right.'

'About what?' The idea that the old man was backing down on something was nearly as amazing as his sober state.

'About Carter. About the deal. It *was* a cheap rip-off. I've sat here near all afternoon and I may have finally figured it out.' Pop sighed unhappily. 'Carter screwed me.'

'Well, you're not the only one who can make that claim this week,' Zach muttered. 'I thought you two were buddies. Like, he was the son you never had.'

He regretted the words instantly the minute he saw deep pain shadowing Pop's eyes. 'Now that's a funny thing for you to say, Zach. Much as I'd like to lie about it, I think I was using Carter to make you jealous.

300

Stick it to you, because we've never been able to be close.'

'Thanks.' Zach couldn't help the sarcasm in his tone. It disguised the pain he was feeling.

Pop shrugged. 'Chickens always come home to roost. Only this time, there ain't no home to return to.'

'What are you saying?'

'The limited partnership was very limited. Carter came here today to collect on my share of the money for the land deal. I have no money, so he owns my house now.'

Sadness glimmered in Pop's eyes. Zach swallowed, realizing the old man was trying desperately to hold back tears.

'If I can't come up with the money in three days, I have to move out. What a sorry end to come to. Old as I am, and I'm going to be evicted from the only home I've ever known.'

Disbelief curled through Zach. He'd been right from the start; Carter's pretense of friendship with Pop had been a means to get to Zach. Firing Carter was turning out to a costly gesture to just about everyone Zach cared about. His vice president – and college friend – had thought out all the twists to this game. Any way Zach turned, he was discovering a precipice.

Sighing deeply, he decided he would try to figure out a way off this Monopoly board later. For the moment, Zach had to consider Pop. 'What are you going to do?'

'I don't know.'

Zach rubbed his forehead, thinking. 'Do you want any help?'

His father tiredly swayed his head back and forth in a helpless gesture. 'Think I'd be damned grateful to get any help from you that I could, Zach. I wasn't going to ask you, because I know I don't deserve it, but . . . hell, yeah, I'm in hot water here.'

'Okay.' He rolled his shoulders, trying to ease the tension Carter's maneuvers were causing. 'Get your stuff. We'll move you into my house tonight.'

'What are you talking about?' Pop was totally shocked.

'I say if Carter wants to own this house, then let him. He couldn't sell this rat trap if he wanted to. The house is only fit to be pushed over. He may get a little money from the sale of the property, but not much, with that bingo parlor over there and the crime rate in this part of town. Carter's counting on you having no place else to go, so he can extract more blood from you. But, Pop, I'm telling you that you have a better place to go and to hell with Carter.'

'You would do that for me?' The gratitude on Pop's weathered face made Zach feel miserable. He would have done so much more for his father over the years, if only he would have let him.

'Won't be any skin off my nose. The house is so big we don't have to run into each other for days, if we don't want to,' he said brusquely.

'Well, hell . . . what about your wife? Can't imagine

she'll want an old sot like me hanging around.' Pop's white eyebrows lifted inquiringly, as if he couldn't believe the offer – as if Zach had suddenly lost his mind.

'There isn't going to be a wife,' Zach said, his voice low, yet determined. 'LouAnn isn't the right woman for me. It'll just be me and you, Pop.'

Now tears did leak from Pop's eyes. 'I don't know what to say. I didn't expect this.' He wiped at his nose with a dirty sleeve. 'Are you certain, Zach?'

Zach stood with a sigh. 'I'm positive this is the only way to keep Carter from trying to bleed you dry, Pop. Get your things. I'll borrow a truck tomorrow and we can come get the bigger items you want to keep.'

'I won't be needing to come back, Zach. Just a minute.'

Pop left the room, shuffling down the hall. Zach looked around the room, knowing in his heart he was doing the only possible thing to keep Carter from manipulating his father. And if Pop had been shocked into soberness by the thought of losing his house and being kicked out into the street, maybe eventually he'd be ready for further treatment for his problem.

Pop made his way back into the room, carrying a cardboard box with some clothes in it and a smaller box stacked on top. Zach didn't ask what was in the box, but he assumed they were mementoes. Taking the whole sorry mess from Pop's hands, he pushed the door open with his foot. 'Ready?'

'Ready,' Pop said firmly. Then he glanced back

down the hall, as if he were listening to something. Pop's stillness was unsettling, with the darkness surrounding them and the noise from across the way. Zach watched his father without saying a word, unsure what he was thinking. But it was obvious some last emotion was hanging him up.

Slowly, Pop turned back around. 'Did I ever tell you that you were born in this house?'

Astounded, Zach shook his head. 'I didn't know that.'

Pop nodded. 'We were too poor for a hospital. A church lady came over and helped your mother.' He stared back down the hall, his eyes wide open, looking. 'She had a tough time of it. But she was brave . . . so brave. I was afraid. Her shrieks scared me to death. There was so much blood. But I couldn't take her to the community hospital, because she . . . because I hadn't married her. She wasn't legal, and I was afraid . . . it was 1966. The law and attitudes were different then. I didn't know – '

Zach shifted the boxes to one side. Gently, he took his father by the arm. 'Come on, Pop. Let's go home.'

It didn't take much to get Pop settled into one of the guest bedrooms. The old man and the boxes had gone quietly, gratefully, into the freshly painted room. There was a connecting bathroom, so Pop nearly had his own apartment, except for whatever he needed from the kitchen. When he could slow down a little, Zach planned on having a television put in

304

Pop's room. Then he'd have everything he needed to feel settled in.

Zach walked into his own room, not tired despite the late hour. What he was feeling was keyed-up apprehension pouring through his veins. His answering machine had been blank, though he'd expected a venomous reply from LouAnn to his message that there wouldn't be a wedding. Feeling numb, Zach crossed to the mahogany bureau, and reached into his pockets. Slowly, he placed the earrings down on the shiny wood. Then he pulled out the snake jaw Cody had given him, looking at the skeleton for a moment before putting it beside the glittering jewels. A sudden, distressing thought paralyzed him as he realized where Carter's other shoe might be dropping from.

In the beginning, Carter had claimed he'd never met Annie. Never been to her farm. Couldn't make any progress buying her land over the phone. So, he'd lied, talking Zach into going out there. Yet, Carter had tangled with Annie and knew he would never get what he wanted.

But Carter was now the sole owner of the deed to the land south of Annie's. And now that Zach had fired him, Carter would be a dangerous neighbor for Annie to have.

Though she didn't feel rested, Annie had gotten up at six this morning, having chores to attend to around the farm. Through the rest of the early hours, the day warmed up steadily, with every sign of being one of

305

the hottest days on record for this summer so far.

Deciding that a cranberry loaf and iced tea would be a refreshing snack in the afternoon, Annie went inside and prepared it, her mind only half on her work. When she finished that, she turned her thoughts to fixing lunch. Cody and Mary came into the kitchen to say hello, and Annie was relieved to finally be able to put her mind on something other than Zach.

'Mmm. Smells great. Am I invited to lunch?' Cody asked, sitting down.

'Sure,' Annie replied, slapping some potatoes down in front of him. 'Start peeling.'

A knock at the door kept her from hearing his reply. A man she didn't know was standing on the porch.

'Are you Annie Aguillar?'

'I am.'

'I need you to sign this, please,' he instructed, handing her a pad.

She did, then accepted the package from the courier with a hesitant smile. 'Thank you,' she murmured, closing the door and walking back into the kitchen, where Cody sat at the plank table eating the cranberry bread she'd just baked. Mary had run down the hall to check on her grandfather and Gert.

'This is certainly the week for surprises,' Annie commented. 'This package was sent all the way from Austin by courier.'

Cody grinned. 'Wonder who would make such an expensive gesture?'

'I have no idea,' Annie said. Her heart was racing.

306

Though she was still angry with Zach over paying her taxes, the feminine side of her was irrationally delighted and flattered by this sign of interest. Maybe she'd been wrong about his motive for paying off her taxes.

'Well, open it,' Cody commanded gruffly. 'Let's see what Slick's up to this time.'

'Maybe I won't show you,' Annie teased.

'Maybe, hell. Maybe I'll just have a look-see myself.' He made a pretend swipe to grab the package.

'All right,' she said, laughing. 'What *does* that man have up his sleeve this time?' Tearing open the envelope, Annie pulled out a handwritten note on cream paper. The sloping, delicate letters read, *Thought you might be interested in these.*

'Hmm,' Annie said, laying the letter aside. Cody swiftly snatched it up, but she didn't notice. Underneath the note were a couple of pictures, of Zach in the arms of a stunning, naked woman.

Date-stamped the day he'd made love to Annie.

Shaking, Annie sat down at the table. She was too frozen to think, too shocked to cry. 'Apparently, Zach had more up his sleeve than I imagined.'

CHAPTER 20

Silently, deeply embarrassed, Annie handed the pictures to Cody. He whistled low and long. 'She's a hot piece, isn't she?'

Annie wrapped her arms around herself, mortified at the realization that the man whose hands had brought her such joy and wonder had touched this big-breasted, ivory-skinned woman the same day. 'I guess that's his fiancée. She certainly looks the way I'd envisioned her.'

Cody glanced up from the pictures, concern etched in furrows across his forehead. 'Annie Aguillar, don't you start making comparisons and finding yourself short. You've got more going for you than this Playboy bunny any day.'

'Except Zach,' she said unhappily. At Cody's questioning glance, Annie explained, 'He told me they'd broken off their engagement. I assumed he was free.'

Her shamed expression told Cody the rest. 'Ah,' was all he said.

'Obviously, they're still very much together,' she

finished. Unable to meet Cody's sympathetic gaze, Annie looked down at her hands. 'The humiliating part is that Zach paid off my tax bill while he was in Desperado.'

'Playing Santa Claus that day, was he? And now you feel bought.'

Annie winced. 'I suppose I do.'

Cody put the pictures down and reached across the table to take Annie's hand in his. 'Annie, Zach didn't bring that carousel to Desperado himself to try to get you in the sack. He brought it to appease his conscience where Mary is concerned, because he truly cares about that child. And he paid off your taxes because he's got more money than he knows what to do with. And he cares about you. My theory is, he couldn't stand to see you hurting. Any more than I could.' Cody grinned comfortingly. 'His visit and these pictures are not connected events, Annie. I'm sure Zach very much wanted to develop a deeper relationship with you, or he wouldn't have come down.'

'He wasn't free like he claimed,' Annie said bitterly.

Cody picked up the pictures again, analyzing them. 'I don't know about that. My hunch is that Zach's very free, and Blondie here isn't too happy about it. That's why she sent you these.'

'They're together. He took her clothes off – '

'Ah, but wait,' Cody said, holding up a hand. 'You must read the body language involved. If a picture is worth a thousand words, then look what Zach is

309

saying.' He pointed at the couple. 'Look at his neck. He's got his head cocked back, like he's gotten too close to poisonous fumes. Now, if he wanted this floozie, he'd have been nuzzling on her neck, or somewhere.'

Annie considered Cody's words. Zach certainly hadn't had his head turned away from *her* body. He'd buried himself eagerly in her breasts, the curve between her neck and shoulder, beneath her hair – warm shivers fluttered over Annie as she remembered Zach's hunger for her.

'I suppose you could have a point,' she said, still unwilling to be convinced. The sight of the voluptuous woman nude and so near the man Annie wanted made her stomach clench painfully.

'Let me show you something else.' Cody stood, gesturing at Annie. 'Come here a sec.'

She got up and walked to Cody's side of the table, stopping in front of him. He laid the picture beside them, where they could both see it. 'Now. Note the position of Zach's hands.'

'I do,' Annie murmured. 'They're on her body.'

'Yes, but the position is critical. See how his hands are forward, thumbs down on her hips, as if he's . . . I don't know. Either trying to push her away, or hold her up. For all we know, she's drunk and incapable of standing.'

'You're not making me feel any better.'

'You're not paying attention,' Cody said with a grin. 'Stop looking at the skin and pay attention to the

310

details. *If* he wanted to be with this woman, Zach's hands would be like this,' he said, placing his big hands on her waist, 'fingers down, thumbs up, pulling her *closer* to him. Like so. Get the difference?'

Annie pulled in her breath sharply as Cody pulled her tight against him. A sudden memory of Zach holding her just this way, his hands sneaking into her panties to cup her bottom, engulfed her.

'Uncle Cody, what are you doing with my mommy?' Mary asked.

'I'd like to know the same thing,' Travis chimed in.

Gert and Travis stood in the kitchen entry, with Mary in front of them, holding a stuffed animal to her. Annie and Cody grimaced at each other, and she surreptitiously slid the telling pictures under the plate of cranberry loaf.

The nut-brown of Cody's skin had turned a bit ruddy around the facial area, Annie noticed. Mary's question had thrown him.

The stillness in the room was taut as wire. 'I'm just trying to see what's in your mommy's eye, ladybug,' Cody said gently, glancing down at the child who'd come closer to inspect them.

'My eye?' Annie asked.

'Her *eye*?' Travis repeated. 'Why're your hands on her rump, then? She learning to see with her legs?'

More color washed into Cody's neck, just above the collar of his denim work shirt. Annie's smile widened into a grin.

311

'Oh, for heaven's sake, Travis, come back to your room. You're stirring the pot,' Gert complained, dragging him with her down the hall.

'If Uncle Cody has fixed your eye, Mommy, can I have a drink of water?' Mary asked.

'My eye's fine, sugar,' Annie said, slipping away to get her daughter a drink.

'Thank you,' Mary said, taking the cup. She drained it, then clutched her stuffed animal more tightly. 'I'm going to watch TV.'

'I'll call you in a little bit for lunch,' Annie said.

'Ok, Mommy.' Mary darted out of the room.

'Well, wasn't that exciting?' Cody said dryly.

'Not as exciting as these.' Sitting back down at the table with the pictures, Annie riffled through them one last time. 'I want to think you're right, Cody,' she said. 'What do you think I should do?'

He took his customary seat across the table, as if the embarrassing encounter hadn't happened. 'About Zach paying your taxes, or the surprise delivery?'

'Either.' She waited for a suggestion.

'I don't know. I'm not sure old Slick's figured out what he's doing himself.' Cody went back to eating another huge piece of cranberry loaf, his expression thoughtful. 'I wonder if she's told him about the pictures?'

'What difference would it make?' Annie was curious.

'Maybe none. But if this little courtesy on his fiancée's part was designed to run you off, then she's

312

running scared. But scared enough to do more than make you cry, I wonder?'

'You're worrying me. What are you talking about?'

He pulled his hand along his braid, then scratched his head. 'I presume the fire was intended to put Zach's ass in a sling.'

'I know you do. Evidently, you convinced the sheriff, because he doesn't even talk about the fire and Zach in one breath any more.'

'So, did Zach have a guess as to who was out to get him?'

Annie rubbed a finger lightly over the image of Zach's face in the picture. 'Carter Haskins. An employee at Zach's company, who happens to be disgusting and dishonest.'

'Okay. So, we have the fire, a possible suspect who has motive – though we don't know what it is – and blue-movie pictures of Zach and his socialite fiancée, yet another noose designed solely for Zach's neck.'

Annie narrowed her gaze, staring at Cody. 'How do all these events line up?'

'We'd have to ask Zach for that answer. I wonder if there's any way the fiancée and Zach's friend could be in cahoots. What's Zach done that might piss either one of them off real bad?'

She shifted on the bench, shaking her head. 'I can't call him up and say, "Zach, what gopher hole did you step in"?'

'I guess not. But I could.'

'What makes you think he'd discuss any personal details of his life with you?' Annie asked.

Cody reached over and thumped her finger gently. She quit tracing Zach's image immediately. 'Zach and I understand each other,' he informed her with a smile.

'Well, that's more than I can claim,' Annie replied, not smiling.

'Honestly. First of all, Zach trusts me. I could say "Hey, what's the meaning behind these pictures?" with all the big-brother bluster I can manage, and likely, he'll tell me. Second, I have the protective instinct surging through me right now. I don't like anybody trying to hurt you, Annie, especially not some silly blonde twit. Zach trusts that I'm going to take a chunk out of his hide if I get disappointed in him.'

'I must have missed some bonding between you two,' she commented wryly.

Cody grinned. 'You must have. But you've been real busy lately.'

Annie sighed and got to her feet. 'I think I should just leave Zach alone for awhile, until some of the static clears from the air. After all, it's not like we had agreed upon any relationship between us,' she said quietly. 'I don't really have the right to question him.'

'Oh, Annie, bull. You have every right to call him up and ring his ears about this little gift his lady had hand-delivered to you.'

'That's true. But then I'd have to ask him about the

314

taxes. And to tell you the truth, Cody, I think I'd just rather wait. Give Zach some time to decide what he wants to do, what he wants from me. If you're right, and he's got all these different problems, all he needs right now is a . . .' She couldn't bring herself to say *extra burden*.

'Nagging woman.'

She smiled. 'Right.'

'You may have a point,' Cody said, getting up from the table, too. 'Hate to run off the only man that's come calling for you in a long time,' he teased.

'Oh, thanks. You spend half an hour building me up, then tear me back down right before you leave.' The words were complaining, but Annie was laughing.

'I've got to keep your feet on the ground, Annie Aguillar. See you later,' he said. 'Bye, Mary,' he shouted down the hall. 'Bye, Travis, Gert!'

Annie watched from a window as Cody got into the hearse, waving goodbye. Instantly, she let her hand fall to her side, because he never looked back. Though he'd been joking and smiling in the kitchen with her, his expression now was determined, hard. His eyes lacked the laughter they'd had a moment ago. Underneath the black cowboy hat Cody had slipped on, he looked dark and fierce.

Not like the man she knew at all.

Zach sat in the easy chair after Pop had gone to bed, trying to decide what to do. If LouAnn sprung her trap, it was going to be the end of him and Annie. The small flower that had begun to blossom between them would be ruthlessly nipped off at the bud. Yet, how could he call Annie and try to explain the pictures? He'd sound like a fool. LouAnn was counting on that.

It felt like she had him right where she wanted him.

Lost in a hazy world of worry and regret, Zach barely realized he'd reached for the portable telephone beside him. Dialing the operator, he requested a number, memorizing it instantly. Hesitating only one second more, Zach dialed the number.

Cody answered immediately, despite the late hour. 'Hello?'

'Cody, it's Zach Rayez.'

'Well, Slick. *Cómo está?*'

Zach started at the sound of Spanish in his ear. He registered two things: one, no one had spoken the language directly to him since his mother had left, and two, Cody had used the formal tense . . . as if they didn't know each other very well . . . Which didn't sound much like the man who'd given him a friendly chewing out over spending inappropriate time with Mary. Zach's antennae raised.

'I'm fine,' he replied. 'Wanted to bend your ear about something.'

'Bend away.'

Although the farmer wasn't gregarious by nature, neither had he always been short with Zach. His antennae began to quiver. 'I had an unfortunate

316

incident occur with my ex-fiancée. The bottom line is, she's found out about Annie and decided to make trouble.'

'How do I fit into this scenario?'

Zach winced at Cody's brusque tone. 'I'm hoping you can tell me the right way to approach this with Annie. As I see it, either way, I'm going to lose her respect and trust. But I don't want to see her hurt. If I can avoid it at all, I'd like to try.'

Cody sighed. 'I see.'

Zach took a deep breath, preparing to color in the rough sketch he'd just given Cody. 'LouAnn was angry that I'd called off the wedding. Deciding that she needed collateral to make certain I'd be the willing groom, she arranged to have – '

'Suggestive pictures of the two of you sent to the unsuspecting third party,' Cody interrupted.

'Yeah,' Zach said. 'How did you – ? Damn it to hell! She's already sent them.' He cursed fluently under his breath. He'd underestimated LouAnn's determination to cut him off at the knees. A sudden thought speared his brain. 'Oh, my God. What about Annie? Is she all right? Does she want to kill me?'

Cody chuckled slightly. 'Hold on, Slick. Don't give yourself hives. Annie's fine, I think, right now. The pictures were . . . a shock, to say the least. They were very revealing.'

'Shut up, Cody,' Zach said, his mood not lightened at all by Cody's joke. 'Tell me about Annie.'

'I don't think she has murder in mind, although

317

she's very distressed. I sort a figured there was sabotage involved – '

'How in the hell did you figure that?' Zach barged in impatiently.

Cody paused for a moment. 'Don't really know, Slick. Might have been your body language.'

There was dead silence for a moment. 'Cody,' Zach said finally, 'you *are* crazy.'

'Yep. Well, I gotta go, Zach. I've been spending too much time running around doing other people's stuff and mine's suffering. I'm a farmer by career choice, and this farm doesn't take care of itself. Oh, but about Annie,' Cody said in a quiet, straightforward tone, 'she's no fluffball like the one who was trying to snare you. She's not going to enjoy intrigues and low-rent special effects like she got today. You'd have been burned out of her life like a hole in a cloth if I hadn't been there. It wasn't a Kodak moment when those little squares of film arrived, if you follow. So, if you're as smart as I believe you are, you'll do your best to keep Blondie's nails trimmed. Cody's Lovelorn Hotline, signing off.'

The phone went silent. Zach turned the phone off, sighing deeply. What little bit Cody told him let Zach know Annie had been hurt deeply. It was too late to call tonight, because with his luck – and the phone being in her kitchen – he could wake up Travis or Mary. He'd have to wait until tomorrow. He closed his eyes, rubbing the lids tiredly. Damn. He'd never played such emotional roller derby in his life.

The thing to take his mind off the whole situation for a while was to bury himself in world events, Zach decided. He snatched up some loose change, noticing that the light was blinking on the answering machine. It could wait for a few more minutes.

Zach went outside, walking briskly down to the corner newspaper cage. Sticking in the coins, he pulled out the paper.

LOCAL BUSINESSMAN SUSPECTED OF EMBEZZLING, the headline blared. 'Sam Lindale moved fast on that,' Zach murmured to himself. Reading swiftly down the column, he suddenly stopped, his heart in his throat, his chest beating wildly.

According to a high-placed source within Ritter International, Zach Rayez has been mentioned in connection with thousands of missing dollars, stolen from the brain child he created, read the caption.

Zach staggered home, feeling like he'd just taken a bullet through the chest. Pain and fury mingled together in a cocktail of emotion that dizzied him. His name splattered in such a manner, in the newspaper where no prominent person – businessman or social chairman – could miss it.

He was finished.

Nothing he could do, no retraction he could ever force, could take away this black stain and resurrect his reputation. There would always be whispers in boardrooms, and doubt. Everything he'd worked for all his life in his desperate drive to escape his past

319

had just gone up in smoke.

And Annie. Though she was far removed from Austin, he had no doubt that some considerate person – like the one who'd sent her the pictures – would make certain she got this day's informative edition. What conclusion could she possibly draw, other than what was written there in black and white? She was going to believe the worst. And if he would commit a crime against the company he'd started, how could she know that she would fare any better? That he hadn't been lying to her all along?

Without being aware of his actions, Zach stumbled inside his house, slamming the door behind him and just barely remembering to lock it. His breath was caught deep in his chest where he couldn't draw it up comfortably. Zach put a hand against his ribcage and made for the privacy of his bedroom.

Tossing the paper on to the bureau next to the emerald earrings and snake jaw, Zach caught a glimpse of himself, eyes wild, black hair askew. He looked tortured. Shutting off the light, Zach fell back onto the bed, to stare upward in the darkness.

He *was* being tortured.

'Zach, you've got to get up,' Pop said, his voice holding a note of concern that Zach registered but ignored. 'You've been rotting in those sheets for the whole morning. Phone's been ringing off the hook, and I ain't no damn secretary. If you don't get the hell out of those shucks, I'm having some paramedics come and rescue you.'

320

Zach turned over, but other than that, didn't move. He couldn't. The tightness in his chest had returned, though it had subsided during his sleepathon. Still, he'd been up all night trying to think of a way out of the maze, without any luck.

'Zach, damn it! If anyone should be lying in a bed, it's me.' His father's voice came closer. After a moment, Zach felt an aura, like something was close to his skin. He opened one eye, to see Pop staring anxiously into it.

'Ah. You are alive.' Pulling up a chair, Pop sat down and glared into Zach's only open eye. 'It ain't gonna get any better, you know, sitting in here and hiding from it.'

'Oh, hell. Am I going to get a pep talk from the man who's spent most of his life hiding inside a liquor bottle?'

Pop snorted. 'My, we are going to have a pity party, I see. Well, I'll be here as long as I need to be.'

Zach heard the steely determination in Pop's tone and groaned.

'I may as well begin by giving you your messages.' There was a rustle of paper. Zach closed his eye wearily, realizing there was more than a page length of phone calls. 'There was a message from a reporter at the newspaper, wanting to confirm some details. 'Spect you shoulda picked up your messages sooner,' Pop stated in an ironic tone.

When Zach grunted, Pop continued, 'Then, a man named Sam Lindale's called about five times. He's frantic. Says he's got to talk to you right away. Told him you'd caught the flu.'

'In August,' Zach commented without opening his eyes.

'Well, could be stomach flu. The man wasn't looking for specifics on your health. He wants you to know that's he's placed all the calls he can to pertinent folks, but the damage is probably done.' Pop nodded decisively. 'That's what he said.'

'Like I needed anyone to tell me that.' Still, the fact that Lindale was trying to help soothed Zach's pride. He could use a few friends like him right now.

'I 'spect he's talking about this little eye-opener in the paper,' Pop said blandly, pulling out the damning article. 'Got me a paper the next day, 'fore I knew you'd bought one. Could have saved myself two quarters.'

'Oh, for crying out loud, Pop,' Zach complained. 'It's fifty cents, not a million bucks.'

'Still. Wasn't any need of wasting good money on a paper that's gonna report lies.'

Ah, another supporter in his corner. Not that it would do any good, Zach thought sourly, but it did appear to be true that one's real friends came out when the chips were down. It was a nice change from the filth-spewing father he'd learned to accept.

'Speaking of the newspaper, you've got about ten calls from different reporters wanting to hear your side of the story. Wanting to know if you're going to jail, if you're going to skip the country, small details like that.'

Zach snorted.

'LouAnn called, wanting to know if you'd changed your mind about the wedding. Said that it looked like marrying her was the only way to save your reputation now, because obviously a Harrison wouldn't marry a criminal.'

A wave of sardonic laughter wanted to burst from Zach, but he held it in ruthlessly. Of course not. His lily-white ex-fiancée would never get her delicate fingers dirty by marrying a criminal. Because they all knew Zach was innocent.

'I asked that bimbo if she was behind this stack of bull dung, but she said no. Actually, she said an extremely rude thing to me that has to do with a sexual act.' Zach opened his eyes to see Pop sitting up stiffly in the chair, looking affronted. 'I don't think I want her for a daughter-in-law,' he said primly. 'Your mother could yell my ears off, but she would never have dreamed of saying such a thing.'

'Let's not forget you've used that same language many a time,' Zach said mildly, though he was trying not to laugh at Pop's disbelief over LouAnn's choice of words.

'That's different,' he said. 'She wants to be your *wife*. I don't think you ought to marry a woman who talks like a whore.'

'Thanks, Pop. I'll keep that in mind.'

'Anyway,' Pop continued with a sigh, 'some business acquaintances called, leaving messages for you to call them. You're probably going to lose some contacts over this.' He slid Zach a warning look.

'I think I can count on that.'

'Well, that takes care of my receptionist duties. I haven't written so much in ten years, and I know I haven't talked on the phone so many times in my whole life.'

'Thanks, Pop. I appreciate it. Unplug the phone now, if you don't mind. I'm not going to return any of those calls.' He lifted his head up from the pillow suddenly. 'Nobody named Annie called, by any chance?'

Pop consulted his list again, frowning. 'Nope. And I was very careful to take names and numbers, if they'd give them to me. But there was no Annie. In fact, the only woman who called was LouAnn.'

Zach let his head fall back onto the pillow. 'Figures. Of course, I really wouldn't expect Annie to call.'

Pop didn't reply, and silence hung between them for a moment. Slowly, because it felt like his muscles had begun to atrophy from pressing grooves in the sheets, Zach sat up. Giving Pop a hard look, he said, 'How come you're still sober? Have you been sober the entire time I've been in here?'

Pop looked astonished. 'Didn't I teach you better manners than to insult a house guest?' he asked. Zach looked at him warily. His father shrugged. 'I've stayed in a pretty even stupor ever since your mother left. Now that I've lost my house, it's become clear to me that drinking wasn't solving anything. I lost her, I lost my house, and I damn near lost you. Way I see it, I'm at the end of the road here.'

'Last Chance Hotel, huh?'

'Feels like it to me. Though it hasn't been easy. The first day, I felt like the only thing that was going to make me feel any better was the hair-of-the-dog remedy. But I shut my door and waited till the urges passed. I've taken a few walks around the backyard to feel the sunshine. I'd nearly forgotten how good the sun felt on my skin. I've gone through most of that gourmet coffee you keep in the house, and I want you to know that stuff tastes like shit.' Pop wagged a finger at him. 'We've got to get some real coffee in here.' A sheepish expression came over him. 'And I've ordered a helluva lot of pizza, Zach. I hope you won't mind that I took some money from your wallet to pay for it. But you were in here a long time, and I was getting hungry.'

'Oh, hell, Pop,' Zach said, stretching out his legs, 'it's not like there's a whole lot to eat in this house, anyway. You're not supposed to eat paint chips just because you're living here.' Rubbing the back of his neck, he said, 'Since I was getting married, I wasn't laying in lots of groceries. Just enough to get me by.'

'Looked like peanut butter and beer was enough to get you by, then,' Pop sniffed. 'This ain't no four-star hotel, is it?'

Zach eyed his father. 'Now, that sounds more like the man I know.'

Pop gave a short flip of his hand Zach's way. 'I'm not complaining. I just meant that I spent all these years being jealous of you, thinking you had it all, were living the high life. I had no idea your life was so stressful, Zach.'

Zach was silent. Pop's words hurt.

'It's lonely around here, too, isn't it?' he continued. 'There's no noise, no neighbors totting around to get into your business.'

'Or to steal you blind, either, Pop. If you miss the bingo parlor, you can go back.'

Pop shook his head. 'You're mighty sensitive today, Zach. Lack of natural light's affecting your mood.'

'Ah, hell.' Zach leaned into his hand as it rested on his knee. 'I'm being an ass. I don't mean to be. Ignore it if you can. I really don't want you to leave,' he said, meaning every word.

'I didn't take you seriously. Besides, there are benefits to being here, Zach. I didn't mean to point out bad stuff, just that it's different. Which is good, because I've had some time to think. Damn, it's so quiet, all I could do was think.'

'You could have turned on the TV in the den,' Zach reminded him.

'I did that some. But mostly, I just sat and thought. And there's something I think I should tell you.'

'Oh, boy.' Zach's tone turned ironic again.

'I loved your mother, Zach. She was the most special woman I'd ever met in my life, even now.' Pop looked uncomfortable with his revelation. 'Truth is, I adored that woman to the point that I smothered her. I didn't want another person looking at her, or sharing any of that generous soul she had. I can't explain it any better, than to tell you that Cati was like no other.'

Zach bent his head. He knew what his father was talking about. Annie held a piece of his heart that no other woman could ever touch.

'I was so jealous,' Pop continued, his voice sad, 'that I became insecure. I was certain I wasn't good enough for Catalina. She was lonely, I know, because she didn't speak good English. I didn't care, though.' Pop laughed softly. 'I understood every word she said. It was total, emotional communication.'

Shifting uncomfortably, Zach bent an elbow to lean on his knee, grasping his chin in his hand. All his life, he'd wanted to know the truth. Now, he was going to hear it. Though it was going to be just a little more salt rubbed into his fresh wounds.

'But my doubts about myself led me to start acting dumb. I mean, here was this beautiful woman I'd met when I was on leave, when I'd gone into Matamoros to drink. And we had a few dates – well, I ate dinner with her family a couple of times and those were dates, because she was from a good family – and we fell in love. Most incredible, she agreed to come back with me.'

The disbelief on Pop's face was nearly comical. Yet, Zach felt saddened by the whole sorry tale.

'Right away, I suspected she was doing it just to get

327

legal. Then the whole family would eventually come over.' He took a deep breath. 'And instead of thinking, yeah, that's a great idea, I'll marry Cati, and she can become a legitimate citizen and her family can come over eventually . . .' Pop paused for a moment '. . . I let my jealousy talk. I thought she might leave once she got legal. So I used it as a weapon, a chain to keep her with me forever. In short, I was a bastard.'

Zach wanted to agree, but his father had spent too many years living with his regrets. 'So, then what happened?'

'Well, she became pregnant with you and for a while everything was fine. Except then I learned from a neighbor that the fellow down the street, Pablo, was slipping by to see her while I was at work every day. And I saw red in shades I never knew existed,' Pop said quietly. 'I wanted to kill that son of a bitch, though I knew, in my heart, that . . . my Cati loved me; that she was lonely and wild for someone to speak with in her own language. But that just infuriated me more, because it was a part of her I couldn't have.'

He paused for a moment to gather his thoughts. Leaning back in the chair, Pop said, 'In my heart, I knew you were my child, but of course, in my suspicious state, that was something I let myself begin to doubt. I quit coming home at night, starting hanging out at bars. It infuriated Cati, of course. There were other ways I could have dealt with the situation. But, I was selfish. I wanted her to love only me, not to need Pablo. I began coming home fresh from other women's arms, just to show Cati two could play the same game.'

Shaking his head, Pop said, 'I was building up my own ego, trying to convince myself that I deserved this wonderful woman. But,' he said, sighing, 'this went on for many years. We were locked in a stalemate and by the time your seventh birthday rolled around, Cati's patience wore out. She'd figured out I wasn't going to marry her. I was treating her like dirt, and she'd decided to return to Mexico. I said, "Fine, but leave the brat on this side of the border," once again, thinking I had the upper hand. She wouldn't leave you, I knew. Or, she might leave for a few days, but she'd come back. You were Cati's only happiness, I'm ashamed to say.'

Zach pursed his mouth, not knowing what to say. But he watched Pop silently, seeing the age guilt was stamping on his face as he spoke.

'To my shock, Cati did leave. One day while I was at work, she had Pablo drive her to the border. I know this because he told me so.' Pop's eyes dimmed. 'Came by to tell me he'd never laid a finger on Cati, that she wouldn't have let him though he would have married her in a second. Apparently, Cati felt allowing Pablo to be more than a friend would be compounding her sin. Whatever that was, I'm not sure. Cati was a good woman,' he said quietly.

A memory of loving arms holding him, while a lilting voice sang in Spanish, filtered through Zach's memory. 'I have a hard time believing Mama hasn't tried to see me in all these years.'

'Oh.' Pop frowned sadly. 'She's written many times. She has sent little Mexican trinkets and photos of herself.' Getting up heavily, Pop walked out of the room.

Zach took a deep breath and ran his hand through his hair in an angry motion. Damn Pop for being such a pitiful case, he thought. His father came back into the room, carrying the box Zach had seen when he'd brought him home. 'These are all the letters and pictures she's sent you over the years.'

He handed the box to Zach. 'Please don't go through it right now. I don't think I can bear it yet.' Sadly, he said, 'I don't think enough years can pass until I will be able to bear it. But it's time you knew that you were right. I drank as much as I could trying to forget her. Trying to live down the knowledge that I'd run her off, not because I was a worthless person, but because I'd acted like one. I didn't deserve her, not the way I treated her. As long as I live, I'll never forgive myself.'

Pop looked at the ground. 'But as much as I regret what happened with Cati, I regret more that I took it all out on you. You were always a good boy, Zach, but . . . I couldn't let go of my misery long enough to tell you that. I was proud of you when you graduated with honors from high school, and I was proud of you when you won your first college soccer game. I was proud of you when you graduated *magna cum laude*. But I knew none of that had anything to do with me. It was all Cati

330

inside you, keeping that spirit inside you that I couldn't break no matter how much that demon inside me tried.'

'And you're especially proud of me now,' Zach said mockingly.

'That's what I'm trying to tell you, son. I *am* proud of you. Whatever is happening to you, don't let some bozo drag you down, but especially, don't be dragged down by your own self-pity. I let somebody box me in, and I don't know what I would have done if you hadn't rescued me from myself. Worst of all, my self-pity cost me Cati. And I'll live with that the rest of my life.'

He knew what Pop was trying to tell him, but he felt overwhelmed by his father's story. He felt sad about his mother. Mostly, he felt a crushing sense of tiredness weighing in upon him. And somehow, Zach felt like he'd been physically destroyed, bit by bit, by everything that had happened in the past couple of days.

'Tell you what,' he said after a moment, 'I'll think about what you've told me, if you'll leave me in peace for a while.'

'Going back to sleep?'

'No. Going to shower and get dressed.'

'Good. I'm never talking on the phone again,' Pop said in a token complaint as he shuffled out.

'I'll take over after I shower,' Zach called. As far as he could see, he was damned.

But that didn't mean he was going to go down without a fight.

CHAPTER 21

Annie stood in the field with her father, who'd insisted upon taking his daily exercise with her instead of Gert. Annie knew the lure wasn't so much herself, as it was the chance to get out and see how the land was mending from the scorching devastation of the fire two weeks ago. She'd become almost used to the dark, flattened appearance, although she was still sad – and concerned – that anyone had deliberately tried to ruin her. With any luck, that person had realized she was too tough to be burned out. And no matter how much she'd resented Zach paying off her taxes without discussing it with her, the fact remained his gift meant she no longer had to worry about hanging onto her home.

Now she had to turn her thoughts toward the future. Overhead, crows were circling, flapping black wings and cawing as they looked for food. Travis turned over a dirt clump with his cane, and dozens of earthworms wiggled deeper into the moist blackness.

'I can see your wheels turning, Annie. What's it going to be?'

Annie crossed her arms, staring thoughtfully into the distance. 'I'm checking into the subsidy situation on wheat, Papa. We've still got time to get some of that in, and it would be a good use of the soil through fall and winter.'

'Wheat's a good crop for this part of Texas,' he agreed.

She was glad he liked her idea. 'I'm considering saving about an acre behind the house for a huge vegetable garden as well.'

Travis squinted at her. 'Expanding, are you?'

'Maybe. I'd like to grow tomatoes, jalapenos, maybe try some of those new brown onions everyone's saying are so good. Then I might run some cilantro and other herbs closer to the house.'

'Sounds to me like you're giving Slick's idea some thought.'

Annie walked forward a few steps, wrapping her arms around herself though the day was warm and the sun shone brightly. It wasn't that she was cold. But the mere mention of Zach was enough to send shivers running in little electric currents over her body.

'I am,' she confirmed. 'Initially, I believe it would be best if I stuck with enlarging the process I'm already using. That's why I'm expanding the garden. There's a few kinks I want to iron out, to completely smooth out the recipe before I try to sell it to a gourmet public.' She rubbed her arms without

333

really feeling any warmth. 'Although I couldn't allow myself much time to dream about my own business before, with Gert being here and my financial worries eased slightly, the salsa idea has really begun to take root in my mind.'

Travis nodded. 'So, does Slick know you're thinking about it?'

Annie shook her head. 'As Zach said at the time, it was an idea he was giving to me, to use if I wanted. There'll be some start-up costs involved, which I'm going to have to figure out a way to pay for. But other than that, I see no reason to discuss this with Zach. Especially since I'm still very much in the planning stage.'

Her father listened, remaining silent for a moment after she'd finished speaking. He rubbed his chin, then swung his cane back and forth half-heartedly a few times. 'Haven't heard you say you've talked to him lately, Annie,' he said gruffly. 'Not that it's any of my business.'

Annie lowered her eyes. Papa was wondering the same thing she was: why had the phone been suspiciously, conspicuously silent where Zach was concerned? It had been a little over a week since she'd last seen him.

Over a week since they'd made love.

A week since she'd received those astonishing pictures. After listening to Cody's practical comments, Annie had ripped those pieces of Polaroid into shreds, burying them into the trash can where

Mary could never accidentally see them. But the images were cut into Annie's memory with shard-like intensity.

'Don't suppose he changed his mind and got married after all, do you?'

Pain shot through Annie, a combination of jealousy and fear and doubt all wrapped up in one. Miserably, she shook her head. 'No. One thing I know about Zach in my heart is that he didn't . . . become involved with me with any commitment still owed to someone else.'

Travis stamped down a dirt mound with his boot. 'Seems odd he ain't calling. I'd just about gotten used to his ugly mug popping up every time I tried to sit down at the kitchen table.'

Annie laughed, though she didn't feel any deep release of joy. It was true. Zach's lack of communication was uncharacteristic. Briefly, she replayed the string of events in her mind. They'd made love, and he'd gone from the foreman's cabin to pay her taxes. He'd gone to see Mary, and to take her the carousel before returning to Austin. The pictures had arrived soon after, but Cody had eased her fears about that.

She'd managed to exterminate the white-hot apprehension even more so when later Cody revealed that Zach had called him, wondering how to alert her that the pictures were coming without upsetting her. Cody had believed Zach's story about a furious ex-fiancée.

Strangely enough, Zach had never called *her* to explain about his ex-fiancée's little surprise, never called or wrote to reassure her in any manner. At this point, even a postcard might appease her worry that Zach, for whatever reason, was quietly calling off the relationship that had been building between them.

'Who knows about Zach, Papa?' she said airily, not feeling that way at all. 'Maybe someone else is feeding him.'

She'd meant it as a joke in response to her father's remark about the kitchen table, but it fell flat. Travis observed her, concern in his weathered gray eyes.

'Maybe you oughta call him, Annie.'

Annie's lips parted in surprise. 'Why would I do that?'

'To ask him if his finger's broke, gal! Hell, to ask him the same thing you're wondering, which is why hasn't he called? Put more politely, of course,' Travis muttered.

She crossed to her father, rubbing one hand soothingly over his back. 'You shouldn't worry about me so much, Papa.'

'Can't help it. And I know it ain't any of my concern, and you're too old for me to be mother-henning. So, I'll keep my mouth shut from here on.'

They walked forward together, Annie accepting the little of her father's weight he would allow her to carry. 'I might call him some time, Papa,' she said. 'The thought hadn't occurred to me. I know he's had a lot to straighten out, and I guess I knew Zach would show back up again when he was ready.'

'Yeah, well, we ain't a home for stray animals,'

336

Travis complained as they reached the steps. 'He shouldn't be bringing his bowl around here just when he's hungry.' Slowly, carefully, he stumped up the steps and opened the door before turning back around to look at his daughter. 'It's the nineties, gal. Give him a call and maybe a piece of your mind, if you think it's right.'

Travis went inside and Annie sat down on the porch. She'd never considered calling Zach, because she'd understood he had a lot of personal stuff to deal with. But by now, she had been hoping for word from him. For clarification on whether she had a part in his life or not. Whether there was any reason Mary should continue to ask daily when Mr Zach was coming back. What Papa said was true, though. Zach had been more constant than he was being now.

Annie sighed. If she called him, those questions might be answered. Somehow, that was just as unnerving as being in the dark.

There was no way now that Annie could continue to avoid dialing Zach's number. She'd called the agricultural extension to ask questions about subsidies on wheat. She'd called Jim Crier to see if there were any further developments on the investigation. There weren't, and they both knew there wasn't going to be. The rain had pretty much taken care of matters, not to mention that the culprit had been fairly careful not to leave evidence around. Then she'd called her insurance company, as well as her father's doctor's

337

office with a progress report. There simply wasn't anyone left to call, though she would have rung anyone to avoid hearing Zach's voice answering his phone. Would he be glad to hear from her? Or would he be stiffly polite, embarrassed that she hadn't understood the parameters of their association?

Annie closed her eyes, knowing that, just as she was going forward planning new crops and a new venture in her life, she needed also to go forward with her personal life. There was no point waiting around for something to happen if it wasn't going to. Opening her eyes again and taking a deep breath, Annie dialed Zach's number.

'Hello?' a rough and rather craggy voice shouted at her when the phone was picked up at the other end.

She raised her eyebrows in astonishment. 'May I speak to Zach Rayez, please?'

'He ain't available. Take a message for you, though.'

Grimly, she pressed on, trying to ignore the growing tremors in her stomach. 'Do you know when he might be available?' she asked.

'Nope. Can't say that at all. Give me your name and number, and I'll tell him you called.'

'I . . .' Her message was too personal to leave. Still, leaving some word would be the right thing to do, she supposed. 'I . . . could you tell Zach that Annie Aguillar called, please? He has my phone number.'

'Hang on a second, while I get the spelling. Annie . . . Ag– Wait a minute. Annie? This morning Zach asked me if you'd called.'

338

Relief washed into Annie with the speed of a torrential downpour. 'He did?' she asked. 'I would have called sooner if I'd known – '

She cut off the sentence, realizing that finishing it with 'if I'd known he wanted to talk to me' wasn't going to sound right. 'Well, I'd be grateful if you'd pass the message along.'

'Say, hold on, Annie,' the man said hurriedly. 'I . . . uh . . . I can't say as to when Zach might call you back. I don't suppose you'd want to pay him a visit, you know, just a quick, social thing.'

Her eyebrows raised again at the suggestion. She sensed hesitation in the man's words, as if he wasn't sure he should be mentioning the idea. And it was obviously an off-the-cuff invitation.

'I don't really do quick, social things, sir,' she replied. 'Is there a reason I'd want to?'

'Well . . . Zach's been kinda ill. I'm his father, so I've been here looking after him. But, to be honest, he might feel better if you came by, since he was asking for you and all. Might cheer him up a bit. He hasn't had many visitors, you know.'

Every fiber of Annie's body sprung to awareness. 'What's wrong with Zach?'

His father paused. 'Don't rightly know.'

'You haven't taken him to a doctor?' Annie was becoming more worried by the moment.

Another pause. 'He won't let me.'

'I see.' Zach could be extremely stubborn, she knew, as most males were when faced with seeing a physician. Papa didn't exactly go quietly and docilely when he was sick, either. But she had no car, no way to get to Austin. Annie was quiet for a moment, her insides knotted with indecision. 'I'm not sure I can do anything to help,' she murmured, throwing up a last resistance. How did she know Zach would welcome her?

'Can't hurt anything,' Zach's father replied. 'You don't have to stay long . . . but please, Annie. I think it would do him a world of good.'

The indecision caved. Zach had done more for her and her family than anyone besides Cody. And if his father said a visit from her might make Zach feel better, then by heaven, she'd find a way to get to Austin. Gert could keep an eye on Travis. And they wouldn't mind watching Mary for the evening, or Cody could probably be counted on to pinch-hit. 'I'll be there tonight,' she promised.

'I'll order some pizza,' he replied, before hanging up the phone.

Annie stared at the receiver for a moment, pondering that strange remark. Something very mysterious was going on. Trickles of alarm fanned through her, as she wondered if something worse than sickness had gotten to Zach. Something more like a person whose mind was bent with revenge. Cody's words came back to her: *I wonder if there's any way the fiancée and Zach's employee could be in cahoots. What's Zach done that might piss either one of them off real bad?*

It was a haunting question. She squinted, thinking

340

hard. The fire. The cigar in the field. The fable of oil under her land. The pictures.

Zach's sudden silence.

Zach had fired Carter Haskins – and also broken off his engagement. And now he was suffering from a unknown malady that Zach's father thought a visit from Annie might help.

Because he'd asked for her.

Annie's hands were shaking. She dialed Cody's phone number, absurdly relieved when he answered immediately.

'Cody,' she said abruptly, 'I was wondering if you'd lend me one of your vehicles. I need to go to Austin.'

Annie wasn't surprised by the size of Zach's house, nor by the obviously wealthy neighborhood he lived in. She parked the junky old hearse out front with a small grin to herself, thinking some noses would certainly be pressed against windowpanes. As she got out of the car, Annie realized with a pang that she was stepping into Zach's world. A world totally foreign to her, a place where she likely wouldn't fit in. There was light-colored brick everywhere and shiny brass lamps and mailboxes, and actual paved, cobbled sidewalks all adorning the houses, signaling affluence.

Feeling self-conscious, Annie ran her hand down her long braid, making certain it was still neat despite the harried rush in which she'd left Desperado. Tendrils had come loose around her forehead and along her cheeks, but it couldn't be helped now.

341

Either Zach was going to be glad to see her or he wasn't. And there wasn't a way to gauge his reaction. She had to see him to know.

Ignoring the anticipation racing through her, Annie walked on to the porch and rang the bell. To her surprise, Zach himself came to the door.

He didn't seem especially shocked to see her, nor particularly enthusiastic. At least a day's growth of beard darkened his chin. Annie had never seen Zach without the utmost attention paid to his grooming. Somehow the unkempt hair and shirt hanging out of his jeans was troubling. Still, he didn't look as ill as his father had represented.

'Hello, Zach,' she replied.

'Hi, Annie.'

Not nice to see you or, what a surprise. 'Did you know I was coming?'

He shrugged. 'No, I didn't. But that's all right.' Motioning her inside, Zach said, 'Have a seat.'

She walked to where he pointed, asking, 'How are you feeling?'

'Fine.'

She hadn't expected open arms or Zach doing rebel yells at the sight of her, but she certainly hadn't expected this laconic person. Perching on the sofa set at an angle to the seat he was taking, Annie told herself it was all right to try to move the mountain with a little more directness. 'How have you been, Zach, really?'

Zach nodded. 'Fine. Quiet, actually.'

But he didn't look at her. Annie noticed Zach kept his eyes trained on the teak coffee-table, every once in a while his gaze darting to the hallway. Annie's heart began slowly sinking in her chest. If he wasn't glad to see her – and if this monosyllabic conversation was an indication of how her visit was going to go – Annie knew she shouldn't have come.

He didn't want to see her.

Worse, she wasn't sure she knew him anymore.

'Mary's enjoying the carousel,' she said tentatively.

Interest flickered briefly in Zach's eyes. 'I'm glad.'

Annie pursed her lips. Obviously, she was going to have to use less finesse to get some real answers. 'I missed hearing from you. We all did. Papa wondered if you'd gotten lost.'

His gaze stayed with her. 'Somewhat,' he said mysteriously. 'A lot's happened since I saw you last.'

Annie nodded. 'I thought it might have. It's been crazy lately, hasn't it?'

Zach appeared hesitant. 'I know I'm ready for a change.'

'How much of a change?' Annie asked softly. 'What's happened, Zach? Your father said you were ill, but you don't seem sick, maybe just unhappy, or something. Can you tell me what's wrong?'

Is it me? she wanted to ask.

'I was going to call you. Some time.' He paused. 'I don't know when. But I would have, Annie. Between canceling a wedding and – '

He sat quietly for a few minutes before getting up.

343

Annie watched him disappear down a hallway, then return with a paper in his hand which he gave to her. 'Don't suppose you got this edition of the newspaper.'

'Paper boy would have to have a pretty strong arm to throw the paper all the way to Desperado from Austin.' Annie scanned the article in shock. Looking up, she met Zach's eyes. 'This is only fit for the bottom of a bird cage.'

Zach nodded. 'Yeah. But I sure didn't see it coming.'

'This is Carter's work?'

'I've got some calls in to find out, but I'm pretty certain he's the highly placed official they're quoting. Only, he's not part of the company any more because I fired him, but obviously, that fact didn't get checked. Or wasn't significant enough to include.'

'This is because I wouldn't sell my land to that miserable monster.'

Zach shook his head. 'This is happening because Carter's a greedy bastard. Everything was fine as long as I fit into the pattern. The instant he realized I really was going to leave the company, I became useless to him. By then, he'd gotten it into his head to cheat you out of the supposed oil, and thought I was just the person to strike the deal. It's been a one-upmanship game with Carter all along, only I didn't realize I was playing.'

Zach shot her a smile that seemed threatening and determined at once. 'But I do now.'

'What a terrible price for you to have to pay,' Annie murmured.

'What a terrible price for *you* to have to pay,' Zach returned, with more hard-edged spirit creeping into his voice. 'I can't stop thinking about everything you've lost because of me.'

Annie lowered her eyes. 'I have gained because of you, Zach.'

He snorted. 'If I'd never shown up at your door, your father would never have had that heart attack.'

'That's not – '

'And that's just the beginning. As long as I live, I'll never forget the sight of that corn field blazing, Annie. It's painted in a fiery yellow-orange picture in my mind. I caused you to lose your livelihood, your security.'

Zach's voice was anguished. She sensed that nothing she could say could erase what he thought he'd done to her. So she shrugged. 'You paid my taxes. Wasn't that enough to make up for everything?'

'Maybe in part.' Zach sounded uncertain. 'I could help, and I wanted to. But, yeah, it was the least I could do.'

Annie sat stiffly, not wanting to hear her own assumptions confirmed. She'd known Zach had probably felt obligated. Still, it hurt. And that taunting voice inside her screeched mockingly, *Not because he's in love with you*!

'The thought was kind, but unnecessary. You shouldn't feel any responsibility for me. I've always managed, even before I met you.' It was true, but injured pride made Annie say the words more spitefully than she'd intended. But she wished the differences between them weren't so obvious. She didn't want to seem so helpless to a man like Zach Rayez.

'Oh, I know that,' Zach said swiftly. 'It was just that – '

The doorbell rang, cutting off his words. 'Excuse me,' Zach's tone was brief. He got up and opened the door. Annie leaned back into the sofa, trying to pull in a deep breath that might relax her when shrill words reached her.

'Mr Rayez,' the woman said, 'My bridge circle is due to start arriving any moment. Do you think your maid could park that . . . her car in back of your house?'

CHAPTER 22

There was a pause. Annie's mouth dropped open in astonishment.

'Annie, love,' Zach called, 'my neighbor has something she'd like to ask you.'

Without hesitating, Annie rose and went to stand beside Zach. The plump old woman lowered her eyes briefly, before trying to steady her gaze on Annie. Even wearing little-old-lady heels, the woman didn't reach Annie's shoulders. Annie stared down at the triple strand of pearls adorning the woman's fat throat and the sheen of her silk dress as the sun danced on the fabric.

'I'm not a maid,' she said quietly. 'If your guests can't park their cars near mine, then I guess they'll have to jog up from the end of the street.'

'Well, I never!' the woman sputtered.

Annie sized up the woman calmly. 'No, it doesn't appear that you do get much exercise,' she said, not releasing the woman's stunned gaze as she stepped back.

Zach closed the door. A grin lit his face, then he laughed. 'Oh, Annie. I've missed you so much. You're so different from anything I ever thought I wanted, and yet . . . you're exactly what I need.' He pulled Annie into his arms. 'Where were we, before we were so rudely interrupted?'

'Not *here*,' Annie said angrily, trying to pull away, but Zach's grip was a gentle vise.

'Ah, yes. You were telling me how you could fight your own battles, weren't you? Man your own cannon? Go toe-to-toe with snobby people?'

'That's not funny, Zach,' Annie shot back.

'No, it's not,' he said, smoothing a kiss along her shoulder. 'It's also not funny that you seem to think I paid for the privilege of holding your body, of loving you. I can't help feeling some responsibility for your troubles, Annie, any more than you can help feeling some self-righteous anger that I do.'

Annie slowly ceased her struggles as Zach's ministrations started weaving their effect on her. A warmth she remembered well began creeping through her body, a warmth that only Zach could create.

'You don't want me – ' she began.

He interrupted her with a mind-sizzling kiss. 'I do want you. You've just come at a time when my life has completely turned upside down. I don't know where the past has ended or the future is going. But, oh, Annie, if you think I don't want you, you're badly mistaken.'

His hands searched her back, smoothly undoing the

348

buttons of her cotton blouse before finding the metal clasps that released her bra. Immediately, impatiently, he slipped underneath to encircle her breasts with his palms. Gently, he squeezed her nipples, which brought them to instant tautness. A moan escaped Annie. 'I want you, too,' she whispered. 'I just want it to be on my terms.'

Zach lifted her, carrying her down the hall to his bedroom. Laying her on top of the bed, he said, 'I know. So do I.'

At first she thought he was agreeing with her, and then Annie realized Zach was talking about his own terms. But he was doing wonderful things to her and she was returning every emotion she was experiencing to him and somewhere along the way it wasn't worth saying that they wouldn't be making love in his big bed if they weren't caught in a game where everyone wanted everything on their own terms.

Zach knew his life had been splintered, broken into jagged pieces until Annie had come to him. He looked at the sleeping woman beside him, tremulous lips full with sleep, ebony hair undone now and tangled over her pillow and his, and thanked his lucky stars she'd come to show him what he'd been in danger of forgetting. He'd needed to be touched by reality again, and Annie was that. Annie's honesty and basic goodness had steered the desperation he'd been struggling with right out of his mind. She didn't allow herself to be ruled by money or status or any other thing – all factors which he'd nearly let suck him under.

Annie was real. And her strength brought him strength . . . And conviction. Lightly, he kissed those slightly open lips, and was rewarded by the fluttering of her eyes.

'Hello, again,' he murmured with a grin.

'Hello, yourself.' Annie pouted teasingly. 'You woke me up from the most wonderful dream.'

'Did I have a starring role in it?'

'No.' At his purposefully sad frown, Annie laughed. 'But I give you top billing in bed.'

'Only in bed?' Zach raised his brows.

'For now.' She slanted him a provocative look. 'But you've always been a hard worker. You'll probably move up if you try enough.'

He gave her the gentlest slap on the rump, before pulling her over and up on top of him. 'I'd rather let you have top billing for now.' Lightly, he reached up to tease her nipples. Annie's eyes glowed at his touch and, as she settled herself against him, every cell in Zach's body came tantalizingly alive. *Just once more*, he promised himself, *before I let her go*.

It was the sound of paper being pushed under the bedroom door that brought Zach unwillingly out of his sex-induced slumber. With one eye, he peered toward the stack of notes, realizing with regret that his wonderful escape into Annie's arms was coming to an end.

'Okay, Pop,' he muttered to himself. 'I get the message.'

Annie opened her eyes. 'What did you say?'

He bent over to give her a quick but thorough kiss on the mouth. Reaching down, he grabbed up his clothes. 'As beautiful as it's been, I can't stay a fugitive in here. It looks like I've got about thirty phone calls to return – and then I've got to go – '

Zach stopped himself from saying, *kick some butt.* 'I've got to go talk to someone.'

'Oh.' She sounded disappointed.

Zach sat down on the bed, allowing himself to run a hand along her thigh. 'I'm sorry, Annie. I'd stay in bed with you until Christmas if I could. But I don't have anything to offer you until I settle some things.'

'I know.' She pulled herself into a sitting position, wrapping her arms around her knees, and gazed at him. Seeing her sitting there so unconsciously sexy in his bed nearly made Zach detour from his plans again.

But he couldn't. Not if he was going to be earn this woman's love forever.

'It's not very romantic, me running off on you, but – '

She laid one finger against his lips. 'I think we've re-established connections to my satisfaction.'

He smiled, wondering what he'd ever done to deserve this woman. 'Thank you for understanding.'

Annie shrugged. 'There's not that much to understand.'

He thought there was, but Annie possessed essential

backbone. Her breasts had swayed enticingly with her shrug and Zach swallowed hard. 'Okay. I'm going to shower now. If you want to sleep some more, feel free.'

She shook her head. 'I really need to get back to Mary and Papa. Thanks, though.'

'You could always shower with me,' he suggested, knowing she wouldn't accept but a part of him wishing she would, even though it would obviously mean another lingering, loving delay.

'Next time, maybe.'

'Next time, *definitely*,' Zach replied. He rose to head to the shower. 'Help yourself to anything you need,' he called over his shoulder. 'I think Pop's got several different kinds of pizza in the refrigerator, if you're hungry.'

Annie smiled, thinking her hunger had been appeased for the moment. She got up and dressed quickly. Glitter caught her eye and she paused in the act of putting on her shirt. Feeling a little guilty, Annie walked over to Zach's dresser. Her eyes widened as she looked at the stunning emerald earrings tossed down casually next to a snake jaw and an old, ragged box. Small shivers ran along her arms at the odd array. But it was the earrings which drew her gaze relentlessly. Zach must have really loved his woman at one time to buy her such a valuable gift. Shooting a look at the closed bathroom door where Zach's lusty baritone voice was pouring forth in song, Annie picked up the earrings.

They winked at her, their color bold against the

earth tone of her palm. Slowly, even though what she was doing would be embarrassing if Zach were to come out and see her, Annie lifted the gems to her ears and snapped them on before staring at herself appraisingly.

Shaking her head a bit to set the smaller stones dancing, Annie was beset by the heavy feel of the earrings. They were like weights. And though the jet of her hair complemented their greenness, her hair was too long and too wild to look right with them. Hesitantly, she took her hair, pulling it into an upsweep on top of her head, imagining for a moment what she would look like if she were to ever accompany Zach to one of those fancy dinner parties he no doubt frequently attended.

With a sigh, Annie let her hair fall and pulled the clips from her ears. It was no use. She wasn't the glamorous type and nothing was going to change that.

But Zach had said she was exactly what he needed. Carefully, she placed the earrings back on the dresser and finished dressing.

Zach needing her was the reason she could return to Desperado, believing that there would be more between them. Eventually, anyway. Her heart much lighter than it had been when she'd first knocked on his door, Annie walked out into the living room.

'You must be Annie,' a sandpaper-rough voice said.

She jumped, turning jerkily toward the voice. A little old man, probably Papa's age but not nearly so robust-looking, gazed at her stoically.

'I am,' she replied. 'You're Zach's father.'

There wasn't much family resemblance, she mused, not in looks or in bearing.

'Yep,' he replied. 'You can call me George, if you want. Want some pizza?'

She shook her head. 'No, thank you.' Pinning him with a stare, Annie asked, 'Why did you tell me Zach was sick?'

'He is.'

'He seems in fine health to me,' she stated.

The old man shifted slightly on his feet before tapping his head with a finger. 'His illness is up here.'

She shot him a suspicious look. 'What are you saying?'

'I'm saying he was down, depressed, fighting but not kicking ass.'

'That's not how you made it sound on the phone. Anyway, he probably would have come around without me.'

He crossed his arms stubbornly. Zach's hearty voice boomed down the hall in a loud rendition of 'Amazing Grace'. 'Seems there's been some kind of change since your arrival,' the man remarked. 'Course, you'll pardon me for causing you any trouble.'

Annie pursed her lips wryly. Zach's father was perfectly aware that her trip hadn't exactly been for nothing. But he wasn't about to let her nail him down into admitting any fault for his actions. 'Maybe I'll have some of that pizza I hear you've been hoarding after all.'

'Sounds good to me,' he said. 'Sit yourself down at the kitchen table.'

She did, listening to him open and close cupboards and turn the microwave on. Seconds later it dinged, and he brought out a plate with so many pieces of pizza she'd never eat it all and a glass of iced water.

'I'd offer you something else to drink but all Zach's got is beer and gourmet coffee. I don't drink the hops anymore and I'm trying not to drink that damn coffee.'

Annie smiled in commiseration as he sat across from her. Taking a bite of pizza, she watched him watching her.

'He asked for you, you know. Maybe knowing that, you can forgive my little bit of stretching the situation.'

Annie raised her brows, not about to let him off the hook that easily. Zach's Pop seemed pretty cagey to her.

'Don't suppose you care to know that you're not exactly what I was 'specting,' he told her.

'I'm not surprised,' she said, thinking about the earrings and the pictures of Zach's ex-fiancée she'd received. 'I'm not much like the woman Zach nearly married.'

'Thank God,' he replied with spirit. 'What a shrew. What a she-troll. Ugh.'

Annie tried not to smile at the relief in his voice. 'Thank you for your support,' she murmured.

'Support, hell. I want the same thing for my son that I had.'

'What is that?'

He paused for a moment, his eyes lowered, before he met her gaze fully. 'You remind me of my Catalina, Zach's mother.'

Annie hesitated. The memory of Zach sitting with Mary at the edge of the pond filtered back to her, misty and tinged with sadness. She remembered how gentle and soothing Zach had been as he'd rubbed Mary's back. *I have a feeling neither one of them wanted to leave us that way*, he'd said.

Obviously, this was sacred ground she was treading on right now. 'How do I remind you of her?' she asked softly.

'Well, you're dark, like she was. You're taller, though,' he said, squinting across the table at Annie. Her pizza lay on the plate, completely untouched now, as the old man glanced down the hall. Zach had finally quit singing, which somehow Annie missed. He'd sounded so lighthearted, it pleased her to think she'd done that for him.

'Course, she was a looker, my Cati,' George continued, lost in his own reminiscences. 'You're pretty, too, though I guess Zach's told you that.'

Annie smiled. 'Thank you.'

'And she was kind and gentle, but she had pride you couldn't bust with a rock.' He was quiet for a few moments before speaking shakily. 'And she loved that boy of hers.'

356

Annie was astonished to hear what sounded like a sniffle. 'Ah, hell,' the old man said, getting up from the table. 'I'm sorry I tricked you down here, Annie, but I ain't sorry you came. Guess I'll be off to my room, if you'll excuse me, 'cause I'm embarrassing myself. Besides, nobody wants to hear the ramblings of an old man. Though I appreciate you listening,' he said, walking slowly out of the room. At the doorway, he paused. 'Now that I've thought about it, you're exactly what I should have expected, Annie.'

He disappeared and Annie took a deep breath. The pizza had turned cold and unappealing, but she'd lost her appetite, anyway. She drank some water and got up from the table, too, putting her dishes in the sink. Slowly, she gathered up her purse and keys as she thought about Zach's father's regrets.

Zach's door opened and he came down the hall, nicely dressed in trousers and a blazer. Her breath caught at the sight of him, his hair still slightly wet but shining ebony in the light. He was so handsome it hurt. Somehow it was hard to believe that this man might one day be all hers.

'I see you got something to eat,' he told her.

'Actually, I wasn't very hungry.'

He glanced into the kitchen before looking down at her. 'It's pretty slim pickings around here.'

'Depends on what you're picking,' she replied.

Zach smiled, but Annie could tell he was anxious to be off. And, for that matter, so was she. 'Well, I guess I'll be going now,' she said reluctantly, not knowing how to end their leave-taking gracefully. She felt so awkward.

Lightly putting his hands on her shoulders, Zach pulled her forward for a lingering kiss. 'I'll let you know something when I can,' he promised when the kiss finally ended.

She could only hope he would. 'Good luck,' she said, before turning toward the front door. Walking outside into the day that was passing into late afternoon, Annie looked back as she reached her car. Zach was right behind her, his expression protective and serious as she got into the hearse.

Annie fought back the strange and overwhelming sensation that this might be the last time she ever saw Zach. Although she desperately wanted to hear him say he'd call her tomorrow, or this weekend, or whenever, she had to make do with the fact he honestly seemed to think they'd be together soon.

'Don't take any wooden nickels,' she said, forcing herself to sound light.

He gave her a quick kiss through the open car window. 'Drive safely,' he replied.

Annie started the car and drove to the end of the block, where she made a cautious circuit around all the cars that had come to the bridge circle at Zach's neighbor's house. She waved as she drove past Zach and he did the same.

In her rearview mirror, Annie saw Zach standing on the sidewalk watching her drive away until she could no longer see him. Taking a deep breath, she headed toward Desperado, feeling like she'd just left half of her soul behind.

Gert and Travis were playing cards at the kitchen table when Annie got home. She peeked at both their hands, saw that Gert was going to trounce Travis soundly, and went to get a drink from the refrigerator.

'Was Mary good?' she asked.

'Of course,' Travis replied. 'When isn't she?'

Annie smiled at her father's praise of her daughter. 'Thanks for looking after her. Where is she, anyway?'

'Tucked safely in bed,' Gert replied. 'I'd brought over some books from my house and she wanted to hear every one.'

'Oh, thank you, Gert.' Annie's gratitude was palpable. 'You sure have been heaven-sent for my family.'

'I'm glad.' The woman nodded and laid down her hand of cards. 'I guess now's as good a time as any to tell you I've got to be getting back to work at the hospital.'

'What?' Travis sounded stunned. 'What do you want to do that for, woman?'

Annie stared at her father. He sounded as if he didn't want Gert to leave. Was this the same man who'd once called the nurse a grey-haired battle axe?

'It's not that I want to do it, as much as I have to,' Gert replied serenely. 'You may know that a paycheck and health insurance and retirement benefits are necessary if I want to continue to eat.'

'Ain't you getting enough to eat around here?' he demanded.

'That's not what I mean and you know it.'

Annie thought Gert's calmness was admirable, considering her father's rudeness. Obviously, the thought that the nurse needed to return to her own life bothered him. Setting her drink down, she walked over to Travis and sat down beside him. 'Papa, if Gert needs to go, we can't stop her. We've been lucky to have her so long.'

'I don't feel lucky right now,' he complained. 'She's beat me at every hand – '

'Fixing to beat you at this one, too,' Gert inserted.

'See? And she pushes me around and makes me do things I don't want to do, like wear short pants! Which I'm doing to please her, but do you think that matters? No!'

Annie held back a smile. It was good to know that her father had found someone he liked. Because it was plain as day to her that Travis was fighting like a fish on a line so that he wouldn't have to face Gert's leaving.

'I'll come around once in a while to see you, old man,' she said placidly. 'You'll still have to do what I tell you.'

Travis got up, stomping jerkily across the kitchen to the doorway with his walker. Then he circled back to stare down at Gert. 'No, I won't. Just for once, Nurse Gert, I think the patient ought to have a chance to tell *you* what to do.' He took a deep breath. 'If you have to return to the hospital, fine. But I think you ought to come home here at night.'

Annie and Gert were silent, as they stared up at Travis. The quiet dimness of the kitchen seemed to shroud the three of them in a frozen frame of surprise.

'What are you saying, Travis Cade? That you want me to work all day and then come here and take care of you at night?' Gert sounded like she might be working herself up for some anger of her own.

'Hell, yes! I mean, hell, no! You're twisting me around, Gert! I'm trying to ask you to marry me, but you're making a fine mess of the whole thing.'

Travis looked completely unraveled by his speech. Annie slid a glance at Gert, who looked as shocked as Annie felt. But she smiled, thinking that her father deserved a good woman like Gert. He'd been without a soulmate for a long time.

Too long.

'Well, Annie, what do you think about this astonishing turn of events?' Gert asked. 'You're too old to have a stepmother, and I wouldn't want to horn in where I wouldn't be wanted.'

Annie smiled, pushing back warm tears of happiness. 'Oh, you're wanted, Gert, if you feel like accepting my father's rather unique proposal.' She gave the woman a hug, which was returned gratefully.

'Well, old man, I guess you've got yourself a wife, then.' Gert looked pleased and somehow younger as she stood to look him in the eyes. 'Though, you should know this doesn't change anything. I'll still be wearing the long pants around here.'

She nodded at his compliant silence. 'Now, off to bed with you.' As was her normal brisk manner, Gert pushed past Travis, leaving him to follow behind her. But he reached out, snagging her arm and turning her around as she got to the doorway.

'You may wear the long pants, woman, but I'm still the one making the important decisions. And I say, I ain't going till I get a proper kiss for my marriage proposal.'

'Well, then.' Gert leaned over, careful of Travis's walker. She gave him a quick peck on the mouth. He frowned. Thoughtful for a moment, Gert leaned over and gave him a kiss that lasted a full five seconds longer and which he appeared to return. Annie lowered her eyes but couldn't disguise her grin.

'There. That's all the excitement you're getting tonight, old man.'

Gert turned and headed down the hall. Travis hurried his walker behind her, calling, 'I love you, too, old woman.'

Annie sat alone in the kitchen, listening to the noises of Travis resisting Gert's attempts to settle him into bed to sleep. They made a good couple and she couldn't have wished for a better woman for her father.

But in spite of her happiness for the newly engaged couple, Annie couldn't help hoping – wishing – that she and Zach might find their relationship heading down the same rosy path. She flipped over one of the abandoned playing cards absently. The queen of hearts turned up, content in her allure, and Annie put her back down. Was she the queen of Zach's heart? Annie didn't know. Suddenly, she remembered Grandmother Day's journals, long forgotten in the attic. She'd been a woman who had completely possessed the heart of the man she'd chosen.

If there was ever a time to read about the two lovers who had turned their backs on everything but each other, if there was anything Annie could learn from her grandmother's words, now was the time to find out.

CHAPTER 23

Zach watched Carter leave the upscale condo where he lived. His eyes narrowed as he observed the man's confident swagger.

Well, he wouldn't be cocky for long. It was time to give Carter what he had coming to him.

'There he is. Come on,' he murmured to the man standing behind him in the darkness.

'Hey, Carter,' Zach called. 'Wait a minute.'

Carter halted at the sound of his name, standing stock-still with a goofy grin on his face the moment he realized Sam Lindale was with Zach. Which was exactly what Zach had expected. With Lindale being a stockholder, and Carter knowing of the close relationship between Zach and Sam, no doubt the egotistical idiot assumed that they'd come to offer him his job back.

The two bigger men stood on either side of Carter, staring down at him in an intimidating fashion. Carter's grin started to fade a bit.

'What's up, Zach?'

'I wanted to talk to you about a little article that showed up in the paper yesterday,' Zach began.

But he didn't need to continue. 'Hell, Zach, I didn't have anything to do with that!' Carter looked at Lindale beseechingly. 'You know I wouldn't have taken any stories about Ritter outside!'

Sam nodded grimly. 'Maybe. But who else could it have been?'

'I don't know. But it wasn't me. I wouldn't have done that to you, Zach, man.'

Zach commanded himself not to shove Carter's lying tongue down his throat and to let the cooler head – Lindale's – prevail.

'That's not what LouAnn Harrison says, Carter.' Sam kept his eyes trained on his ex-employee. 'She says you've been out to get at Zach since day one. That you've always been jealous of him, and the first chance you got to tear into him, you did.' Sam frowned down at Carter. 'I guess I'd have to believe her, since she was sleeping with you while engaged to Zach.'

Carter's eyes bugged. 'She's lying. She just made that up because Zach dumped her.'

Zach had to look away for a moment in order to keep from strangling Carter on the spot.

Sam crossed his arms. 'I don't know. LouAnn's father is one of the most respected businessmen in the community. Don't know why she'd need to make up lies about you to get her kicks. You're not going to say that LouAnn had something to do with the article, are you?'

'No, I – yes, I am saying that,' Carter said hurriedly. 'She convinced me to talk to the paper about Zach after he broke their engagement. I didn't want to. And then they twisted around everything I said. I never told them anything about you embezzling money from the company, or – '

'I wasn't embezzling from Ritter.' Zach's expression turned harder. 'Don't say it again or I'll kill you on the spot.'

He hadn't meant to make the threat, but it came pouring out of his mouth like lava from a volcano. Carter and his lies and deviousness had filled him with a burning anger that might explode any second.

Sam put a restraining hand on Zach's arm. 'Tell you the truth, Carter, we have enough information on your involvement in this matter to go to the authorities. And Zach here can sue you for libel, and win easily.'

Carter blanched. 'Please . . . don't do that. I'll call the newspaper and have the article retracted.'

'That's not good enough. A man's reputation has been ruined and a simple retraction isn't going to do the job. Zach has suffered a lot of damage because of you.'

'Tell me what you want, Zach. I'll do whatever you want.'

Carter seemed terrified now. Zach became intensely aware of one thing: if Carter was this frightened of the authorities investigating him, then he no doubt *had* been embezzling from Ritter. No doubt he'd stolen enough money to give himself vacation time in Tahiti for the rest of his life.

Harshly, Zach said, 'I want the deed to the property in Desperado that you bought.'

'No way.' Carter shook his head, trying to look brave again. 'No can do, *amigo*.'

'Shut up, Carter,' Zach hissed. Carter calling him friend in Spanish was more than his temper could stand. 'Give me the gun, Sam.'

'All right, all right!' Carter capitulated instantly. 'You can have the damn deed!'

Zach pulled from his pocket the worthless deed that his father had given over to him. 'I've already got the deed. And my name's on it. What I want is you signing your name off this deed, and authorization for total ownership to me.' Zach's smile was thin. 'Here are the legal documents, all drawn up nice and neat.' He handed Carter a Mont Blanc pen. 'Start signing, you son of a bitch.'

Carter paused for a moment. He stared at Zach, then at Sam. 'He's crazy, you know,' he said to Sam, as if Zach weren't standing on the other side of him. 'You won't let him make me sign away property I bought without giving me some payment, will you?'

Sam pointed at the documents Carter held in his shaking hands. 'I suggest you sign fast, Carter. Zach's been dying to take a chunk out of your hide ever since he discovered who'd talked to the newspaper.'

Reluctantly, Carter lowered his pen to the paper. 'Hey, this says I deed over your father's old shack, too.

You're leaving me without anything.'

'It's not worth a dime, so why do you care?' Zach asked.

'Because I've just about got it sold to a guy who – '

Zach's mouth thinned to a grim line. 'Who what, Carter?'

'Well, it's a bad section of town, Zach. And across from that bingo parlor, the land is nearly worthless, unless one opens a . . .'

Carter's voice trailed off. A curious sensation hit Zach that Carter was afraid to tell him what his plans for Pop's house were.

'I believe what our friend is trying to tell you is that he's going to open a little house of whores, Zach,' Lindale finished. 'Isn't that right, Carter?'

Zach stared, disbelieving. He ground his teeth as his eyes met Carter's and saw the guilty truth in his expression. 'God. You don't care how you make money, do you?'

Carter didn't reply, obviously becoming petrified of Zach's burgeoning rage.

'Sign it,' Zach commanded. 'You'll just have to find a way to make a profit somewhere else.' No way in hell was he going to allow any sex shops to be opened on the ground where his mother had once lived, had once raised him with her gentle love.

'What good is it to you?' Carter asked, still unwilling to give up his investment.

'I don't know. I'll probably give the property to a church or a charity, where it can be used in a suitable

368

manner. That area of town could use some spiritual uplifting. Now, sign, damn it.'

Reluctantly, Carter obeyed. 'Are we finished conducting business, now? I have an important meeting to go to.'

'You sure do.' Lindale tucked his beefy arm securely through Carter's. 'As a matter of fact, the board has thoroughly examined Ritter's financial records, and we've discovered that we are indeed missing a bit of change in the company. Coincidentally, we also found a like amount in your bank account.'

'So,' Zach began, taking hold of Carter's other arm and leading him forward to Zach's car, 'we think the police will be interested to hear your tale of how you became instantly rich.'

Carter struggled between them, but Zach's grip was determined and fierce. 'And,' Zach finished, 'when they're through talking to you, the Desperado sheriff is sending someone to discuss a little bitty fire some firebug set down that way.'

'I didn't have anything to do with that!' Carter screamed. 'You'll never be able to tie me to the fire on that bitch's land. And anyway, that Indian woman had it coming to her. She thinks she's a frigging queen. But I'm too smart to leave evidence lying around, and even if the two of you try to pin it on me, it won't stand up in court. You'll never tie me to it.'

Zach looked down at his prisoner. 'I don't have to. You and your filthy mouth just did.' He flipped out a recording device that had been in his pocket. Carter stared, shocked, before hanging his head. A police cruiser that had been waiting for Zach's appearance with Carter rolled to the curb, and two officers got out.

Sam and Zach handed Carter over to them. Carter went peacefully, obviously realizing the futility of struggling now that every angle had been completely covered by Zach. Before getting in, he turned to look at Zach one last time.

'This isn't what I thought would happen, back when we were in college,' he said.

Zach looked at the man who had once been his friend. He shrugged. 'Me, neither.'

Carter nodded. Then the policewoman helped him into the car. Zach handed over the recorder to the officer's partner. 'We'll be getting in touch with you, Mr Rayez,' the officer said.

'You do that,' Zach replied.

Within seconds, the cruiser had disappeared, taking away the man who had tried to ruin Zach's life. He stared after it, glad the whole thing was over. But deep inside, it sickened him that it had ever had to happen.

Sam slapped him on the back jovially. Zach turned to look at his friend. 'I can't thank you enough for coming with me today, Sam. Carter wouldn't have cooperated nearly as well without you.'

Lindale chuckled. 'You seemed to be doing fine to me. Although you worried me a little with the gun business. Couldn't figure out what I was going to have to pull out of my pocket for that one.'

Zach laughed. 'Sorry. I got a little crazy.'

They got in Zach's car. 'Well, now what?' Sam asked. 'What are your plans?'

Zach didn't hesitate as he started the car. 'I've got a few more loose ends to tie up. But as soon as I do, I'm heading toward Desperado.'

'Time to fire up your salsa factory?'

'Yeah. Feel like attending a wedding any time soon?'

Sam laughed out loud. 'Hell, yeah, I feel like it. I just got my tux ready for the wedding you were supposed to have last weekend.'

Zach smiled. 'Keep it out. If I have my way about it, I'll be eating wedding cake very soon.'

In Desperado, Annie and Mary sat by the fish pond, quietly feeding the fish. The smaller ones were beginning to be cautious about humans, but they still weren't as shy as the bigger fish. The corn kernels were just too enticing to be passed up.

Mary laughed happily as a fish splashed in the water. 'They're playing,' she said.

Annie smiled, gazing at the daughter she loved so much. 'Yes, I think they are,' she replied. After a moment, she said, 'Mary, you didn't have a chance to know your grandmother. But she was a beautiful woman who loved your grandfather very much.'

'I know. But she got sick,' Mary said. Sadness stole into the little girl's eyes.

Annie wrapped her arms around her daughter and pulled her into her lap. 'Yes. But I have some good news to tell you. Ms Gert and Grandpa Travis are getting married.'

Mary turned around to peer at her mother. 'Are they really?'

'Yes.' Annie nodded at the delight in Mary's eyes.

'Can I go to the wedding?' she pleaded. 'I'll be really good and not sleepy or anything.'

Annie laughed. 'Better than that. Gert wants you to be her flower girl.'

'Oh, my,' Mary breathed. 'Will I look just like Cinderella? With flowers and everything?'

Tears jumped into Annie's eyes. 'With flowers and everything. It's going to be small and simple in the chapel at our church, but Gert has even picked out a flower halo for you to wear in your hair. You'll be every bit as beautiful as Cinderella, sugar.'

Mary clapped her hands. 'I'm so excited! I can't wait!' But just as quickly her face fell. 'I'm happy for Grandpa, I really am. But I wish it was you, Mama,' she said softly.

Annie lowered her head, brushing a kiss against Mary's little forehead. Zach had never mentioned marriage to her. It wasn't likely that he would choose her to be the woman to fit into his world. But she said to Mary, 'Maybe one day, sugar. But if I ever do get married, I promise you'll be my flower girl.' Then she hugged her daughter close, and wondered if she'd ever hear from Zach again.

* * *

Thirty minutes later, Mary ran up to house to get a soda. Annie stayed where she was, lazily enjoying a moment of contentment by the side of the pond.

She might have even started to doze off, but a masculine voice spoke out in the stillness. 'You look just the way I always think of you.'

'Zach!' Annie sat up quickly, repressing the urge to throw her arms around his neck. 'I didn't expect to see you so soon.'

'Did you doubt me, Annie Aguillar?' Zach asked. 'Did you think I wouldn't come back?'

Annie didn't really know what to say. He looked so tall and wonderfully handsome standing there, his mouth quirked into a cocky grin that she hesitated. She wanted to tell Zach how glad she was that he'd came, but the words stayed inside her. 'Um . . . it wasn't so much that I doubted you, but I knew that there were a lot of things working against us.'

'Precisely why I had to come back.' Zach sat down next to her, pulling a piece of paper from his pocket. 'I have a lot to tell you. First, I think you'll be happy to know that the plans for the state highway were redrawn some time ago, I discovered. From the looks of it, the highway will run in a northwest line, only marginally close to that line of your property.'

'I can breathe a sigh of relief about that,' Annie said. She was grateful to have the news.

'Second, I have a gift to give you, that I hope you'll accept.' He extended his hand, holding out the piece of paper to her.

'You shouldn't give me anything else, Zach. You've already given me so much,' Annie protested.

He didn't say a word, but his hand stayed where it was. Gingerly, Annie took the paper, quickly scanning it. 'This is the deed to the property south of mine?' she asked. 'Why is it in my name?'

'Because I'm giving it to you, if you want it,' he said. 'I ah, talked Carter out of it.' Annie raised her brows and Zach shrugged. 'He wasn't cut out for country living, anyway.'

'Hmm.' From the pleased expression on Zach's face, it seemed that there were parts of the story she wasn't going to hear.

'Me, however,' Zach said, 'I'm looking for a new enterprise to back. Somebody gave me a tip that a smart, sexy, beautiful woman was looking for an investor in her salsa business. I happen to think salsa's an excellent venture to back right now.'

Disappointment flooded Annie at his words. She was glad to see him, but apparently, he only had business on his mind. 'Oh, Zach,' Annie said softly, 'You don't have to do that. I'll find a way – '

He interrupted her with a long kiss that stole her breath and made her heart beat faster. 'I have to have something to do with my time. Otherwise, I'll just lay around and make love to you every day, and that won't put money in the bank, you know.'

'It would be nice if it would,' Annie agreed, pulling away after a moment, 'but I guess you're right.' She looked down at the paper again. 'But, Zach, you shouldn't give this to me. It's yours.'

He shrugged. 'Nah. I'm not interested in becoming a landowner.'

Intently, he leaned over, to take her in his arms, tracing his fingers over her hips. Annie tried to ignore the thought that Zach's interest seemed focused on her – sexually. 'If you're sure about giving this away, can I give it to Papa? With him and Gert getting married, they might like to have a place of their own. It would be so convenient, just a truck drive across the fields.'

Zach paused to look into the distance. 'I think giving the property to Gert and Travis is an excellent idea. Honeymooners should have their own place to move into.'

'Yes. They'll be delighted with your generosity.' Annie took a deep breath, not trying too hard to get away from the searching kisses Zach was trailing along her neckline and shoulders. 'By the way, you may have been right about the oil.'

He lifted his head and looked at her, instantly alert. 'What are you saying?'

Annie took a deep breath. 'I'm saying that I appreciate you wanting to back my business, but you may want to go into oil production instead of pushing salsa. I read my grandmother's journals and,' Annie stared at him solemnly, 'apparently, she and my grandfather had always known it was there.'

CHAPTER 24

Zach was stunned. 'Are you positive? I mean, could your grandmother have been certain?'

Annie nodded. 'According to what Grandmother Day wrote, her parents – who had disinherited her from the family when she married my grandfather – were sure that there was oil under their land. They drilled, but nothing ever happened. In fact, my great-grandparents were nearly broke from the expense of it. And dreadfully disappointed, because the rumors had been so persistent for so long that they'd begun to believe they were going to become oil barons.'

Simultaneously, their hands touched, then wrapped together. 'They'd really counted on it, then?' Zach asked.

'Well, as rich as they were, and owning half the county, I wouldn't think they needed to be any richer. However, from my grandmother's writing, it seems that her parents were rather greedy and liked to lord their wealth over everyone.'

'Including the daughter who didn't marry to their standards,' Zach stated.

'I got that impression, too.'

'So, they were feeling the financial effects of their treasure hunt and needed a strike to keep up their lifestyle.'

'Yes. And my grandmother and her husband, Two, were living on the fringe edge of her parents' land, several miles away from her family and with no contact between them – this land we're on now – with no real income and nothing more than what they could grow in the ground.'

Annie sighed. 'One day,' she continued, 'a man went to Grandmother Day and told her he'd miscalculated the property line. That he'd accidentally drilled on a portion of her property.'

The hanging willows edging the foreman's shack blew softly in the light breeze. Zach looked at her silently, waiting for her to continue. 'Although any place that had been drilled on her parents' property was dry, for some reason they hit oil on Grandmother Day's side.'

Zach chuckled. 'So, the daughter they were so ashamed of came out the big winner.'

'Yes. Grandmother Day swore the man to secrecy and told him to cement the place where they'd drilled. Apparently, he never violated her trust, because her parents never suspected that the small parcel of one hundred acres they'd given to their daughter to assuage their consciences was the most valuable piece of their land.'

'I think I would have liked your grandmother. She was smart,' Zach said.

Annie smiled up at him. 'This is the best part of the story, though. When she told my grandfather about the oil, he sat down and laughed for two days. He said that her parents shouldn't have disowned their only daughter and that everything had happened just as it should have. According to Grandmother's journal, that's why she nicknamed him Two Days Laughing.'

'Or it could have been two Days laughing,' Zach murmured, 'if you consider that Nancy Day probably found the whole situation as amusing as her husband did.' He gave Annie a kiss that was meant to be supportive as well as loving. 'So, why didn't she ever have the oil brought up?' he asked.

Annie shrugged, before standing up and walking on to the porch of the shack. She led him inside, turning on the lamp on the small table where Mary's carousel had once sat. 'It was her idea to save it for future generations. She wrote that she liked to think she was keeping something for her daughter, or granddaughter. And Two felt that the earth's natural resources should be left as they were, anyway. Grandmother Day wrote that, because of their love, they wanted for nothing.' Annie sat down on the bed, an intent expression on her face. 'Remember when I told you that Mother once allowed drilling on the property, just to satisfy the gossipmongers so they'd leave her alone?'

At Zach's nod, Annie said, 'Mother led them away from the spot that had been drilled before, closer to the original existing property line. Nothing was found, so it was never mentioned again. And she never told me, though she'd probably intended to one day. But when she got sick, she died so fast that . . .'

Annie's voice trailed off. Zach sat down beside her, taking her hands in his. 'So now you'll have a story to tell Mary one day.'

She looked into his eyes. 'Yes. I like knowing that my daughter's inheritance is greater than I even dreamed. The land was enough, but . . . this is amazing.'

He was quiet for a moment, just looking at her. Then he turned his gaze away. 'I'm just glad you didn't sell out to me.'

Zach looked so distressed that Annie took him into her arms. 'Oh, Zach, don't even think about that anymore, unless you think of it in a good way. After all, if you hadn't come here to buy me out, we would never have met.' She drew near to him, nearly touching his lips with hers. 'And I would have lived my life without you,' she whispered. 'I don't even like to think about that.'

They kissed, long and sweet, as quiet settled over the cabin. After a moment, Annie pulled back just enough to look in Zach's eyes again. 'Would you think I was terrible if I said I would like to see what was there, just once?'

She saw he knew exactly what she was talking about by the understanding in his eyes. 'You want to see the oil.'

Annie nodded.

'But it's your grandmother's soul you're really going to see, isn't it?' he asked. 'And her dreams for the children of her line, who would inherit the wonderful legacy she'd left them.'

This time she didn't nod, because he understood her need, and it was enough to know that the bond between them was this perfect. Somehow, she had known it would be this way between her and Zach.

'Well, if oil did come in, you could have it capped and plugged later. But no,' he said, pausing to brush a kiss against her cheek, 'I don't think you're terrible at all. I think you're a woman of rare insight and wisdom.'

Then he gently pushed her back against the pillows and Annie pulled him against her, telling herself to be content that she could be with Zach for now.

It was later in the evening when Annie finally uncurled herself from the protective cocoon of Zach's warm body. He put out a hand to stop her, but Annie gently pushed it away with a smile. 'I have to get dinner on,' she said.

'I'll help.' He stood up and began dressing. Annie did, too, somewhat regretful that they had to leave their enchanted moment behind.

Five minutes later, they strolled outside and made their way up to the house, holding hands. Suddenly, Mary came running outside to hurl herself into Zach's arms.

'Mr Zach!' she cried. 'You came back!'

He gave her a tight hug, laughing at her joyous greeting. 'Did you think I wouldn't?' He gave her a fake-stern look.

'No. I knew you would.' Mary's answer was assured.

'Good. Because I've come to ask you a very important question.'

Annie saw Mary's expression turn pensive. She felt anxious as well, as she looked at the handsome man kneeling down and holding her daughter. *Please, please*, she thought, *let him stay this time forever. My little girl loves him almost as much as I do.*

'I was wondering how you think I'd rate as father material,' Zach said.

'Father material?' Mary looked puzzled as she repeated his words, then hopeful. Annie's heart leapt in her chest.

'Do you think I'd be any good at it?'

Mary didn't hesitate. 'Good at it? You'd be the best, Mr Zach!'

Zach chuckled, catching Annie's eyes. 'I don't know about the best. But I'd give it my best shot, if you'll let me.'

'Oh, Mr Zach, I would like that more than anything. I'll help you all I can.' Mary hugged his neck tightly once more.

Zach patted her back, never releasing Annie's gaze. 'Then there's something I have to ask your mother, Mary.' He drew Annie down to kneel beside them.

381

With Mary still in his arms, Zach said, 'Annie, Mary seems to think we'd make a pretty good family.'

Annie smiled. 'I agree with her.'

Zach cleared his throat before looking deep into her eyes. 'Well, then, will you marry me, Annie Aguillar, and make me the happiest man on the planet?'

Joy sparkled through Annie at hearing the words she'd only dreamed of hearing. But she wanted to know that the past was behind them. 'What about the problems you were having in Austin? What about everything that was turning your life upside down?'

She held her breath.

'I've cleared up the problems that were in the way,' Zach said, his expression earnest. 'But without you in my life, I don't think my life would ever be whole.'

A luminous smile lit Annie's face. 'Then my answer is yes, Zach Rayez. Marrying you will make me the happiest woman on the planet.'

'Besides me!' Mary chimed in.

They all laughed. 'I have something for the two ladies in my life, then,' Zach said. 'Mary, would you reach into my pocket – ' he pointed at his denim shirt '– and see what you find there?'

She put a small hand into the pocket and pulled out a grey velvet jeweler's box. In wonder, she held it up.

'I had something I needed to return to the jeweler's,' Zach said, taking the box from Mary. Annie knew he was talking about the emerald earrings that would never have been right for her. 'And while I was there, I saw this ring.' He held up a stunning sapphire, nearly the shade of Annie's eyes, that was surrounded by diamonds.

Annie gasped and Mary's mouth dropped open. 'I thought about how beautiful this would look on your mother's hand. What do you think, Mary?'

'I think you're right,' Mary breathed.

Zach smiled and slid the ring on Annie's finger. It was a perfect fit.

'It's lovely,' she said. 'The most beautiful ring in the world, Zach.' Leaning over Mary's head, she gave him a kiss that promised greater rewards later.

'You're welcome,' he whispered. He held Annie's gaze for a second longer, before turning to Mary. 'But while I was at the jeweler's, I also saw this.' He pulled a smaller ring out of the box, gold with a heart on the band and a tiny diamond inside. 'And I knew this was perfect for the other lady in my life.' Gently, he slid it on Mary's little finger.

Mary stared at the bauble adorning her hand. 'It's so pretty. I've never had anything like this. Look, Mama. It even has a little star inside the heart.' She looked up at Zach. 'I'm going to love having you for a daddy. I can tell.'

Annie and Zach laughed together, then hugged Mary tightly between them. 'You've answered her prayers, Zach Rayez,' Annie whispered into his ear.

'I'm glad.' He gave Annie a loving kiss. 'Because you've more than answered mine. I love you, Annie Aguillar. I always will.'

'And I, you, Zach Rayez.' And as they stood outside, the three of them wrapped together with the night sky gathering outside, Annie knew that she had at last found what her grandmother had possessed as well.

Splendid, never-ending love.

EPILOGUE

Three weeks later, Annie and Zach stood in the fields, watching the drilling procedure. Mary ran and played nearby, but not too far from Annie's protective sight. Cody looked on with interest, as did Travis and Gert. Annie eyed the newlyweds with satisfaction. Even her father's heart attack had turned out to have a silver lining.

There had been many wonderful blessings since Zach had come into her life. Annie looked at him, her eyes gleaming with happiness. He was a wonderful husband, and a better father to Mary than he'd probably ever thought he could be. Their wedding had been a wondrous, candle-lit affair, so much more special because Mary had been a precious flower girl. The three of them had stood at the altar, with Gert, Travis, Cody, and Cody's mother looking on. Zach's Pop had sat watching proudly as his only son married the woman he loved.

Since then, Cody had been patiently teaching Zach the rudiments of farm life. Zach in return was instructing Cody in financial investments. Between the two of them, some venture was always being cooked up at the kitchen table.

Zach had sold his home in Austin. Since Pop hadn't been too partial to it anyway, he'd moved into the foreman's bungalow Annie and Zach were renovating. Annie could tell George enjoyed living on the farm, but what he was loving most was forging the bond with Zach he'd missed all those years. Best of all, Zach's Pop adored Mary, and she him. Mary had more people who loved her than Annie could have ever asked for.

Annie's eyes widened as she heard sudden rumbling. She glanced toward the sky to see if lightning would follow the thunder. After a protracted tenseness when even the earth seemed to pause, oil spouted up, coming down in fat, black spatters. Annie gasped, amazed by the actual sight of what she only previously imagined. The ground turned ebony and slick, with wondrous streams of oil spreading over the land. Zach reached out to take her hand, grinning at the delighted awe on her face.

'There she is,' he said.

'I think you're right,' she said, barely able to breathe. 'I feel her spirit.' She brushed back the tears of happiness and gratitude that were filling her eyes.

Annie's grandmother's own tears had been shed on this ground, for the family who had forsaken her in shame. Nancy Day was surely looking down with a bittersweet smile, knowing that Annie had made the same decision she once had herself, choosing love in the face of overwhelming odds.

Annie smiled at her husband, before looking toward the geyser once again, nodding her respect. Then she put her hand in Zach's, and together they walked toward the silver-roofed, gabled old house, and a future rich with promise.

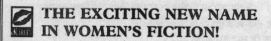

THE EXCITING NEW NAME
IN WOMEN'S FICTION!

PLEASE HELP ME TO HELP YOU!

Dear *Scarlet* Reader,

As Editor of *Scarlet* Books I want to make sure that the
books I offer you every month are up to the high standards
Scarlet readers expect. And to do that I need to know a
little more about you and your reading likes and dislikes. So
please spare a few minutes to fill in the short questionnaire
on the following pages and send it to me. I'll send *you* a
surprise gift as a thank you!*

Looking forward to hearing from you,

Sally Cooper

Editor-in-Chief, *Scarlet*

*Offer applies only in the UK, only one offer per household.

QUESTIONNAIRE

Please tick the appropriate boxes to indicate your answers

1 Where did you get this Scarlet title?
Bought in supermarket ☐
Bought at my local bookstore ☐ Bought at chain bookstore ☐
Bought at book exchange or used bookstore ☐
Borrowed from a friend ☐
Other (please indicate) _____

2 Did you enjoy reading it?
A lot ☐   A little ☐   Not at all ☐

3 What did you particularly like about this book?
Believable characters ☐   Easy to read ☐
Good value for money ☐   Enjoyable locations ☐
Interesting story ☐   Modern setting ☐
Other _____

4 What did you particularly dislike about this book?
_____

5 Would you buy another Scarlet book?
Yes ☐   No ☐

6 What other kinds of book do you enjoy reading?
Horror ☐   Puzzle books ☐   Historical fiction ☐
General fiction ☐   Crime/Detective ☐   Cookery ☐
Other (please indicate) _____

7 Which magazines do you enjoy reading?
1. _____
2. _____
3. _____

And now a little about you –
8 How old are you?
Under 25 ☐   25–34 ☐   35–44 ☐
45–54 ☐   55–64 ☐   over 65 ☐

cont.